Praise for

The Exchange-Rate Between Love and Money

"There aren't many debuts with this scope. Leveritt's take on 2003 Sarajevo is a nutty, funny and constantly inventive ride."

—Matt Thorne, author of *Tourist* and *Cherry*

"Part love story, part hilarious political send-up, Leveritt's debut is hectic, intense and verbally dazzling."

—Catherine Taylor, *The Guardian*

"[An] impressive debut . . . a beguiling blend of thirtysomething angst, political polemic, lyrical description and, towards the end, boy's own adventure."

—Brendan Simms, *Sunday Telegraph*

"A tumult of avarice and violence and romance: at once brutal, crazed and hilarious. Leveritt's command of language and narrative makes this a highly promising debut novel."

—Jean Hannah Edelstein, *New Statesman*

"Leveritt's Sarajevo, circa 2003, is a modern version of Burroughs' *Interzone*, a new Tangiers where everything is permitted to a busy and self-regarding clique of Western do-gooders. . . . Leveritt is adept at capturing the strange atmosphere of post-war Saravejo."

—Marcus Tanner, *The Independent*

"[A] diverting debut that is audacious enough to broach questions of heroism and justice."

—Hephzibah Anderson, *Daily Mail*

"At once a love story and a portrait of a city, this book teems with life and the hurly-burly narrative reflects the chaos of the post-war Balkans. Sarajevo is awash with hustlers, hedonists, and humanitarians buoyed up on a tidal wave of European cash. A . . . humorous debut in which money and lovers change hands with abandon."

—Sebastian Shakespeare, *Tatler* magazine

"Radiates a certain clued-up, slacker intelligence . . . serving up political farce and human tragedy side by side, his story of a city in which everything has its price unravels at breakneck speed."

—Claire Allfree, *Metro*

"Merges the explosive coupling of love and war, which produces a gripping, tense and thoroughly satisfying read."

—Sam Noakes, *Aesthetica*

"[A] strange concoction of thriller and satire . . . Leveritt's style is youthful, energetic and a little florid."

—*The Sunday Business Post* (Ireland)

"[Leveritt] has crafted a nuanced fictional debut, both humorous and harrowing, and provides a vivid, vibrant portrait of a society rebuilding in the wake of genocidal brutality."

—John Paul Holden, *The Big Issue* (UK)

The Exchange-Rate
Between
Love and Money

THOMAS LEVERITT

Simon & Schuster Paperbacks
NEW YORK LONDON TORONTO SYDNEY

Simon & Schuster
1230 Avenue of the Americas
New York, NY 10020

Originally published in Great Britain in 2008 by Harvill Secker

Published by arrangement with Random House UK

The author and publishers are grateful for permission to reproduce
the following copyright material: Nine lines from "Lady Lazarus" from *Ariel*
by Sylvia Plath. Copyright © 1963 by Ted Hughes.
Reprinted by permission of HarperCollins Publishers.

First Simon & Schuster edition April 2009

SIMON & SCHUSTER PAPERBACKS and colophon are registered trademarks
of Simon & Schuster, Inc.

For information about special discounts for bulk purchases,
please contact Simon & Schuster Special Sales at
1-800-456-6798 or business@simonandschuster.com

Designed by Paul Dippolito

Manufactured in the United States of America

1   3   5   7   9   10   8   6   4   2

Library of Congress Cataloging-in-Publication Data

Leveritt, Thomas.
The exchange-rate between love and money / Thomas Leveritt.
p.   cm.
1. Postwar reconstruction—Bosnia and Hercegovina—Sarajevo—Fiction.
2. Postwar reconstruction—Economic aspects—Fiction.   3. Bounty hunters—Fiction.
4. Triangles (Interpersonal relations)—Fiction.   5. Sarajevo (Bosnia and Hercegovina—
Fiction.   I. Title.
PR6112.E8864 E93 2009
823'.92 dc—22   2008044893

ISBN-13: 978-1-4165-9726-1
ISBN-10:   1-4165-9726-3

For Mom and Dad,
the two best people

The Exchange-Rate
Between
Love and Money

The Girl in the
Gingerbread Blizzard

PRETTY WELL THE first thing Bannerman did after moving to Sarajevo was fall in love with his best friend's girlfriend. No, worse: his only friend's only girlfriend. Bannerman had always been clumsy, but this was a pratfall many, many pots & pans more impressive.

His best friend was Frito, a big surly mother with a ton of money, Disinhibited Personality Disorder, and a knack for girls—none of whom, perhaps as a result, had ever interested him long-term. But he'd been looking for the one that would. Thoroughly. He'd heard about this amazing thing love, had been trying to score some for years now—he'd painted a target on every girl he met and shot himself out of a cannon at them, but none ever withstood the impact.

Until that autumn of 2002. Frito was down in Sarajevo on business when he finally met someone. He kept it quiet for a few months, behaving a bit odd admittedly, commuting back and forth across Europe to see her, until one bleak afternoon back in London, in the dregs of that year, he finally faced up to the responsibilities that true love demanded. He dug Bannerman out of the back room at The Rottweiler and told him they both needed to move to Sarajevo, on account of the substantial killings to be made in that city.

"Zat so?"

"*Substantial*, I'm telling you, Bannerman," which, with his on-off New Zealand accent, he pronounces to rhyme with "cinnamon." Frito explained it all. The dotcom boom hadn't died, it had gone to live in Reconstruction. Guilt money was raining out of the Dayton Peace Plan in lumps the size of a fist. The European Bank for Reconstruction and Development (EBRD) was going nuts with grants and loans, desperate attempts to get the Bosnian economy breathing. Likewise with the World Bank and the IMF. Western governments would match your investment like for like. Then there were the UN refugee and resettlement programs, the Organization for Security and Cooperation in Europe (OSCE), the Office of the High Representative (OHR), the International Criminal Tribunal for the former Yugoslavia (ICTY), plus the entire captive market of NATO's Stabilisation Force (SFOR), with all of the subcontracting opportunities they represented, and a whole slew of lesser acronyms rattling along in their wake like Just Married cans, and all of *those* needing to subcontract . . . cans on cans . . . and meanwhile fifty percent unemployment in Bosnia, highly educated workforce, and no import tariffs with the EU. "Mate, we can't make money out there? we deserve to go into *banking*."

"Maybe we do deserve that," said Bannerman, nuzzling tenderly at his pint.

But Frito, with his shaky understanding of personal space, just sat there, inches off Bannerman's left cheek, nodding eagerly. Bannerman made a face to register how impressed he was by this barrage of datapoints. "Does sound amazing," Bannerman agreed.

"Yep." Frito stood up, but frowned at Bannerman's inaction. "Come on then."

"Come on what?"—"Come on, let's go."—"To Sarajevo?"— "Right."—"What, now?"—"Better now than later."—"I don't think that's how the saying goes, Frito."—"But we need to go now."— "What are they, after us?"

"No, they're before us, Bannerman!" suddenly too loud, drinkers turning to look, "there are substantial killings out there Bannerman, and they're being swallowed up by those before us!"

"Killings."

"Beyond your wildest dreams!" his hands in starbursts.

What was Bannerman going to do? He didn't have wild dreams. He didn't even dream, much, mostly he just lay there. On recent form Bannerman couldn't consult his way out of a paper bag, whereas Frito had made several killings in various sectors over the years. Bannerman had made zero in the whole thirty sorry years, and he'd kind of planned on catching half of Frito's next one.

Plus Frito was in love. He hadn't said as much, but Bannerman had wheedled out of him that there was some girl he had met, Swiss no less, based out in Sarajevo, named Clare Leischman. Seemed she did something or other for the UN in the High Representative's office, and, from what Bannerman could gather, something for Frito in her own office. Hard to say what. Frito was cagey about such things. So Frito wanted to pursue something with a girl finally, for the first time ever. Why would Bannerman not do this for his best friend in the world?

Bannerman looked around The Rottweiler, with its outsize plastic snowflakes stuck to windowpanes, the fruit machines, the institutional burgundy carpet that looked like someone had opened a pig on it. With a sigh he swallowed his London Pride, wiped the scum from his face, and stood up. "Frito pal, let's do it."

There have been a number of such jinks. Originally both computer programmers, Frito and Bannerman realized early and hard that there was no money in doing it yourself, and for the last few years they've pursued various wild schemes, mostly in Frito's case successful, and mostly in Bannerman's case not. Ethical business consultancy had abruptly given way to online pet food, then to pharmaceutical B2B schemes, then online realtors, computer peripherals, back to pharmaceuticals . . . New York to San Mateo, back to New York, London . . . it's not easy scraping a living outside the mainstream of corporate protection; co-option and moral release have built-in gyms, health plans, pensions. At the other end of their twenties it seemed such an obvious choice, to drop out of the Sleepwalkers' Parade and go find themselves a fortune. Assume ten killings to the fortune, and Frito's halfway there. Bannerman's still looking for the ignition. Now in his thirties and still looking for it, well—still—he's just about holding on to that rising balloon. The boys are brave and, let's face it, not old. But Frito's had to come back in and merge their companies, to form F&B Consulting Ltd., to stiffen Bannerman's resolve. Because the nerve comes and goes, as does the height at which Bannerman's been aiming: the warehouse in Barking, East London, has become crammed near solid with remaindered crap of a wildly varying assortment lately, soaking up much of Bannerman's life, and all of it governed by one of the great eBay-era laws: there is no product so mean as to be without value, in or out of its wrapper, though crazily more so if its clear polymer hymen is still intact. Hence, this trusty laminating machine.

No shortage of explanations for the lack of killings. Excuses include 9/11, obviously, the dotcom crash, and that there was a worldwide services industry recession on. Well sure. It had been slow even at The Painted Lady, their local café, which was strange because even in a recession Londoners still needed to eat badly. But despite Bannerman's sincere attempt to help, Fatima, The Lady's manager, refused to cut her prices in order to capture market share. There was no consulting some people.

Yes, business is slow. In November this happened: Bannerman spent three whole weeks doing an Ethical Consult for some pissy little outfit, just a couple of guys in Shoreditch doing nothing in particular—still it was work—when they, the crappy guys, served him, Bannerman, with an invoice, for *their* three weeks' consulting.

"No, see, it's you two, ethically consulting *us*," Bannerman assured them. "Honestly."

"Exactly," goes guy 1. "And we expect to be paid for that service."

Bannerman was like "yeah well," and there followed a lengthy and unbusinesslike exploration of one another's shortcomings.

How could this have happened? Bannerman wanted to know, in a pub session afterwards. The guys sighed that they didn't know either, that they arranged it all very thoroughly with Bannerman's partner, the big Kiwi bloke, what was his name again, Frodo or something.

"Guys," Bannerman had said, clapping them both on the shoulders, "I understand completely."

But how could he complain? Frito wasn't so much about the hassular paperwork side of things, he was more into the hunter-gatherer fundamentals of Trade. He'd taken to moving alcohol around the Eurozone, arbitraging his way around the excise situation. In August he had a breakthrough at a sushi bar: idly peeling the label from his bottle of beer, he discovered that the UK version of premier Japanese lager Asahi is actually brewed in the Czech Republic. A revelation. Which told him that:

Cheap as international shipping was, East European beer was cheaper.

"And it's the best in the world, Bannerman!" So in September, rummaging around Eastern Europe for options, Frito came across a more than usually cheap beer: Sarajevo Pivo, a golden Czech-style pilsner brewed from its own mineral water, which he started selling at a horrendous profit in Hackney that next week. "Sarajevo" having exactly the right branding for your arty East London crowd: heroic, grime-stained, kind of FTW, hints of Trade for Aid about it, and buyable at £0.12/33cl bottle, cases of 20, half-container shipments, EXW Sarajevska Pivara, dd., 15 Franjevačka, Sarajevo 71000, Bosna i Hercegovina.

Declare for excise in Calais, bring the shipments across in unmarked vans, to be distributed by Reza their hollow-eyed delivery guy. Frito's been getting a markup of 35p a bottle. Sweet as. Though that was only possible as long as the authorities didn't look into all these private weddings Frito's been having, which wasn't a worry, except that Frito had started drinking again—which interferes with his antipsychotics, and the old Disinhibited Personality Disorder started playing up around Customs officials. "Gentlemen," Frito waggling Sarajevo empties at them, "I have of late, wherefore I know not, foregone all Customs & Excise . . ."

Bannerman was aghast. "You taunted the *authorities*?"

"Don't get your knickers in a knot," Frito waving a hand through it, "Customs are used to that kind of thing. They enjoy it." With something like 50 percent of all London alcohol smuggled in on reduced excise, Frito's contribution is—they told him so, shaking their heads at his presumption—"small beer, mate."

Well. Bannerman knew all along that something else was up. Between September and Christmas Frito made maybe a dozen trips down to Sarajevo, with only Reza's limited conversational palette for company. Supposedly there were exclusive distribution deals to negotiate, marketing splits, labeling issues, organic accreditation, etc. Which shouldn't in the normal run of things be enough to interest Frito—he's a high-stimulus guy—but he was *very* interested by something down there. He was drinking again, sure, getting blasted nights down The Rottweiler, but on Sarajevo Pivo no less, buying back at retail the wonderbeer he'd sold them wholesale. Very alien behavior. Diagnostically, it was hard to separate psychotic disinhibition from love. Bannerman confronted him about it, tapping at Frito's chest, "think someone might have a cru-ush?"

"Right enough bugalugs—Hilmo Selimović!" The owner of the Sarajevo brewery.

Frito claimed, defensively, that Sarajevo Pivo did golden things for his "mana"—he wears his Maori mysticism pretty heavily—and generally affected the delicate state of his psyche so joyously and deeply that eventually how could he not get to thinking it maybe had some kind of narcotic content, "like early Coca-Cola, mate!" sidelong leer at Bannerman, nodding, "you know what I'm saying?"

Bannerman knows where to file all this. When you're on antipsychotics for Disinhibited Personality Disorder, a lot of things affect the delicate state of your psyche. Drugs that wreak major changes on a persona, this is not a small thing. With a corresponding swathe of side effects that some see merely as side effects, and nothing more sinister, poor fools. But Frito was educated better than that. The old Maori cosmology had a lot to it that was quaint, vagina-spelunking myths and so on but some deeper truths had found their mark in him, and Frito's wise to the spiritual dimension that Western medicine refuses to acknowledge—knows that mind-altering drugs will necessarily change a man's relationship to his god (whatever that is) and to himself (if that's a different thing), and that the side effects of antipsychotics are in some way penalties exacted for having to purchase, rather than achieve, state of mind. On his own terms, he's a failure.

Bannerman has needled him what the relationship is between the facts that Frito's on antipsychotics and that he sees it this way. Frito wriggles against it but okay, if Bannerman wants it that way, fine. Anything to force his major point through. Conservation of Emotion:

His assumption is there's a whole Mephistophelean exchange rate out there, administered if you like by spirit-world *atua*, or sprites, for the whole or part sale of souls. Frito's is out on leasehold. Take anti-psychotics like Zyprexa, for stability, and the price includes reduced cognitive speed. Hypersensitivity to the sun's another one, plus amusing brain effects like uncontrollable pattern recognition, diminished concept of body safety and indifference to the emotions of others . . . Frito's got all those. Bundle them up behind a face looks like it could hammer in nails and a voice like an idling lorry, and the girls go down like skittles. Not that he *minds*—sex is great stuff—he's just bemused at how readily they throw themselves under the wheels of a boy's indifference. Ego. A need to perturb.

Which would all be perfect, if only those atua let him give a damn.

"Admit it. You are in love, aren't you," Bannerman says once they're on the road. Around Augsburg, Germany. It's a two-day drive in the Transit van, gray-green in all the windows, F&B crap jammed solid in the back, and a little Christmas tree dancing from the rearview.

"I . . . *am* feeling things I've never felt before," Frito confesses.

"Yeah?"

"It's so pure, I can't tell you. And it feels *wetter* than everything else, if that makes sense, actually *wet* on the inside . . . I suppose that's because it's made from its own mineral water, y'know?, that has percolated down through the rugged beauty of the Dinaric Alps to an underground lake, whence it is drawn by the brewery's three artesian wells, which may draw water at a rate of a hundred litres per second."

Bannerman scratches his head testily. "Not sure you need that figure in there."

"But what a brand! Sarajevo—the reluctant hero, the cosmopolitan warrior, the hedonist, an intoxicating whiff of dissent . . ."

"Intoxicating Whiff?" Bannerman frowns. A new addition to the basic template Frito used to use on bar managers back in London, trolling his wares round the trendy drinkeries of Shoreditch and Hoxton.

". . . what about 'Plucky Underdog,' Bannerman? You think that works?"

"Dude, why are you still doing this? You planning on selling it back to the Bosnians?"

But Frito doesn't reply. Only the hum of tires on the German road and the rain on the hood, very uterine.

"Sorry," tension flowing at last from his body. "It's just, there's something funny going on. I keep getting these shivers, mate. Started in the autumn, when I'd go through the sales pitch. It was no use saying parts of it. I had to do the whole thing, like the Nicene Creed, and at the end I'd get this whole—bellyful of—fantastical feelings inside my mana. It was the order of the words. A magic spell I guess. A poem."

"Fantastical feelings?"

Frito rubs fat fingers through his sandpaper jaw. "Take this plucky underdog thing."

"It works."

"Yeah maybe . . ." shaking his head.

"Sure it does. Bar managers love it, right? The British anyway, rooting for the underdog, Dunkirk and all that?"

"Forget that. Think of it for a second not as a sales pitch, but— let's say—an explanation. Can't help wondering, Bannerman: how did Sarajevo survive?"

"Them underdogs had pluck."

"Seriously."

"Uh," Bannerman narrows his eyes at Frito, thinks he may have missed the tone here. "Is this a quest?"

"Sarajevo couldn't survive, Bannerman! I just don't think it could have. Listen to this. On the one hand, right, you've got this vulnerable little town, see? two or three hundred thousand people, a small town the size of like Chichester, surrounded by high ground on all sides. And they had no defences, army, no weapons, nothing. Mind-ing their own business. So this undefended little town is attacked, right, out of the blue, by this enormous army of homicidal rednecks, all of em ideologically motivated, veterans and armed to the teeth. Tanks, artillery, planes, everything. And the Yugoslav army just *emptied* itself on them. They let em have it, right, for four years—they besiege Sarajevo for four *years*, Bannerman—and they still can't capture it." Frito pauses. "So my question to you, Bannerman," throwing an index finger at him, "is what the fuck?"

An expectant pause. Bannerman knows his cues. Frito will wait for him to begin speaking before cutting him off. "Probably—"

"It *isn't* possible. Sarajevo was *surrounded*. They had no access to weapons, food, ammunition, diesel, water—the Serbs were poisoning the river—and they held out for longer than anything in the Second World War."

Bannerman doesn't really know about these things. "Maybe they—"

"It's not possible, Bannerman. I'm telling you."

"Personally I put it down to their remarkable pluck."

"And every time I gave that little speech, to every bar manager in town, I'd get to that point and see it begin to work on them, and they'd be like: oh yeah, that *is* good going, good old Sarajevo—except—every time I said it, it was also working on *me*." Frito listens briefly to the echo of his own words. "Some flip paradox I been peddling around, that now *I* have to solve. The biter bit. I'm like, *hang* about: how *did* they? Longest siege for four hundred years?"

"Th—"

"It isn't possible. I'm telling you. They had more *men*, sure, I mean, they were living there, right? But no weapons. There was the arms embargo, they couldn't get any, I just don't see how they could of held out." Banging a fist in a palm. "There's something we're missing, Bannerman. It just isn't possible."

Which has a note of finality, but Bannerman's not fooled. Frito has form here. "Impossible?"

"Not explainable by *science*, anyway."

Bannerman nods knowingly.

"And sure, you nod your scrawny little nod all you like mate, but saying something's not explainable by science doesn't mean it's *supernatural*. Necessarily. Might mean it's just explainable by like, history or geography or something. Latin."

"Sorry wait, you think it's *not* supernatural?"

"Well just—hang about a minute. Let's not even prejudge that whole issue, alright? Let's just call it something 'Other' for now. So there had to've been some kind of 'Other' thing that kept the city protected. Am I right?"

"Wasn't that the UN?"

"So—" Frito pauses to look at Bannerman doubtfully, decides to ignore this egregious lapse of taste, "—so I was thinking, I wonder what that 'Other' thing might be? If someone were to find out? what that thing was? maybe harness that power? well, that'd really be something, wouldn't it? If only someone knew what it was, Bannerman." And Frito, holding a Sarajevo Pivo with its label pointing at Bannerman, drinks meaningfully.

Bannerman drives on, chin on chest, lets the noise of the wind outside have a whole minute to itself, then two, but Frito's getting impatient, okay better get this over with:

"Frito," looking up, "do *you* have any idea what—"

"As a matter of fact, I do. Because, and I found this out only the other day, during that entire time, for that entire siege, you had men and boys going to the front line with like single rounds in their rifles, and guns made of bloody *plumbing* Bannerman, and during that entire time—listen to this—during that entire time, half the city was already captured by the Serbs, and during that *entire* time, you listening, mate?"—Frito seems to require more attention than Bannerman can single-handedly provide—

"During that entire time, the brewery never stopped producing beer."

"Who doesn't like beer?"

"They barely had any *water*!"

"So they must have been thirsty. Nothing like a beer when you're thi—"

"No! It takes like five litres of water to make one of beer. They were using their precious water to make beer with, Bannerman! What's that tell you?"

"They like beer?"

"Tells *me* that it was incredibly important. More important than can be accounted for by just being, you know, *beer*—" fatly pinching his lips "—that it must have had some 'Other' significance . . . and when you put that next to this indomitable little town, inexplicably holding out against the invaders . . ."

"Holy shit," Bannerman suddenly getting fantastical feelings of his own, featuring physical harm to his business partner, "tell me you're not thinking like, magic potion?"

Frito spreads his hands. "I don't want to be the one to say it—"

"Jesus god." Bannerman heating up fast. "At least tell me this is not why we're moving to Sarajevo fucking Bosnia? Tell me at least it's because you're in love with some girl? Or boy—Christ, even a boy would do at this point?"

There's a pause while Frito maybe weighs up the admissable answers here, before his shoulders drop and he mumbles, like a child who knows he's done wrong, "because of the substantial killings."

"That's more like it."

And the rest of the road trip passes without incident, through Austria and out of the Schengen Area, down the Croatian coast, into Bosnia-Herzegovina and up the Neretva Valley, motoring past Mostar and Konjic and up into the snowline and soon a darkening watercolor east, cloudbank high above the mountains still lit pink by a western radiance that flashes from the wing mirrors, the indigo shadow of their own vehicle four or five lengths ahead and swinging away across the brown-iced road. And singing along to The Breeders' *Drivin' on 9,* pulling on Sarajevo Pivos, and approaching the idea that this strange feeling might be happiness. Bannerman's going somewhere new, with all the corresponding illusions of progress, it might just be what the AA—that's drinkers not drivers—calls a geographical cure, but he's ambitious and optimistic and alone with his best friend in the world, with a new life opening in front of them, and possibilities in every direction.

* * * * *

"Clare," they both say, shaking hands.

"At last, the great Bannerman," she says, "Frito's told me so much about—"

But Bannerman's only half there and unable to deal with what he's seeing, there's something different-species here about the intensity of freckles, all over her forehead and ears and *on her lips*, skin-colored lips of a beauty not thought possible, not by anyone, not until now—a girl short and minty and highly evolved for camouflage in brown sugar, save for those intense black-lined eyes and those lips, soft brown-dotted lips, which incidentally might as well be talking Bosnian for all he can register what they're saying—

Almost two weeks in and this is the first time he's been allowed to meet her. After the bleak numbness of London he's suddenly drastically alive, and through all the Sarajevo Pivo he knows a Class A girl when he sees one. An instant dependency. He knows; he's had enough first hits by now. She's amazing. Dragging a hand down his face, suddenly he absolutely must have the one girl in the world who is out of bounds. A strangled hunchback moan leaks out of his mouth, a slow mournful noise that starts with a "cr" and heads lugubriously toward a "p."

"Excuse me?" Clare's eyebrows are all ears.

"Sorry, just a—quick, moan of pain, there."

"You're in pain?"

"Yeah no sorry, I just—remembered something, about—ethnic cleansing. Anyway, you were saying?"

Clare smiles sweetly. "I was saying don't you hate it when people moan while you're talking."

New Year's Eve in Sarajevo. People are promenading in their hundreds up and down the wedding-cake splendor of Ferhadija Street, just seeing and being seen, from the Eternal Flame past all the lingerie shops and bars, along the low medieval bazaars of Sarači Street to

Pigeon Square, and back again. Clockwise. It's a Sarajevo thing. They're all fleece hats and pink noses and sexy glances, a good-looking town, done up tonight in exotic party kit: transparent moon-boots, feather boa hats, spray-on jeans and stained-glass handbags, an entire gentleman's suit made of a fabric that says Sretna Nova Godina in pink on black—and all of it something else for Bannerman to feel too old for, being only a slight formalization of the situation he'd been facing back West, where teenagers also speak a different language. Enormous music pulses in everyone's ankles. Smoking is absolutely compulsory.

And Bannerman has remembered it all. This freckled girl has crashed down on him like toys from a forgotten closet, unopened for twenty years . . . there are memories in his head he didn't even know were there, about *this exact girl*. And, now, having leapfrogged the small talk in one easy bound, International American accent, a sarcastic eyebrow expectant as a microphone, *this is her*.

"No, I like it when people moan," says Bannerman, quick riposte, "frankly any way I can get someone to moan's fine by me."

"Sexual double entendres, okay," Clare nodding, "I can see how you might want to, throw out a few of those, to—let everyone know what kind of person you are."

"Yeah, they are great," Bannerman bares his front teeth thoughtfully, "and when I can't think of one? I cold drop *sack* on a dude's ass."

Clare blinks. "This phrase has not come to Switzerland yet. But I think I can visualize—"

"Violence," hurriedly, "that one was a violent entendre. Not sexual. Really."

But she's looking doubtful.

"Plus it was a single entendre! 'On someone's ass' is a preposition of violence, see, not like *affection*, you're not *balancing* something on, you know, the Cheeks—and 'sack' is—. No one really knows what sack is."

"I think I do."

"No you don't."

"And I think you do too."

"No no no it's violence. I'm American, see, it's *always* violence."

"So, say,"—searching the crowd for a suitably handsome man—"if *that* guy told me he wanted to drop his sack on my ass, that would mean . . . ?"

"Just 'sack,' not 'his' sack."

"Okay fine whatever," shrugging it away, "clearly it's none of my business, it's between you and your therapist."

"I'm not in therapy!"

"Evidently."

She sparkles. Bannerman winds up for a thumping comeback but she's not letting him off the back foot: "A therapist might suggest you confuse sex and violence—"

"I'm pretty clear on the difference."

"—which of course you're in denial about, but nevertheless you tell a girl you've just met that you like to beat people up?"

"Well but hey that's just a standard hip-hop type—"

"A girl you are attracted to, no?"

Bannerman goldfishes. "What, you?"

"When you say you like to beat people up, you're advertising your sexual suitability, I think?"

"No! It's just an ironic whiteboy sort of—"

"Meaning you'd like to have sex (I have to assume), with *me*, correct?"

"Whoa now Doktor Fräulein, enough with the—! *Crazy* wide of the—. I mean, you're cute and all but—. Let's move on."

"You don't get turned on by violence, Bannerman? Guns?"

"Guns a device for Sticking It In from a distance, sure."

"Fights?" leaning closer, *"Beatings?"*

"Is this like the *Am I A War Criminal* questionnaire?"

"Nationality test. Real Americans are turned on by violence."

"How am I doing?"

"You tell me," frowning, "you tell me if you wouldn't like," eyes all sarcastic childlike innocence, "to come round to my apartment, middle of the day some time," finger trailing down her neck, "and beat *me* up?"

Bannerman freezes.—Caught in the highbeam of those eyes

burning with an impotent rage, stuck for answers, and wondering what do you do when the girl of your dreams turns out to be a man-hater?

Finally: "inflamed rotator cuff," regretfully massaging his shoulder.

Clare collapses into a smile. Her sudden bitterness cleared with a single line. "Poor thing," tilting her head the other way.

"Yeah. No strength at all. I haven't successfully pulled a Christmas cracker all winter."

"Have you pulled anything all winter?"

"I see Frito's briefed you."

Shaking her head, "Feminine intuition."

But she has a glittering smile for him anyway. He's passed some sort of test. "Bannerman listen, great to meet you and all this, but how about we get to know each other while we look for Himself in front of the band?" and leading him by the hand through the street parties, the burek stalls, the goldfish vendors trying to keep their stock defrosted, and up the decibel contours toward where The Seams are playing in front of the Catholic cathedral.

Jesus. He's heard, this is how it is with stage hypnosis. Nominally you're in your brain, perfectly alert—just dragged along in a slip-stream of charisma, without the energy to disengage the grip of that white wrist, too thin, too fine, an epidemic of freckles and a long straight vein up the bone . . . disappearing into a fitted gray ski jacket, the reflector patches down front and back observing the curves of her body . . . a mind as agile and defenseless as deer, an articulacy of soul wasted on a coarse world, her breath colder than ordinary air, and with a touch more oxygen, and his own togetherness beginning to flow easier, rather than the strangled hunchback moans that nor-mally crawl dead from his lips . . .

"Cool kind of *fiesta nevada* they got here!" Bannerman calls out to some passing Spanish soldiers. The garrison in town is Spanish, this year.

"Well maybe tonight you'll get lucky," Clare turning round at him, "you can't hook up on New Year's Eve, you're in all kinds of trouble."

"Not sure I've ever hooked up on New Year's Eve."

"Good idea," considering him, "a sympathy play probably is your best bet."

"Specially at this sort of *fiesta nevada*, here."

"Yes *okay*. 'Snowy party,' the only two words of Spanish you know, clever."

"So acknowledge it then!"

"What, you need people to acknowledge what let's call, for the sake of argument, your jokes?"

"I like obsequious laughter as much as the next guy."

Clare does what will turn out to be her standard sly smile, with lazy eyes following a moment behind. "All right," accusatory finger on his chest, "only I have this bee in my bonnet about girls doing all the giggling. I'd like to see equality of laughter, you know? Basically what I'm saying is: you can take it, but can you dish it out?"

Bannerman has a stab at a tinkling little laugh.

"Amateur." She does hers, and Bannerman's head explodes. The blast directed upward into the starry sky, his headless body with singed neck tumbling slowly into the snow . . .

"Coed boarding school," and Clare launches into a no doubt familiar tirade about gender roles and submission through giggling. When she's finished: "All right, you can stop your fake, little—tittering now."

"That's my real laugh," says Bannerman.

And Clare stops plowing through the crowd, and turns to look at him again. A re-evaluation, searching from eye to eye, for whatever's real, in there under all the clown . . . until it slides off at last, crumbling into amusement again, not without sarcasm and in a high register: "dick," she says, with a chuckle and a shake of the head . . .

And twenty yards of crowd away are The Seams, playing the first bars of their eponymous breakout track, These Are The Seams Along Which You Will One Day Rip: and here are girls in FK Željo tops bodysurfing on the crowd, here are barbecue embers fluttering like tracer rounds into a starry sky, and here is Clare Leischman smiling out of fat dotted lips, clean against a jostling world, with confetti butterflies fluttering around . . . and here now an electric-green lens flare from the stage lights, sliding out of the night sky and down between their faces . . .

Five minutes in and this is the best girl he has ever met.

But how can he avoid seeing in hallucinogenically vivid detail the thing, the one unavoidable thing here: the thing involving Frito's shimmering Polynesian buttocks, eyes rolled back into their sockets, swinging strands of saliva hanging from a depraved German Shepherd leer, small feminine whimpers beneath him?

Bannerman lets out a strangled hunchback moan.

"Genocide this time?"

"Listen, Clare," conspiratorial, "can you bear with me a second?"

"Sure," expectantly, little smile, perfect gums candypink above whitewhite teeth.

The call center brushoff. Bannerman nods her thank you and turns, drifts vaguely away, on undirected feet though the subzero boozing, and disappears into the crowd.

"Oh there you are Leischman," says Frito, rocking up with his hands full of the wonderbeer, "what have you done with my friend?"

And so the crowdian motion carries Bannerman off into the Great Sarajevan Promenade, past hat stalls, happening bars, čevapi shops and frizerski salons, a girl in fur chaps and holsters dispensing slivovic, some kind of graffiti-off down an alley, paramedics freeing the frozen lamp-post kissers. But his eyes are all inside, sadly reading the writing. The message couldn't be clearer: the less time he spends with that girl, the happier he'll be in the long run.

Because the unopened closet, the one he didn't even know was there, has told him everything. *She* is the girl who has made love to him, and who never said anything. When Bannerman has lain back over the years, eyes screwed shut and wanking onto his stomach, an array of different women will have passed through all possible and impossible positions in his mind, not just fantasy women but also women that existed—and of all these pure & applied impersonations astride him, looking around at him over perfect rumps, undoing incandescent white uniforms, leaning with palms flat on his chest, on their backs gasping in a horror of pleasure at the splendid carnage he's making of them, looking down flat stomachs, shaking out cascades of hair, crisp slickbacks, angular eighties buzz cuts, gloss-red mouths, plump bloodless heroin-colored lips, cracked dried lips, lovebites on jugulars, runs of icewhite hair up the golden spines of California girls, the white-magenta mottling of inner thighs, sharp conical tits, tits with perfect spherical undersides, swinging tits as big as a head, beautiful faces gone ugly with orgasm—his mind sifting fast through this whole fantasy Rolodex for the one that's going to work tonight—

There will have been phases when he kept settling on:

A slight, bright girl. Maybe a little awkward. Painted in very high definition skin, so bright it's flirting with hospital-scrub green, thread-count beyond anything he's felt before and absolutely *dipped* in freckles: tiny and beige on the forehead, maturing to bold sienna summers on her nose and cheeks, a fall of brown inkblots on angular shoulders; with sleek lateral panels, under her arms, less freckled. Sometimes freckles is *all* she was—all of her gone except a wireframe shell of freckles that bucked and writhed against him . . .

In these fantasies their ages have been variable. Often he was fourteen again, back in his mom's house in St. Paul, Minnesota, and she was a friend of his sister's, eighteen, leaning in the doorjamb, popping gum and full of amused contempt. Sometimes *she* was the kid, a little sassmouth playing at womanliness but with nothing to say but a giant O when she wriggled down onto his haggard twenty-nine-year-old cock.

Mostly they were both older, lean undergraduates in someone's four-poster, or later on yuppies in a white duvet awakening somewhere on the rainblown shores of a gray sea, weather smeared up against all the windows, and she would screw him leaning back on her elbows, facing him, the outside curves of breasts dancing in break-beat syncopation with her hips, sinews defining the corners of her neck, the slack lassitude of a gorging hedonist but doubt always about her, even when she came, which she did silently, eyeballs fluttering behind closed lids, her chin set to "imperious," and a vague smile on her mouth. Though rarely of admiration.

He absolutely recognized her. This being from the perfect dimensions, transposed into the crummy phenomenal world. Everything in him wants to reach out and protect her, save the winter-fresh optimism inside her from every kind of shittiness, protected as she is only by the thinnest of cynicisms, an ill-fitting persona worn just to get by. He knows exactly who she is already.—But he didn't know that she would come out Swiss—yes, that was a surprise.

Oh, crud. The one Frito finally falls for, is his. An imperfect situation. He wanders, muddled by snowy alleys and Sarajevo Pivo, tries to eat a čevapi, the local sausage sandwich, but even shitfaced his mouth won't allow it and it crawls out of his mouth and into a bin. Instead he sits at the water fountain in Sebilj Square, frozen for the winter, and smokes wistfully, and considers how to handle this—but it's not long before he finds his thoughts turning to the correlation between alfresco wistfulness and warm weather, and he has nowhere else to go but back.

"Colorscheme of Hazardsigns" is, as advertised, a nightclub in black and yellow, where the tables and booths revolve—a lovely u.s.p., but more importantly it's too expensive for the locals. Instead, it's a lazy ebbing and flowing of Westerners, catapulted into Society-grade wealth by dint of exchange-rate. Everything is cheap. Not least, consequently, jokes about the host culture ("You ate čevapi darling, you'd have to be Lucky Pierring with starvation and insanity to eat one of *them*"). But these are well-meaning people who didn't even go home for New Year, who are out here helping this country and just trying to have a good time like anyone. *Polako* is the name of the game, which literally means "slowly," but which translates somewhere between "mañana" and "non preocouparti," and that's how life is taken by this rump contingent of Embassy staff, lawyers, soldiers, engineers, Irish girls in pointy shoes who press their cheeks together at regular intervals for the benefit of a camera, auditors, guidebook writers with a bad case of Bosnia Is A State Of Mind, some slick new MBAs, quiet Frenchmen in yellow sweaters and boat shoes, Swedes and Australians swapping bloodthirstiest warcrime stories . . . each with their place in the vast system of Dayton Money, and all smoking as though they've got Serbs for lungs.

"Nice place," shouts Bannerman.

"If you like this kind of thing," shouts Frito.

But that's all right. In the main room, there's little scope for talking anyway. Bannerman has to scream in some Portuguese girl's ear to offer her a drink, and she says yes, and the dull lust in her eyes is keeping him motivated all the way to the bar and back, though he has to fight through a dreamscape of pounding bass, writhing limbs, soulful rock songs from a few years back, and people screaming, though from exuberance or what, it's not clear. In this room there's any number of twentysomethings dry- or possibly wet-humping on the dance floor. Fighting back through the throng, holding his drinks above the crowd, Bannerman's easy prey, and disembodied hands rake up and down his back, his face, one down the front of his trousers, another through his wallet, by the time he's back to the Portuguese girl his jeans are around his knees and both glasses are empty. Oh well. Portuguese girl is then grabbed by some guy with cheekbones like he's got a weapons cache in there, who starts grinding himself against her pelvic floor. Her eyes slide shut, her head lolls back, and they disappear into the crowd.

"What's not to like!" shouts Bannerman.

"Hey—where'd you get to!" shouts Clare.

He leans down to speak into her ear, nose brushing her cold hair, "I had to go take care of this thing!"

"I didn't think so!"

Bannerman smiles lopsidedly.

"Come on then, start over!" she says.—"What?"—"Start over!"—"At what!"—"Impressing me!"

Bannerman steps back to frown at her. Her eyes challenge him to deny it. So he leads her by the wrist through an obstacle course of dancers, scrimmages, revolving tables and waitresses to a quieter bar at the back, still crammed as full with people, though not with sound. "So—what?" he says, "you're offering me a second chance at first impressions?"

"Why not?"

"Well, uh," Bannerman frowning at this weirdness, "is that yours to offer?"

"In this town, you don't have to have something to sell it."

Nodding, "Sounds like Frito's rubbing off on you."

"We did that the first night."

"Classy." But he felt it all right, and throws back some more slivovic to neutralize. "I don't know about this meeting each other again thing . . . wasn't so bad the first time?"

She's like "speak for yourself," with large comic eyes.

He shines. Already with the affectionate abuse. "So how do you like Sarajevo?"

"Fantastic! Love it!"

Bannerman takes another look at her. "Didn't think so."

Clare clinks her glass against his. "All right, I admit, sometimes it gets a bit . . ." waggling her head.

"Sure."

"There's only so much raping a girl can take."

An old line around her office. Where the humor is for obvious reasons very gallows. She's with the International Criminal Tribunal for the former Yugoslavia's Office of The Prosecutor (OTP), specializing in violence against women. But Bannerman doesn't rise, just nods thoughtfully, wise enough to the thin ice here to know that while she can make wisecracks about such things, he can't. Such wisdom suddenly. Just her presence makes him competent, and somehow he knows not to doubt the taste of such comments, no not even with his eyes.

"The usual stuff about coping mechanisms," with a wave of her hand. "Come on, let's do this right. Buy me a drink."

"I totally would love to?" peering into his wallet, mysteriously empty of Bosnian Konvertible Marks, "you ever get the feeling your wallet metabolizes cash straight into receipts, without any human intervention?"

"Got a good metabolism, your wallet?"

"One of those metabolisms girls like to pretend they've got."

"Oh, that's so annoying," Clare puts on an annoyer's voice: "I eat like a horse, me, and never put on *any* weight. Haven't a clue *where* it goes!"

"Right," agrees Bannerman, "straight down the toilet."

Clare pauses, a little movement of the head, squints at Bannerman. "Isn't that where it's supposed to . . . ?"

"Straight *back* down the toilet, I mean."—"*Back?*"—"Not, back as in: having come from there—I mean, they don't pass it *through* their digestive systems, it's just visiting, in and out, toe-in-the-water—fuck," deep breath, start again: "I suspect many girls of recreational bulimia."

"Recreational?"—"Sure. It's fun, in, then out again."—"Fun though?"—"Course. Don't you like putting food in you?"—"Are you referring to eating?"—"Actually, that's not a bad business model," Bannerman's jaw set to one side, "so the contraceptive pill gave women sex without consequences, if you gave people *eating* without consequences . . . double the target market for starters . . ."

"Olestra?"

"I was thinking more some kind of throat condom. Or femidom, I suppose. What drug mules do. You go along for a nice dinner party, you'd have to get all the alcohol in first—then everyone would fit their throat femidoms, awkward, bit of retching, then you throw back all this food, and at the end, everyone pulls theirs out, like a colostomy bag see, and you all compare how much you managed to keep down."

"Appealing image."

"I'm an appealing guy."

Clare blinks slowly. "You are, somewhat."

Bannerman smiles, and she smiles back, and the room is filled with stars. Oh man. He has to get out of there, and tells her so.

"You're ending our conversation?"—"I am."—"Why? I thought it's going okay."—"It is."—"Why, then?"

Bannerman tries to wriggle out from under this one.

"Because I'm Frito's?"—"That'll do."—"What, you're not even *interested* in speaking to me if I'm not sexually available?"—"That's not it."—"You can always go home with Victoria, the French one, you know."—"That's good to know."—"It'll only take ten minutes at the end of the night. She's into you."—"That's great."—"No? What then?"—"Bye bye, Clare."—"Tell me!"

Bannerman rubs his hair, frustrated. "Just—let me speak to someone else."—"I'm boring you?"—"So not."—"You think it's not a good idea?"—"Roughly."—"Not a good idea, like throat femidoms are not a good idea?"—"They are an excellent idea."—"Not a good idea, like you're *wary*?"—"I am a naturally wary person."—"You're wary of your best friend finding out you were *speaking* to me?" shrugging at an invisible jury. Bannerman smiles and shakes his head. Clare arches an eyebrow. *"Wary of the intensity of your feelings?"*

Bannerman can't keep a smile down. "Take it easy, you."

Clare shines at him. "The Prosecution rests."

But he can't tear himself away. "Where's it resting tonight?" real casual.

Clare smiles and screws him in the eyes for maybe five seconds straight. "With Frito," she says at last. "Your best friend."

"Oh yeah," and he gives himself a mock slap upside the chops.

Clare reaches up to massage his shoulder. "At least your rotator cuff is better."

And that's pretty much how the expat scene plays for Bannerman: at cocktail parties, dinners, gigs, farewell bashes at CityPub, Embassy receptions of one flavor or another—always in permutations drawn from a pool of maybe fifty simpatico First Worlders, of whom Clare Leischman is overwhelmingly his favorite. A slow underwater grace takes them both; he anyway feels like an elite conversationalist, the jokes are effortless and lighthearted, and always pressing up against the walls of what's acceptable . . .

It's a welcoming scene. Memory and judgment smeared by all the excellent and cheap alcohol, everyone living in the same acre of city and not disinclined to physical companionship, life in Sarajevo quickly becomes a motion-blur of people hanging onto decades-long adolescences. Relationships form and dissolve with college intensity.

Couples go up to Park Prinčeva restaurant for sundowners over the city, and wave at the couples at the neighboring two tables, all six having been there before in a different combination. It's a campus, and that's family enough. All stiffened by high daytime ideals and a weirdness that never really goes beyond the eccentric. Like this Danish character Joren, from the Office of the High Representative, who's decided Bannerman's going to be the recipient this year, all year, of his observations on women. "See this girl here!" dragging him away, "I think she is an Aviation Blonde, yes! You know what this is! Yellow hair, black box! Ha, ha! Yes, you think so!" elbowing him keenly.

"Colorscheme of hazardsigns," says Bannerman.

And for a few weeks reluctantly fending off Clare Leischman, mornings at the literally Byzantine apartment he now shares with Frito above the Turkish quarter, Clare comes into the breakfast room all shower-fresh hair and a grin that lets you know it's been freshly fucked. "Sleep well?" she says, knowing full well that Bannerman has lain awake all night watching the lightbulbs swing.

"Morning, Ban-O," Frito sweeping through with a hunk of toast in his mouth, peeling off some hundred-KM notes for Clare, "mate, would you mind driving Clare to work? Got to see a man about a dog" and out the door again, leaving him alone with her eyes.

And little respite outside in the city. Because there seem to be three or four Clare Leischmans now, at least one at every party and all speaking different languages, brief floodlit moments of mascara and killer smile before glancing away again, dissolving into chitchat . . . nothing more than torturing him, and not only because she can. Seems to be a genuine pleasure for her, stretching in front of him first thing in the morning, holding her hair up so he can clasp necklaces, making sure she is seen again and again in improbable places, glowing from within her constellation of freckles, fingertips like butterflies across Bannerman's back as she insinuates herself into his conversational circle, some quickfire exchange of sass between them before Bannerman can move out of range and try to disinfect his heart with alcohol, but she's already somewhere else when he arrives, gloss lips wide open and laughing at another man's joke.

Aw c'mon. Frito's his *best friend*. Bannerman makes listless attempts to console himself with other girls that collapse with spectacular damage to everyone's ego. But it always comes back to Clare, she's the golden thread, every evening his eyes scan for freckles in the Promenade. He cannot stop from doing it, and his heart lurches before he even knows what he's seeing—oh just a Bosnian girl, freckles, hijab on, seventeen tops. When the real Clare's lashes flick up with a clang he is twice as alive, twice the data between them, in her every hint of eyebrow semaphore which he implicitly understands, and which she understands that he understands.

And so in not too many days, after a going-away party at which he watched Frito treat her with an indifference bordering on scorn, he'll sit up all night in the window-room of their apartment over Baščaršija, smoking and watching the city-valley and its galaxy of streetlights fade to nothing under the dawn's maybe three inches of snow. Muezzins will call the morning in, hatchbacks and trams will clang along Marshal Tito Street, and he'll contemplate his monochrome world: dead black trees on the white slopes, white carapaces on a chaos of Ottoman brickwork, grades of cast iron and steel, a nobility of minarets and towerblocks undulating into the hazy western distance, and the roof of every building blessed with snow in the night, transfigured by the white of peace.

Or ceasefire, anyway. Fuck it. Reckoning his odds at 40 percent, and even though just the attempt will end his friendship with Frito, he'll finally give up not trying to get her. He's going to move in on his best friend's girlfriend. Contemplating this most taboo of betrayals with that special equanimity given by the last cigarette in the pack, smoked at dawn—which soon he'll stub out and head to bed, and wake up after lunch, stretching like a dog, and feeling absolutely awesome.

ViKA, d.o.o.

FORMERLY ONE FIFTH of a financial services team that went long in handheld weaponry in the summer of 1991, Vedad Alimović cleaned up when the Bosnian government found itself staring down the barrel of a neo-Nazi invasion with no weapons, no army, and a UN arms embargo that prevented them from defending themselves. Vedad had seen which way the wind was blowing. The cartel, known as the "Parejevo Lobby"—a schoolboy play on *pare*, meaning money—smuggled 7.62 and antitank weapons in and charged astronomical markups, and were considered patriots for doing so. "If we survive, UN will forgive the debt," they shrugged to each other. Resolution 757 prohibited all funds transfers to the former Yugoslavia, and, as with the arms embargo, there's a bit of embarrassment about that now.

Each of the five shares of the cartel represented enormous fortunes. Tragically the other four members didn't survive the war, three catching frags in spooky circumstances, which was all very suspicious, but who wanted to have a word with Vedo about that? And what, frankly, wasn't suspicious about that war?

But Vedad Alimović, now pushing sixty, is a man of naturally expansive mind, with unofficial easements over a great variety of Bosnian property, and whose raft of interests these days runs to an industrial-conglomerate scale—canneries, restaurants, reinsurance, publishing, German-language call centers—everything having been incorporated under the umbrella ownership of Vedad i Kara Alimović Poduzeća, d.o.o., ViKA for short. Which, ever on the lookout for new enterprises in which to be investor of first refusal, holds networking soirées on the first Tuesday of each month.

For there are the usual obstacles, imported from diplomatic uglinesses elsewhere, against certain nationals gathering in certain embassies, which however irrelevant inside the Protectorate of Sarajevo must nonetheless be observed. And many of Vedad's closest associates, having in the past decade become enthusiastic not to say fervent Bosniak nationalists, are not exactly posterboys for the kind of interentity harmony that High Representative Ashdown has started forcing down Bosnia's three throats—while relatively few of the businessmen in Bosnia as a whole enjoy a full and frank relationship with the law. That's just what happens when Stability goes. But everyone has a friend in Vedad Alimović. The upshot is that, if the exchange of business cards is your thing, the ViKA soirée, "Enterprise Initiative," at Stakhanova 4 is the only game in town.

Stakhanova is a short dead end off Skenderija, and number 4 faces you from the end: five stories of gloss-black brick with tinted windows, and curiously spared the graffiti that covers every other building in this neighborhood. Only the city's compulsory number sign, a big white 4 on a small green square, interrupts the blackness, and doesn't seem too happy about it.

Inside reception, lady employees clatter high-heeled across an underlit floor, shiny black pantsuits with lipliner to match, severe male counterparts with buzzcuts and clipboards standing by the entrance. Once past, steps lead up to a mezzanine level of dark carpets and muted lighting, save for the spots shining down onto perspex cubes, meticulously labeled and containing weatherbeaten old stećaks, architraves, columns, other fragments of medieval architecture. Among bookshelves, and mounted directly against the brick walls, are antique Federov and Schmeisser machine guns. Soft library-volume conversations going on between balding men and twenty-year-old women. Dust particles, gold against black, dance in the columns of light. At the far end of the room, guarding the entrance to the soirée, is Vedad himself in a biznis suit, set about with hangers-on, and receiving visitors with a grand-, not to say god-, fatherly charm.

"You go," says Bannerman. "I'll stay here and find out about machine guns."

"Relax," Frito driving him forward by the upper arm and standing, Bannerman can't help but notice, almost directly behind him. "Hey, Vedo!" calls out Frito, "been at the pie cupboard again, anya, ya fat bastard?"

A moment of heart-stopping silence while an associate whispers in Vedo's ear. Then Vedad smiles. "Frido!" he says, and he and Frito break into some kind of mutual Heimlich Maneuver. "Sretan Božić, thank you for your gift, my wife she is very happy. Welcome to Sarajevo! This will be good year for you, I think! O.K., nema problema! And this is your little friend!" as one of Vedo's hands swallows Bannerman's up to the wrist.

Bannerman deals with it. Looking Vedo in the eye, he fields a few questions, tells the consultant-on-the-landmine joke, customizing it for maximum local flavor, which goes down well. Hell, with this kind of panic management, maybe Bannerman would have made a good soldier himself. Here, where everyone got to find that out about themselves, it seems okay to wonder.

Then Vedo looks over their shoulder, receives a whisper from his aide, and bellows, "Eh, jaran! Thank you for your gifts! My wife she is very happy—" and the pleasantries are over. Frito and Bannerman are ushered gratefully past and into the sudden loudness and thick, steam-thick, cigarette cloud of the main room:

A full-spectrum crowd. Contractors, translators, exporters, politicians, smugglers (the flashing of diamond ear studs, tiepins), foremen, journalists, security people, manufacturers, enforcers, engineers, UN monitors, programmers, marketing consultants, restaurateurs . . . and a slew of bareknuckle tycoons involved with mines, some bauxite, some tin, but mostly anti-personnel.

Frito's eyes glow. "I'll take this side of the room. You go that way."

Bannerman knows he can trust Frito here. "Pallet of Sarajevo Pivo to the most business cards."

"Done." Frito will have sold €50,000 worth of prescription pharmaceuticals by ten o'clock—stock he does not, naturally, own—while Bannerman launches himself into a bewildering waltz of conversations:

DANIEL FLEISCHER, CORRESPONDENT, *FRANKFURTER ALLGEMEINE ZEITUNG*

"Have you met Vedad before?"—"Sure. He's schizo, you know."—"I can imagine."—"No, for serious. Schizotypal. Clinically."—"Yeah?"—"Worst case of Bosnian Psychosis I've seen. Strain of the war, supposedly."—"Understandable."—"Story goes, the injustice of the UN arms embargo versus the moneymaking opportunity it set up, generated this internal conflict that pulled his mind completely in two."—"Gosh."—"Severed his corpus callosum."—"Corpus . . . ?"—"Yes this is the neural structure that joins left and right brains. Vedo's broke. Now he has none."—"Golly."—"Yes this is what enabled him to beat his partner Fehim Bičekević to death while begging himself to stop."—"Is that a fact?"—"Yes this sounds crazy, but I swear this is true."—"No I totally believe you, it was nice meeting you."—"You too, dobro dosli in Sarajevo. Let us hang out!"

EMO ADONIĆ, BRANCH DEPUTY MANAGER, AGROKOMERC

"Like Ibrahim, I trust God to stay my hand." Emo downs a tumbler of whiskey, then looks forlornly at its ice cubes. "Again he forsakes me."

LUDOVIC VAN EISLEY, INTERN, OSCE

"No, it is strange. They don't make a big deal about it, but you feel it. The seething. They have a nose for nationality. Maybe it's easy with us, with our red cheeks and orange hair and Dutch accents and all this stuff.

"In America and England, you do not like to put the dots in UN, yes? On the sides of trucks, it says UN, no dots, yes? Virtual dots, let's say. Everyone knows the dots are supposed to be there, but it looks cooler with no dots. Yes? Well. Bosnians don't read signs like this. They don't understand no dots. Unfortunately it was the Americans and English who put the sign outside Potočari Base in Srebrenica which said, UN SAFE AREA SREBRENICA."

"Holy shit." Bannerman's cheeks redden in sympathy.—"Yes."—"I never thought of that."—"Yeah, well. It is very hard now to persuade a certain type of Bosniak that this is not what was meant. Not even subconsciously. They are . . . superstitious people."

Bannerman stands, knocking back whiskey, a contemplative bubble in the hubbub of the party. "Yeah but hey Ludovic—can you persuade *yourself* that that's not what was meant, even subconsciously?"

Ludovic smiles again, red round the eyes.

EDGAR RADFORD, JR., DIRECTOR,
FILE 13 SECURITY CONSULTANTS

"Hey what do you know, an American! Good to know you. Edgar Radford, Jr., Alexandria, Virginia." Edgar is an enormous beefy guy, who is surely either gay or an Abercrombie & Fitch model or both, and who presses his card into Bannerman's hand.

"Bannerman Tedus. St Paul, Minnesota."

"A Twins man! Well all right. You know they used to be in my town, DC, before we kicked em out to yours!"—"I did know that, yeah."—"So tell me, how'd you make it in *here*?"—"Into Sarajevo?"— "ViKA."—"No idea. My business partner organized it."—"He did, huh? Just like that? *Damn.*"—"Why, was it a hassle for you?"

Edgar puts a hand to his head. "Oh man, you got no idea. I been trolling through the gray economy for weeks, I swear to god, I have to do two hours of coffee with like one more garrulous old dude, I'ma lose my shit."—"I'm sorry to hear that."—"Wouldn't be so bad, apart from the coffee. You tried the coffee?"—"Some."—Edgar shakes his head. "*Man.*"

Bannerman nods thoughtfully. "You wanted to get in here pretty bad, I guess."

Shrugging, "Security consultants, we need to put ourselves out there. Can't do anything in this town without the help of one lobby or other. Vedo's is the most, ah, energetic."

"'Security' being a euphemism for . . . ?"—"No euphemism," innocently, "private security details for politicians and bureaucrats, risk assessment, that sort of thing. A lot of standing around looking mean and hitting on translators."—"Gotcha."—"Bannerman, I'd like you to meet my boss, Andrew Elliot-Maitland. A Scot. Animal, this is Bannerman. Minnesota man. Just arrived."

Another enormously tall man, this one bald on the front half of his head, wearing a navy guernsey, corduroy pants and desert boots, shakes Bannerman's hand, gives him his card, and scopes him up and down like he's estimating his calorific value.

ANDREW ELLIOT-MAITLAND, DIRECTOR,
FILE 13 SECURITY CONSULTANTS

"Hi there Andrew, for a minute there I thought Edgar said 'Animal'!"

Elliot-Maitland smiles. "A school nickname. It stuck." Fatless cheeks. "Nothing to do with sexual prowess, if you're about to ask."—"No no."—"People do. Now let me see . . . if I'm not mistaken, you're the chap who goes about with the Maori?"—"Right."—"With a ware-house in Dobrinja?"

"That's," Bannerman's eyes check the exits, "correct."

"Yes," by way of explanation, "you've been seen around."—"I have, have I?"—"We were wondering who you were."—"We?"—Air-ily, "People talk."—"No they don't!"—"Oh, but you'd be surprised how much they do."—"When interrogated, maybe."—"Sarajevo's a small town . . . Bannerman, was it? The expat community's even smaller. Get used to it."—"I been here a matter of days!"—"Plenty of time. Expats stand out a mile off, you'll see. Feel at home yet?"—"I don't know, what does your psychological profile say?"—"You should. It's very American, this town."

"Yeah?" Bannerman looks doubtfully around, "haven't seen that many of us?"

"Not so much in that way. International, I should say. Like early Manhattan, under the Dutch. Ironically enough."—"Why ironi-cally?"—"We're still under the Dutch."—"A lot of them around?"—"Plenty."—"Well, haven't seen any of them, either. No wait—let me guess—you're about to say, but they've seen me?"

Animal smiles. "One ought to assume so. The country's crawling with Dutch commando. Some sort of repentance after Srebrenica. You'll hear the name Jens Asselijn bandied about, their commander, look sharp if you do. A serious gentleman."

Bannerman squints up at him. "What are you, running intelligence for Paddy Ashdown?"

"In my dreams. File 13 has a Ministry of Defence contract, personal security details, few other SFOR bits and bobs, but we're just a start-up. Always open for new business. If you're thinking of doing anything risky, speak to us." Handing over a card.

Bannerman properly freaked out by this point. "I'm thinking of going over and talking to that girl?"

Animal looks over at the indicated, wrinkles his nose. "I wouldn't."—"No?"—"See that man hanging around like he owns her? He does. Not a figure of speech."—"Okayy."—"Stick to the expats. Safer. Quicker, anyway." A handshake. "Now Edgar here went to some lengths to get us invited, we should mingle. Good luck, Bannerman."

And Bannerman drifts away to the bar, where he orders three whiskeys and attempts to tip them, triple-barreled, into his face.

"Useful?" Edgar asks Animal.

"Sorely doubt it," replies Animal. "How's my audience coming along?" Privately chatting over a foot above the rest of the crowd, these two soldier-entrepreneurs are a forbidding sight.

"They asked could you speak to, ah, man called Jasim Bukić first."—"You let them palm you off?"—"What can I say Animal, I insisted, they insisted."—Animal exhales noisily. "Alright. Let's find this Jasim Bukić."

A lady with a clipboard confers with Animal and Edgar, floats off. They move toward to a matinée-looking Bosniak, thirties, a light gray suit, and hang fire until his present conversation draws to a close. Animal moves in afterward with a gigantic hand and a dazzling smile. "Izvinite, ante li Gospodin Jasim Bukić?"

JASIM BUKIĆ, SENIOR VICE PRESIDENT,
VIKA SPEKULACIJA, D.O.O.

"Yes, Colonel Maitland, I am Jasim, and I thank you for making effort, but please: let us speak English. Sometimes I think," Jasim nonchalantly letting his expensive gray suit hang open enough to show the handle of a pistol, "this is—only language you people understand!" Uproarious laughter, Jasim gripping them by the shoulders for dear life.

"Very good. Very good." Animal and Edgar sharing appreciative looks. Gangster humor.

"You are having good time, yes?"

"Excellent time, Mr. Bukić. The food is excellent. Now forgive me, did Mr. Alimović get my fax?"—"Ah. Yes. I have read your fax."—"And Mr. Alimović?"—"I have described this to Mr. Alimović."—"I see."

Apologetically, "Mr. Alimović is busy man."

Animal puts a finger against his lips, thoughtfully, sizing up this Jasim Bukić. Supposedly Vedo's head of Domestic Relations. "Mr. Bukić, from this I understand that ours is not an interesting proposition?"

Jasim chews a canapé, assumes a look of deepest sincerity. "You understand, it is necessary we have . . . nothing involve with your project."—"I understand this."—"We do not touch this."—"Yes."—"Nothing at all."—"Absolutely. I quite appreciate, that if it were to become known that Mr. Alimović had in any way helped—"

"I—no, Colonel Maitland, forgive me. I did not wish to interrupt."

"No no, go on."

"I think you are not thinking in accurate way. You think you can keep this secret. In the West, CIA, NATO? ok, maybe you have secrets. In Sarajevo? no. There is no difference between helping in secret and helping in public. Everyone knows everything." Putting his two index fingers alongside each other. "It is same."

Animal reddens, not accustomed to receiving lectures. "I understand. Thank you for your time."

"Colonel Maitland, you are quite welcome. No? You are not satisfied?"

"Just one more question, Mr. Bukić, if you don't mind."—"Of course."—"Why, given Mr Alimović's political stance, his well-known difficulties with *Dani* magazine, his financial support for the SDA and so on, why is it such a bad thing for him to be seen helping to capture Persons Indicted For War Crimes?"

Jasim Bukić cocks his head doubtfully at Animal. "Because this is war."

"Not to fight, just to help apprehend—"

"This is war," showing empty palms.

"Merely to provide *information*—"

"Colonel Maitland. Here is the 'real thing.' ViKA has looked at your fax carefully. You are very brave soldier, and you are intelligent man. No one says this is not true. But it is necessary for you to under-stand that Mr. Alimović cannot help you. He hopes very much you capture Bosnian Serb indictees, that you get huge rewards from America, that you have big party and he is invited. But he cannot help. If he helps you, there will be retaliation from certain persons, and then retaliation to *that*, and this takes us back to our 'problems.' No one wants this. This is also why he will not speak to you. If he speaks to you, people will see this, maybe someone gets angry. Then there is no escape. 'Juka' Prazina was shot in Amsterdam. For this reason also it has been difficult for you to be invited to this ViKA soirée. But the persistence of your colleague," bowing at Edgar Radford, Jr., "is remarkable."

"Obliged," says Edgar cheerfully.

"You understand, Colonel Maitland?"

"I understand."

Jasim Bukić gives him a wink, says "sretno," good luck, and thins into the crowd.

"Nail in the coffin, boys?" says five foot four of Harvard Yard lounge lizard, sidling up in dinner slippers and tuxedo. Andy Garcia hairdo, circular eyeglasses containing herring eyes, a smile that's all gums and no teeth.

"Ciao, Mudhill."

AL MUDHILL, OFFICE OF SPECIAL PROGRAMS, U.S. DEPARTMENT OF DEFENSE

"Ciao boys—miss the goldrush again? You can still make the next one, if you hurry. You got three months, max, before kickoff. Brown & Root just got COMSFOR to stump up for free Arabic lessons. Building 113, evenings after school, all contractors welcome. Little bit of DiFac scuttlebutt for you. That the kind of thing you were looking for?"

"Our offer stands, Al. Anytime you want."

Al Mudhill squirms delightedly. "Boys boys, read the writing on the *wall*. You'll have to think up something much more delicious than boring old money to buy Al *Mud*hill," placing five exquisite fingertips against his shirt front, and simultaneously drawing attention to his gold elephant shirtstuds, whose glittering trunks stick out the best part of an inch.

"Better than money," Edgar's got a toothpick in the side of his mouth, John Wayne style. "Any hints?"

"Edgar Radford, use your imagination! Honestly. Officially, the only way to interest Defense is with major dope."

"Dope?"

"Not *your* kind of dope, you big dope, *inside* dope."

Animal looks at Edgar, Edgar looks back guiltily. "I don't use!" he protests.

"Oh but I do like that. Edgar Radford, Jr., the outside dope. *Sensational*. I must tell Ariel. Very interested to know how you boys get on. If you get anything really juicy on Vedo's more colorful contacts— you know," nodding around the room, "the Iranians, Maktab Al-Khadamat, all that AQ stuff—give a call," pressing a card into Animal's hand, "I'll roll right over, let you tickle my tummy."

"Unofficially?"

"Oh *you*," Al Mudhill wrinkles his nose, "don't make me say it!"

"Say what?" Animal genuinely puzzled.

Al Mudhill slides a fingertip vaguely up Edgar Radford, Jr.'s, pant leg. "That I have my price, same as anyone," and wandering off, gummy smile thrown over a parting shoulder.

"—" Animal begins.

"I am totally dedicated to File 13," says Edgar Radford, Jr. "But no."

"Ah, New Zealander, are we?"

"Yep, hold on. Got a card here somewhere—"

L. FRITO COOPER, DIRECTOR, F&B CONSULTING LTD.

"'Frito,' how'd you do? Al Mudhill. What an enchanting name. *Does Frito lay?*"

"Oldie but a goodie," Frito nods. "You're what, some sort of spook?"

"No no. Just a penpusher. But we like to keep our fingers in everyone's pies, yes."

"Uh-huh," warily, "so you know who everyone here is?"

"I like to keep my ear to the ground," then Al leans forward conspiratorially, "*from a standing position*, you understand."

Frito nods this one past too. "Know anything about me?"

"I know you're new. And now I know you're forward. Do you always push yourself forward so?"

"Mate, cut it out. You're gay, great, move on."

Al Mudhill peers sexily over the top of his glasses. "But what I don't know is: *who* does Frito lay?"

Frito sighs. "I'm seeing this girl at ICTY."

"Is that so?"—"It is."—"Not Sophie den Uyl?"—"No."—"Clare Leischman?"—"The same."—"Aha, the lovely Leischman, you as well. Nice for you, if you can deal with all those," wiggling his fingers, "*things* on her *face*."—"You don't go for freckles?"—"Eoo, *no*," Al squeals, "diet cancers."

Frito puts a hand on his shoulder. "You're alright, Mudhill."

"Still, makes a change from everyone lusting after Sophie den Uyl, who once had a *fourway* with Jens *Asselijn* and two of his men!"—"Is that right?"—"Scout's honor. A dose of the Psychosis won't be all she goes home with, that one."

**DMITRI LAUTZ, FEDERAL MINISTRY FOR ECONOMICS AND
LABOR, GERMAN EMBASSY**

"Bosnian Psychosis?"

"Ah, well. Everyone gets it eventually. Everyone," Dmitri indicating the entire room. Tanned, sleek Italian threads, perfectly at ease, Dmitri's the epicenter of the party. Frito doesn't trust him an inch.

"And this is an exciting field also, Frito: psychological problems with external symptomology, the way social class is indicated against anorexia, you know? And shell shock and so forth. This time it's geographical. A decrease in rationality comes first, then paranoia, apophenia, und so weiter. You can see it in the eyes. Helen from ICMP has been here so long she wants to restart the war, to finish the Serbs."

"Crikey."

"Removal leads to a lessening of symptoms."

Frito nods thoughtfully. "Antipsychotics any defence?"

"Who knows. The Psychosis has deep roots. Back in the siege you see, the Serbs broke into the mental hospital and let the patients loose in the city. There's an interesting paper on it. It seems they were trying to break Sarajevo's sanity, not individually but what's called the *Gruppengeist*, that beyond a certain level it will be degraded beyond use, and the city will go completely mad . . . remember the Serb leaders were psychiatrists, Rasković, Karadžić, and so on. They knew what they were doing, they'd already started a retaliatory war with propaganda only, now they'd moved on to a new theory, of breaking a city without weapons. Grind down their sanity," unnaturally white wolf-teeth, "a brilliant insight."

"Didn't work though?"

Dmitri looks about him, amused. "What do you think! Though yes, I am not sure that insanity really obstructs an ability to kill in large numbers," with a practiced wryness that has already accepted whatever you have to say about Germans, in this regard—"Rest of their work, though, pioneering. Textbook."

Frito squints at Dmitri thoughtfully. Spies everywhere. "So why *didn't* Sarajevo fall?"

Dmitri only laughs at this one, mutters ja very good, chucks Frito on the shoulder, and dissolves.

MAK PLANINOVIĆ, SDA DEPUTY, SARAJEVO KANTON

"Sarajevo never fell because of our arms smugglers. For this we thank Alija Izetbegović, our great president."

"Thought Izetbegović *disarmed* Bosnia before the war?"

"This is true. But then he was smuggling weapons in, all days. Alija and Hasan Čengić. They bought many weapons from the Americans and the Iranians. The Unholy Alliance."

"In violation of the embargo?"

Mak Planinović gives a smile that says: *come now.* "Vedad Alimović will tell you he has saved Sarajevo, but I think Hasan Čengić has smuggled more. Hasan had Iranian suppliers you see, Vedad only Afghanis. The Afghanis are," how to word it, "enthusiastic spiritualists, but their infrastructure is—piece of shit."

"Well but so, how'd any of it get in, before the tunnel was dug?"

"Aha!" a politician's stage laugh, "this I cannot tell you. But that is why Vedad Alimović and Hasan Čengić are rich men, and I am only—poor deputy for Sarajevo Kanton."

Frito nods. "That a Rolex Oyster?"

"Naturally."

CHRISTIAN WESEL, ECONOMIC ANALYST, EUROPEAN BANK FOR RECONSTRUCTION AND DEVELOPMENT

"Herr Wesel—"

"Oh, please, *don't.* Just go away."

"But—"

"No, do not deny it. You think we don't recognize this look? It is very particular, this lust in your eye, your scrupulous manners, look at you! You are desperate for EBRD money, yes!"

"I just—"

"You have no idea what it is! I am an economic analyst, this only, and I cannot walk freely in this town! Each time I get into a taxi, the driver tells me his proposal. A colleague of mine was mugged the other day in Mejtaš, mugged you see, they handcuffed a *business plan* to her wrist! It was bound with chain and printed on Tyvek, this is unbreakable paper, she had to *shower* with it!"

"Jesus." Frito cools off. "What was the plan?"

Christian relaxes as well. "Tyvek printing." He shakes his suit jacket back into a natural fit. "I am sorry if I am mistaken of your intentions. But you see how it is."—"I get it."—"In information terms, the city is Pareto optimal. It is *the* model economy. Everyone has perfect information!"—"But imperfect sanity."—"Yes, ha ha! O.K., you know this one already."

ZANNA AGNERI, ASSOCIATE LOCATION MANAGER,
MAGASINS SANS FRONTIÈRES

"It's totally the coolest thing? Rapid Reaction Economics. We bring *factories* to *people*. Mostly textiles, sewing pants together, handbags, that kind of thing? What with the whole tax deal in Bosnia, makes it totally this worthwhile thing, right?"

"Like a maquiladora?"

"No! maquiladoras exploit, everyone knows that, whereas we are helping these people."—"Fair enough."—"We are a registered charity."—"Rightyho."—"We have factories made from shipping containers? that we carry around, drop in some very bad warzone? where people will work for practically *no* money. Almost nothing! It's awesome."—"Sounds awesome."—"Yes, it is! If you had the choice to starve or work?" shrugging, "what do you choose?"—"I'd choose work."—"Exactly! So we give them this choice. Soon as we get through the manifest, we pay everyone and move on. Our client list includes some *top* brand names in the West. T-O-P, top. Harvard Business School made us a case study."

"Does sound a *bit* like a maquiladora."

"Oh please. Working is fundamental human right. We give people money *and* pride." Frito feels the antipsychotics take the strain, and inhibit him from saying anything more brutal than "Work sets them free, huh?"

"Totally."

KHAN KERENSKY, FORMER YUGOSLAVIA ANALYST, PERPETUA ASSOCIATES

"Dude! Having *nothing to do* with that Zanna chick. She went camping up on Bjelašnica last summer, where she claims she was made love to, right? by a *djinn*."

JÓVAN AMARANZIĆ, ADVOKAT

"So what's the deal with Sarajevo Pivo?"—"Sarajev*sko* Pivo."—"Right. Sorry."—"What do you mean, the deal?"—"Why's it magic?"—"Magic?"—"I suppose . . . why did the brewery keep brewing it all during the war?"

Jóvan Amaranzić looks at Frito with some amusement. "You come to ViKA, you start conversation, and first thing you say is the war?"

"Oh get over yourself, mate, you're going to have to face up to it *sometime*. Sorry anyway." Jo-Jo waves it away. "With me, it is okay. But in general, you should not do this."—"Well, so, I'm interested in finding out some things about the beer and the brewery, Sarajevsko Pivara."—"Sarajev*ska* Pivar*a*. Our language, ironically, is one that has to agree."

Frito grins. "Nice."

"I don't know if I know what you mean. The brewery produced beer because this is what breweries do."—"But during the world's longest siege! Without water! And electricity, and diesel, and ammo . . ."—"Oh, it wasn't so bad."—"Really?"—"Not for Sarajevska Pivara. They had water."—"They were the only ones that did."—"Yes, okay."—"And because of that, the Chetniks went for it, actively tried to destroy it."—"We say VRS."—"Sorry?"—"Not Chetniks. This is like 'nigger.' Also 'ustaše' and 'balija.' Maybe if you are Naser Orić, big war hero, okay, you say Chetniks, but as member of the Colonial Overclass, you should say VRS, Army of Republike Srpske."

"Was that, 'Colonial Overclass'?"

Smiling, "Yugoslavia is Communist for fifty years. Marxist-Leninist roots are not far below this," waving a hand around the room's swanky decor, "topsoil."—"Okay."—"You have spoken to Hilmo Selimović?

No? You should. He is managing director of brewery during war."—
"Yeah, we're old mates . . ."

HILMO SELIMOVIĆ, CHAIRMAN, SARAJEVSKA PIVARA

"Wotcher Gospodin Selimović, sta ima?"

"Kako si Frito . . ." Frito nods through the wave of Bosnian that comes back at him. Mr. Selimović doesn't really speak English. Nor Frito Bosnian. End of.

"Hey, Bannerman! Bannerman! We're going to need a translator."—
"Gotcha. I'm going to need someone inside the police."—"I'll keep me eyes peeled."—"Likewise."

Bannerman claps his friend on the shoulder. "How you doing?"

Frito nods, *not bad*. "Half cut. You?"

"Shitfaced. Who was the ah, Robert McNamara's shorter, eviller brother?"

"Al Mudhill. Republican. Avoid."

MAZA CUKIĆ, TRANSLATOR,
DEUTSCH-ENGLISH-BOSANSKI-HRVATSKI-

"Mr. Frito Cooper. My name is Maza Cukić. I hear you're looking for a translator."

"Blimey, that was quick."

"A girl must be quick. The competition is very strong."—"But there's got to be a ton of translating work, no?"—"There is a lot, yes, in total . . . but working for strong, good-looking men? not so much."

"O-Kaay . . ." Frito scrapes a hand across his jaw. "Muslim, are you?"—"I am Bosniak."—"Know Sarajevo pretty well?"—"I have spent my life here."—"During the war?"—"Yes."—"And you speak English good, do you?"—"I speak quite fluently."—"Is that American quite or English quite?"

Maza tilts her head, puzzled.

"That was kind of an interview test, see."

"American quite or English quite . . ." Maza searching the ceiling for clues, but none apparently forthcoming. Soon a flush gathers beneath her collar bones, rising up her neck and pushing into her cheeks.

"Don't worry about it, it's a bit of an obscure—"

"No, I will answer. Please wait one moment."

Frito takes the opportunity to look around, check the curves on that liter bottle of Sarajevsko Pivo.

"Mm, O.K. I have answer for you: this is English quite."

"You sure?"—"Yes. English quite means 'very much.' American quite means 'only a little.' "

"Cracker. You're hired."

Maza breaks into spectacular laughter, and throws her arms around Frito. Men look. "Thank you thank you, Mr. Cooper, I will be a very good translator for you."—"Call me Frito."—"You didn't even ask me my rates!"—"You didn't ask me mine." Maza looks momentarily distressed. "Aw, don't get your knickers in a knot. We'll do the going rate."—"Oh, I am so happy, Frito."—"All right, all right. First off, could you ask that chick for the other half of my beer?"

There's an awful lot of this, culiminating in dinner somewhere, dancing somewhere else, drinking everywhere, at least three packets of cigarettes and a couple failed attempts to eat čevapi, ultimately spinning out onto the river frontage, where big dudes go back and forth in tracksuit tops, ARBiH soldiers in camoflage, typist-looking women in penciled eyebrows, and mustachioed old-timers with necks retracted into parkas in apparent surprise, like the cold's a practical joke someone's just played on them and which'll be over in a minute—all walking home or waiting for a late tram, which will arrive presently, clattering against its inadequate-to-no suspension, cheerfully decrepit, covered with graffiti and the backings of ripped-away stickers for gigs—and we will all go merrily home together, crashing into each other and each time lifting our hats in apology.

Shiny and Jamie

ELSPETH "SHINY" DRYHTEN has been here since last spring and she still hasn't got a grip on the Old Town. It's constantly rearranging itself. Gets tiresome, chasing around after her favorite restaurants, kiosks, bakeries; new ones emerging from nowhere, sudden squares with cafés that were simply *not there* yesterday, roads paving and unpaving themselves into piles of loose marble, backdrops appearing grandly Romanesque and already floodlit, low medieval rows rotating with the moon, leaving behind spiral staircases that go nowhere, solitary colonnades standing for nothing, unexpected mosques, Baroque fountains dribbling water, cathedrals swapping places with octagonal Orthodox follies, minarets that point at different constellations every night . . . Shiny has heard that the very walls are built of tombstones. In the desperations of siege, down the centuries, effendi and pasha have had no choice, but which has surely unloosed eldritch powers . . . and now what look like graffiti tags but could equally well be runes of Bosnian Cyrillic, thought to have fallen extinct centuries ago, crawl onto and off of facades, negotiating their way around lintels, window bars, gathering under bridges to observe their own social-insect laws. Addresses rarely lose themselves entirely. It has happened, but around here there are easier ways to disappear buildings.

Not least under snow. Tonight an almighty occluded front is rounding on Bosnia, temperatures are diving through the zero, followed closely by a battlegroup of waterlogged clouds. People are talking about ten centimeters in the city, maybe twenty on the pistes, the first flurries have already started, and everyone's hurrying to get indoors. But first, twenty minutes of promenading.

Hotel Alija, on Štrosmajerova Street tonight, is the setting for an occasional poker evening Shiny runs with her husband Jamie, in these early days of the global poker craze. So here we sit around our black-baized table, alone in the exact center of the Šamac function room, classic low-hanging central lamp, a darkness of invisible spectators pressing around us like railbirds. But our stout campfire of laughter, tobacco and late-period John Lennon albums, playing for Animal Elliot-Maitland's sake, holds those hollow-eyed presences back—when at a joke from Animal, an old friend of the family from back home, about "been working like a Bosnian bricklayer," how can Shiny not spill abruptly sideways out of her body as the rest of us chuckle, see herself suddenly to be what she hates: one quite comfortable above the apartheid, thank you, with all its possibilities for carelessness toward those beneath? She can barely tolerate the existence of waitresses, her instincts run so strongly to helping. And looking around, the local population is visible here only to tiptoe in and out in red vests, lashes lowered like the palm fronds of fan-wallahs. Possibly not even visible to some here, gliding amongst them easy as djinn and shaitan.

Oh but come. It's only cards. That doesn't take away from what we're all trying to do, does it?

Shiny and Jamie are in their early thirties, fresh-faced, fresh-hearted. Jamie O'Ryan—freckly, masses of black hair—runs a small de-mining organization, methodically clearing the Former Confrontation Line (FCL) of UneXploded Ordnance (UXO). That's in the summer. When the ground is frozen, he fund-raises. Shiny Dryhten (she kept her maiden name) has picked up an internship at the International Organization for Migration (IOM), helping trafficking victims. Anything to avoid worrying whether he'll come home tonight. But Jamie doesn't go about prodding the turf with knives so much, not these days; there are plenty of locals who are happy to put a price against that task. Which is—Jamie's not proud, but it's a not-for-profit company, and they only had three Incidents last year—€4 an hour.

They're not rich. De-mining costs a euro per square meter, whether you find one or not; so there are powerful reasons to "de-mine" innocent land, and consequently millions of euros pour through an industry now rife with fraud and gangsterism, against which Jamie takes a conspicuously principled stand. He will draw only €28,000 this year, plus pension contributions. Shiny will make that go further than most. The finances might have created awkwardnesses in their marriage if they weren't as in love as they are—Shiny's from a grand old family of Scots Catholic recusants; Jamie's just a poor, decent Leinster boy, who's by no means keeping her in the manner. But he's the goodest man she has ever met. And if it took a comfortable upbringing to free her to know the value of that, then fine. She won't disown it. She is proud to be the dutiful wife of Jamie O'Ryan. For how can his fierce pride, his flat refusal even to discuss putting a price against certain of his principles, for all its practical difficulties, not make a red-blooded woman love him more? Each time she veers near the idea of letting her parents help them out—the anger and shame that redden his cheeks, a stammer that comes on—oh it breaks her heart, and all she knows is, she loves him, she loves him.

They make a little extra organizing the poker games. Jamie's one vice. And excellent networking anyway, because as often as not characters like Erika Dreizen, from the IMF, can just about pull enough strings to get more donation funneled their way. And it was through the medium of poker that the Sufi Child came to them.

It was January. A shady Maori entrepreneur called Frito was losing money less rapidly than usual. After some medium-to-heavy betting, he'd made it to the flop without obvious enthusiasm. Then when Queen-5-5 hit the table, he actually knocked the table leg in surprise. Chipstacks danced. But he blamed it on Shiny next to him, and looked round at everyone rolling his euphoric brown eyes in exasperation. Checks all round back to the ebullient Maori, who checked as well, his other hand playing air piano. Shiny bet a timid €2, everyone folded back to Frito who made a show of considering, before raising her to €10. Shiny folded in a second.

"Bloody hell," Frito said, throwing down 10–5 off. "Why does no-one bet when I hit my hand?"

At the phrase "hit my hand," Edgar Radford, Jr., spat beer in a fine aerosol into his lap.

"You had a feeling double 5 would come down, didn't you?" said Jamie O'Ryan, peering out from under his mop of hair.

"Indeed I did," Frito scooping his meager chips. "The magic beer told me."

"Sounds like the beer talking," Jamie agreed.

Which turned the conversation to the strange verbosity of alcohol, at which Ketyl Gaarder, a quiet red-faced Norwegian girl with the European Union Police Mission, told the table: "Oh I saw one of the Drunk Monks earlier! A sweet-looking boy, absolutely drunken. He can't have been more than fourteen. He was passed out, right there in the cemetery."

"Blinds," said Edgar Radford, Jr., dealing. "Jamie?"

But Jamie's attention was caught: "Sorry, what?" at Ketyl: "Drunk monks?"

"Oh, you haven't seen em?" cut in Francine Petersen, a middle-aged Australian lady with the World Bank, "they're just the cutest thing," and Francine told him all about the men who drink alcohol in order to become closer to God, a sort of mystical Islamic sect—

"Dervishes," said Ketyl Gaarder.

"I know," with a glare, Francine's enjoying Jamie O'Ryan's attention herself thank you, "they're dervishes, like the lady said, and they believe God speaks to em through the medium of alcohol, and oboy they just *loove* speakin to God! You'n see em now and again, lyin around, chuckin right there in the street and trying to do that chant thing?"

"Allah Akbar," said Ketyl Gaarder.

"Thank you," Francine said firmly, "Allah Akbar. You'n hear them late at night sometimes, they're just kids, but they make a hell of a noise, once I swear I thought it was the Serbs coming back for seconds, I thought, uh-oh, Francine, they comin gitcha—"

"And there's one out there, tonight?" Shiny twisted to see out of the window. It was snowing thickly. "Where was this?"

Ketyl looked troubled. "In the cemetery, up by the stadium."—"Which cemetery?"—"Oh, I . . . one of the Muslim ones . . ."—"Please remember."—"Let me just, remember," flustered, "I think the big one. On the left."—"Left of where?"—"You know, with the big metal spike?"

Jamie and Shiny looked at each other. "You stay here," Jamie putting a hand on her shoulder as he passed. "Ketyl will show me where she saw him. Come on, Ketyl."

"You want me to—?"

"Come and show me where you saw him."

Ketyl stood uncertainly.

"Your chips will be safe."

Ketyl looked miserably around at the other players, many of whom were suddenly involved in intense sotto voce conversations, picking their teeth with the corners of playing cards, restacking chips.

Ketyl got her scarf and coat, and followed Jamie from the room.

You can't save everyone, he has told Shiny before now.

—I know, she has sighed, her skin never more thin.—It's just . . . when these things are put right under my nose, I can't keep turning my head away so I don't see.

Jamie has his sadnesses too. Her life is being taken over by a doomed rearguard action against one of the nastiest paradoxes of charity: no matter how far into it she goes, there'll always be someone she lets down. There will always be someone in whose face she must shut the door and say: no more. I can't take any more. The face will be empty and innocent and won't understand Shiny's callousness, its bewilderment will haunt her, Shiny will suffer from it, and there is no way Jamie can stop it from happening.

"He was somewhere against these railings," Ketyl said.

Fat gobbets of snow hung in the air. Jamie was in sneakers rather than boots, and his feet turned first wet then numb. "Well, you know what Shiny's like, Ketyl—if we come back empty-handed we're going to have to be *positive* he's not here."—"Yes."

For ten minutes they hacked among the Muslim tombstones, white marble obelisks, blizzard-blind and singing whatever old songs they shared for warmth and attention, lonely protests in the dead acoustics of snowfall.

"Jamie?"—"Yep?"—"I'm not a bad person."—"Oh Ketyl."—"I just want you to know." Her face an intense crimson from either mild rosacea or bad winter sinuses. "Oh Ketyl, I know you're not."

Finally she found the boy, curled up in the lee of a large stone tablet, just a comma in a sleeping bag, gashes in its fabric mended with duct tape, and the drawstring of an anorak hood pulled tight around the tip of a small pink nose. "Govorite li engleski?" Jamie asked the nose. But it didn't reply. A spot of foot-nudging and the sleeping bag stirred. "You a Drunk Monk?" nudging him harder, but still no answer. Jamie untied the drawstring. "Oh!" said Ketyl.

He was appallingly light. Jamie carried him to the street, nylon sleeping bag whistling against his own waterproofs, and bundled him into a taxi back to his and Shiny's flat. In the blast of the car heating, thick driver eyebrows frowning in the rearview mirror, small gloved fingertips appeared around the opening of the sleeping bag, and the zipper was pulled halfway down. Ketyl took off the boy's wool beanie and vigorously rubbed his crewcut with bare hands. Even allowing for the boy's vaguely Asiatic looks, Chechen maybe, which might shave a few years off, he can't be more than eleven. Pre-puberty, anyway. It was only then, in the taxi, that he began to shiver.

"That's not a good sign, is it?" Ketyl said.

"Well, it *wasn't*." Ketyl looked a wreck. Jamie felt bad for her. "But if it wasn't for you raising the alarm, this lad would have been in dire straits."—"Yes."—"Don't look so glum Ketyl, you saved his life."—"Yes."—"Aren't you happy? Isn't that what we're here to do?"—"Yes."

Presently the boy opened his eyes, red in the lids. It took him a few moments to blink, focus, and register Jamie, Ketyl, and the taxi whirring along beneath them. He sized up Jamie and Ketyl wearily. "One hour, twenty euro," he said.

Shiny is already home when Jamie and Ketyl arrive.

"Thank God," says Shiny, rising from the kitchen table.

"Congratulations!" says Jamie, carrying the sleeping bag into the flat, "It's a monk!"

They get him in a warm shower, and twenty minutes later he emerges, flushed pink and exhaling in a giant dressing gown of pink toweling, rolled up several times at the sleeves, and trailing behind him like a wedding dress. "Hello everybody," he says, waving a limp sleeve.

"And he speaks English! Kako se zovete, malo?"

"I learn to speak English at tekija."

"He speaks *good* English!"

And he was beautiful. A dark crewcut that starts too low on his forehead, glittering green eyes with bruise-colored halos, and whose eyebrows are now opening up like drawbridges, in cartoon helplessness: "I thank you for warmth," in the tiniest, cutest voice, "I have very cold . . ."

Oh, the sheer weight of cuteness. Shiny goes "oh," hand on her heart, clasps the boy to her waist, and rocks him side to side. At that moment and for several after, Jamie cannot take his eyes from them.

Jamie sorts out the youngster with a dry hoodie and a pair of jeans, wraps him up in blankets on the sofa, feeds him tea. Ketyl has a big day tomorrow, she'd really like to stay and help, but, you know— and she leaves among undertakings to drop by after work.

From the sofa: "I thank you profusely for chocolate."

"Quite alright," says Shiny, "we're just glad you're inside instead of out."

"Also me!" with a sheepish grin.

"What were you doing out there anyhow? Don't you have somewhere?"

"Habitually, yes. But there is argument with my chum."

"Your chum, eh."

"Yes," darkly, "my chum tried to thieve my money."

"Well! That's not very nice of him."

"He is not nice. He is scallywag."

"That's ah, that's some fine vocabulary you've got yourself there, young man."

He tilts his head, blank forehead rucked up where there are no lines yet.

"Oh Jamie," Shiny going over to hug the boy some more, "can we keep him?"

It turns out he's been educated by the tekija, or Dervish monastery, that he has been in since before he can remember—namely, the war— and which, a few months ago, forcibly graduated him. This is the Tekija Prnaša Esoterika, an imaret, orphanage, school and inn all rolled into one, some way out of town, and run by an obscure order of Sufi devotees, known as the Drunk Monks—who do, yes, subscribe to a certain "alcomancy," or divination through alcohol, in their pursuit of Enlightenment. This young beneficiary of the tekija is evidently practiced in summarizing its teachings, and he adopts a stance not unlike that for the National Anthem, and recites, in a sing-song voice:

"How Better to Open of Gates of Consciousness than by the Annihilation of Self, which, is it not True, is that which Stands between Yourself and Allah?"

"Like it," says Jamie.

The boy nods. "I have said this many times. Mevlevi Dervaša, you know these gents?"

"Yep. The Whirling Dervishes."

"These gents spinned until they fall over, this helped them to open Gates of Consciousness. Now, Tekija Prnaša Esoterika has— better technology," with a shrug.

"Well, quite," says Jamie.

"In vino veritas," says Shiny, and they all clink their bowls of hot chocolate.

The child doesn't blame the tekija. Nor will he go back there; he has his pride, and he's not the only one hanging on to the bottom rung of the market economy. The order's not a large one, and not well endowed, just a handful of part-time dervishes and acolytes up on a hill, weekend toilers-in-the-soil and distillers-of-the-plum, able to provide housing and education for only so many orphans. He spent ten years there, and that's more than most. The little one said roll over, and it was his turn to go.

In that decade of grinding agricultural labor, amid painful lessons in English and German, the Prɳaša dervishes also paid attention to his spiritual welfare. They provided unlimited free slivovic for all orphans, provided they drank responsibly, and didn't just stop after five or six glasses. Annihilating enough Self to achieve the ecstatic presence of Allah, the Omniscient, the Vast, the All-Encompassing, was a serious undertaking, and not to be approached lightly, in some *recreational* frame of mind.

"Sounds like quite the high school," says Shiny.

"I've the most fond memories, yes," infectious grin but sad eyes . . .

But there were down sides. A renunciation of material possessions being the big one, which included, for the orphans, the legal instrument of possession itself: the Name.

"So, what, you've got no name?" says Jamie.

Sufi Child solemnly shakes his head.

"None? Seriously? What do your friends call you?"

"Happy. Sad. What I am at this time." Shrugging. " 'We speak not to the Self, but to the soul inside the Self.'" He has obviously had to field this question before now, and has also gotten used to saying this: " 'The Name is that which the Self clings to.' "

Jamie nods coolly. "That's a given."

"But that's simply . . ." Shiny puts her hand over her mouth, but appears not to be able to express what it simply is.

"The monk that dare not speak its name," says Jamie.

"So—you drink, clearly? How much? Enough to access, what do you call it, the 'Seven Skies'?"

"Not habitually. Seven times per fortnight?"

"Good god. And you have access to the Seven Skies?"

Not entirely understanding the question, "Yes—?"

"What do you see? Do you see God? Allah, rather? Angels?"

Sufi Child wags his head noncommitally and a classically evasive

answer ensues, even to some extent hiding behind the language problem. It is not apparently a question one can ask; or, if one has the callousness of heart to push it, the answers are all subjunctive.

But as Sufi Child expands on his theme that night—Shiny and
Jamie too fascinated to let him go to sleep quite yet—his arms grow
animated, reaching up to describe the many layers of universe asserted
by his order, the cosmic machineries and symmetries, it occurs to
Jamie it's all sounding very . . . Timothy Leary . . .

"So do you do acid as well?" Jamie says, "you know, drugs?
LSD?"

"No!" Sufi Child recoils at the thought, "this is—very bad."

"Oh."

"Drugs are—very bad. Devilry!"

"Alright alright."

"No drugs." Sufi Child's really quite horrified, pushes himself a
little further away from Jamie, a little closer to Shiny.

"Quite right," Shiny murmurs in Sufi Child's ear, a snarky glance
thrown across at her husband, her voice gone falsetto and everso
Morningsade: "*Gaelic devilry.*"

Shiny made it clear to the Sufi Child that he could stay as long as he
wanted.

In bed with Jamie, she wrestled with the problem that they were
happy with this beautiful young boy staying in their home, yet would
they not feel different if it was an elderly woman?

"Wee beastie: shh," Jamie coos at her.

As so often before, Jamie has had to hug the anxiety out of her,
grab hold of his own wrists around her and squeeze it all out, the full
weight of him on her until she can breathe deep again, can kiss him,
can accept that what she is doing counts for more than what she is
not. "Wee beastie: shh."

She lies on her side, asleep. He's awake. Not from anxiety, but
impatience. He does not want to waste time near her being uncon-
scious. He will grow tired and old soon enough. Instead he is awake,

breathing in the world around her. He can wave a hand through it, and comb it into contrails of incredible clarity, through which his own hand can be seen rendered in godlike resolution: he sees not just surface, but visible inside every wrinkle, scar and callus is the complete catalogue of everything he has ever touched.

Then the contrails dissipate, and the world is hazy again.

One palm supporting his head, he trails the other's fingertips over the shifting sinews of her rib cage, so lightly, listening to where her back is murmuring to be touched. Lightly enough not to wake her, but enough that she will dream of butterflies. In her sleep, she mumbles out her love for him.

Even so, after a few days Sufi Child runs away. Or rather: fails to come back one evening, and one of Jamie's fleece jackets to the better.

"He knows what he's doing. Let him be," Jamie holding out a hand for her. "Come to bed."

"Selling his *body* for *money*?"

Shiny can't countenance that, in fact is gearing up for the fury, and Jamie knows he'll be out on the streets again before too long, whistling for a child. He sighs, reaches for his coat.

"Go away," says the Sufi Child, when Jamie finds him.

"There's a hot dinner waiting for you."—"I have ate."—"A nice soft bed."—"I don't need it."—"Do you also need that rather smart fleece you've got on, there?"

Sufi Child takes it off, gives it back to Jamie. "I don't need you." Lighting a Drina.

"Nor I you, god knows," Jamie accepting an uncharacteristic cigarette himself, "but my terminally charitable wife, bless her cotton socks, has swallowed your whole 'I'm such a defenceless wee child' routine, which, frankly, is a bit of a disaster for me, because the reality of the situation is, *I'm* not going to get any sleep until *you're* safely tucked up in bed, with a water bottle into the bargain I shouldn't wonder. So, my lad: resistance is useless."

"Twenty euro."

"Get in the fucking car."

A pattern that repeats itself several times over the course of February. Shiny grows more hysterical each time the Sufi Child doesn't come back to what she's already calling "home." Jamie has to raise with her the prospect that he might not *want* to stop turning tricks.

"Prostitutes do what they do because they like sex, is that right?"

"That's not what I said, Shiny. Please calm down."

"Sounded like it."—"It wasn't what I meant."—"Then what *did* you mean?"

"Maybe he just—would prefer to earn his way in the world, rather than have it handed to him?"

"By *selling* his *body* for *money*?"

"Oh, drop the body thing, beastie—it's clearly not such a hurdle for him as it is for you."

"Hurdle! Listen to yourself, Jamie O'Ryan!"—"Well it clearly isn't!"—"You sound like a pimp!"

"Oh leave off will you! Look at the way he gets through the slivovic, woman. Listen to his teachings! No name, no ego, he's practically all spirit as it is—the boy's body is *not* a temple. More like: a wrapper."

"James O'Ryan!"

Jamie knows where Shiny's raft of maternal instincts comes from.

As it seems, does Sufi Child, who looks up from his defensive hunch over dinner one evening, and says apropos of nothing, straight to Shiny, "Why have you no childs?"

Shiny is thirty-two.

Shiny is rosy-cheeked and brown-haired. She has a special beauty—not of youth, or cheekbones or animal grace or anything like that—really, she's quite plain—but the pink chevron that passes from jaw to jaw over the bridge of her nose glows from the inside. It *emits* light. Her kindness can be felt, the calmness of trees. A wild child in her youth, she takes her wifely vows seriously, and cuts now a prim, maternal figure. The lads about town don't fancy her; the two ideas of her and of shagging will not bond. And, indeed, her failure to have had children by now has certainly excited Sufi Child's question in other people, though none so directly. And now the red in her face deepens.

The answer is they've been trying long and hard, but have yet to conceive. It's a sorrow for them both, not just for Shiny, which has been putting other strains on the marriage besides the financial ones. Though not unrelated. One of Shiny's favorite koans, or focuses for fretting, is whether they could even afford to raise a child if she did get pregnant.

A point that strikes Jamie as moot. "I never knew children were so expensive, Shines. It's a wonder the human race was ever started."

"Be serious."

"I always thought it was, 'it takes a village to raise a child.' I see I misheard—it was actually 'twenty thousand pounds a year.' "

These are the seams of anxiety that run through them. Which Sufi Child, with his green dog-eyes looking from Shiny to Jamie and back again, seems to have an uncanny feeling for. "Why you don't give her children?" to Jamie.

"I have," replies Jamie, "seven. She's eaten them all."

Sufi Child dodges, lets it sail past his shoulder. "You don't love her?"

Jamie frowns. "I love my wife very much."

"Why you don't give her children?"

"That's a private matter. Between me and my wife," waving with his fork. "Eat your broccoli."

Sufi Child leans over toward Jamie, beckons his closer, and talks in a stage whisper. "Maybe there is something—not good with you, Jamie," whispering, "in your . . . little man," waggling his little finger.

"Quite possibly. Shiny—have you noticed anything wrong with my little man lately?"

"Seems fine to me," with a brave smile, her eyes squeezing thanks to her husband for keeping the tone light.

"O.K., O.K.," Sufi Child still conspiratorial, "But maybe. Maybe—to find out there is something not good with you, I try."

Jamie pauses, like he's listening hard for something. "Sorry: you try?"

"Yes. If you like, I try."

"*You* try?"

"To give her children."

"You'd like to try? With my wife?"

"If you like," Sufi Child spreading his hands, sitting up straight again.

Jamie nods thoughtfully. "Well that's a terribly generous offer."

"It is no problem. When I try, if she gets children, then we know, there is something not good with you. If no children, then something not good with her. Yes?"

"Crikey. Yes. That's quite a . . ."

"I believe I shall try . . . six or seven times, when she is quite ready, and if she gets children from me, then O.K., it's no problem, you—" giving it the finger-across-the-throat gesture, with accompanying sound effect "—then it's 'plain sailing' for you. O.K.?"

"Golly, you've—you've really thought it through. Hasn't he? So what do you reckon, beastie?"

Shiny dabs her mouth with a napkin. "It would save us a spot of money at the fertility clinic."

"Elspeth Dryhten, *you* are not allowed to joke about this."

"Sorry."

"Sufi Child, it's a generous offer, meant well, but I must decline. No. In fact, I must do more than that. Let me make this clear: If I catch you so much as thinking about my wife in any untoward way whatsoever, ever again do you hear me? by the grace of God I'll thrash you to within an inch of your life. Is that clear?"

" 'Untoward?' "

"You understood. You'll feel the sharp end of O'Ryan's belt. Eat your broccoli."

"O'Ryan's belt?" Shiny says.

Jamie nods proudly. "My father used it on me."

But Sufi Child had caught hold of something in that exchange, a loose thread in the fabric . . . which thread he tugged at, after dinner, while doing the washing up, when Jamie was in front of the TV and Shiny came back out to the kitchen to fetch the whiskey. He apologized to Shiny for any embarrassment his little joke had caused.

"Not at all. You're the perfect guest." Moving back out with the bottle and glasses.

"Shiny—"

"Yes?"

Sufi Child wrinkled his face somewhat. "You are lying to Jamie?"

"Sorry?"

"You are lying to him about," running his hand over an imaginary tummy, "children." It started out as a question, but, once out in the open, it's not really. He's just telling her.

Several times she collects the breath to begin speaking, but doesn't. Doesn't quite know where to put herself. In the face of this certainty, her denials stall.—And for such a long time that presently her silence answers for her. Eventually she tears herself away from that troubling pair of eyes, muttering "nonsense," and returns to the living room to pour her husband his evening dram.

Three days later, a bleary afternoon with the flat to themselves, she brings it up with the Child.

"What did you mean by that?"

"I see you are lying," he shrugs.

"Lying about what?"

"I see it is you who has not—have not—give Jamie children."

"That's the impression you got?"

"Yes." Direct eye contact. "He wants children and you do not, but you do not confide him." Shrugging. "This is easy to see."

Shiny Dryhten searches in his face.

"You do not love him, Shiny?"

"I love him so much."

"Then why?"

—a long silence. Shiny twists the ends of her long dark hair, turns an agonized gaze out the window, at the block of flats and the railway line beyond, where snow has covered the sleepers but not the rails, leaving a vista of pure design, a barcode wheeling off into white perspective.

"We can't afford it."

"So you," making a horizontal cut with his hand, "you take pills."

Her eyes, brilliantly lit by snowglare, search for something in the landscape. She shakes her head, timidly, but what she's shaking against is the possibility of Jamie finding out.

Sufi Child says nothing; waits for her to look back at him, to verify for herself that he has received her plea.

When she does, the softness of her eyes is leaking out. Her cheeks are red, and a single fluorescent braid hangs amongst her straight dark hair.

"You are beautiful, Shiny," says Sufi Child.

*   *   *   *   *

Well. At the next poker game, there's developments that require sitting up and looking at. Shiny Dryhten strides into the Šamac room, pushing through invisible saloon doors that flap behind her, her hand resting on the shoulder of a skinheaded little runt in a metallic-green quilted jacket.

"But this game is for," Bannerman Tedus starts to say, ". . . *us*, right?"

"It's my game," says Shiny.

"Sure . . ." Bannerman's not convinced.

"Alright, then. Please supply an acceptable reason why you'd not like to play against a Bosnian child, and we'll talk."

Bannerman squirms in his seat, but none of his buddies, so friendly only moments ago, are helping him out now. "'Cos they have like—powers, right?" As articulate an enunciation of American Europhobia as any. Specially out here, off the eastern edge of smooth highwayed Europe, where the map begins to crumple and fold in unexpected ways, where time flows funny, nursing recidivist pockets of history whose actual existence no amount of Googling, even in this information age, will be able to establish one way or the other . . . "And Dracula comes from round these parts, y'know . . ." looking to see who's with him.

"Complains about playing a *little boy*," Shiny adds, with a cluck.

"Go on fella," Jamie O'Ryan pulling a seat aside for the Sufi Child, who clambers adorably up into it, gawking around at the ring of faces. Shiny lays out ten €20s in front of Sufi Child, and pats the stack when she's done. "There you are. Enjoy yourself, *malo*," kissing him on the head. Sufi Child tries to wriggle away, embarrassed.

A brisk trade in significant glances around the table.

"The kid with no name," Edgar Radford, Jr., says, "and no money."

"Ignore em," Shiny murmurs in Sufi Child's ear, and he nods, pulls a crumpled piece of paper from his jacket pocket, and smoothes it onto the table. Written in a gawky cursive, it's the ranking of poker hands: High Card, One Pair, Two Pair, Three of a Kind, etc.

Everyone frowns, and some wisecrack aborts halfway out of Khan Kerensky's throat. That is not a good sign. What that piece of paper traditionally says is: My Friends, You Are About To Get Hustled.

But no, this is genuinely the third or fourth time Sufi Child has played. Everyone has to keep reminding him, "Big blind," "Any raise?", he's slowing up the play, and though he's really trying and blushes each time he's caught unawares, the guys still turn heavylidded eyes onto Shiny. Shiny meets such looks with equal seriousness, and hands them back, with two or three seconds' more attitude.

And the Child drinks like the damned. Bottle after bottle of anything colorless comes and goes. But he never loses composure, it's an amazement to see, and pokerwise he barely puts a foot wrong. Never bluff a beginner, is the adage, and the guys fold whenever Child shoves any chips forward.

But even beyond that. He catches a couple people on bluffs. These are bold calls for a pro. It's a slow accumulation of money, and it's proportionally hard to trash-talk someone with more money than you.

Then Bannerman gets dealt a pair of Jacks.—Holy shit. The Hooks, dude. They look good in Bannerman's fist, sensational in fact. You can't not bet Jacks, right? But for Bannerman they're cursed, it's the Blue Screen of Doom's hand, he basically can't not get beat with a pair of Jacks. But this time they look so good Bannerman could eat them— slightly blurred from the shaking of his hand, but they're telling him he's going to win. Yes he can feel it. We are your friends, Bannerman. Honestly. You can trust us.

So he plays it slow, puts in a small bet, waits to ambush anyone who steps up.

Folds round to Sufi Child.

"It's on the Child," Edgar Radford, Jr., sighs heavily.

"Yes." But Sufi Child won't be hurried, he's just sipping most carefully while staring at Bannerman, which is weird, bubbling loza in his top lip like a connoisseur (filthy Herzegovinan stuff, 90 proof, made of tires and old boots) then, get this, now actually *tipping back* in his chair and open-mouth gargling it. Finally he sits up, swallows, and bets €20.

Well all right. Finally, Bannerman's turn to school this little so-and-so: he pushes all his chips in. Folds all round back to the Child, who counts Bannerman's stack down, that's €125 altogether, and puts same into the middle himself.

Bannerman hesitates, first stirrings of disgust. The Child uses one card, a Queen, to turn his other Queen over.

"Anti-safe," Bannerman sighs, dumping the Jacks face-up.

"Luck of the Bosnians," Animal Elliot-Maitland agrees.

But it's not over yet. Animal does the honors with the community cards, which come 5–K–10, then a Jack ("*Safe!*"), then 8. Bannerman's made Three of a Kind in Jacks, ducked the straight, and Sufi Child yields the €250 pot with an easy shrug, like that's the sort of thing that happens every day, with no reason at all to blame his miserable lot in life.—A popular win. No one minds that they're playing with a penniless orphan with melt-your-heart eyes, this is poker, after all, recently gentrified yes, but without a certain heartless avarice it wouldn't have no soul.

"The O'Ryans aren't going to be real happy about that one," Bannerman tipping back in his chair, eagerly taunting the boy, whose hands can barely reach around a chip: "How'd you persuade them to back you at cards anyhow? Told em it was for charity, I bet. Don't get me wrong, I think you're in the clear, you're perfectly justified, blowing someone else's money on cards and booze. Teach em some sense. Seriously. I wish *I'd* done more of that sort of thing when *I* was four."

"Ignore him," Shiny murmurs to Sufi Child.

"He is cursed in love," says Sufi Child quietly.

And Bannerman tips over backward, disappearing below the line of sight with a distant scream.

"Four legs good, two legs bad," says Jamie, shuffling the deck.

But the Child *does* have powers. He's been making incredible calls all night. He looks at you and in his childish purity of heart he just knows. He pours back the loza and rolls his eyes into his head and everything in him relaxes, and when his irises pop back out again, already focused on you, *through you*, he knows. He has annihilated his Self and he has weighed your soul in the balance, and found it wanting a fifth spade. And then 200 euro. Which the little shit is only going to piss up against a wall.

Or half of it anyway; Shiny Dryhten (canny Scot knows an opportunity when she sees one) gets the other half. Presumably she has a deal something like that.

Which pays off in a big way at two in the morning when Sufi Child makes an impossible call on Animal Elliot-Maitland. Animal's a steady player, takes few risks. A rock. He's gone all-in on the flop, no straight or flush possible, just the two of them—so Sufi Child does his thing with the loza, leans back and so on, but notices Animal's empty glass and asks a waitress to get him a new one. Animal says no thanks. Immobile. "Please, says Child," let us drink to cards, however Allah plays them." But it's no, really, he has to go to Foča first thing, he mustn't drink any more, etc. The Child then *won't leave the issue alone*—is making quite a scene, gets Animal animatedly pissed off, until eventually, more out of bemusement than anything else, he gives in, says *živjeli*, takes a sip, serves him with a tight thank you, and the Child is satisfied. He then calls Animal's all-in and lays down bottom pair.

"What!"

"Animal's gonna school *him*," commentates Bannerman, so drunk by now his mouth works like a stroke victim's, "*he'll* show him which way the wind blows . . ."

Animal just sits there for a long time, jaw muscles working, before showing bottom pair with an even worse kicker.

"Holy communion!"

But Animal still has outs—but the next two cards do nothing to help either one of them, and so Sufi Child wins all his money. A €700 hand. Sufi Child pulls the chips in, and doesn't bother to stack them. Everyone a bit fazed, nodding distantly. Shiny Dryhten's eyes do a lightly sportive round of the table.

Later that night at Colorscheme of Hazardsigns, the whole gang is hanging out, lots of talk of Sufi Child's ability to access the plane of shared human consciousness through alcohol, and how the O'Ryans have weaponized it. Jamie and Shiny are kissing and cuddling at the bar and buying drinks for everyone, and periodically ruffling the Child's hair.

Frito's heard all about it and hovers nearby, keeps pestering the boy about magical beer. But Shiny's protective. Frito's a man of unproven scruples but clearly has a nose for business, which is to say, he stinks of money. Meanwhile Jamie has one Khan Kerensky to fend off.

"He's your ticket to fame and fortune!" Khan exclaims. Khan Kerensky is a slick financial type, a naturalized German, who wears the sort of pointy sunglasses favored by football coaches. He's an analyst covering the Former Republic of Yugoslavia for a Frankfurt-based hedge fund, and is frequently in and out of Sarajevo, Zagreb and Belgrade, vector of gossip and share tips for all.

"We got lucky this time," agrees Jamie. "Can't imagine the Child will want to play with a backer forever, though."

"He does not have much of his own money, I think."

"He will soon."

"But but," Khan Kerensky's poor banker's mind can't get itself around this, "you will make a killing being his manager! You have to, man! If you don't, I might!"

"Go on then."

"What! Jamie, you *cannot* pass this opportunity!"

"I'm no poker manager, I run a de-mining charity," shrugging. "It's Shine's thing anyhow, it's her money. And why should the lad pay someone else half of everything he wins? It's him that wins it."

"Because you . . . you persuade him that . . . you will manage his interests . . ."

This goes on for a while, but Jamie's unbudgeable. "I don't care how you phrase it, Khan, exploiting children is not what I'd care to spend my only life doing."

Shiny takes her cut that first time, and the time after, but from then on Sufi Child's playing under his own steam, and making good money. He's a natural. He's got something. It's not luck—there's some combination between the bright clarity of a young mind and a sensitivity to certain liminal human frequencies, ones usually ignored, which gives him his edge . . . but only when his rational mind is too sodden to get in the way . . .

So much so the expat poker scene is soon too small for him, and before long Frito Cooper—who gives him some sort of day job at his warehouse in Dobrinja—has introduced him to the card circuit surrounding the gangster Vedo Alimović. Serious dudes. Serious money.

By August, Sufi Child has a Mercedes-Benz. A heartwarming tale of everyday Bosnian-Herzegovinan folk.

"So it seems," Shiny draping her arms round her husband, a lingering smile, "we got the boy out of prostitution and into gambling."

"You old missionary," Jamie kissing her neck.

*

Even by the summer, with Jamie's de-mining outfit in full swing up in Bjelašnica, operating capital running short, domestic finances a little tight, Jamie still won't hear of accepting any money from the boy, by way of thanks or anything else. Oh Shiny's proud of him, but sometimes he can be so pigheaded—the money situation is really a worry. Is it impossible Jamie could see a way to receive at least *some* money, a token, for giving the boy his start in life?

"Damned if I'm going to come out to Bosnia to accept handouts from *them*."

Well, she knew this when she married him. Shiny will get on with her life with Jamie as best she can, and make them both as happy as she can.

Sufi Child will come round to play with the expat crowd now and again. The story climaxes in June, a night back at the Hotel Alija. By this time Sufi Child's hair has grown out, a luxuriant Van Dyck brown, which flops in his face when he looks at his cards. The days are enormous, and the windows still bright when play starts at 2100.

Shiny is not in town; she has gone back home for a week to see her family.

The familiar crowd plays regular Hold'em poker for the first three hours. By midnight other games creep in, at first standards like Omaha and Stud. Sarajevsko Pivo is flowing freely, and by two in the morning it's degenerated into freeform Dealer's Choice—and monkey games are taking hold, things like Flaming Cross, Barbary Beetle and Fucking Nuns—wild cards, void cards, cards stuck to foreheads, cards thrown in the air. Part of the impetus is undoubtedly that Sufi Child's advantage withers to nothing in these games, when the psychological element is replaced by blind luck. Good old luck. Read *that*.

Still, he's got some sort of chip where Jamie O'Ryan's concerned. All through the night, whenever Jamie O'Ryan has a hand, Sufi Child comes out all guns blazing, slaps him back down. Again and again it happens: Jamie O'Ryan raises the bet to an aggressive €20, say, and Sufi Child's all in for €400.

"It's just a bit of fun, for fuck's sake," says Jamie, throwing his cards in. Again. He can't risk that sort of money.

But it clearly gets to him. He's been playing more and more erratically against Sufi Child, there's some sort of private vendetta going on that everyone else round the table can only guess at. At Omaha Hi-Lo, Jamie bets big before the flop, Sufi Child goes all in, Jamie growls "sod it" and calls for €260. Jamie's the clear favorite with AA52 but somehow—*somehow*—that mithering Child pulls both sides away from him.

"Chump," chuckles the Child, as he rakes in the chips.

"Forgive anything except a good turn," Animal Elliott-Maitland murmurs to Daniel Fleischer, the journalist. Dan nods, and squints at the bitter taste of the idea.

Jamie O'Ryan takes slugs of whiskey and digs out another few hundred euro. He won't take this from the Child. People have not seen this side of him.

"Mate," begins Frito, "are you sure—"

"Leave it." Jamie's head is lifted uncharacteristically high, so Frito can see his shy eyes in all their seriousness. "I'm fine."

Frito backs off, eyebrows up.

At which point begins the game in question:

COJONES

1. Everyone (7 players) posts a €2 ante, and receives two
   cards.   €2
2. Everyone takes a peek, a deep breath, then holds their
   hands out, facedown over the center of the table, and
   on the count of 3: either drops their cards or holds on.
   For dear life.   €14
3. (a) Those who dropped their cards (3 players) are
   out & forfeit their money.
   (b) Those who held on to their cards show them.
   The highest hand (Animal) takes the money. The
   lowest hand (Sufi Child) posts *double that amount*.
   The guys in the middle hang on, as before, for
   dear life.   €28

4. Round 2. Re-deal. Those that drop their cards (Animal)
   are out. The lowest of the 3 remaining hands (O'Ryan)
   posts double that pot.   €56
5. Round 3. Re-deal. Those that drop their cards (Frito)
   are out. The lower of the 2 remaining hands (Sufi
   Child) posts double that pot.   €112

A geometric progression, see. It's basically high-carding each other, but if you pull a pair, you're almost guaranteed to win. The pots soon get rather meaty, especially when you have two stubborn bastards after a long and liquid evening going toe-to-toe over some inscrutable offense from months ago . . .

Hands come and go, quickened by a ferment of high merriment, until, only three rounds and a few minutes later—at the €896 pot, still neither player has admitted defeat.

"Now, steady on, Jamie," Animal Elliot-Maitland has said.

"I'll thank you to butt out, Andrew." An extraordinary thing for Jamie to say. Animal is more his parents' generation.

"Jamie—"

"What."

"I've known Shiny her entire life," says Animal, "she'll ask me how I let you do it."

Jamie just looks at him, not speaking until Animal shows both palms in surrender.

Jamie's down €600 already. An insolent leer hovers about the Child.

Both turn over their palms, slowly . . .

Jamie, with an otherwise promising A–5, loses to Sufi Child's 3–3.

"Oof," says Frito.

"Nine hundred euro is not so bad!" says Khan Kerensky.

"That's not what he's saying oof about," says Edgar Radford, Jr. "Takes a while to hit the brakes in this game."

Khan goes *oh*: because now Jamie has to post double the last . . . *scheiße*.

Jamie scratches the back of his neck a long time. "Khan?" he says at last.

"Anything you want, pal."

So Jamie O'Ryan lays €1,792, in chips and notes, in the pot. This is a month's pay, after tax.

Animal deals. Jamie and the Child look at their hands, and then each other. Jamie O'Ryan is flustered and taking all this rather heavily. Jamie extends his hand. Sufi Child's eyes are on Jamie O'Ryan like a blanket.

Silence.

"Hey Frito," says Sufi Child.

"What's up?" grunts Frito.

"Do you think," not taking his eyes off Jamie, "Shiny Dryhten has—best bosom in Sarajevo."

By now no one's looking at each other.

Frito's treading carefully. "Just play the game."

"Really! Have you seen from near?" holding a flat palm an inch from his nose. "She does not use bra, because they are so—" using his hands to demonstrate.

"Just play the fucking game."

Jamie's hand, out in front of him, is trembling.

Neither player drops.

The table can barely bear to see the hands turn over.

Jamie lays down J–8. Sufi Child flips only one card onto the table, a King.

Finally Jamie pulls out a checkbook. "ViKA Speculacija," says Sufi Child. "€3,584." Then, while Jamie is writing out the check, with perhaps a bit more care than most that he writes, Sufi Child adds: "Quickly." Jamie stops, fixes him for a long time, before completing it and laying it in the middle of the table.

A waitress appears at the door, reads the atmosphere, and leaves.

Animal deals again. Jamie looks at his hand, then at the Sufi Child, who has not looked at his. They hold out their arms. Sufi Child's eyes are cold and steady. Jamie is trying to work out what this means for the odds of victory. He probably shouldn't drop. Should he drop? He shouldn't. He must. Should he?

"Don't drop your cards," says Sufi Child.

Jamie says nothing.

"You must not lose now. You must reclaim your money. What will your beautiful wife say?"

"___."

"Your beautiful wife with the beautiful bosom."

"___."

"The beautiful bosom with disgusting mole on it."

"Right, I've heard enough you miserable little shit," Animal Elliot-Maitland leans across to the Sufi Child, grabs him by the front of his shirt, enormous fists inches from his face, "if you don't belt up, this instant, we'll throw you out, with or without your money."

Sufi Child flicks a smile at Animal. There's no danger of that, not after the name Vedo Alimović has been invoked, and everyone knows it. But Animal's said his piece, and it's his pax that settles over the room.

Jamie's in real trouble. Who's to know whether that detail about the mole corresponds to reality. God, we hope not. Oh god, peeking out from our fingers, we hope not.

*

"Ready," says Jamie.

"Oh, you are keen now? If you win this, you are only two thousand down, not bad, eh Jamie?"

Jamie shows his cards.

But doesn't look at them, just watches the Sufi Child—who looks, leaps up clapping, bangs the table, slaps Frito on the back . . . who sits motionless, flexing his jaw muscles, eyes on the table: 10–7 to K–J.

Jamie immediately pulls out his checkbook, starts filling it in in silence. No one can watch. No one can look at each other. No one can say anything, or leave the room, or breathe.

"You don't have to—" begins Khan Kerensky.

"Yes he does!" Sufi Child practically shouts.

Jamie looks up, about to ask something.

"Seventy-one sixty-eight," Frito and Edgar say, simultaneously.

"Thank you kindly," Jamie bending down to write.

Again, Sufi Child doesn't look at his hand before extending it out over the table.

"Confident?" says Jamie.

"No," shrugging, "but you are—'born loser.' Why don't you see this? Drop your cards, Jamie, go away, go be in your life."

They count to three, and neither player drops.

Jamie loses. Goes for a walk. Rubs his jaw. Comes back. Writes a check for €14,336.

Sufi Child pummels the table with his palms in excitement. "Pretty good, no?" Again, he doesn't look at his hand. We all sit and watch, numb, helpless, thirty minutes between hands, but utterly unable to leave.

*

Jamie wins. K–2 against 4–3. Takes the check from the middle of the table, and with shaking hands tears it to atoms. His head lolls back. But he's still €12,000 in the hole. All he has to do is win one more hand, and he's in the money.

"I am with Vedo," says Sufi Child, "he will pay all."

The expats look over to Frito, well known to be thick with Vedo Alimović himself.

"Vedo does back him . . . I guess if Child says it's cool, it's cool." Jamie O'Ryan shrugs.

"Not sure I'm happy with that," interjects Animal. "Vedo bankrolling him for tournaments is not the same as Vedo covering unlimited losses at monkey games."

So a 3 a.m. call to ViKA ensues.

"That was Jasim Bukić," Frito flipping his phone closed, "says the Child's credit is good for this hand."

"Good. Then let us play the game of," Animal rubbing his hands together eagerly, "Cojones."

So it's an IOU, witnessed in triplicate, and bearing the Sufi Child's thumbprint, for €28,672.

Edgar Radford, Jr., deals. The cards slide across the baize. Jamie's cards sit in front of him, at right angles to each other, for a long time, in dramatic silence—Jamie savoring the adrenaline, Bannerman taking photos—before he puts them together, settles them in his palm, and holds out his fist.

"You don't look?" says Sufi Child. "You think my ruses work against me? You don't have ruses that belong to you?"

"This way you can't get a read on him," says Khan Kerensky.

Sufi Child waggles a mischievous finger at Jamie. "Slowly, you are learning, Jamie O'Ryan."

Jamie wins.

"Jamie, you *have* to drop. You're sixteen thousand up. Have to." Jamie surrounded like a boxer between rounds. There's plenty of time to talk tactics while they wait for Jasim Bukić, who's with-held the next round of funding until he arrives to see it for him-self.

"Eh, jarane!" when Jasim arrives, "having fun? And what are *you* doing, little friend?" clapping a severe hand on Sufi Child's shoulder, "Excuse us a moment." Jasim and Sufi Child disappear from the room.

"Sufi Child'll come back in with, like, two black eyes."—"Yeah, and with a bleeding stump where his left hand was."—"What he said, Jamie, don't let it get to you. It's just trash-talking."

But when Jasim Bukić and the Sufi Child do reenter, an en-dorsed ViKA check for €57,344 hits the table. Jasim is doing his best to look cheerful, but his poker face isn't as good as the Child's.

This time, Jamie looks at his cards. Then holds them out.

"Oh, you look now? Now you are done, you have your money back, you go—one look from curiousness—you—." But Sufi Child stops. Jamie is evidently satisfied with the situation, and doesn't care who knows it. They hold out their hands, eyes locked.

"Okay," says Edgar, "drop your cards on three. One, two—"

"Wait," says Sufi Child. "More time." Staring at Jamie O'Ryan. Jamie doesn't flinch.

"Ready?" says Edgar. "On three, then. One, tw—"

Sufi Child drops his hand.

"Sweet Jesus," Jamie exhales, collapsing into his chair, muscles useless. He's won by default. The rush of exhaustion and pleasure across Jamie's face belongs to any smack addict. Frito picks up Jamie's cards, 4–3, then goes for Sufi Child's cards, but the Child slides these back into the deck.

Khan, hedge fund analyst, fingers the check. "This is more than *I* make."

"Thank you, everyone," Sufi Child scraping his chair back in its place, "it is time for my bedtime." Then: "And Mister Jamie"—he puts his hands together, blushes, the assured swagger's all gone— "you are proud man, and hard to thank. Thank you." And he and Jasim are gone.

Everyone looks at each other, pulses knocking, wondering to themselves what the hell, no seriously, just happened.

"Sure, *now* he pretends it's on purpose," says Edgar Radford, Jr.

Foča

JUST BEYOND THE airport, straddling the Inter-Entity Boundary Line, lies the SFOR Headquarters at Camp Butmir—a vast installation of reinforced concrete, razor wire, flagpoles, containerized housing, and only slightly fewer uniforms than nationalities: because apart from all the Armija Republike Bosna i Hercegovina (ARBiH) and Vojka Republike Srpske (VRS) guys, now getting along better and known collectively as the Armed Forces (AF), every NATO and Partnership for Peace nationality is represented in this sprawling barracks, as well as some other UN and PfP-affiliated forces—South Africans, Romanians—plus nations with observer status, people up from KFOR, Commonwealth Forces by special arrangement with the UK—and Koreans, Armenians, a little tension in the Dining Facility between the Greeks and the Turkish Platoon (TurkPlat)—themselves often accompanied by a wide spectrum of Muslim colleagues, in the form of PakPlat, MalPlat, and EgPlat; and Russians and Poles trading ancient facial insults undetectable to anyone without postgraduate work in the field—and frankly bizarre shit, what look like Uzbek marines in the corridors of Building 200; Chinese space program people; military attachés passing envelopes under tables; contractors from dozens of private military companies like Kellogg Brown & Root, DynCorp, and MPRI, all apparently running a Gaudiest Shoulder Patch competition; freaky sunglasses-and-bandana types hanging out in the Millennium Bar with subscriptions to *Soldier of Fortune*; auditors from the U.S. Government Accounting Office, plus journalists, pilots, ambulance-chasing PTSD counselors, chaplains of all flavors, and CID men, army lawyers, dentists, medics, private-sector surgeons, cooks and clerks; and of course nowhere on earth is beyond the reach of pharmaceutical sales reps, in this case from local pharmaco Bosnalijek, flicking long salon-fresh hair around, hitching skirts up, and pushing this or that painkiller onto anyone involved in medicine, however junior, and however battlefield first aid.

The already high numbers boosted by the quarterly Joint Military Conference (JMC) that has just taken place, to chew through how the Dayton Peace Plan, known round here as the General Framework Agreement for Peace (GFAP), is coming along, and boosted further by the imminent arrival of Supreme Allied Commander Europe (SACEUR), who's coming to town February 4 to kick him some ass. The JMC has pretty clearly shown that GFAP is not coming along well at this point. Rapprochement isn't happening; the Serbs won't allow Bosniak refugees to return; the leaders of the Federation and the Republika Srpska are at each other's throats; "Democratization" is a farce; Property Restitution has been abandoned even as a goal by Paddy Ashdown; and just recently, in what have to be the last weeks before Gulf War II, the Republika Srpska (RS) has been caught selling arms, *actual guns*, to Saddam Hussein. Breathtaking foreign policy, if not the very core of the Serbian Pariah Complex.—Tensions are consequently high. Not least *inside* Butmir, where suddenly it's all talk of WMDs, material breach, and cheese-eating surrender monkeys. And everything exacerbated by the fact that SACEUR is a U.S. Marine, and if that needs clarification an asshole, who's expected to arrive running the fingers of his white gloves along the backs of everyone's shelves.

Which means that down by the National Support Entities—the euphemism by which bars are known—things can get lively, as tonight, with what appears to be an Old versus New Europe fight brewing in the alley. Inside the French NSE meanwhile, getting outside of some *pressions*, flipping through the List of Acronyms (LOA) handbook, and listening vaguely to the din, Edgar Radford, Jr., and Animal Elliot-Maitland become slowly aware of a camouflage presence next to them. They look over to see a gaunt officer who seems to have been talking in a low monotone, presumably to them, for some time.

"Ah—Commandant Sommantier, I presume?" Animal holding out a genial hand.

He stares at Animal's hand impassively. "Jens said this might happen."

"Jens Asselijn?" frowns Animal. "What might happen?"

But Sommantier just murmurs *follow*, rises from the table and glides out the door. Edgar and Animal down their drinks and scramble out after, just glimpsing Sommantier slaloming ghostlike through the thronging crowd, where a Carabinieri jeep and a Bulgarian Military Police detail have arrived simultaneously to deal with the aggro, but, language being a constant headache, look like they're about to start policing each *other*—Animal and Edgar bumping into soldiers at every step, finally bursting out, scrambling across yards rutted with frozen mud furrows, past the National Intelligence Centers, bristling with aerials, dishes, radio masts, and a giant radome, and eventually running down their 2100 appointment, Commandant Jean-Jacques Sommantier, late of 22e RI French Army, at a small Portakabin behind a Motor Transport yard. Peeling dymo tape on the door says LIAISON CIMIC-AF.

"Thank you for comingue after hours," J.-J. Sommantier says from his desk in the Portakabin, clasping his knuckles in a way clearly intended to be businesslike, but which comes across as more supplicatory. "You understand, during the day, I have AF sergeants here— I can say nothingue before them."

"You couldn't send em on a mission?" tries Edgar.

Sommantier shrugs. "They fart higher than their ass. All day they play solitaire on the computer. They will not perform any 'mission.'"

"We're just glad to be here, Jean-Jacques," says Animal firmly. Edgar gets the message.

"Good. Then if you will both read and sign this Non-Disclosure Agreement."

Animal and Edgar belt up and sign the fucking thing. File 13's finances are shaky, they've done nothing but spend backers' money for a year now, and even bounty hunters have to eat bread and butter. This Sommantier maybe has a job for File 13, paying actual money, and since you don't get jobs till you've done jobs, if it's halfway decent, they'll do it for anything. But first, as with so many people in Bosnia,

Sommantier's going to make them sit and listen to a rant in three parts, this one subtitled "The Dayton Peace Plan Is Worse Than The Treaty Of Versailles."

". . . must be helped. This is the why all this is here, yes?" Sommantier waving a hand at the base. "What would our daughters think? It is a question of either morality or immorality, is it not? No?" staring at them both, settling for staring into Edgar's eyes with a tenacity positively ancient & marine. "Eh? I am askingue you!"

Edgar Radford, Jr., nods agreeably back.

Sommantier straightens, opens a file. "So. The Liaison CIMIC-AF has orders inflexible and naive, restricting me from any involvement with the black market, the gangsters, or anythingue deemed Anti-Dayton from the remote safety of Brussels," Brussels being NATO Headquarters. "Pouf. The heads-of-desk are happy to let these people 'stew,' that they deserve each other, but I was out here duringue the war, I became inoculated against such abandonments."

"Think he meant infected," Edgar will say later. That's the primary indication of Bosnian Psychosis, right there: zealotry. File 13's boys know that this is the kind of thing that in other wars would get them fragged. Still, for twenty-seven months now this Bosnian Psychotic has been siphoning off extra budget for "local initiatives," parking it in Euronext tracker funds, and has just closed out with enough money to mount his own covert operation, using NATO clearance but private military company manpower. "Just a small one, for reasons you will see. Under conditions of secrecy the most absolute and complete."

"We understand."

"My office co-ordinates security details for the construction companies—you know—they are buildingue the houses for the returningue refugees, but these keep beingue dynamited . . ."

"Building sites," Animal visibly deflating.

"We're a special forces outfit, you know," clarifies Edgar Radford, Jr.

Sommantier sits back, blows cigarette smoke into the air, watches them both. But neither Animal nor Edgar gets up to go, or adds anything. In fact there seems to be a sort of Thousand Yard Stare competition going, and the lone Frenchman is crushing these two elite Anglos. "Leave if you wish," he says.

"I apologise," says Animal. "Please continue."

"Because SFOR requires the same religion of peacekeepers as the area, we must route Ukrainian, Russian, Greek security details in Foča. But still the houses are dynamited. Deduce what you wish."

Sommantier refreshes them on the history of Foča, a small town near the Serbian border at the top of the River Drina: the prewar population had a Bosnian Muslim majority of something like 55 percent. In April 1992, in response to the Bosnian declaration of independence, Karadžić's hardline SDS Party rounded up the non-Serb men and imprisoned them in the K-P Dom, a former federal prison, where they were tortured and starved; and rounded up the women into the "Partizan" sports hall, a small gym in the center of town, where they were systematically raped. Meanwhile, all of Foča's sixteenth- and seventeenth-century mosques and minarets were destroyed, and, to signify the complete purification of the town, they changed the Muslim-sounding name "Foča" to "Srbinje," meaning "Serbtown."

"That a fact," says Edgar. He didn't know the name change was like *that*.

"A 'fact,' "chuckles Sommantier. "The idea of 'facts' in this place . . ."

Animal and Edgar share a look. Inverted commas are not, prima facie, the sort of thing you want a man on the other end of a contract putting around the word "facts." *This better work out*, Edgar's telepathing to Animal . . .

Sommantier's merriment ends abruptly, and he goes on: "Under Dayton, one permits the fruits of atrocities to persist. Foča is still held by Republika Srpska. The Muslims are all gone. The SDS, you know— the Serb "Nazi" Party—this is the same men as duringue the war, they dynamite refugee homes when they are rebuilt. We rebuild, the Fočaks dynamite. They will not permit non-Serbs. They don't even permit *Serbs*, who lived in the Federation before the war, to go *back* to these Muslim places! Oh yes this fantasy of the pure Volk, this is very healthy in Foča. A shitty place. Everyone is scared. They burn OSCE cars. But you understand, rather than confront the RS, in the face of reports absolutely incontrovertible from E-Say-Air-Say, the international community has backed down. Again. In the name of Stability." Sommantier looks from Animal to Edgar and back again, clasps his hands to one side in a rustle of waterproofs. "Old habits die hard."

His eyes are narrowed against invisible weather, and fine wrinkles beneath them curve out onto his cheekbones. He's a weathered old man of forty. He doesn't seem comic or desperate now.

"I want this sabotage to stop," he says.

The stakeouts are tedious, as interesting as these redbrick repairs going on against the treeline at the top of the Muslim quarter of Foča. A dilapidated collection of traditional rustic houses below, the usual war damage and collapsed roofs and dust that only bloated jackdaws stir any more. Amongst which there is the K-P Dom itself, a depressing, scarred, municipal installation. Close enough for the interned men to have been able to hear their former homes and women being taken. A sinister place. The stillness of other centuries. People in the street stare for too long.

Dark pine hills rise precipitously on all sides, and drop to the dreaming River Drina, an electric-blue purity to the water. The ostensible SFOR presence, Ukrainians, come by now and again in camouflage windcheaters, watching the idle rate of progress, getting drizzled on and accepting coffees, straight trigger fingers laid on the outside edges of rifles. Nothing happens. Occasionally the builders get spat at by villagers. Other villagers go up the hill to apologize for the spitters, with maybe some meat for the lads. The builders down tools at each of these episodes, and only slowly and with obvious misgivings take them up again.

Nothing will keep J.-J. from achieving at least one victory, however small and personal. The contract provides for one File 13 man at a time, strictly not personnel from the Former Republic of Yugoslavia, to keep J.-J. company at the site, sometimes only over the phone from a Rear Observation Post in the hills overlooking, but more frequently side by side at the Forward Observation Post. Currently a Honda Accord. Low-level muttering goes on, and the boys can only sit tight while J.-J. takes full opportunity to express the deep discomfort of his insomniac soul, hissing insistently about the corruption inherent in the concept of organization, about death, love, the immutability of human nature, how much worse everything is now that La Langue Française is no longer the lingua franca—

"It is not somethingue you feel, you Anglophones. Your language has two words for everythingue, one with an etymology Teutonic, one Romance. In the fleet of language, all our ships—rowboats, galleons!—have one hull, but yours is catamaran. You have grandmothers, we merely bigmothers. Okay. But really this is—very bad thingue. So for you Anglos, the brothers 'morality' and 'mortality' are very far from your immediate Norse 'death.' With everyone else, death is here," holding a palm to his nose, "mortalité, la mort. Imagine if instead of 'mortality,' you had 'deathness.' You would feel this, I think. But instead you are insulated, you see 'morality' as a choice, a concept abstract—not a battle for your soul in the imminence of your own death. As consequence, you are frequently immoral."

Brick Lahoussaye, File 13 stalwart, nods for a while, then offers over a packet of biscuits. "Squashed fly?"

Periodically the RS Policija roll by to exchange barely civil platitudes. In the scheme of things, episodes of whiteknuckle interest. Anything to take the fun out of watching the most *polako* builders in the world: construction being the exact opposite of what soldiers are really for. By the end of the first month, Flameproof Cooper is seriously suggesting that File 13 sneak out in the middle of the night, like elves, and build the fucking thing themselves.

"Glad you left the real army now, Flameproof?" says Edgar Radford, Jr., relieving him at 2 a.m.

"Fucking right, ye septic homo," growls Flameproof. "Shagged your girlfriend last time you were on stag, said she hadn't had been fucked like that since her dad died."

"Oh, you Brits," goes Edgar. This will go on for twenty-one weeks.

During the days, J.-J. Sommantier watches from behind a curtain of rain, fingers tight around the Styrofoam warmth of a coffee, twitching at nothing. The progress is painful for him too. But somewhere below the breezeblocks and the red mud, it feels right. *Would she be proud*, is the question he asks himself ten times a day, *would she be*— and presently, receiving no answer, squints back up at a horizon no one else can see.

*   *   *   *   *

"Because it feels more alive here," Clare Leischman replies to the question everyone asks. "Like this is what life looks like from the inside."

"And not in Zurich?"

"No," a cyan melancholy, "that's what it looks like from above."

Not her color at all. She's in a key all of her own, a sort of gray ♭ (musical "flat" symbol) with little pink topnotes. An idealized, a hopeful's chord, and which characterizes her apartment by the Markale streetmarket. She's done her best to make it soft and homey, with modulations of salmon and peach against the sanitary zincs, soft rugs over carpet-tiles made from some near relative of steel-wool, flaking plaster walls, sofa and duvet the color of shorn lambs. A number of scented candles-in-a-glass methodically lit when she gets home, ostensibly for "atmosphere," but it's proving difficult to keep the secret from herself that they're more about warding something off. Why so necessary to have one in each corner, hmm Clare?

Maybe something to do with what she whispers to herself during office hours at the UN Building, back against the sixth-floor window, collecting her hair into a band for another push through the photographic evidence. Not so much the forensic shots—sheer archeology—as the family shots: scarved old crones in warehouses, having recognized a shoe, sobbing at skeletons' feet. They send her tumbling out of her composure, face wrinkling and ten fingertips up over her eyes . . . It could so easily be her. It would be the teeth. She would recognize the chipped teeth of her father on a black and shriveled corpse.

So, scuttling around her apartment and its wasteland of improvised chocolate bowls: toothmugs, the tankard, pink Pyrex, even *plates*—sugary schokolade running in a wide Confucius mustache either side of her face—she'll breathe deep against her galloping case of neurotic imposture: the conviction that she's woefully incompetent at her job and it's just a matter of time before she's found out. So she lights candles and creeps mid-evening under her duvet, wondering how she'll continue to fool everyone, never more in need of protection, small wet nose twitching at the latest shipment of *Paris Match* until the woodland fear passes, and the facade feels more than a few layers of skin thick.

She applied for the International Criminal Tribunal for the former Yugoslavia's Office of The Prosecutor more out of boredom than a wish for advancement, and boredom not so much with work as life. Zurich is a small town. Her entire existence had turned in on itself, everything was self-conscious and at least half-ironic; she danced with the same boys to same tracks at Kaufleuten; there was no one new to meet or kiss or *make friends with* that everyone else in Seefeld wouldn't know about within a week, form their own mocking subgroups, gossip about, recalculate the implications for the grand social schematic. Paths were turning to rails. Against which her best friend at Freiburg had taken a medical lizenziat, got in her three years at the University Hospital, and escaped to Afghanistan and Médecins Sans Frontières. But as skills go, knowledge of the Strafgesetzbuch and Cantonal penal codes wasn't as internationally useful, and by the time Clare noticed that life as a Zurich bourgeoise wasn't what she wanted, she was twenty-nine and stuck, her life unfolding to such a preordained pattern that the problem of free will had become moot . . .

Until the Anwaltsverbände, the Bar Association, sent round one of these OTP ads.

An easy decision. She had once lived in Belgrade, in the holidays anyway, where the EDA—the diplomatic corps—had posted her father. She hadn't minded it. But there was always going to be the catch: and upon arrival at Churchillplein, ICTY's headquarters in The Hague, this poor little brainy girl was faced with the high likelihood of fumbling cases many times more crucial than anything she'd dealt with before. If she got a technicality wrong now, mass murderers would go free, the *Neue Zürcher Zeitung* would cover the story, most likely with a photo, the Gymnase one with The Spot, and an inset flow diagram on HOW RETARDED LAWYER SLIPPED THROUGH NET.

So her discovery of Foča was both burden and relief. Burden because Clare could not *believe* what she was reading—that such things should happen, in Europe, in her lifetime. The massacres at Srebrenica were almost reasonable by comparison. Internally coherent, at least. But *raping* hundreds of women? Institutionalized rape—there were military units set aside: some for beatings, some for rape. And it wasn't ethnic cleansing either, because they didn't let the women go. It was slavery. But as of last summer, when she was up at The Hague, there had only been eight indictments raised against Foča. Eight men put on trial for raping an entire town. This wasn't a dilemma, this blew straight past the sonderfall Swiss compromise she'd been born to. This was pure fury, and something she simply had to do something about.

And relief because she could get away from those courtrooms. A flurry of internal lobbying and Clare got herself transferred within OTP from Prosecution to Investigations, and dispatched to Bosnia to look into raising more indictments around the Foča case. Previously hampered because many of the Muslim victims of rape refused to testify, Clare argued that perhaps a female investigator would have better luck. So now she's out here, a lawyer in a policeman's unit, working under a former major in the Koninklijke Marechaussee— the Dutch Military Police—one Marc van Xanthe. Surfer-haired and laser-eyed, Marc has the sharpest instincts for weakness she's ever encountered, which was somewhat unnerving, watching his darting eyes meet her subterfuges of competence. But as it turned out those male eyes were easily baffled by womanly exteriors. In Zurich, at twenty-nine she was a girl, but out here she's a woman, as long as she keeps it chic. Another warding-off.

So it's crisp lines, sharp toes, tailored shirts and any tone between white and charcoal. But maybe she doesn't count or notice her father's weathered old Bellinzona scarf, once burgundy and now a weather-beaten pink that manages somehow to be rugged—and in which she nuzzles, blowing warm chocolate-breath into on the way to work, a mobile defense against this desolate winter city, where many different flavors of cold blow through her . . .

Otherwise, it's head down and babysteps, during Collection of Evidence she makes everyone write down and sign everything in the presence of witnesses. Even, once, directions. She keeps her little OTP stamp and inkpad in her handbag, talismanic protection against discovery.

FLAVORS OF COLD
1. absence of family and best friends.
2. horror at what people, and by extension herself, are capable of.
3. anxiety about fumbling case.
4. complex glances from eyes more ancient than buildings, make you feel very young, silly.
5. a bald Balkan coldness, whole kingdoms east of her own snug Röstigraben . . .

Maybe she's too cautious, workaholic, easily chilled. For there are safety nets and warmths. Frito, for one, whose instincts are all protective. Like that time Rachael Drikkevand (some Dane) said, apropos of something trifling—these new Ugg boots, in fact—"they're an atrocity." Frito put down his beer, leaned his huge handsome head very close to hers, and growled, "Rachael. You are not allowed to use that word in that way." Rachael stared at him, bemusement bordering on disgust, about to give him the whole *whatever* treatment—

"Not around Clare," he clarified.

And Rachael looked at Clare, and Clare looked at her own shoes, and despite herself, glowed. Everyone else might think he's a maniac, but for her: this is why Frito completely rocks.

Plus he's sex on wheels. And *yes* she's aware he's less into it than she is. But she doesn't mind that, for now. Does her good to be on the back foot now and again, it sharpens the longing—it makes the ghost of him moving inside her more solid than any daydream . . . she can't control when the riptides will take her pelvis, aching for the big dark hands that make her so delicate. At the office she keeps slipping away . . .

So yes his brusqueness hurts, but the resolution to homekey is all worth it, when he wraps her in his arms and they sleep together . . . even when it borders on abuse, when Frito gets back to his flat, drunk and hours late for an appointment she thought they'd made, "Sorry babes, busy just now," Frito barely stopping to run a hand up her back, being passed some pinetree schnapps by Sufi Child, "we're almost at the shared plane!"

"First: empty your head," says Sufi Child. "Now, the bottle."

Leaving Clare feeling stupid and alone, and with only Bannerman for company. Times like this, it almost feels sour. Almost. But she knows the corresponding rush when Frito does take her again will more than compensate. It's amazing how he does it. The cycle of tension and release, the geometry of orgasms, that most people can only sustain for what—an hour at best? But Frito's got her tension mounting for, goodness, *days* in advance . . . her heart knocks just to think about what's coming. She clockwatches from 1300 all the way to 1800.

"I'm at the File 13 house," he says.

"Working?"

"Shooting the breeze with the fellas."

"We still on for dinner?"

"Just ordered burek. There'll be masses, come on by."

So irritating. He promises exciting weekends, restaurants, the high life; but always this. He must know that there is no universe in which burek, a coiled turd en croute, will pass Clare's lips.

File 13's headquarters is a gated compound on Ašenova Street, on Vratnik hill, north of the Old Town, bustling with Bosnian employees and security guards in the distinctive File 13 pale blue. There's also a private side, where its expat employees all have bedrooms; Clare gets buzzed in and makes her way to the living room, which looks much like any room lived in by eight men and no women, to find Frito's there not just with the boys but also Maza Cukić, his fat annoying language assistant. Flameproof Cooper and Eddie Geddes on sofas barracking with Frito, and Brick Lahoussaye teaching Sufi Child some card game in the corner—whose object, by the look of things, is to bury your opponent under a pile of money. Brick has almost succeeded. Andy Deuchar playing *Halo* on the Xbox, courtesy of F&B Contraband; Maza Cukić watching the screen carnage with hollow eyes, cuddled up a little on the close side to Frito. Takeaway cartons everywhere.

"Ciao guys," Clare taking it all in, "getting in touch with our inner children?"

Flameproof Cooper cackles dirtily. "I'll give you inner chil—ow," as a beer can bonks off his head.

"We are not being children, we are discussing thee, applications of Sufi Child," says Maza Cukić. Flameproof and Eddie Geddes interglance uncomfortably, Flameproof does a little catspaw gesture. Clare just looks at her. In the distance, Brick says oh bugger.

"Wotcher Leischman," Frito knows how to behave, goes over to Clare, gives her a kiss. "Looks like you had a heavy day. Glass of wine?" Getting up to go to the kitchenette, this situation is looking like it might get filed under "Girlfriend, hassular" . . .

"No thank you very much."

Settling in moodily for half an hour, tops. Frito gets the message, and at the next lull announces that it's been great fellas, but he's going to have to take Clare home now and fuck her to bits. Flameproof and Eddie Geddes and Brick Lahoussaye and Deuchar pausing the video game all turn to look at Clare thoughtfully.

And anger is metabolized straight into lust. He's good.

By the time they get back to her place she's clenching with anticipation, almost contractions . . . she puts her keys in the glass bowl that sits to one side of the door, goes around lighting her candles, shielding the flame with a hand delicate as verse, lowering it to the soft cream wax—

But Frito is all over her, great spam hands holding her head like a basketball, sucking at her mouth, another hand fumbling around below with either his or her buckles and buttons, it's not clear, Clare's kind of struggling but it might just be the flailing of desire, at some point her toes leave the ground, Frito may not even know that he's picked her up but he has, soon he chucks her down on her low thin bed, and stands looking at her, snorting clouds of lust while he de-jeans. Clare lies on her bed, limbs turning in their soft fabrics, fingers at her lips, watching Frito grow naked. Soon his cock is out, big fucking thing, he stands at the foot of her bed wanking, looking down at her in all seriousness, hand making the slow journey from one end to the other, the intensity of what's coming somewhere between a promise and a threat. Clare's writhing is getting worse, her quail rib cage rising and falling under clean cotton. His stare is better than most guys' hands. Then he picks her up and undresses her, slowly and like a doll, holding her in one hand while he peels off a sock, then the other, Clare letting herself hang uselessly, putting her over his great thigh to slide her skirt off, her pants as well . . .

One hand smothering her eyes and nose, she's biting at it dreamily, his other between her legs, fat fingers sinking into her, but tonight's not a night for foreplay, so he's sitting up on the bed, lifting her by the armpits, her shins cocked to clear his lap, and biceps quivering brings her slowly down on his great red cock, her thin arm going around behind to guide, her lips pinned with teeth but popping open anyway when he starts going in, by now she's used to him, knows how to handle the intensity so it registers as pleasure, and soon she's filled right up, head back, throat exposed, glowing behind her freckles and a galactic sigh directed at the ceiling along with the exhalation of everything in her . . .

Oh, god. And then Frito is fucking her to bits, she's pinned face-down on the bed and he's an immovable weight on top of her, gold-brown hair smeared against her wrinkled eyelids, blank inner thighs wedged open by his knees, her worn-down fingertips searching for a handhold on the headboard until with a low almost regretful groan she enters the pattern, begins to shake and kick, but Frito's way too heavy, she's utterly in his control, and as her face melts into a silent scream Frito redoubles his pace, he was only fooling, he's nowhere near coming, and won't be for, oh, hours yet . . .

*

Alone with Clare in Baščaršija, Bannerman nods, exhales, and with shaking hand takes a sip of water. "Thank you for sharing that with me," he croaks.

"Hey—you asked," she insists, "and I didn't hear you trying to interrupt me, either."

"No, that's right. I do love hearing about my buddies having sex."

"I *bet*," flaring her eyes.

"What?"—"I've seen the way you look at Frito. You're in love with him."—"I am not!"—"Are too."—"So not!"—"He's the most important person in your life."—"Doesn't mean I love him."—She looks momentarily horrified. "You're saying there is *no* love in your life?"—Bannerman squirms, "But not in a gay way!"

"Not sure it needs classifying," a fingertip touching the edge of her smile, "there's always a sexual element. He's a sexy guy. You must have seen his, ah, *service trois pièces*, why don't you admit that, sometimes, you do think about it—getting screwed by him . . ."

"Dude!"

"All right all right," laughing, "I mean, not like—oh, I don't know . . . sometimes . . ." dreamy now, "sometimes you know *I* wonder what it would have been like . . ." a look away, a fall of hair, "in the rape camps . . ."

"Hey. Hey." Bannerman reaching out to touch her.

"You get used to it apparently," vacating her own eyes, "like anything."

"Clare," grabbing her shoulders, "come back."

She looks up, blinks at him, and her face melts into tears. He brings her into a hug.

This time she didn't go far, and there was Bannerman to come back to, Bannerman and his freely given warmth. But what if one day there's no one around to catch her heel as she floats away, over the mountains and the years to see for herself what she missed, to float in the windows of that pathetic little gym, just to *be there* with the huddled girls and their tear-stained mothers, and what if once there she finds herself unable to desert them, and her expensive gray clothes collapse empty and she never comes back . . . ?

In a February 2001 pre-ruling on the Foča indictments, the Tribune established the principle that rape and sexual enslavement were crimes against humanity, and by extension always had been. It's a brave step, legally speaking, requiring plenty of deep breaths, and one which contravenes the *nulla poena* principle of not passing retroactive laws. Shaky and ordinarily open to all kinds of appeals *fine*, and technically Milošević is right, he wasn't signatory to those laws, but in the grand symphony of humanity, did not such rules *deserve* to have existed?

"Of course. Fuck it," Marc van Xanthe doesn't lose any sleep over it. "Law isn't science. It always comes down to force. You were at Freiburg, you've read Max Weber, the state defined by its legitimate use of violence . . . this is always the way at the beginning of legal systems, and with International Law we're back at the start. Pioneers." A smile. "Now tell me the latest on Ranković."

So it falls to Clare to be the pin-striped and caring embodiment of UN repentance, to move sympathetically amongst the ex-Foček community—those who stayed in-country now resettled in Sarajevo if they're lucky, the Displaced Persons camp at Tuzla if not—collecting testimonies, promising retribution, the absolving and avenging angel. But, to add to her feelings of imposture, she knows she has no real vengeance to offer. Jails are supposed to rehabilitate, not punish, but the UN Detention Center does neither. The commanding officer at Foča, convicted on both command and individual responsibility, was sentenced to fifteen years in, essentially, a municipal gym.

Fifteen years for murder, torture, enslavement and rape. Get caught stealing three times in California and you'll get twenty-five. With that kind of justice, Clare can sympathize with the angry matriarchs amongst the Muslim Fočaks, moated by their own pain, who view the Tribunal as a lugubrious irrelevance, consuming vast amounts of money better spent on the survivors than on the agonizing prosecution of maybe a half percent of those who deserve it. As if there's some zero-sum assumption somewhere that locking up a smattering of Chetnik officers in extreme comfort will make it better for the matriarchs, many of whom view her personally with coldness, practically contempt, who want nothing to do with revisiting the years of suffering from, what, a decade ago now, who only want their families to be happy, for the new generation to play in the parks and cheer for FK Žejlo and go to discos and fall in love and live the good life, like you Švicarskinja do . . .

With a finger, a former slave's finger, pointed at Clare, herself.

*   *   *   *   *

Doubts, about the point of anything, are also indicated. Edgar's getting that as well. After a more than usually intense night with Sommantier in the Honda Accord, he gets back to the File 13 offices in Ašenova Street, 9 a.m., and confronts Animal about it.

"There's no way this is cleared with Brigade."

Animal's at his desk, removes one iPod earphone, glances briefly at the language assistant sitting opposite, she's busy with stacks of paper and her own iPod. He peers at Edgar over his reading glasses. "It isn't."

"It can't be."

"No, it actually isn't. I checked."

Edgar spreads icy hands. "So what the fuck?"

"The money's good."

"Fine, and we all like money, but—can't we blow this open? Leak it somehow, get Brigade to cancel the contract, and we keep ahold of the money, I don't know, force majeur?"

Animal removes his reading glasses, leans back in his swivel chair, and lets his eyes close, basking for a moment in the Beatles' "Revolver". "I've considered it," eyes open again. "It's an option. But we're building relationships. And besides, a spot of stakeout never hurt anyone. Good for the soul."

"You planning on improving your own soul some time?"

Shaking his head, "Mine's already sold. But don't you agree with old J.-J.? Don't you think you're doing a good thing?"

Edgar turns on his heel. "I been awake twenty-eight hours now, I need a good thing doing to *me*."

He takes a coffee from the machine, checks his email, and heads down to the Centar, gripping the handrail carefully down the stone steps set into the hill. He avoids a Serbian Flower. All over the city, water collects in Serbian Flowers, the old impact sites of mortars, and at night hardens into ice-traps. Likewise, murderous icicles form on the eaves of roofs and then weep about it all day. Alternately pathetic and lethal. Much more of this and Edgar Radford, Jr., will be getting that way himself. As hard to resist as not to comfort your own weeping mother. He suddenly expects to see *her* round a corner, taking coffee with friends, or alone and sobbing against a wall in her beige raincoat, liver-spotted hands quivering at her face, jewelry a-clatter as she fumbles for a pill, Edgar Junior approaching to tuck her fallen hair gently over one ear *c'mon cheer up mom*, but when she looks up she is seen to be someone else, very much younger, a woman whose cheekbones are slick with sweat and whose eyes have gone luminous, international movie symbol for Possession. And whose sexuality, which over the course of a woman's life has to peak sometime, happens to peak at the exact moment Edgar Radford, Jr.'s, fingers brush against her ear, in fact not just peak but supernova—blast rings rolling out through the city, Edgar Radford, Jr.'s, world suddenly blinding white and all sound reduced to a tinnitus just at the top edge of audible . . .

Edgar shudders, shakes his head free of it, grips the handrail tighter and walks on. It's only a daydream, a micro daydream. A flash hallucination, really, played out in the interval between one step and another. An amalgamation of the Booby-trap Nightmare, common to any serviceman who's been in a hot zone, and—well, some kind of oedipal shit. Nothing to worry about. They happen *to* you; the city's full of them. As full of them as it is of Serbian Flowers, or, as the Mine Awareness Committee keeps telling everyone, UneXploded Ordnance. With "Complacency Is Your Enemy" being drummed in at every turn, how can Edgar Radford, Jr., stand down his hyperawareness to the possibility of antipersonnels, Claymores, culvert bombs, Improvised Explosive Devices with hair triggers . . . hidden in every loose flagstone, drainpipe even . . . and how not draw a connection between Serbian Flowers and these flash hallucinations? Psychic booby traps? The city can cover over scarred tarmac, same as with any IED, but doesn't some kind of disturbance linger, that those who've developed an ESP-grade sensitivity to danger can pick up on?

Dear lord. Clearly the old thinking machine's just a little playful and wanting attention, E.R.Jr. you might want to medicate the edge off it some.

Edgar Radford, Jr., hustles among the weeping eaves of medieval Baščaršija, where hang kettles, bedpans, trays, teasets, and other fruits of the coppersmiths' quarter. Around a permutation of corners lie other demarcations: the silks sector, a street for chessboards, gold- and blacksmitheries, rugs, furriers. Everything suave and polako. Anything will be sold by the Old Town's mellow tradesmen to the interested visitor, including their own personal versions of history. Or, for Edgar Radford, Jr., primary psychiatric care.

Didn't take Edgar Radford, Jr., long to find the narcotic quarter. Fieldwork. All along this street hang bongs of brass and silver, cedar-wood pipes, ornate miniature spoons are set out on display, some fancy-painted signs saying ČARLIJ and SMAK; even old Warsaw Pact 7.62mm shell casings, their brass burnished back to martial splendor, and converted into hypodermic plungers.

"How long you are here, capitan?" says his vendor, Dejvid.

"I been in-country eleven months," replies Edgar Radford, Jr. "And please don't call me Captain."

"Ah, eleven months! Ok. You see this things every day now?"

"Yes, sir. Most days, anyhow."

"Most days . . ." Dejvid rubs his unshaven jaw, "and your father is very strong man, capitan? You don't like your father so much, I think? Not when he fuck your mother, hmm?" doing it with forefinger and OK sign.

"I ast you before, don't call me captain!" Edgar has to be firm with these people. Only thing they understand. But Edgar softens at the old man's surprised face. "Look. Fact of the matter is, I don't want folks round here knowing I'm American military, see?"

Dejvid, three and a half limbs of stringy Bosnian cannonfodder, looks up at this two-meter-tall American sirloin, mid-brown buzz-cut, and draws his own conclusions about the coherence of this here person's self-image. "O.K., mister. I think maybe you have Bosnian Psychosis only. No problem."

"Bosnian say what now?"

Dejvid explains the symptomology: which, vivid hallucinations and compulsive weapons-caching aside, is basically a persecution complex of unusual virulence. "We are attacked by everyone, yankee, and everyone says: yes please Karadžić, yes Tudjman, you have permission, kill this Muslimans—only Beal Clinton stop this ah, 'Projekt.' Only Amerika. And now in Amerika? Muslimans are—not so popular," with a yellow grin.

"But aren't you—Jewish?" Edgar tries uncertainly.

"How you know?" Dejvid shouts. Biznis-men, unemployed cleaners, ginger girls in headscarves, turn to look, and see Edgar Radford, Jr., scion of a long and valorous line of servicemen, buying drugs.

"Your skullcap?" whispers Edgar Radford, Jr.

"Oh," Dejvid relaxing and fingering it, but still a little suspicious, "I forget. Here is your hašiš. Twenty euro."

Hair triggers. Affects everyone, it seems. Edgar Radford, Jr., hustles away with his baggie and his shame, and only later, esprit de l'escalier, remembers to bridle at the diss. Why is the world so determined to mock and undermine Edgar Radford, Jr.? Animal Elliot-*Maitland* doesn't get shouted at by pushers.

"Ciao," says Ariel Alkali, dumping her stuff in a chair.

"Oh hey ciao," says Edgar Radford, Jr., waking up red-eyed on the sofa.

"Watcha doing?" says Ariel, smiling down at him from long legs, shaking out a tangle of glossy hair, and removing an overcoat to reveal an olive-green vest ripped open from bellybutton to collarbone, but held together with maybe fifty gold safety pins. Eyes as blue as perfume ads. Something of a rarity, a half-Croatian half-Czech Ashkenazi artist, and stone cold the most beautiful woman in Sarajevo.

"Hooking up with some important paperwork," Edgar waving at a stack of manila files, multi-colored tabs sticking out on all sides, some of which do indeed say IMPORTANT. On top of the files sits an ornate Turkish bong, its insides bubbling like a stomach, and one end of whose hose is being held, unobtrusively behind the sofa's armrest, by Edgar Radford, Jr.

"Uh huh," says Ariel, and wanders into the kitchen to put groceries away.

"What's that mean, uh huh?"

"It means, yes honey I see that."

Edgar narrows his eyes thoughtfully. "Yeah but I'm not sure that's how you were using it, sweetie."—"Well, how was I using it, honey?"—"You were using it like: I doubt you, Edgar Radford, Jr."—"Oh baby, I don't doubt you!"—"You were using it like: and I'm not sure I *respect* you, Edgar Radford, Jr."—"Oh baby—"

Ariel comes hurrying back through, jumps on the sofa knees-first, folds herself into him. "You get so much respect from me."—"I do?"—"So much."

Edgar Radford, Jr.'s, head lolls back onto the sofa, and exhales a pillar of smoke. "That sure makes me feel better."

"I'm all about making you feel better, honey."—"You are?"—"I sure am."—Edgar Radford, Jr.'s, body sinks a few inches further into the sofa, like he's kept it going on piss & vinegar all day. "That sure makes me feel better, too."

Ariel snuggles deeper into his hug, kisses him softly on his thick neck. "I love you, Edgar."

"I love you too, Ariel," says Edgar Radford, Jr., "you make me feel so good." They lie curled up in each other, for a few wonderful moments of world peace.

"I do love to make people feel good," says Ariel.

Edgar Radford, Jr.'s, eyes flick open. "People?"

Well there are father issues. Edgar Radford, Jr., Operations Officer of File 13 Consulting, is thirty-four years old, divorced, hellish tough, churchgoing, and can bench 480. When he quit the Special Forces last year to work for this start-up PMC, he was combining two great American traditions: Business and The Gun. Surely the retired General Edgar Radford, Sr., now working for MPRI himself—the daddy of private military companies—would be proud.

But he was not. He told Edgar Radford, Jr., that he always knew he was a quitter.

"Oh fuck him, dušo," Ariel has assured him more than once, "he is projecting his issues onto you."

"Yeah, I know. Still."

That "Still" is where Edgar's at, she's told him, where he's stuck— it denotes his acceptance of his father's disapproval and his own refusal to move out from under it.

"Yeah, you're probably right," Edgar Radford, Jr., sighs, pulling on a Sarajevsko. "Still."

Edgar Radford, Jr.'s, priorities do not lie in the direction of sitting down with his dad and talking about feelings. His priorities lie in the direction of ensuring that Ariel Alkali is not getting fooled around with. But she won't tell him if she's getting fooled around with or not, because, she says, if she was, she wouldn't tell him anyway. Twisted Eastern Bloc stuff if he ever heard it, and another thing screwing with his whitebread Virginia mind.

"So, listen, Ariel, hon. What were you getting at the other day, when you said that you're all about making people feel good?"

"That's what artists do, sweetie."

"But you make them feel good in a different way, right?"

She smiles and leans in close. "I just like making people feel *really good*," hot breath on his ear.

Edgar Radford, Jr., wriggles away uncomfortably. "But aren't you supposed to like, challenge their concept of identity and so forth?"

"Sure," pursuing him breathily, "by making them feel *fantastic . . .*"

"But . . . I mean . . ." Edgar Radford, Jr., paces the room.

Ariel watches him from the bed, wondering what's up. "What is it honey?"

"You haven't actually . . ."

"Say it. Say whatever it is."

"You haven't actually been cheating on me, have you?"

Ariel smiles a secret smile and goes through to the next room.

Animal Elliot-Maitland had been a familiar face on the Special Forces circuit for years, an outstanding officer, leader, and problem-solver, who had a habit of making things happen. He approached Edgar Radford, Jr., in the summer of 2001. Was he interested? Edgar Radford, Jr., was. He looked around him from the endless cycle of training at the U.S. Army's Task Force ———— , Fort Bragg, and saw nothing but peace in every direction, and as he was about to get kicked upstairs to desk officer anyway, he decided to go for it. He resigned three weeks before 9/11.

Still. Animal had some kind of ancestral British premonition about Afghanistan, and wanted nothing to do with that first leg of the War on Terror. Well, that was fine with Edgar: Bosnia was still rich pickings. They'd concentrate initially on personal security details. Animals has friends in the Ministry of Defence, Edgar in the Pentagon, any amount of financial backing all lined up, and a three-year business plan: workaday Dayton contracts for the biscuit base, with the chance of some lucrative bounty hunting into the bargain. "Toppings."

He arrived in-country in the spring of 2002 and it wasn't a few weeks before he'd hooked up with Ariel Alkali, spectacular beauty and human quilt: Adriatic eyes, Czech skin, Jewish hair and a Berlin art mind as tangled as any map of Bosnia.

Making them the most beautiful couple in town. Or in the expat scene anyway, which is all anyone cares about. She was into him, right from the get-go. Of course. Edgar's got a U.S. passport. Edgar can bench 480! Edgar's got a clapboard mansion in Virginia coming to him, full to the attic with pre-Revolution fortune—there's a pretty sweet dynasty there, all right. Radford boys have been righteously kicking ass all across Virginia since four years before Massachusetts saw its first bootbuckle, and he fully believes this extraordinary art-

witch can see that, somehow, somehow when she's astride him, fingernails in his pecs, bucking with Central European magics he'll never understand, burning a hole clean through his brain with those wolf eyes.

Which was fine by him, whatever worked. This was always going to be a temporary arrangement, make his life in this shithole a little comfier. A lot comfier. He's basically moved into her apartment, a whole lot better than living in the File 13 house, sharing a bathroom with Flameproof Cooper and Brick Lahoussaye, former SAS colleagues of Animal's, both of whom, Edgar swears, have bacteria in their colons the likes of which medical science has never smelt.

But here they are, Edgar and Ariel, nine months into a life together, and godammit but Ariel has worked some spell on him. It's beginning to seem like it's *him* who wants *her* more. Hoo-boy, Dad wouldn't be happy. Edgar Radford, Sr., has a foible for announcing, at the table and in front of guests, while Mom brings through the food, his preference to shit fireflies before letting a woman get the better of him.

"Face it sweetie, your dad's an asshole," Ariel has said, curled up in bed at night.

"Now, Ariel," Edgar stiffening, "please don't make me speak to you again about disrespecting my father."—Ariel makes small simpering noises. "Would you be forced to punish me?"—"Quit fooling. That's my family pride you're trampling around on."—"I thought *this* was your family pride."—"Well yeah, we are proud of the Radford penis."

"Eooo-wuh!" an explosion of bedsheets, and Ariel's on the far side of the bed, "You say it like you and your dad share the same one!"

Edgar is thoughtful.

Ariel's fingernails make themselves felt in Edgar's forearm.

"Edgar, you say right now that you and your dad don't share the same penis."

But Edgar Radford, Jr., won't let little old pain push him out of a bargaining position. "I will, if you tell me you haven't been cheating on me."

"You kidder," Ariel pushing him away.

*

The truth was, Edgar Radford, Jr., would have had to leave Task Force —— soon anyhow. He was at the peak of his strength and his training, he was respected and liked, but his mind was giving him trouble. It had stopped being the hard BB pellet required of Task Force —— officers and had developed fuzzy edges. Doubts. He bore the niggles in manly silence but in the end he'd had to see the doc. A common enough complaint. "Doubts" was the second most common injury causing men to drop out of Task Force ——, after the anterior cruciate ligament.

But then it didn't quit from getting fuzzier. Getting involved with someone as off-base as Ariel is a whole new type of strain; he keeps getting visions of her, middle of the day, having sex with people! *Great* sex, too! And now, wouldn't you know it, further compromised by a dose of Bosnian Psychosis. The new Gulf War Syndrome. Well, he can't get himself transferred out now, he ain't in the Army no more, plus he's invested time and money in File 13 Consulting, and he isn't about to be a double quitter.

So he's not proud, but he's started using. Marijuana, valium, sleeping pills, oxycodone, anything to stop his mind from running all by itself. Now sometimes it can't even tell the good guys from the bad guys. So he clings to Ariel for comfort . . . not too smart. She's slippery, she doesn't fight like the girls back home. If she's mad at him, she don't reach for the crockery. No ma'am. She pretends everything's just fine, slips into her darkroom for a few hours, hangs up prints of other men all over the apartment. To "dry." The girl is guerrilla.

And then with File 13's difficulties getting contracts—or getting intelligence reliable enough to locate war-crimes indictees—the whole enterprise doesn't feel real secure either. And now with Sommantier's course of Bosnia Is A State Of Mind lectures—*Jesus*—seems like Ariel is his only firm ground anymore. So when he starts worrying about her fidelity—*is nothing for sure?* he wants to scream, wants to be back at West Point, anywhere to know for certain he's in the right place at the right time, to be able to put a number against his performance. Instead, he's contracting a mind fungus off of this country, in whose grip the clarity of everything rots, and even such a thing as the Stars and Stripes—the saviour of this city!—no longer seems as primary-colored as it used to. Not that he's admitted that to any-one. Apart from Dejvid.

"Bosnian Psychosis?" muses Sommantier, in the Honda Accord, "I do not believe in this. But one cannot say it is definitely false . . . [*shrugging*] there is nothingue definite here. Everything is in the sub-junctif."

"*You* don't trust facts, J.-J.—*I* only don't trust my girlfriend."

"Same thing. The futile need to believe not just in the thing but also the intention behind. Are you a *child*, Edgar? You must be told you are the only little boy in the *universe*? If she is there when you arrive home?"—raising his shoulders—"who cares what else she does? Maybe when you take her back to Fortress America, O.K., things are different. But who cares about 'trust' here? Take your hap-piness, my young friend, while you can."

Edgar takes the hint. Every night the release is immense, holding her after sex and fading away next to her, and every morning is the most beautiful he's ever seen—but by midmorning, at his desk or at Butmir or training on a mock-up with the File 13 boys, the doubt comes seeping under the doors again. He's started turning up at the apartment in the middle of the day, supposedly to pick something up but really to catch her out . . .

"So how's your day going?" he'll ask real casual.

She'll be just sitting around the house in a towel, flushed pink, ostensibly from the heat of the shower she's just taken. "Fine." She smiles.

"Do anything?"—"Not much."—"See anyone?"—"Not much."—"Not much, huh. What's that mean, you only saw part of them, or you saw them entirely but not very well?"—"Who?"—"Whoever you saw."—"Jens?"

Edgar's cool caves in. "*Jens?* You're seeing Jens *Asselijn*?"

"I don't see much of him."—"Not much of his body, or not much of his time?"

Ariel gives a merciless little snicker.

"*You haven't been cheating on me, have you?*"

"Like I'd really tell you."—"What!"—"Why would I tell you?"—
"Don't say that! Just say no! All you have to do is say no!"—"What's
the point? If I wasn't, I'd say no, and if I was, I'd still say no."

"Say it anyway!" urges Edgar Radford, Jr., racked with pain. "Say
it! Say no!"

Ariel sighs, exasperated, toweling the smooth inside of her biceps.
"No."

Edgar Radford, Jr., relaxes against the wall. "Thank god," he sighs.
"I knew you hadn't been cheating on me."

"I mean, no I won't say it."

"What!" Edgar Radford, Jr.'s, eyes grow fearful. "*What!*"

"Why should I say it? It's meaningless."

"Can't you just *lie?*"

"Why would I want to lie? If I've been cheating on you, I wouldn't
want to lie to you as well. One is bad enough."

"Thank the Lord," sighs Edgar Radford, Jr., "that's good to know.
So you haven't been cheating on me, then."

"That's not what I said," Ariel stepping into her pants, "I said I
haven't been lying to you."

With a mutilated cry Edgar Radford, Jr., throws himself on her.
"Say it! Say it!" he cries, as he drags her to the bed and throws himself on her again.

Ariel squirms and kicks. "Make me."

Edgar Radford, Jr., tries hard, but he can't make her say it. He can
however pin her down on the bed and make her squeal like an animal, after which he feels much more at peace in his heart.

"I feel much more at peace in my heart," sighs Edgar Radford, Jr.
"It's amazing, the jealousy has gone right away."

Ariel, red-faced, curls up fetal, kissing the side of his big sweaty
arm. "That's good. It's important you trust me," 55'ing inside him.
"Why don't you trust me, dušo?"

"I trust you, I totally trust you baby. I only want to make sure no
one's fooling around with you when I'm gone."

"Aw. Baby." Ariel turns round and burrows in closer. She pushes
his hair all the way back and kisses him on his forehead. She curls her
knuckles through his hair and pulls, and the relief in his scalp is

wonderful. His fingertips describe the twin struts at the base of her spine, and she pushes the flat of her against him. His eyes close, and he thinks if this keeps up he might be able to get some peace of mind for once.

"Does me fooling around bother you so much?" Ariel asks.

Edgar Radford, Jr.'s, eyes open with a clang.

"The *thought* of it, I mean . . ."

*   *   *   *   *

Named for the helicopter part hanging from the ceiling, ROTOR is the most authentic Japanese restaurant in town—look, they even have a framed photocopy of Hokusai's *Great Wave* on the bare brick walls. The place has come to be known as ROTOP, however, because persons unknown, presumably Dutch, keep editing the R into a P, *rot op* being a colloquial injunction to go away in that language. After a number of attempts to hold back progress, the proprietors have evidently let it go, and even started calling it Rotop themselves. It's not so much vandalism as "customization," the City Psychotic adopting this place as its own.

Which it already was, of course. Rotop's only the latest incarnation of a restaurant that has stood on this spot since the Pig War of 1906, and these old bricks have absorbed a sonority from generations of Sarajevans taking their pleasures here, infused them with rich chords of chitchat, laughter, živjelis, smoldering come-ons. Plus these hip proprietors have clearly learned there's few places can't be made suggestively sexy through judicious use of darkness, which hangs above the candlelit tables here like chandeliers. Or aeronautical hardware.

It was supposed to be a double date, but Frito hasn't shown, and his phone's off. So it's just Clare and Bannerman and Bannerman's date, Zanna Agneri: the Magasins Sans Frontières woman, statuesque and with a highly visible chest ("pile of wood outside *that* door," murmured Clare), but with an acne problem that has rumbled on into her twenties, and a corresponding skepticism that anyone could ever want her. She's attractive but for romantic purposes not even at the table.

Clare on the other hand: a gray cotton-Lycra wraparound hanging from the delicacies of her collar bones, a wineglass with outsize bulb held up to her smiling cheek, the wavering shadows of its droplets playing amongst her freckles. Eyes more blackly lined tonight, and because of her makeup, both psychological and otherwise, she's hogging the only boy here and sees nothing wrong in that. *She* doesn't know this ghastly Italian.

How It's Going With Frito was the initial title of their discussion, inevitably. Bannerman's being charming and funny, trying to involve Zanna when he can, recapping for her benefit the triangular situation that's developing, in the course of which he introduces them to the Second Law of Romantic Comedy: He whose shoulder gets cried on, gets the girl.

"Ohmgosh, that's so true!" exclaims Zanna happily.

"Zat your plan?" Clare narrowing her eyes playfully.

Bannerman begins to deflect it in some typical way—but through her narrowed eyes, everything's blurry and his face is in shadow and she can't make out his features, when she's hit by a flash hallucination: and she's seeing *through* that goofy surface to a dark malevolent interior, where the ideas of sexual desire, and girls crying, intertwine like lovers . . . .

She jumps, terrified. Pretends to have dropped something on the floor. Goodness, she's getting quite ill from this job. From the safety of the UN Building, dark malevolent interiors seem to be everywhere. Her desk is two inches deep in paperwork on the Foča Crisis Committee, the SDS Party apparatus that in April 92 orchestrated the detention and rape of non-Serbs in Foča. Like dozens of others across Bosnia, it included the mayor, a military officer, a lawyer, two literature professors, and the head of the primary school. Hard to find a more respectable clutch of exteriors.

ICTY has dealt or is dealing with the direct military commanders of the K-P Dom and the Partizan sports hall—the male and female prisons respectively—but not their political masters, the Crisis Committee. Velibor Ostojić, for example, one of the literature professors, was the man who gave the non-Serb Fočaks fifteen minutes to turn themselves in or suffer the consequences. For most of the war he was

RS minister of information, responsible for the propaganda that kept the Serbs fighting for what they thought was their lives. *Newsday* published reports from people who saw Ostojić playing football with a severed head. At the end of the war Radovan Karadžić promoted him to deputy prime minister.

Marc van Xanthe shook his head with a smile. "You can't go after Ostojić."

Clare has found these barriers everywhere. "Et quelle raison cette fois-ci?"

" 'Art of the possible.' I've had long arguments with the Chief Prosecutor herself, about Ostojić, Maksimović, all these shitty guys— she is not any happier about this, believe me. With Crisis Committees, proving chain of command will be a nightmare. Plus, Ostojić is a big cheese in the RS. You know after the war he was head of Parliament's Human Rights Council?"

"Yeah. That's just terrifying."

Marc smiled, capped his pen. "A lot of the evidence is gathered. You have seen the files, I think. Realistically there's no more time for guys like Ostojić before the mandate ends. These more political cases will go *eleven bis*."

"Sure. If State Court ever gets going." *Eleven bis* being the instrument of transfer to the Bosnian State Court's jurisdiction.

"Hey, come on *you*," leaning back, a sunny relaxation. He's expert at managing Clare's little anxiety fits by now. "State Court will be great."

"Ostojić was minister for information! He was the Serb Goebbels! If we don't indict *him*, who will we?"

"Clare. Listen. They know the politics. SDS, SRS, SDA, HDZ—all this. Let the Bosnians try it."

"It's been ten years," a daughterly whining, "what if they never do?"

Despite increasingly firm warnings over the winter, she wouldn't leave Foča alone. Things grew frosty with Marc van Xanthe, right up to the day of her breakthrough, November 2002, when she negotiated witness resettlement for an inside man, a Serb Fočak and SDS member, who essentially "defected" to ICTY with a wealth of official documents—Jugoslav National Bank, Crisis Committee, Elektrodistribucija, VRS organizational charts. It was a deluge. Up to then, Foča had been a creepy, recidivist black hole, little information passing either to or from a population brutalized into silence, and cut off from the outside world—from the world's newspapers, TV—by its SDS captors. They had only recently learned about what happened at Srebrenica. At a stroke, Clare was OTP's blue-eyed girl.

First man indicted is RANKOVIĆ, Petar. Nom de guerre (all the colonels had them) "Banko," ostensibly from his profession, but with overtones of majesty about it, the Bans of Bosnia being its ancient viceroys. "Ko" a suffix denoting bloke. But he's small fry. In the scheme of things, anyway: the U.S. State Department has agreed to a $500,000 reward for information leading to capture. It's not much, compared to $5 million for Mladić, Karadžić, and half a dozen others; themselves dwarfed by Osama bin Laden, currently at $25 million. Theoretical values of course: American colleagues here tell her the tendency in the State Department's upper echelons is to discourage bounty hunting in favor of rebuilding economic stability. Meanwhile Defense is overrun by maniacs subject to no known laws, and payouts are by no means guaranteed. So everyone's waiting for the Democrats to come back in next year, sanity to percolate back down the ranks, and with it some kind of commitment to justice.

Small fry but the center of her universe, and she's developing a rather un-Swiss monomania about him, maybe more so than about Frito. Of course. Frito's only got indifference and a seismic ability to get her off, not acts that unravel everything Clare thought she knew about people. The cute old dichotomy back in chambers, that crimes are committed out of either greed or desperation—well not in Foča. Raping Muslims with legs of pork—Clare's more intrigued than horrified, genuinely. How do you get there? What's the process, the descent? Ranković is a graduate of Belgrade University, head of the Foča branch of the Jugoslav National Bank, (JNB), a civic leader, a family man, a good neighbor, a patriot; by all accounts he held many high ideals, and continues to do so. For Clare it's a full-blown mystery, in the Oberinspektor Derrick sense: something to be solved by methodical approach, a closing-in on the prey—not a whodunnit, of course, or even a how, these are givens—the prey here is something abstract, a certain state of being, maybe, something ancient and Pharaonically terrifying . . .

The feeling is of chiseling away at a slab of limestone, tapping through Jurassic veins of calcite and dolomite, slowly to reveal a marble core in broad smooth curves, sealed when all this was on the Tethys seabed. The marble shapes resolving—*no*—yes—undeniable, this here is an elbow, and this a bicep . . . her hairs will stand on end. It's not going to be Ranković himself. What she's after will already have left him. It will be something else, something worse . . .

Rancović was Foča's moneyman, and instrumental in the administration of the "Izvor" program, laundering money from Serbia proper into the otherwise bankrupt RS to fund the war. But even Izvor wasn't enough to fund it completely, and the RS took to printing money, both primary and gray issue, in order to pay the army— not printing the enemy's or a third party's money, like all sides did in the Second World War, but printing their *own* money. Not too smart. And something that Ranković, the consummate banker, repeatedly railed against in a series of increasingly desperate memos. The smoking gun is one such memo from July 1992, circulated among JNB managers, exploring different funding options available to Crisis Committees across the RS, and proudly citing his own pioneering examples. The general strategy advocated was to monetize systems already in place; so, after rattling through road tolls, logging and a few other creative ones—selling sniper shots to wealthy foreign tourists—he came to sale of detainee possessions, sale of detainee man-hours (chain gangs) and, by extension, sale of detainee woman-hours:

> Everyone knows that defending our way of life from the evil Islamic jihadis is difficult and costly undertaking. Therefore it is not only prudent to increase profits to fullest possible extent, beyond what is considered "polite" in time of peace, it is moral imperative . . .

VII. Woman-hours. Our boys will always take the females they desire. This is not an opportunity to miss, much as water will always flow downstream, if there is a mill or not. Initially in Foča we instituted payment system for our boys to take females they wanted, but our experience was this was tiresome to administer and the quantities too small to have substantial effect on war effort. Instead, Instruments of Possession have been drawn up to establish ownership, and the females have been sold outright to our soldiers. Our experience is that for the most desirable and youthful specimens, DM800 is not too high a price. Further we have found it expedient for buyer confidence to undertake to buy back at half-price if buyer is dissatisfied. In this way we may reclaim from our own soldiers the money we have paid them to neutralize enemies of Serbs in the first place.

The man knew how to sweat assets. This was not one of Paddy Ashdown's "town-hall thugs." So what Clare's after is an active ingredient, a mortal terror maybe, that made such things possible, even necessary. She has no idea even what category of thing it is, "demonic possession" is the closest she can come, explaining it to her more nuts-and-bolts, and probably more effective, colleagues—"but it's *not* that, it's not—it's," shaking her head, marveling at her own inarticulacy, "it's wider than that, broader, less obviously 'evil' . . ." giving that word air-quotes. Course she *says* that, rationally, she dislikes even using the word "evil," it gives her the Fear. A word vastly more malevolent than her own German *böse* or French *mal*, neither being as jet-black in its refusal of any possibility of redemption . . . a word powerful as a spell, that removes all restraint or decency. And in its major public uses embodying a corrupt fundamentalism attached to policy goals, and normally a redflag that something *really* bad is about to happen . . . Ranković had to draw up legal documents to dehumanize *his* opponents; the Anglos did it with a word. No, her instincts are that the word "evil," the very word itself, is toxic to those who use it. Even Hannah Arendt. It removed all possibility of *her* being it.

"Et quant à Vojislav Maksimović?" Clare calls through into Marc's office. Ostojić's sidekick.

"Onze bis," Marc calls back.

Because maybe what's inside the limestone is indeed some burnt winged creature, mutilated face frozen somewhere between a maniacal laugh and a scream of pure agony, I AM EVIL tattooed across its knuckles . . . But it won't be that. That would be easy. It is much more likely to read THEY ARE EVIL, and to look absolutely normal. That will be the most terrifying thing of all. If it even, to a degree, looks like herself. That's what she sees, when she disappears into this fugue state, a hideous spectrum of suffering, that she herself, either deliberately or through a failure to object, is complicit in—and which comes over her at unpredictable intervals: twice now actually during sex, with Frito.

But these are only dreams, a dose of the Psychosis. She does come back to her body eventually, like Dorothy, to find everything as it was—only exhausted and grieving for a cigarette. She's pretty sure there's nothing really bad there. But, sitting back above the table at Rotop, she's getting uncomfortable about how cleanly separated the area of her brain that deals with rape camps is from the area of her brain that deals with boyfriends . . .

"I get it," Bannerman mulling this over, "you're brave."

"Not sure it's *bravery*." An unspecified Sunday afternoon, Frito not around again, Clare and Bannerman have gone for a walk. They're on the rural south side of the valley, high above the snowbound city. One of those slow, thoughtful ambles, where the view is mainly of their own shoes. All the fields up here have turned to cemeteries, forlorn djinn-haunts, caretakered by what are either big jackdaws or small ravens. To the west, the sun has ripped itself open on Mount Igman, and is spilling a rich bronze dusk all down the white valley, slow as molasses. "More like paying attention."

"Have you told Frito this?"

"Ahh," dismissively.

"Seriously. He's interested in, you know. Depth."

"Yeah, but he's just like, '*You're* not evil babes. Don't be such a big sook.' "

"Really?" Bannerman can't believe this.

"He's always . . . away, making money.—He calls me 'Edelweiss,' you know, I keep telling him that that's Austrian, he's like, 'yeh sure it is.' "

Nodding thoughtfully. "That's a really good impression of him though."

Clare smiles. "Aw thanks mate."

Soon they're ambling back through the deep dusk, returning to its oceanic blue, sodium fairylights coming out all over town, occasionally larger ones at the mosques. Distant loudhailers on the minarets call the faithful, church bells toll, trams ring. Back into a residential zone, rooks decking the boughs of naked plane trees, the sleepy barking of dogs, callings-in to supper, the smell of frying onions and lamb. Stumbling down steep cobbled roads, cinderblock houses patched up with bricks, the occasional slab of sheetrock plain nailed to an outside wall, and everything covered in graffiti in lighthearted designs, all gathered into the voice of this city. Looks lighthearted, anyway. They don't see the old war slogan PAZI SNAJPER, "beware of the sniper," once.

The tender mood is broken when Bannerman gets beaned with a snowball, plumb in the back of the head, and a little high-pitched celebration comes from behind a row of parked cars, six or eight impish eyes peering over at them—and Bannerman's like "Right," fucking *pissed* and gathers up some ammo, turns into a snowball *machine*, getting a rate of about three per second, accuracy a little off but excellent suppressing fire, keeps their urchin heads down, but they dart from cover to cover, natural guerrillas, hiding in shadows, skipping his shots, lobbing them back, calling out obscure taunts that make each other snigger. Clare's out of it for laughing until they get *her* too, then she's gasping for air and wiping ice off her collarbones, "*slay* the little shits—" Bannerman does eventually capture one of them, "got a squealer here," dumps him over a fence into four-foot snowdrift, and commences burying him alive in the snow; but it's difficult, as the little anklebiter won't stop wriggling for laughing, and course during all that Bannerman's become a snow-magnet for the others, and what else is there for it but to beat a tactical retreat, throw Clare over his shoulder and make a run for it . . .

Further down the road, some older kids try to run them over.— Accelerate their battered old Yugo straight at them until swerving away at maybe an inch and a half, and screech off into the night, cackling.

"Guess teenage kicks have to be a little more exciting round here," Bannerman helping Clare out of the trash they have dived into, trying to cover the tremor in his own voice. A hundred yards further on, he's still holding her hand. But it's Sunday nighttime in Sarajevo, the blue is deepening to black, the hillsides have come alive with streetlamps, the people are inside and the melancholy is out, and, for the time being anyway, neither is letting go.

*   *   *   *   *

"We ah—had some visitors last night," Animal Elliot-Maitland mentions to J.-J. Sommantier in March.

"Yes?"—"Yeah . . ." rubbing his chin thoughtfully. "Local lads. Andy Deuchar followed em home. They came and had a poke around the building site, stole a few things."—"You arrested them?"—"No no. Just watched. Let them get comfy."—"Ah."—"Thought you should know."—"Thank you," distantly.

"We . . . understand you're going out on a limb here, J.-J."

"Somewhat."

"If you want to call it off, I totally understand. We can work something out."

But J.-J. doesn't acknowledge this, just reaches with practiced hands into the breast pocket of his combat jacket, pulls out some Lucky Strikes, offers one to Animal. Animal takes one, but does not light it. He stands about, wondering what more to say.

"A daughter, I gather?"

Not looking at him, J.-J. digs into his other breast pocket, the pocket where NATO forces keep a first field dressing, pulls out an old photograph leathery with creases, and hands it to Animal.

"Beautiful," Animal says.

J.-J. nods, a smile full of sadness. He accepts it back and returns it to his jacket.

Animal stands about a bit longer, and presently goes away.

"You can't trust anyone," says Al Mudhill, sipping a Mountain Dew at Ašenova Street, "except me."

"Ah yes, the Liar Paradox," says Animal. "Though we're not really in the business of trusting anyone."

"Just their intelligence, not their intentions," says Edgar Radford, Jr.

"Well put," says Animal. Edgar glows.

"Semantic," says Mudhill.

"No, he's right," Animal going to the window, "we don't expect unswerving honesty. We just want to be pointed at a pifwick," a Person Indicted for War Crimes, "and we don't care if it's because of an old feud, a gangster spat, unpaid debts, whatever." Animal's big hands are trembling from caffeine, cigarette stub flicking itself, as he leans his dome against the panes. On the other side, black and white trees tap at the glass to be let in. "As I said before, we'll pay well, and in cash."

Mudhill brushes aside such talk. "But you're never going to know, are you? You can't know if it's good intelligence until after you haven't been ambushed."

Animal and Edgar don't reply to this one. "We just want a local fellow, preferably a Bosnian Serb but not necessarily, to work alongside us, share the payout. There's that Miko fellow for instance—"

Mudhill snorts. "You trust him, you'll wake up dead."

Animal reluctantly moves. "In a city of a quarter million, there has to be someone."

Mudhill shakes his head. "It's too interconnected. When Naser Orić and a friend decided they'd go after Karadžić, claim the five million dollars, the friend—who'd fought *on the Serb side* in the war— got drilled. By his own people. Before they even *began*. Naser was lucky, he was still in jail in The Hague."

"Hadn't heard that one," Animal confesses.

"You'll never know. Not out here. Besides, there's a strong case you *shouldn't* know where the intelligence comes from. It's insecure. Didn't they teach you that at Bragg?" at Edgar, "You don't want sensitive data in the field, not even in someone's head—from where, as I'm sure you are both aware, it can be quite easily extracted." Al Mudhill's trademark smile shows his upper gums in their gingivitis-maddened entirety, and just the tops of his front teeth. "No, your only course is to trust those who are really, truly on your side. Namely, Uncle Sam."

Animal doesn't reply for a long time. "Are you, though?" at last.

Mudhill sneers horribly. "I won't take that from the *British*. You declined to lift a finger, even after Srebrenica. It's only thanks to America that Bosnia even exists."

"America meaning Clinton," says Animal.

"Meaning Gingrich," acidly, "Clinton wouldn't have done anything without Congress."

"Your new man has no such scruples."

"Tough times take tough men."

The air sits heavy in the room, an alpha-male staring contest. Edgar looks from one to the other.

"Come on, this is silly," Mudhill breaking off at last, "of course we're on side. Follow the money! We're the ones paying for this entire region to get back on its feet. And you think somehow we're not *committed*?"

"I think you're not committed to rounding up pifwicks," Animal says.

"If you're referring to that canard about Holbrooke promising Milošević immunity—"

"Not just that," a jedi hand silencing him, "America hates the whole idea of international justice."

"I don't. Do you, Edgar?"

Edgar shows his palms, he's staying out of this one.

"The U.S. *government*," testily.

"That doesn't mean we're going to prevent *you* from catching them. We want them as bad as anyone—in fact, *we're* the ones paying out five million bucks, per! Don't see much *pounds sterling* on offer?"

"The point I want to make," rising above it, "is we don't expect you to tip your cards. But we would like you to see that we have a grasp of the larger forces at work. We see that American policy in Bosnia is aimed more at rebuilding the economy than at rounding up pifwicks, partly—*perhaps*—because you want to play down the whole idea of international justice, but *mainly* because arresting them only rubs the Serbs up the wrong way, who do what they do best and destabilize the economy, which, at the end of the day, we can all agree, is what matters most.—And I do expect you to see that within that larger framework, you can have your cake and eat it: we can get in, grab our man, and get out again, absolutely silently. You know how we work. No upset at all."

Mudhill has to take a few deep breaths before rejoining. "So let me get this absurd conspiracy theory straight: you think that the U.S. knows where the pifwicks are, and has the means to get them, but we won't for our own—I don't know—*dastardly* neocon reasons, but we'll happily tell *you* where they are, and then pay you top dollar when you bring them in, which is something we don't even want in the first place? Is that what you're telling me?"

Animal's turn on the back foot. "I don't expect the U.S. government to tell us where they are," pointedly, "just you."

"So we're back where we started. Give me something, I'll give you something. Not money."

Edgar, from behind his desk: "Why not, cos I heard you're skimming like a motherfucker, is that right?"

Al Mudhill peers closely at Edgar Radford, Jr. "If you weren't in the private sector, Radford, I'd likely pass a comment about your pay grade."

"Fuck you, man, you're like twenty-five!"

"And you're just the aging muscle," a heatless smile, "but since we're all private sector now, there's no more getting each other posted to Guam." Deep breath, standing up to go, putting his can on the desk with a hollow clink. "But no, I'm so pleased we had this chat. And I'm pleased to say you've convinced me. Well done, boys. It's a policy objective I'll be pleased to fulfill. I hear of anything, I'll bring it along, we'll do a deal. Trust me," with a wink.

Exasperated, Animal has leaned his head right back over his chair, the sculptural mess of his carotids and Adam's apple jutting thickly out. "What do you want," he sighs, and before Mudhill can reply, "*besides* Edgar?"

So how can Edgar Radford, Jr., not apply the Liar Paradox to Ariel? What are her intentions—what does a Croatian-Czech artist really *want*? A visa? A ring? A nice little divorce settlement with a long wedding train of zeroes? Or should he even *care* what goes on in that twisted brain of hers, as long as she sticks around?

Of course he shouldn't—b-but goddamit Mom, he does! And right now, he doesn't hardly care about the money, he just needs to make sure she's not getting fooled around with. He can't think straight if he's away from her for too long.

Edgar Radford, Jr., charges up the stairs and throws open the door. "YOU HAVEN'T BEEN CHEATING ON ME, HAVE YOU?" he bellows. "SAY YOU HAVEN'T!"

Ariel smiles and turns off the TV and sips a banana smoothie through a straw, tilts her head sexily to one side. Hair rolls down her collar bones. Edgar Radford, Jr., watches, appalled, his five fingertips still splayed against the door, while she considers her options.

"There's no point me telling you I haven't been cheating on you," she says at last. "It's an empty formality."

"What! All you have to do is say no! Two little letters! There's no room for it to *be* empty!"

"And all you have to do is trust me. Any relationship is built on trust. Don't you trust me, sweetie?"

"Trust you!"

"I wouldn't want to go out with someone who didn't trust me. You do trust me, don't you?"

"What!"

"Because if you said you didn't trust me, we'd have to split up.

Wouldn't we? Because any relationship is built on trust. And neither of us wants that, do we?"

"I can't trust you if you don't at least *go through the motions* of reassuring me," groans Edgar Radford, Jr. "Just reassure me, Ariel. Please."

Ariel considers this. "I mean I could say the *words* . . ."

"Yes! Exactly!"

". . . but it wouldn't reassure you really. It's an empty formality."

"Not to me it isn't! It's a formality totally full of comfort and happiness!—Look," he goes on, when it's clear she's not going to budge, "even if you have been cheating on me, can't you just lie, so that way I can at least concentrate on my work?" pointing up the hill toward Ašenova.

"But I never want to lie to you," says Ariel. "Why would I ever want to lie to you?"

"So . . ." Edgar Radford, Jr., frowns. He's getting mixed up. "Just tell me."

"No."—"Come on."—"Why?"—"Please."—"It means nothing!"

Edgar Radford, Jr., takes a deep breath, paces the room. "It's not that I don't trust you."

"But you don't not trust me either?"

"Uh," but Edgar Radford, Jr.'s, mind can't parse all those negatives. "I just need a little help from you, Ariel."

"Great. Tell me what I can do."

"Drahoušku, just lie to me so I can trust you!"

Ariel smiles cannily. "So you *do* don't trust me?"

Edgar Radford, Jr., turns sharply left and headbutts the innocent fridge, which rocks on its rear edge, and rolls back for more. "Just say you haven't been cheating *godammit* and I'll never know the difference!"

"Baby . . ."

"God *damn* that hurt!"

"Aw," goes Ariel, coming up to take a look at Edgar's head, "but you'd never know the difference anyway, sweetie," touching his forehead gingerly, lips coming into a pout, "someone could have been balling me all morning, and you would never know in a million years . . ."

Edgar Radford, Jr., bats her hand away and holds his head in his hands.

For now there's nothing else for it, other than to make love to her as deep and slow as he can, during which times she is at least under his direct physical control, and pray that some of whatever magic is supposed to happen during sex finds its way to whatever black organ she calls her heart—watching while sweat drops off his nose and splashes in Serbian Flowers on the flat of her breastbone—and to come point-blank in each other's faces, and to fall asleep against a wish, as strong as a child's prayer, that she never leave him.

And to keep doing that, as the years pile up, and the teeth fall out, until the very, very end.

"Honey . . ." Edgar Radford, Jr., murmurs in the hot stillness of their bedroom, spooning round the back of Ariel and fading fast.

"Hm, dušo?"

"You're my poison and my antidote."

"That's sweet," as lightly as she can. But her eyes are clenched, and she's holding her man's hands as tight as she dare against her chest.

Something happened on the Foča building site in June. Two men arrived in the middle of the night with an antivehicular mine, enough to make a mess of the meager progress to date. One minute they were taping it to the base of a wall, next thing they were on the wrong end of a Level 5 kicking from persons unknown. Hours later they found their way home, shivering and hurt.

Complaints were filed; there were newspaper reports of attacks on Serbs, talk of a breakdown of what was suddenly not being called "the peace" anymore, but "the cease-fire." There was an investigation, the operation was terminated, File 13 caught flak, the houses were dynamited, and still no Muslims live in Foča/Srbinje.

By the end of the summer Commandant Sommantier was removed from his SFOR rotation and discharged from the army. It was a relief, all told, that he had been removed by authority, and not had to leave under his own willpower.

He peeled off the uniform, an empty man. Within a few months he had secured a job in management consultancy, and, though still living in Lyon, he works a few days a month in Paris. He has rebuilt himself and his finances, and found, broadly, a certain peace of mind. Though there is a daydream that recurs to him, when he's in the big city, between appointments on a boulevard, moving as intangibly among crowds as ever: of all these unknown faces, one, at least, might one day catch his eye, and politely stop him, verify his identity, and, while acknowledging his ultimate failure to achieve anything meaningful, might, nonetheless, for his good intentions, thank him.

Thrill of the Chased

ZMAJA OD BOSNE, Dragon of Bosnia, is the main freeway along the valley floor, where behind curbside barricades of filthy snow, between the addled towerblocks of Novo Sarajevo and the Centar, is a long stretch of university campus, many of whose faculties are still shells, long rows of more or less distinguished old buildings burnt from the inside by their own treasury of books, and now roofless, roomless, set about by skeletal trees tapping at windowpanes no longer there. In these skull-buildings presences linger. Not curses exactly, nothing so malevolent. Maybe the same custodians who have stalked Alifakovac for centuries, the mountain cemetery over the city's east gate, where strangers are buried.

Trams rattle past the university, eyes averted. Graffiti is sparer and less about self-affirmation or fucking the system—only such ungraffiti sentiments as "I Lowe BH." Assumption in the expat scene is this is just the Central European snarl-up around "v" and "w"—until someone pointed out there aren't any w's in Bosnian, and that if you're into downloading your thoughts onto your university, you don't just take a stab at the spelling—so it was as likely a play on the name of Sarajevska Pivara's second beer, Löwe, named after the Austrian founder of the brewery, and pronounced "lova," which as it happens is local slang for "cash." Meanings here are as layered as the baklava, and money's in most of them.

"Poets, all of em, these Sarajevans," Frito says genially, "it's in the water."

Genial but really he resents other people reading it—that graffiti feels like a love letter to *him*, personally. And not the chaste kind, either. He's got such a hard-on for Bosnian beer it feels like there's a spectacular climax offered somewhere in there, if only he would make the effort to chase after it . . .

Well he's trying. But his inquiries into the anomalous production of Sarajevsko Pivo during the siege have elicited little but evasions, denials, and blank Balkan shrugs. Frustrations for a guy not used to getting shut down, even from the Sufi Child, who quickly caught on to how badly Frito wanted pointers in the way of Alcoholic Enlightenment, but who has picked up a few general negotiating principles from his time on the street, and held out for proper money.

"Reckon I'll have to cold *employ* the little tyke," Frito mulling it over over dinner with Bannerman at Libertas, "I want any leverage at all."

"Not on the F&B payroll," Bannerman waving a knife at him.

"Come on, plenty of slack. I'll put him on as a, what—Food & Beverage consultant."

"You want him to teach you how to get so drunk you hear voices, and me to underwrite it?"

Frito lost his temper. "I'll get you back in cash, ya bloody scrimper. It's my money, anyhow. Seriously Bannerman, what's the point even *being* a tycoon, you don't shoot from the hip now and again? Faint heart never won fair maiden, mate," with a significant look whose meaning Bannerman doesn't, or doesn't want to, understand.

So the Sufi Child embarks Frito on a course of Beginner's Alcomancy, using Sufi-grade slivovic, beer being too blunt for the purpose, each session lasting twelve hours and with a recommended thirty-six hour "meditation period" afterwards. The trick is to shed enough self-consciousness to achieve what serious psychonauts would recognize as the Transpersonal Plane. The imagery is all the same: all talk of "ascending" to a stark, almost wireframe landscape, recognizably this one but uncluttered by the phenomena of reality: no colors, no stormblown textures and power cables, no dense white fog roofing the gray valley. Only the glowing pulses of consciousness around us. Only emotional value remains.

"But all I got was shitfaced," Frito groans next day, sliding into a bubble bath Bannerman has run for him and unleashed €20 of suds into, so now the foam superstructure occupies three to four times the volume of the water, and a significant proportion of the room.

"Why don't you just use ketamine, cut out the middleman?" asks Bannerman.

Frito parts the foam like undergrowth. "Int that cheating?"

"The Sufi drink slivovic to see God; he shrugs, "now we have— better technology."

Comedowns hit Frito hard. Like an eighteen-wheeler forced to brake, it's days before he's back to the old momentum, but as soon as he is, he's back at the top of the slide with the Sufi Child and hassling people for the secret of the brewery.

"Hi I'm Frito and this is my yoda," coming up to a couple of local heartbreakers, and concentrating not so much on them as the amorphous thrill blooming around them at being objects of attention. He'd never really noticed it before, but it's there, it is there—a whole attack, decay, sustain and release in translucent moods, as clear-edged for the heartbreakers as any other stimulant, and defining a time envelope in which Frito must either get them sexually focused, or move on.

Clare knows he's like this. Toying with lesser creatures and because he can—these are terms she has accepted, and she just has to reassure herself that he knows these girls are not what he's looking for, just traps in his path. "Booby traps," he grins.

A price worth paying. For her, it's all Frito. Analyzing her emotions is difficult; the trick to burning through indecision is to find the right question to ask. And what that is, for now, is if Bosnia went nasty again, who would she cling to? Bannerman's a sweet boy, but a boy.

But she's powerless to protect Frito in return. After sex there's not the quiescence she's come to expect. His mind spins like a motor screaming for a clutch, when he's not actually fidgeting there's a forced stillness, in between dozes she catches glimpses of his unguarded unhappiness, she turns over, fractionally awake in the nighttime musk, and when she turns over a second later, the duvet is empty.

"Schatz what are you doing . . . ?" She comes into the kitchen in a dressing gown. Frito's sat at a full ashtray and writing in a note-book, pages and pages of desperate wizard-scrawl, which he'll shut guiltily and get up and hug her and presently lay her on the table and screw her.

She doesn't get it. He's not kidding about this brewery story, she doesn't understand his urgent need for it to be true. There's even some fairy tale he's dug up about it: among the many myths and superstitions crowding the valley is a clutch of more recent ones con-cerning the siege, one of which apparently features a "beer fairy," a being invulnerable to sniper fire who flitted around town during the first months of the siege, distributing bottles of Sarajevsko Pivo. If he left a bottle on your doorstep, it was a sign that you were not going to die. Not that day, anyway. And that's as much as Frito has heard: just a fairy tale.

He pursues it into monomania. Asking people about it, eyes nar-rowed, searching for a tell. On some level it must be about himself, about what private pains may be locked up in that great head, fear of shortcomings, memories of failure. And she definitely doesn't under-stand his refusal to share these fears with her. And now there are ster-ile syringes and boxes of 0.45mm needles around the flat—and worse, if possible, the foils on his antipsychotic medication go unpunched for days in a row.

"Have you stopped taking your medicine?" smoothing his hair down in bed.

He flinches. "Just—" but stops himself.

Her stomach turns to stone. She's learned, the hard way, never to hassle a boy about *anything*.

"Messes up my ability to feel," he says presently.

She doesn't know what to say. "To feel me?"

"Sure yeah."

Leaving her classically trapped. Maybe his failure to have formed bonds of love before now is a side effect of the antipsychotics? It's plausible. So something she should welcome, possibly?

But as he stops taking them, over these weeks, disinhibitions creep in, disinhibitions and insomnia and an accelerating paranoia.

He fidgets, he walks around naked, he keeps getting up to open the door because he's sure there's someone else in the flat.

"Coulda sworn . . ."

For much of January the city is cut off by the maglai, the white fog that sits in the valley. Above a sharp fog ceiling at 700 meters there's blazing winter sun; from the mountain highways above you can see the maglai's roof flat as a lake; while down inside the weak visibility turns everything to dreamscapes. Hunched figures stumble into and out of Clare's world, their eyes' intention not clear until they're already too close. She wants to make Frito right so he can hold her, make all this dissociation romantic and not just scary. But the more he is unperturbed by her, the harder she tries to shake him out of it . . .

Even Sufi Child wonders, "Is Frito going to be ok?"

This was at the top of the UNITIC tower, hanging out in Ludovic van Eisley's place, Shiny Dryhten and Ludo and Clare all chatting over coffee, the Child leaning spreadeagled against the plate glass to better absorb the amazing blankness. Just visible twenty floors down was the abstract shape of the parking lot, eaten by the white oblongs of snowed-on vehicles.

But Clare didn't have an answer ready to go and, caught unawares, began the slide toward tears. Eventually, eyes shining: "Don't *you* know?"

"No."

"He'll be fine," Shiny intervened, firmly sensible, "once he finds what he's looking for."

Perhaps having learned disinhibition off his mentor, Sufi Child piled right in with what not to ask: "He has not found it?"

Clare tried to smile, but her hands made a prayerbook for her face to fall into.

Bannerman spends the working day with Frito, in and out of taxis, hustling among the city's grand delapidations, Frito being very on during business meetings and equally detached in between. Bannerman can read these undulations well enough. Their emotional conversations are rarely overt, but for all that they're precise enough.

"You feeling out of sorts?"

"Nah fine."

"How are things with Clare?"

"Just fine just fine."

There's a small footbridge over the river built by Monsieur Fiffel, in a style similar to his famous tower in Paris. Frito pauses on it, hunched into a donkey jacket, to look down at the river shallowing over terraces on its way west to the River Bosna.

"You're coming off the Zyprexa though?"

A pause. "How'd you know?"

"Clare said."

"She tell you everything?"

Bannerman shrugs. "Unknown unknowns."

"What's that mean?"

Brushing it aside. He's getting thicker-witted, no doubt about it. "Is that a good idea, though, coming off?"

Frito turns around. "Can't be a lot worse."

"Really?"

"Well." Walking on. "You know that real estate deal, up at the west end of the valley?"

"Up at Vrelo Bosne? Euro a square meter?"

"That one. So I was up there the other day to take a look around, and the maglai's *real* thick up there, and you know how sort of haunted it feels round the old front line anyway? Well I was just pacing around, sticking to the path and all that, and I was in this weird little village called Vruci, completely silent at midday, and in the middle of the road there's this lady there, your pretty standard old crone, and we got to chatting, and I was all, must be a bit odd living under Mount Igman, I mean *right* against this almost vertical wall of rock, you know?, which the sun goes behind, *sets*, at midday, right? So like half of the entire lives of the people who live there is spent in twilight. That's got to be attached to some pretty strange behaviour right off the bat."

"Got it."

"But she said, get this, she said yes but we have the water. She explained how the Bosna comes out of the ground so pure it looks like the ducks are floating in midair. It's got properties. Keeps everyone living. D'you not find that a bit odd?"

"I do yes."

"Well that's what I thought later. Though at the time it didn't seem odd."

"Your Bosnian's that good now?"

"Completely not mate, and this is the point: the only thing I can speak is English. I kind of squint and I can see her saying the "f" of floating, really getting that bottom lip way in there."

"An old crone who spoke English?"

"Headscarf and everything."

"Way way wait—a head scarf, I thought they were Serby over there."

"This one had a headscarf."

Bannerman looks doubtful. "For real?"

"Well this is the thing right, I remember it clear as day. But when I like disassemble the memories onto the kitchen table, you know, and I look at it all like that—there's no way. There's no way it happened." Frito now looking at Bannerman, nakedly scared, searching for any flavor of comfort at all. "There's no language that can have happened in."

AGAINST WHICH—peeling the cap off a Sarajevsko, aw man does that feel good. The warm company of the Child and Jamie O'Ryan, Maza Cukič and Bannerman all giving the day a kick in the ribs at some speakeasy downtown, he never feels more at peace. It does not work with any other beer. It's tied up with the idea of Sarajevo, the city herself. The name blazes with a heroism that makes him proud just to be here, to have known the city at all . . . it's the a's in it, or something, the first part a fiery red modulating to an emerald-green suffix. All other words are just black on white. He tries it out on a beermat, it works in any handwriting, even in Cyrillic, capajebo still has it . . .

"What are you doing?" Jamie O'Ryan leaning over to look at his doodles.

"Practicing his signature for when he gets married," says Bannerman.

Frito laughs too long at that one.—Because it's true, he digs the town so much, he wants to have it. Zealotry. He gets angry at just the mention of Republika Srpska. When the old crone at Vruci told him the NATO airstrikes were the happiest day of her life, she swept a long Egon Schiele finger across the blank sky and Frito could see the jets, saw the black explosions on the Serb positions and heard the sonic counterpart roll up seconds later—he gasped at a euphoria that expanded in his chest. It made him, so proud. He wanted to encompass it all, to possess it, in what, at the end of the day, he recognized as a fully sexual urge.

But how can he? How do you make love to something that's not even in the Animal Kingdom?

Maui, the champion trickster god of Maori mythology, has form here. He fished New Zealand up out of the sea, captured the sun and invented fire and pulled a few more godly moves, after which he moved on to the secret of immortality itself. He somehow found out that if only he could defeat Hine, the Night Goddess, he would find it. And he also knew—somehow—that if he could only catch her when she was sleeping, and crawl into her vagina, through her, and out of her mouth, he would gain immortality.

More of a precedent than an answer. Maori has notoriously few words, and putaika doesn't necessarily refer to the human vagina. Still, it's the concept of entering, and that's how the legend has come down. Maui's friends, the birds of the forest, giggled as they watched him clambering into Hine's vagina; Hine was woken by their giggling, swiftly realized what was going on, and crushed him to death against her pelvic floor.

A troubling myth, for several reasons. But Frito genuinely feels these anthropomorphisms in the air—the beer fairy, the City-as-Woman, who possibly—he's not ruling it out—assumes a human form—to be the first hazy symptoms of a next level "up," into transcendence and understanding, and away from the tedious preoccupations with love and money that tangle these gene-crazed members of his own species.

But not good old Vedo Alimović. It's a herd species and Frito should have *started* with someone who stuck out above it. Inquiries to him about the beer fairy elicited a sharp response:

"Why you want to know?" Vedo leaning forward across his giant desk.

Frito could not freaking believe it. "He existed?"

A heated confab ensued between Vedo and his majordomo, Jasim Bukić, about which Frito's translator, Maza, later gave him the gist: yes, he did exist, but he died during the war. His son, however, who was something of a war hero, survived—he could theoretically talk to Frito about it, but he'd been indicted for war crimes and was currently at large. Vedo of course knew where he was, and he and Jasim haggled over whether they could trust Frito not to alert the Acronyms to his whereabouts. Vedo prevailed.

"Frito is good man. He wants talk to him, nema problema! Frito understands," Vedo nodding at Frito slowly, and with a heavy-duty subtext that Frito absolutely stood under.

Thus, at the beginning of February, Frito and Maza find themselves at the house of one Vane Novane: unshaven, late twenties, spiked hair dyed blond at the tips and a white tracksuit, the sleeves rolled up beyond a sea-green fading of old tattoos; a fleur-de-lis on his left forearm, crescent-and-star on his right. The sitting room's a palette of the nicotine colors, with teak veneer to offset, the centerpiece of which is a slung foam armchair, in which Vane slumps back down, and grunts something at Frito.

"You want to know about my father, Kemal Novane?" Maza Cukić translates.

"Yes please," says Frito.

"Molim vas," says Maza.

Vane nods. Tall, rangy dogs pad around. Two wiry dudes sit silent, either side of an electric bar heater. A female presence elsewhere in the house. Instructions are given to draw curtains; outside, a white storm builds momentum. A case of Sarajevsko clanks onto the floor between them. Vane lights a cigarette, removes his sunglasses, and clears his throat.

His father Kemal held Yugoslav Communist Party membership card number 38. He was that close to the beginning, to the first stirrings at Belgrade University, the in-crowd's excitable arguments over morning sliva, all the trendies talking dialectics and utopia, hammering forefingers into copies of Proudhon, Marx, Kropotkin—some maniacs *Bakunin*—even before the Spanish Civil War made communism the compulsory undergraduate accessory. But Kemal Novane had broken his knee while cossack-dancing one hoar-slick night outside the Philosophy Faculty, after a session on a new rakija donated by chemist friends, distilled from organic matter found under the Gazela Bridge. The most proletarian rakija, they told him, *dialectic* rakija! Good times are historically inevitable!

Historically unrecoverable, anyway. Kemal Novane woke up mysteriously lame, with a leg that never regained full mobility, and so unlike university friend Milovan Djilas never took to the hills when the Germans and Italians invaded. Which is not to say he didn't fight. He was an asset all right, thrown into a bookish life, employed as a translator for the occupiers in Sarajevo but protected from sanction by Tito himself, whose Partizans gained much useful, and sometimes vital, information from the arrangement.

But that was as close to the dream of power as Kemal Novane ever came. Out of all loops, and against the jockeying for position up in the hills, he was easily forgotten, particularly after the Partizans' formalization into AVNOJ, the Antifascist Council of the People's Liberation of Yugoslavia, and the bureaucratization of a resistance that had been so lighthearted, such a band of brothers. When the woman who ran his dead-letter drops became his wife, Sarajevo became his home.

Then in the fifties, Djilas and Novane both turned dissident against the regime they had helped forge. Djilas was, once, to have been Tito's successor. But the revolution was ever-revolving; and though they began to speak out against Tito, against all expectations neither was liquidated. How or why not is unclear. Djilas and Novane lived out their lives, both suriving Tito, in fact surviving the entire country, living long enough to see the state they had helped build liquidated out from under *them*.

A mysterious protection. Especially through the dangerous period around 1948's break from Moscow, and its annihilating wave of purges. Probably that Novane had once known Tito himself, had touched his robes, might have warded off the local apparatchiks and OZNa secret police agents. For it came as no surprise that soon after Tito's death Kemal Novane was let go from the university, in 1982, the year FK Sarajevo made it two rounds into the UEFA football championship.

"Ha," wild eyebrows, rotten teeth, "finally they find the courage!"

Like many dissident academics before him, he was thrown into menial labor, and elderly alcoholic that he was, took a job with Sarajevska Pivara, d.d. He never drank disgracefully, if only because *that* threshold was impossibly high. He was respected at the brewery, and by the time of the war, ten years later, had become an institution himself, a rickety intersection between relic and mascot, loved across all factions. It was arguably Novane who did most to galvanize the workforce during the siege. Mister Selimović and his management kept the brewery running; but Kemal kept the workforce coming in. Because just getting there to put in a day's work was tough. Crucially, the brewery was on the south side of the river, and crossing bridges was not an easy commute. Sometimes UNPROFOR armored vehicles would ferry citizens across, or at least provide a mobile shield to walk behind. Either way you had to be motivated.

Vane was still at Gymnasium when the siege began, seventeen and invincible. He joined up with "Juka" Prazina's private army. He came back to the brewery to see his old dad, any time patrol and sleep allowed. The brewery's High Imperial courtyard, burgundy stucco with cream detailing, was shelter from snipers, if not from shells. By that time his father had all but abandoned their home on the city slope of Mount Trebević, towering above the southeast; Kemal had moved a cot to the brewery, and spent the winter there, by the boil-

ers, looking after a few dozen homeless. Vane has memories of Kemal
directing workers around, running the artesian screws from the
underground lake, having to repair the engines in a shrieking nighttime hurry, putting out fires in the stores, rebricking walls, organizing the water queue which sometimes stretched fifty yards down
Franjevačka Street. When the Serbs shelled the queue, the injured
would be brought into the brewery's first-aid unit, a stuffy room
underground with one hassled doctor. Many died. Loss ran thick in
the streets.

There were other pressures for keeping the brewery open, beyond
beer: everyone up to the president and beyond, into UNPROFOR,
was adamant about keeping its unpoisonable underground water
source open. Few were as adamant about beer production. There
were enormous difficulties just getting the raw ingredients, malt and
hops, when people in the city were boiling grass for dinner. But for
Kemal Novane, as for the management, it became even more important, when people were starving, to produce beer. A reassurance; normality as important a defense as bullets. "What would Steven Seagal
do?" Kemal knew how to speak to the men. "He fights, doesn't he?
He fights, but you remember what he says? He says: 'I also cook.' We
also, must never stop cooking our beer. It is through this art that
Steven transcends the violent and so becomes the *superman* . . ." New
dialectics running on old rails. The brewery common room had a
pirated VHS of *Under Siege*, highly revered in spite of terrible tracking for its witty repartee and rich source of innovative fighting tech-
niques. And, naturally enough, for Erika Eleniak. Word spread, and
a pair of staff officers arrived in the spring of '93 to requisition it.

Kemal was assiduous about keeping people connected. It was too
easy to cower in your apartment and go slowly mad from the internal
exile. He frequently made the perilous journey across town to ask
after a no-show, ensure the families of those who continued to work
got enough food and fuel. Kemal's courage shared a border with indifference. Whispered stories built momentum of Kemal limping around
town in plain sight, whistling while running errands, maybe pausing
to refresh the spraypaint on a PAZI SNAJPER while chalkclouds burst
on the masonry around him, discordant jackpot-payout noises on the

banks of burnt-out cars serving as ramparts . . . Soon he wasn't just whistling but singing old sevdah songs, ducking around the billowing blue-gray sniper blankets hung from telegraph lines, his unexpectedly deep voice calling out its yearning for the glory days . . . and presently voices hidden inside smashed windows joined in, tentatively at first but soon more confidently, until finally the whole bridge from bass to soprano was complete—as who among us, even now, can resist that fine Yugo-nostalgia?—tunes familiar as your own soul and warm with the decencies of childhood . . .

It was against such a chorus that Kemal brought beer to housebound groups: women, students, sometimes soldiers at barracks; not huge amounts, just a bottle here or there, but it wasn't quantity that made the difference. It set the bars for heroism and complaint very high. Not least for truculent Vane, out in the mountains, given his first command that winter and eager to prove himself. And it also led to a certain dilution of the idea of Kemal Novane as a man, and not something a little more . . . translucent.

"No no," easy smile, "*I* am not the beer fairy. You silly thing." Ruffling some scamp's hair. Implication being that he knew who was, though. This of course was his imaginary friend the djinn-woman, Djelja, which had attracted a certain ribbing at the brewery, before the war, along the keep-sharp-objects-away-from-Kemal lines, for which grown man claiming an invisible girlfriend named "Multiple" can avoid? This ribbing dried up as the siege wore on. May have been nothing more than tolerance, as everyone locked in that city evolved their own personal belief systems—especially after the mental patients were let loose back into the city, that May of 1992, thick with ravings that suddenly didn't seem so paranoid.

He rarely spoke about Djelja. He didn't evangelize but would answer questions if asked. Young Vane asked them all, many times over. Including: if the djinn existed, why couldn't anyone else see or speak to her. With an anger that intensified over the years. Why couldn't *he*, Vane, meet her. Kemal never lost his kind temper, though, even when Vane was raging as only a frustrated seventeen-year-old with a bandolier of Coke-can grenades can. The classic SDA/SDP dichotomy that played itself out between parents and children all over the city. Kemal agreed that yes, the djinn probably was all in his head. "But Vane, my love, my son—where else would it be?" Vane could not be made to understand that that didn't matter. Kemal tried any number of approaches, including the theorem of his own dear Gödel, that provability is a weaker notion than truth . . . but Vane couldn't see. He was developing an idiot's absolutism, demarcating the world into polarities of good and evil. And now, instead of sitting his matura, he was undergoing the formative experiences of life out in the mountains, at the far end of the objectivity spectrum: there wasn't much that was subjective about a 30.06 round. Fighting the Chetniks it simply didn't matter where his head was at, in any but the most physically literal way.

The djinn had become Kemal's personal faith, and if Vane couldn't accept that, the rest of Sarajevo did. The fragmentation of belief sys tems in the city, already advanced by its peculiar history, went crazy during the war, disparate precursors of what would later become codified as Bosnian Psychosis. Everyone had their super- and sub-stitions for keeping alive, sudden blossomings of hospitality, justifi-cations for kindness, rationalizations of murder. The Republic of Bosnia-Herzegovina, for all its youth, was still the representation of a secular ideal, of what America once stood for, of diversity and toler-ance. And it was being exterminated. *Every* mosque the Chetniks captured out in the mountains, every one, was destroyed. How could fiery young Vane respond in any way other than by standing by the religion he hadn't even cared about, by becoming what the papers would soon be calling "polarized"? Wasn't it treason of a sort, irre-sponsibility if nothing else, for his overeducated father to stand by with his philosophical mysticism and watch it die? And to affect shame—*shame!*—at what Vane's unit had had to do in the defense of the people?

The truth was that by the time of the siege, encounters with djinn had ceased to be anything remarkable. The first rash of sightings was explained away as Medjugorje Envy, a common enough complaint in the Muslim and Orthodox communities even before the war—at the Catholic shrine at Medjugorje, just down the road, the Virgin Mary still appeared on a fairly regular schedule, a single tear stealing down a porcelain cheek—or there was always shell shock, PTSD, drugs, sleep deprivation, simple grief to explain it away.

But a few months into the siege and *djinn* sightings were snow-balling out of control. It was the time of the Jugoslav People's Army's most serious attempt to capture the city, attacking on multiple fronts with motorized columns and close air support. Early May. A cascade of heartbreaking evenings on the boundary between spring and summer, that capsized their load of sun across the Golden Valley, while below the ridgeline a darkness that descended like a turning away from God. Bright against this mountain blackness, phosphorus tracer rounds fountained and frolicked, angelic in their trajectories and intent—for most of the tracer rounds were old JNA stock, colored with barium peroxide; though the Sarajevan TO units and impro-vised gangs already had smuggled Iranian issue, colored with stron-tium. Celestial presences, searching: the green for Muslims, the red for Serbs, messengers with summons to the world beyond the world.

"They are not angels," voices hissed in the front lines around Dobrinja and Mojmilo, "but a race of djinn perhaps, for where the Qu'ran tells us that angels are beings made entirely of light, the djinn are of "smokeless fire.""

"But we know that djinn have free will. But these tracers travel in straight lines, and therefore have no will."

"So you think they must be angels? Idiot!"

"Shh! You will summon them!"

"Old fool. The djinn cannot hear."

"They are not djinn! They are tracer rounds!"

"Shh! Iblis himself is djinn!"

"Maybe these are neither angels nor djinn—but *qareen*?"

"No. These are of smokeless fire, they must be djinn."

"Phosphorus is *not* smokeless!"

"What! There is smokeless fire in my Esbit blocks. Do I summon djinn each time I cook?"

"Of course not. But these are convergences. We are thrown out, exiled in our own valley, we live among the bones and animal drop-pings. Shaitan and ghul dwell in such unclean places, where they wait to trap us. In these days we may understand 'unclean' in a strictly military sense. For each of these phosphorus tracer curls, look, has its holy purpose, do you not see? A cord slung from the Seven Skies . . . phosphorus is Greek for "bearer of light," which is also what the Tree of Jesse calls Iblis, you see, *lux ferre*, 'Lucifer.' The devil. He is in each arc, and we know *he* is djinn. Do you dare not say your Bismillah now?"

Vane returned to his dad and cried in his arms, and Kemal stroked his hair, patient, full of love, and gave him some Djelja.

Yes, to drink. There were several stills in the house on Trebević. There was a cellar with three small vats, each one a different recipe: grape, grain, potatoes. There was a larger vat, ЂЕЉА burnt into the side, into which the smaller vats were emptied, forming a strange punch of slivovic, orahovac, wine, cabbage stock, flat Pepsi—anything that would not curdle—making it more soup than beverage, spicy-hot on the tongue, and containing inscrutable lumps best swallowed quickly.

The djinn-woman lived in there. Two years before, during the World Cup, Vane had had a group of friends round to watch Yugoslavia take champions Argentina to penalties. By the end, owing to the long overrun, they'd run out of rakija and had moved on to Djelja. Kemal found them next morning and threw Vane's friends from the house, and shouted at Vane till he, Kemal, had to sit down and hang his head.

The first of two times Vane saw his father angry. "You might have killed her," under his breath as he replenished the vat. For Djelja was to be maintained in the manner of Chinese Old Soup: never allowed to run empty, always kept at least half-full, so that, according to Zeno's Paradox, you would be drinking a brew as old as the very first ingredient. Two hundred and fifty years, according to Kemal. Over the years he'd regaled young Vane with heroic episodes of her passage through history. More fairy stories. Culminating in one of the critical episodes of the People's Liberation War: how the IV Corps of the Partizan Army, retreating with horrendous casualties in the face of overwhelming German and Italian armor, and simultaneously fighting the Chetniks, survived the Battle of Neretva: 1943. Driven back against the chasm of the River Neretva, seven thousand men encircled and all the bridges out, certain death from Štuka dive-bombers coming in the morning, and the leadership stuck for ideas. Against this grim background the punch Djelja made its appearance, and in a last flowering of the Communist ideal was contributed to by all ranks, and the ensuing grand mixture to be distributed equally to every man at supper. A last drink before the end, what the Christians amongst them recognized as Last Communion.

That night: a thick fog fell along the valley; the bridge the Partizan engineers had been failing to secure finally held, though none could say why; the Partizans crossed the raging river while the Wehrmacht failed to press their advantage; and Mihajlović's Chetniks, waiting to ambush the Partizan stragglers on the far side of the river, also missed the escaping divisions. In an asymmetric fight, they survived complete encirclement, through manifestations or transactions that Vane now waves a dismissive hand at. "Who knows how they really did it!"

Well it was known how the Communists felt about religions, both established ones and start-ups. But despite that, and in the light of their miraculous survival, the punch Djelja wasn't destroyed, or drunk down; perhaps in those shifting times Tito needed all the luck he could get. The men believed in it, and there was nothing to be gained from throwing out a rabbit's foot. At the second AVNOJ council that November, running at five liters, Djelja was brought down out of the mountains and given in trust of the Jugoslav people to Kemal Novane, for him to do something with. Even in the years of Muslim suppression, 1945–68, the Jugoslav people never asked for it back.

Vane now grins and spread his arms at his guests, in mute appeal for some sanity, and maybe some fucking gratitude.

The second time Vane ever saw his father angry was that winter of 1992, after the scandal created by Vane "murdering" his Serb prisoners. The same episode, incidentally, for which Vane is now wanted by ICTY. Vane prefers not to talk about it. "And the Dutch accuse *me* of crimes. The Dutch!" He shrugs, peeks through the curtains at the snowdrifts being nourished by the wind.

Predictably enough, Djelja was all gone by that first Bajram of the siege. "Ha! When she was gone, Kemal said she was another victim of the war. The old fool . . . she was not *shot*, the old drunkard drank her all himself, can you imagine this! The most precious thing, he loved this more than his son, who was fighting Chetniks for him, no, he hated his son but he loved his djinn . . . and he became so thirsty he *drinks* her! Ha, ha! Imagine remorse of drinker after this!"

Vane Novane's eyes do not shut when he laughs; they keep steady watch on Frito as Maza says his lines for him.

"He was very old by this time, he was"—Vane tapping his temple—"he was very sad after this. After this, he started giving out free beer. People said, he has moved his djinn into the beer, because the old vat is gone, and he is such a believer in the beer now." Vane shrugs, aims for an insouciance, but there's only bitterness in his voice. "I think he had nothing else to love."

Frito nods for a long time at this, then asks a question.

"Ah, well. This was famous scene, one year later. Your translator knows, probably. He was shot on the Vrbanja Bridge, playing violin. Suicide. He never said goodbye. Not to me. He was still angry about the—you know," a pause, a desolate gaze out of the window, "maybe he wanted to punish me. Or give an apology for me, something like this. Of course that wasn't the reason he told. He told he did not wish to live in world where someone will shoot a violinist!" a sarcastic laugh, "but no, that was not reason either. In my opinion, I think he knew of the photographers by the Vrbanja Bridge, and also the snipers, and that his death playing the violin would be a very strong picture for the American newspapers, and for the Jews in particular, who as you know control America . . . I think he thought it will remind them of Jew violinists in Nazi camps, and maybe the Jews will make America to lift embargo and stop Chetniks from killing us all . . ."

*   *   *   *   *

Ketyl Gaarder wants some attention, too. Everyone's lusting after Sophie den Uyl and Clare Leischman, people like this, but Ketyl gets little beyond polite curiosity. She may not be in their league, on a purely physical level, but nor are most of the boys chasing them . . . only Jens Asselijn, the Dutch army officer, has irrupted into Ketyl's world, one amazing night back in October of soft eyes and hard limbs. She knows this hardly makes her unique, but there *was* some connection between them, that went beyond the merely physical . . .

"A hard man to catch, that Jens Asselijn," Clare Leischman has told her.

"You don't think I can get him?"

"No no, I'm not saying that," hurriedly, "although . . ."

Jens has been with most of the expat women in Sarajevo. Ketyl knows. Even one or two Muslim girls; his charisma is considerable. But Ketyl Gaarder has her secret powers also. She's an officer with the European Union Police Mission, and spends much of her time at the BH Telecom Inženjering Building, an exciting new installation on Zmaja od Bosne, built out of steel, mirrored glass, and presumably, for what it ended up costing, vacuum-packed bricks of hundred-euro notes. She works alongside SIPA, the state-level FBI, establishing systems for legal telephone call interception that might, one day, become compliant with the sprawling hegemony of European policing protocols, a collective headache known as the Schengen Acquis. In practice this means a little desk at the far end of an open-plan office, the reassuring vibe of IT departments everywhere: striplights and inadequate ventilation, garish desktop images, the thick whirr of heatsink fans, stacks of servers blinking in their cabinets, sysadmins blinking in their spectacles. There, she has the power.

For she's been googling the objects of her desire since before Google came out. Extreme Googling being one of very few pros in that sea of cons, policework, as before the EUPM she was with the International Police Task Force, also in Bosnia, and before that back in Norway with Økokrim, the national white-collar crime agency. Never anything major, just running an eye over bank statements, call logs, that sort of thing. And she's found out that Jens Asselijn makes calls to an amazing number of people, not all of them women—he's an officer in a NATO armed-surveillance operation. In the respective secrecies of their work, she and Jens both inhabit an invisible superstructure above the daily hum of the Dayton Peace Plan. A Dayton aristocracy. By imperceptible signs are they known to each other; a certain glint in the eye, a quiet thirstiness for information, even when falling-over drunk at Embassy lawn parties. No other woman, none that Ketyl has identified in any case, attains to her level of access, making Ketyl Gaarder Jens's only option if he is not to enter into a morganatic relationship.

"Only we can really understand each other, you know?" she tells Sophie den Uyl at the Japanese ambassador's leaving party. Sophie flips her hair to the other side and replies that Jens Asselijn seemed to be understanding her, Sophie, rather well last night, thanks.

Bitch.—The Japanese diplomatic crowd, normally so stiff, have turned into a gaggle of teen pink obsessives. There's a lot of magenta hair, stripey fluorescent pink stockings, butt cleavage, tinsel, one guy wearing a fishtank, and girls on rollerskates handing out giri-choco.

"Ketyl, can I introduce you to someone?" Clare Leischman rescuing her from Sophie, leading her back to her little circle of Bannerman, Frito, and the Child.

"I know these guys already," Ketyl says. "I take money from them at poker. Apart from you, adorable little one. The girls had better watch out, eh!" bending down to squeeze the Child's cheek. Child turns into a wind turbine of arms.

"Yeh, I think Clare was just rescuing you from Sophie," says Frito.

Ketyl goes *ah*, without making a noise. "I look like I need rescuing, do I?" rather directly.

"Doesn't everyone, time to time?" Frito puzzled at her tone.

"If you can't look after yourself, then maybe yes."

"Well, I'm dead meat around Sophie den Uyl, that's for bloody sure," then turning to Clare," not that I'd ever *do* anything, you understand. She's just a good-looking woman."

"Don't let Sophie get to you, Ketyl," Clare says. "She needs everyone to want her. She'll end up unhappy."

Ketyl looks miserable. "I just want one person to want me."

"Hey Ketyl, *I* want you," Bannerman taking her by the hand, "*to dance!*"

Clare has come as a Tyrolean milkmaid: corset, blue gingham

miniskirt, pigtails . . . and freckles. She will never be able to pull off the squeaky-clean look. Bannerman, by contrast, turned up at her apartment as a Chetnik, unshaven, complete with camouflage baseball hat and toy machine gun. Clare put her hand over her mouth and said, "No. Just—no." So they went through her wardrobe, and now he's in a gray wraparound dress, thick winter tights, and ewok moonboots. Clare smiles to watch him and Ketyl at it, Bannerman wholly shameless on the dance floor.

The Sufi Child, tweenage-cool in mirrored aviators and rolled-up sleeves, and hanging out with big bro Frito, pulls a toothpick from his mouth and points it at Ketyl. "This girl she knows about you."—"Yeh? Knows what?"—"I do not know. She knows more about you. She is also spy, I believe."

Frito pulls at his Sarajevsko. "Also," along with Al Mudhill, Dmitri Lautz, a few others they have identified as "probables." An invisible superstructure, not so invisible to those with enough alcohol down. "Ketyl's with the EU Police, so, yeah, spoze so."

"The police?" Sufi Child looks up at Frito. "Shall she shoot us if she wishes?"—"Don't reckon so, Sufi kid, even if she wished real hard."—"Shall she arrest us?"—"Doubt even that. She's with the telephone police."—"She is listening to people's telephone talkings?"—"Yep, I imagine that's pretty much what she's doing."—"*Your* telephone talkings?"—"Don't reckon so. Lots of *kriminalace* out there lots more interesting'n me." Frito nods a bit, surveying the surveilling scene, then remembers who he's speaking to here.—"Hang on, sorry, mate: *is* she listening to my telephone talkings? Is that the impression you got? Finding things out about me?"—Sufi Child waggled his head noncommittally for a while before deciding, "I believe yes."

That night in the flat, huddled around the single desk lamp on the kitchen table, Frito and Bannerman were electrified with possibilities.

"Dude, the killings we could make would be so substantial! We'd make like Srebrenica-grade killings with even *marginal* access to call data!"

"You still haven't told me how, though mate. How does it help, exactly? You want to what, trawl for some dudes talking about quarterly earnings reports?"

"We'll figure it out," darkly, "we will."

"Not sure we will . . . most conversations *I* have are bloody tedious, and I'm *in* them! You want to tap someone's line, there are easier ways." Bannerman nods at the sense of this. "You want to tap the *girl*—well now, that's another story . . ."

"I don't want to tap Ketyl."

"Besides, she's not a *kid*. You can't get people to break fiduciary duty, *risk jail*, you know? just by asking em nice."

"I know," Bannerman all defensive.

"Doubt money'd do it, either."

"Right."

"Besides, we won't stoop to bribery."

"We're better than that."

"Nope, only option I can see," Frito shaking his head regretfully, "is we really want to know about tapping people's lines, we're going to have to shag it out of her."

Bannerman nods once, firmly. "Agreed."

"So?"

"So go to it, man. Do what you do best," clapping Frito on the shoulder.

"Rather you than me."

"C'mon, she's not so bad."

"*You* hit it then."

"Well I've got ah, I'm kind of—why don't you?"

"Cos I've got Clare, mate."

"Never stopped you before."

"Well it's stopping me now. She's the one, Bannerman. She's the best girl in the world."

Bannerman sucks at a cigarette, eyeing Frito carefully. "You've mentioned that before."

"Besides, I don't see the point."

"It's listening to the city's *business*! What do you mean, the *point?*"

"Saying it like it's the bomb isn't an argument, mate. And it's your project anyway."

"And you're my partner. I help you on *your* projects."

"Some of em."

"No, we do everything together."

"Not everything . . . I don't ask you to go at Clare from the other end, do I?"

"Just shut up about her, can you?"

"Alright. Keep your hair on."

"Go seduce Ketyl. That's your line of work, not mine."

Frito grows suspicious. "You *want* me to cheat on Clare, don't you? You want me to cheat so you can move in, is that it?"

"No! Nothing like that," Bannerman making an appalled face, "Jesus."

"All right. Sorry." Frito and Bannerman eye each other warily.

"Come on pal. Hug it out."

Bannerman looks at his shoes. "Besides, I'm not clear Ketyl would even *consider* me."

"What are you on about? Course she would, you're the great Bannerman, mate, everyone wants a piece of you! Come on, only way to decide: let's play heads-up for it. Loser shags."

Frito's terrible at poker. Bannerman considers this, eyebrows up, sipping placidly at a small glass of orahovac. If Frito sleeps with someone else, Bannerman stands to win very, very large. "Deal."

So it is that Bannerman finds himself pillow-talking with Ketyl Gaarder a few days later. Two lonely hearts, finding warmth in the darkness. "It's been difficult, I don't deny it," Ketyl sighs. "Jens's work keeps him very busy. He has very little time to come back to Sarajevo, and when he is, he's so tired, we never get to see each other."

"Must be hard to make it work," Bannerman agrees.

She's a sweet little girl of thirty-four, unmistakably something of the noble or inert countries about her. A stability. Full outer shell. Not as loaded down with fate as the Finns, higher up the table—the quiet decency of Swedish lagom, but sparer, windblown, Protestant. There's a tenderness there, but Bannerman finds it hard to believe anyone could dig a gut-wrenching love out of her, something to really bond with, and it feels like she suspects that, too. What they have in common quickly dwindles to their jobs, which though sad is also handy, given Bannerman's mission to get her to talk about her power over the telephone company's computer operating system.

"What platform? NT?"

"Unix."

"Yeah? How's it work?"

"Well I'm not going to tell you that! It would give it away."

"Strikes me you've given away the good part already."

"I don't want anyone else to be able to do it!"

"Well, presumably I can't, unless I'm inside, like, the actual server building itself, sitting at a terminal?"

Ketyl smiles, strokes his hair. "I'm not going to tell you."

Within a few hours, she does. "There are interfaces. Of course. Databases of all sim events. Calls, messages, load-balancing, change of cell. You just need to know the sim number and have the clearance. Easy."

"But it's not online, is it?"

"No way."

"So you actually need to be inside the building to access it?"

"Of course. We can't do it from *home*."

"We?"

Ketyl smiles, turns her head the other way, aware she's been found out, again. "My engineer, Zaim. My own personal IT Department. He works beside me."

"Zaim," Bannerman saying it carefully.

Ketyl runs fingertips down his arm. "That's why you're here, isn't it. To dig these informations out of me."

"No no, I'm totally here for—" waving a hand round at her apartment, "—the sex. But what you do is also just *really interesting*. Course I want to know about it."

A silence. "Are you in love with me, Bannerman?"

"Uh . . ."

"Bannerman, please don't take this the wrong way, but I don't want you to fall in love with me."

"Okay."

"It's not a good idea."

"I see."

"This is only for a good time, you know? For now."

And streetlight is striped vertically down her face, yellow against the blackness—showing Bannerman an iris so pale and aqueous it looks more like a tear, trembling fatly on the point of bursting, and rolling slowly down a cheek.

"SPAHO, Zaim" is the only Zaim working at the BH Telecom Inženjering Building. They will tell you this in the lobby, flicking through thumb-stained ring binders—and give you a phone number, too. Glad to help. Dovidjenja!

So Bannerman sets up a lunch with the young Mr. Spaho (25), the title of which is Getting Head-hunted, at Vinoteka: a wooden chalet restaurant full of German officers in their distinctive flecktarn camouflage, laughing NGO workers, EU people drowning their boredom, journalists huddling with sources, and various other blasé members of the International Salariat who can afford it. Zaim Spaho is a skinny Franz Kafka–looking guy, though with more of a faux-hawk, who has not eaten at Vinoteka before, and who doesn't quite conceal his pleasure at finally doing so.

Bannerman takes him through the plan: F&B Consulting Ltd. is moving strongly into retailing drugs online. Just a little internet start-up, run straight at the exit strategy of getting bought out in one to two years' time. A sprint. Ideally bought by the prominent local pharmaco Bosnalijek, so far lacking an online presence in English, and in which, incidentally, Vedo Alimović has been building share. A tendency commentators suggest points to a long overdue addition to ViKA's portfolio, legitimate drugs, given a certain synergy with fields already mature. Or perhaps Vedo will incubate F&B Consulting, and together look for mezzanine-stage capital. Maybe even buy it himself, then use his leverage with Bosnalijek to get *them* to buy *him* out. Any one of these things.

Since real Reconstruction money only goes to Westerners establishing businesses in Bosnia, not to (heavens!) the Bosnians themselves, and "Frankly Mr. Alimović," Frito Power-Pointing all this to the ViKA Board of Directors the week previous, "you're going to need some Westerners with functional business accents to captain this puppy for you, work with the European Bank for Reconstruction and Development, get the export-credit guarantee thing going, qualify for the loans and grants and all that. If you can dig up someone else willing to engage with," nodding delicately, "the full breadth of ViKA's interests, you're golden. But we're here, we know what we're doing, and we have four million five verified email addresses just begging for your hot and juicy spam . . ."

Zaim S. understood. "You want to be internet arm for Sarajevo gangster?"

"Vedad Alimović is a highly respected *businessman*," says Bannerman with great dignity. "Besides, no. We're going to be incubating our own business, retailing drugs over the internet—"

"Spamming."

"Among other methods."

"Without prescriptions?"

Bannerman genuinely taken aback. "What are you, a doctor?"

"This is drug-dealing."—"Yes, exactly."—"Bad drugs."—"Not like *methadone*."—Zaim shakes his head. "Vedad Alimović distributes heroin in Sarajevo."—"Well we won't."—"What then? Valium?"— "Sure, why not."—"Vicodin?"—"Probably."—"Fentanyl?"—"I don't know Zaim, probably not. Come on dude, you twenty-five-year-olds are supposed to be hardline on this stuff. Your body is your own. Don't know how it works in Bosnia, but the Food and Drug Administration in *my* country doesn't ban food additives just because they kill you.—?"

Zaim doesn't flinch against this tirade. "How do you know I'm twenty-five?"

Bannerman correspondingly relaxes. "I thought everyone knew everything in this town."

"Yes. But not Americans." Zaim toys with his napkin, looks again at this American, searching for a tell. "O.K. So you want me to build the technology for your company."—"Right."—"GUI, database, stock-control?"—"Why not."—"Your whole company, in fact."—"Hey, we can do it, we're just paying you to."—Zaim nods tightly. "But why you think this idea will work?"—"What don't you see?"—"It's a full market. How are you going to," doing it with his hands, "squeeze in?"—"No tariffs. Cheap workers."—"Pay the natives nothing, you mean."—"Less than we'd be paying in the EU, sure."—"O.K."—"Problem?"—"No, no, it's O.K." Zaim with a slow Bosnian weariness, "that's economics."

"Damn straight." Bannerman stares him out, nodding seriously, doesn't want to be getting any more attitude from this guy. Fucking Sarajevans, think just because they spent their Nintendo years getting shot at for real gives them more sass than you. But soon he mellows, and over lunch takes Zaim through various grandiose fantasies for their start-up, including not just retailing but *making our own*.

Zaim Spaho stops chewing, alarmed. "Our own?"

" 'Our' all of a sudden, is it?"

"*Your* own drugs?"—"Why not?"—"How will you do this?"—"With like, beakers? Who knows? Vedo's got all that side tied up."

"Which drugs? Generics?"

"Them or," airily, "proprietary ones."

Zaim cocks his head. "Proprietary?"

"Right."

Zaim frowns, taps fingertips on the table. "Maybe I don't understand. I think proprietary means the patent, or whatever you call this, the "IP," is owned by some big company, Merck or Pfizer or something, who will stop you from doing this."

"That is what it means."

Zaim frowns. "Then what?"

Bannerman leans forward for the punch line: "Bosnia's not in the WTO."

It's a hell of a pitch, brilliant in its audacity. There are actual billions to be made, dittoing blockbuster drugs: Vioxx, Viagra, Propecia, in total defiance of international Intellectual Property Law. Undercut the price, and, as Bannerman and Frito have been showing Vedo, customers find you. Vedo has been unable to resist, and is now throwing money at—"incubating"—F&B Consulting Ltd.

Zaim sits back. The bright day outside is blurred through the steamed-up plate glass, except at the edges, where Zaim can catch glimpses of the iron-and-rivet bridge. Taxis and white SUVs troll down Skenderija Street. This man was clever to blunder into the Inženjering Building and ask for "the hacker named Zaim"—to make things difficult for Zaim at his job. That was certainly a very effective tactic. That's the thing Zaim forgets about Americans, they are much cleverer than they seem. There is always some devilish explanation for the apparently stupid things they do, which is why, of course, they are so rich.

"How much will you pay?" Zaim asks.

"It's a moonlighting job. Ten hours a week, and we'll give you half of what you're getting at BH Telecom."

Zaim snorts. "At Telecom I get nothing."

"Then you'll get half of nothing, which comes out to . . . ah . . ."

"O.K., I get thirty-three thousand KM a year. You will pay seventeen?"

Bannerman waggles his head noncommittally. "Funny thing is, I talked to the registrar? Who said you get twenty-two."

Zaim doesn't blink. "The registrar gets many things wrong."

"No doubt."

"That's my base salary."

"All right all right. Engineer *and* hustler, you don't see many of those. Fifteen's the offer, plus stock."

Zaim looks at Bannerman a while. "I think nineteen is better."— "You do, huh?"—"Yes."—"On the basis of what?"—"It's prime number. I'm superstitious."—"That's a pretty good reason. Even with seventeen also being prime?"—"O.K., O.K., you know some things!" a charming grin, "but nineteen is my number."—"We'll see. First though, a little interview."—Zaim cocks his head. "Haven't we had that?"—"By which I mean test."—"O.K."

A pause while Bannerman chooses his words. "If you know what cards the other guy has, the game's a whole lot easier . . ." thoughtfully playing with a wad of twenty-euro notes at least €3,000 thick.

Zaim sighs. "Not again."

"No no, wait."—"You're all the same, you biznismen."—"I'm not asking you to steal, or defraud, or anything."—"What then?"

". . . How close are you to Ketyl Gaarder?"

Zaim flushes. "She is my boss. That's all."

(*That's all?* Bannerman registers that reaction, all right.) "Well so the two of you are involved in the call intercept process . . ."—"Yes."— "A sensitive job."—"Yes."—"Which you know Ketyl's been *abusing*, don't you?"

"No. She hasn't."

"She has."—"She hasn't."—"Trust me. I know."—"I work at the desk beside her. I would know."—"She's been accessing sim logs on friends of hers."

Zaim smiles, turns his head the other way. "That's not abuse. That is 'perk.' "

"Okayy . . ." Time for a change of tactic. "Accessing sim logs on the guys she's fucking."

Zaim's eyes flick up, suddenly hard, and hold Bannerman's for a full second. "She is not sleeping with anyone."—"No: *fucking*, I said. The guys she is *fucking*."—"She isn't doing this with anyone."—"Sure she is."—"No. I would know."—"No, no, she's fucking like three guys at once. Course she is."—"If you're thinking about Jens Asselijn . . ."—"No no. Old stuff. These are three new guys."—"You are wrong. I would know."—"Why would *you* know?"—"We work together, we talk."—"But she's not going to share that sort of thing with you! A, you're a colleague, and B . . ." tailing off.

"I am Bosniak?"

Bannerman shrugs, like it's not his place to say.

"No. She is a good woman. She is not seeing three guys."— "Fucked one of em last night."—"Last night she was at home."—"No she was out all right, raging for action."—"*Last night*," Zaim with his finger on the table, the first knuckle bent near 90 degrees backwards, "*she was at home.*"

Bannerman gazes at Zaim, commiserating with his eyes. "You got it bad, huh?"

Poor Zaim. The information flows freely. He's been crushing on Ketyl from close range but has never had the courage to act. Bannerman, thinking on his feet today, rapidly rearranges the proposition: Bannerman is going to hire Zaim to do work for F&B Consulting, *and* get him together with Ketyl, out of the kindness of his dumb old heart. But for Bannerman's Plan of Romance to work, Zaim needs to keep his job at BH Telecom, and keep working very closely indeed alongside Ketyl Gaarder. "We can totally make this happen. Just got to do what I say."

That weekend everyone piles into cars and drives down to the island of Korčula, on the Croatian coast. It may be winter but it's still the Adriatic, and you can swim in the sea in your actual skin. Bannerman and Frito arrive in the F&B van with their two Bosnians, Sufi Child and Zaim Spaho, respectively.

"Cos I'm trying to get him and Ketyl together," Bannerman tells Clare, in a private moment.

"Oh it's like *that*?" excitedly. "Yes! this is good. Okay. Ketyl is *so* going to kiss him."

And Clare goes about her work with a savage single-mindedness. At dinner that night, fourteen of them crowded into a villa, candle-lit and the wavering shadows of glasses across the tablecloth, Clare talks to Zaim too much, laughs spectacularly at his jokes, leans in too close, passing a joint back and forth, forsaking all others—it's even working on *Bannerman*, for Zaim has become, tonight, really strikingly handsome, all cheekbones and melting eyes and a dense black crew cut—Clare ultimately leading him away from the table for a walk on the beach and a long, heartfelt conversation about object-oriented programming languages. When they get back to the sitting room, Ketyl is the first person to look up and ask, "Good walk?"

Clare peels off to find Frito, winking at Bannerman as she goes.

*

Zaim took Ketyl to a gig at CityPub. He took her to dinner at To Be Or Not To Be, and he was going to pay but she insisted on halving, and so they went to a gambling club to win back the amount she'd paid, which they did, and afterwards, giggling drunk by this time, after a play-argument over who was less square, to the hotel with the bar in the hammam. They went to their respective changing rooms, got into enormous black towels secured with pegs, and met up at the bar inside the steamroom, built entirely of pine. Visibility about a meter. An unknown number of people sporting a wide variety of bodytypes were lounging in towels and swimming costumes, drinking and attempting to touch matches to soggy cigarettes, chatting, sweating, drawing pictures in condensation that immediately filled in. Ketyl wore a towel around her chest, with cream-colored bra straps showing.

"Belt and braces," Zaim said.

Ketyl was alarmed. "You know how you learn a phrase, and then you hear it three times in a week?"

"Have you actually been *wearing* a belt and braces?"

Ketyl wiped off her glasses and put them back on; they steamed up immediately.

"Here," and Zaim gently took her glasses off, and gave them to the bartender to look after. "Much better."—"But I can't see anything!"—"We are all myopic in this room."—"Oh dear, I suppose my makeup is coming off, too."

Her face was reddening fast, more naked without her glasses than her clothes. She looked at Zaim, uncertain what to do with her hands, eyes unnaturally large, trying to keep composure.

"Much better," he said.

She smiled. The bartender, naked from the waist up anyway, pushed over two glasses of wine, and Zaim led her to a corner to drink and sweat.

She did most of the talking, leaning on a locked elbow, the shiny knot of her shoulder up against her chin—the rest of her a cascade of crumpled black toweling—and across a distance that her own short-sightedness steadily ate up. Pores opened. Sweat beaded on her skin, tentatively running from her seal-black hair, across her forehead, collecting under her nose, dropping, pooling behind a clavicle, over-flowing under her towel. Within half an hour the situation had gotten the better even of Zaim's reticence, and while she was speaking, he put a finger out to the drop of sweat at the tip of her nose.

She paused momentarily but kept talking—just about—as he kept his finger there. Her sweat ran down to his knuckle. He watched her mouth talking. His finger inched down to the corner of her lips. He looked up at her eyes again. She rolled her head sideways and put her mouth in his palm, watching him all the time.

He is ceaselessly astonished about the fact of her. There's something remote, not just the quiet security, the simpleness of her body . . . she seems to be made of something that's itself extremely rare. Partly it's *not* racial. They're both in exotic territory, dating in a foreign language. But her skin is so pale, almost without melanin, he's mesmerized by the veins in her breasts and calves, and the intense redness that swells in her, when her eyes are guarded but her breastbone glows—it's telling, much more so than she is herself—it feels like that is the thing he's falling for, a latent shape of blood, that dresses in skin.

"You legend, Spaho!" Bannerman slapping him on the back, next time Zaim's round at the F&B warehouse in Dobrinja. "You absolute *pimp*!"

Zaim allows himself to be ruthlessly befriended by Bannerman, especially as Bannerman reveals to him, part by part, his shameful plans to reel in his own best friend's girlfriend. A secret to bond them. Zaim sympathizes. "The heart wants what the heart wants."

"She's the one for me, Zaim."—"She is hot, yes."—"I'm throwing everything I can at it. *Everything*."—"Go for it, man."—"Any help you can give, greatly appreciated."—"Me? What can I do."—A smile, a deep breath. "Oh, I don't know. Wouldn't mind seeing her call logs, for starters . . . ?"

Zaim laughs. "No, this is not possible."—"Sure it is."—"No. Sorry, man. Some things are too much, even for friends."—"While *you're* tracking Ketyl around town?"—"What?"—"Sure you are. Following her from one cell to another?"

"What?"

Bannerman's big play. A wild stab in the dark: "You track her, don't you? From cell to cell."

Zaim replies carefully. "Why do you think this?"

"Oh I know a thing or two about GSM," popping two Coke cans open, passing one across to a stupefied Zaim, "You log cell changes. It's a sim event. The data's all there, why *wouldn't* you?"

Zaim slackjaws for a moment, fails to suppress a sly grin, and shakes his head. The city's mobile phone reception is provided by dozens of phone masts, with frequently interlocking areas of coverage, referred to as "cells." As any sim card moves out of one cell and into another, the change is logged. Zaim eagerly confesses. And all it takes is a very simple Unix program for him to capture the data from one *specific* sim card, and to alert him whenever it moves around, and from which cell to which . . . out in the mountains the cells are pretty large, some of them 5 kilometers across, but down in the city, where call traffic is much denser, cells can shrink to as little as 30 meters in diameter—enough to be pretty accurate about where any sim card is at any time . . .

It's not abuse. It's intimacy. Of course. It's a yielding of control, as geared around the sexual appeal of vulnerability as any other feminine wile.

"She must have *guessed* I'm doing it," Zaim tells Bannerman defensively.—"Totally agree."—"It's what we do for a job! She *must* know."—"Absolutely. It's just a flirty little game between two specialists. She's probably doing the same to you."—"Exactly!" cries Zaim. "I think she is doing this to me as well, it would be silly not to do it to her in return, I think!"

Although, Bannerman points out, on the other hand it could be unfair to expect Ketyl to have assumed that Zaim has *also* written a little Unix program to capture the data, encrypt it, and send it out to an external IP address, enabling him to follow her from *outside* the Inženjering Building, indeed, from his laptop—which is to say, all the time?

Zaim looks at Bannerman without moving. A zerosum eyeball-wrestle. It's another educated guess.

"O.K.," Zaim concedes finally, "this part I think she has not guessed!"

The thing is, when Zaim's in bed with and crouching above this glowing woman, her biology pulsing, he just wants to get *inside* . . . sex will allow him to get so far inside and no further. Brushing aside her full outer shell, the entering of her is like a homecoming. One finger in an English-Nynorsk dictionary, he'll roam through her past addresses, tax IDs, Ministry of Health and Care Services numbers, departmental histories, and he'll wallow there, with a great and growing tenderness for what he has potentially destructive access to. Feels like home. Finally understanding, difficult for a foreign-language programmer, how it is that "Enter" and "Return" can be synonymous. With each penetration he feels himself falling deeper—and *so* much more intimate than mere sex, he doesn't know about Ketyl particularly, but which is swapped like CDs by the colonial class . . .

There's a level on which she does know. When she looks up at him, her shell giving way to a certain quizzicality, that's her feeling the fieldstrength of his superior knowledge. He's got her covered. Quis custodiet ipsos custodes, well that would be Zaim Spaho, several iterations above street level: guarding the girl who monitors the police who guard us all. The blood-shape inside her knows it, even if her head doesn't—and knows it doesn't—and maybe that dissonance is what generates the curiosity that keeps Ketyl saying yes to invitations from this strange, geeky Saraj boy, nine years her junior, who feels intuitively the need to control events, lest someone else try to . . .

"Thanks," Ketyl whispers.

"No sweat," says Bannerman, "glad it's working out."

Dinner at a sleek chrome-and-pine place on Radićeva Street, with

Khan Kerensky, Dmitri Lautz, a few others to swell a scene. Ketyl has beckoned Bannerman across the table, to put a hand on his and share a private joy at the first romance she's had out here that seems to mean anything to the other person. She's not so much excited about the future—though she is that, sort of—as exhausted by the journey it's taken to get here. She leans a shoulder against the plateglass, suddenly tired, a severity descending across her, against an occluded and now darkening sky. The reflection of these interior lights hangs orange in the monochrome street outside, over the dead grass, old piles of ice, the balconies of laundry, satellite dishes, sensible cars, and a stray beggar-woman working the sidewalk, with an A4 printout detailing her case.

"I'm thirty-four, I have a good career, I should be able to take charge of my life," Ketyl not looking at Bannerman, "but I just couldn't bring myself to make the first move."

"But you did, though." Bannerman smiles, nods. "That first time you talked about him, I could tell that you were in love."

Ketyl's doubtful. "Don't know about *love* . . ."

"Seriously. You still can't see it, that's the funny thing. But it was absolutely clear to me."

"Hmm."

"And look where you are! He's intelligent, nice, incredibly good-looking—okay, he's not Jens Asselijn, but that guy's a *dick*—what more could you want? You were like a missile aimed at Zaim Spaho, and you don't even know it."

She doesn't respond for a while, but a smile drains up into her face. "Yes," eyes compressing in happiness, "I suppose I was."

"Another job well done," Clare says, later that night at Hacienda, a giant Mexican fire hazard done up to look like a bar.

"Damn straight," says Bannerman, "another?"

Frito's in training with the Sufi Child, and he's appointed Bannerman *in loco boyfriend* tonight. So he's gotten her as drunk as possible, and taken a small hammering himself, and keeps telling people, "Dude—I am so full of well-being? sunshine is coming from my *ass*." And it's not long before he finds himself in a conversation with Zanna Agneri occupying 2 percent of his brain, and Clare just behind him, listening earnestly to someone else with her hip out, one hand on a mojito, the other hanging free—and which he takes in his own. The fear doesn't even kick in until the deed is done.

And she doesn't even look round, just continues listening, and Bannerman thinks he might pass out for happiness.

By the end of the evening they're dancing together, to heartbreaking eighties hits. "So how many birthday cards you get, edelweiss?" he asks her.

"Eight," with her lazy smile.—"Not bad."—"Well, I am a desirable lady."—"Yes, you are."—"Three of them were unsigned."—"Oh yeah?"—"But the writing looked suspiciously similar. Like they'd all come from the same person."—"Wow. They must really like you."—"I guess they must," she sighs, "it's a bit creepy, though."—"Yeah?"—"It's almost needy."—"Needy's not sexy."—"No it isn't."—"I hate it when people get needy with me."—"It's not very appealing."—"I mean, when people come up to me and say they really like me and want to spend time with me, I'm like piss off, needster."—"You know what I mean, Bannerman."—"I mean don't these people get it? We're not attracted to anyone who actually *likes* us."—"That's not true."—"What we want is strong arrogant bastards. Selfish motherfuckers, who really know how to treat a girl mean."—"Oh stop."—"I mean, it's like hello, don't you get it? Indifference is all we ask. Is that too much?"—"Stop it!"—"Why can't all boyfriends get shitfaced with preteens on our birthdays?"

But by this time Clare is giggling and digging her nose into his sternum, her hand high on his collarbone. And then "Africa" by Toto comes on, and it's as life-deep and unironic as anything from back then, or out here, and her fingertips spider-walk round to the back of his neck, and he draws her hips to his, and then they are looking at one another in all Seriousness.

An uncertain amount of time later, whether it's the alcohol or what, her perception has become one long steadycam shot, too much information, too dizzy, spinning periodically to find Bannerman at her side as they make the rounds of goodnights, and out into a taxi, Clare curled up in his lap against the cold, Bannerman absently rubbing her back up and down. And at her apartment, she gets out first, but stands at the taxi door and faces him and tucks her hair behind her ears and says "Um." Bannerman was maybe about to get out also, but looks up at her, and says "night kid."—"Goodnight," she says in a small voice and stands there. He takes her hand and draws her down and kisses her so, so softly on the cheek.

She stands up and they look at each other, but it's *cuh cuh* cold and she says, "Are you interested in meeting a sex slave?"

Bannerman's out the taxi and halfway to her door before he stops himself—that was a pretty odd formulation, even for Clare—and turns around quizzically, "Uh—"

"Tomorrow," evenly, "in Tuzla."

*   *   *   *   *

Standing guard over the Tuzla road is an enormous power station, citadeled around with substations, grids, sentry pylons and cables, as brooding and ill-intentioned an instrument of war as anything in this winter kingdom. Today it's grayed out by the weather, its keep beginning a hundred yards off the passenger side window, other side of a chain-link fence and a field of snow that won't have seen a snow-angel all year. Probably not even a snowman, either. Men are easier to spot, definable as they are by a physical presence in the snow, and not, as with angels, an absence.

The town itself is all projects housing, product advertisements in the forlorn garish style, piles of dirty snow, women with two-inch white nails, and old folk in wheelchairs trying gamely to flee their institutions, world-weary carers catching them back in again. There's some Venn-diagram territory between silence and coldness that hangs over it like a curse. A gang of towerblocks mottled with reconstructive plasterwork. A town collapsed. Literally: the saltwater caverns and sinkholes under this place have grown so large that parts of the Old Town have fallen through to the water-world caverns below. Tuzla, "Salt City," being reclaimed by the springs from which it sprang.

Clare's entourage includes Zoran her driver, Vanda her language assistant, and a chain-smoking Spanish corporal with a bad dose of Generation X.

The Displaced Persons camps in Tuzla are still full of Bosniaks terrorized from along the Drina—Srebrenica, Žepa, Foča, Goražde. They have been in temporary accommodation for ten years. Employable-age men sit around in semipermanent structures, working methodically through their packs of Yorks and Luckies, lavishly overdelivering on their caffeine and nicotine needs for the day. Anoraks, short leather overcoats, goatees, thoughtful silences. Urchins in AS Roma shirts play in the streets with a metallic gold ball.

Clare puts her head in the doors of a half-dozen blocks, people she's taken testimonies from already, just to say hi, how's it going. Some are so exaggeratedly delighted to see her, arms up vertically in surprise, a move Bannerman's never seen outside of cartoons, to begin with he thinks they're making fun. But no, not even a little. The irony washes off pretty quick. Zoran, Bannerman, and the Spaniard's function is to consume a thunderous amount of coffee, cookies and fruit from each household; anything less than 5 items and maybe some cheese, and honor is not satisfied. They all need the illusion of having something to offer.

Building 141 is where Witness H-7 lives. She looks like an old crack addict, her stricken, fatless face combed with vertical creases. She wears a red silk head scarf from which sprays of hair, so thin as to be colorless, leak into the air. She gives a gappy smile, happy at the presence of this small circle of trust that Clare and Vanda have conjured up around her. The mutual female understanding here is very secret-society. You can feel the geometries change. Something to do with any culture where the word for woman, made possessive, becomes "wife." Which leaves Bannerman feeling pretty exposed, even standing over by the window, looking out over the white desolation to minimize his presence. Ordinarily he'd feel so awkward as to leave, go join the other men smoking outside—but there would be a loss, a breaking of some connection between him and Clare, made stronger by his being here.

After some cute preliminaries Clare adjusts for the interview, minidisc all set recording, her demeanor slowing and softening, the levity dampening to zero along with the chitchat.

Witness H-7, Irma Sandžaktarević, is thirty-four. She was twenty-two when she was detained in the Partizan sports hall in April 1992. She was raped for six months in all permutations. In September she was sold to a Šešeljovci, a "real" Chetnik officer moving up to the front line at Pale. He branded her on her shoulder blade. She shows them the brand; an eagle; Clare takes a picture. As a slave, she was allowed to wash but was not fed enough, to keep her the way men liked. She was often beaten, twice seriously. The first time she lost three teeth from her upper left quadrant. The second time she lost movement from her right side. After this second beating she was no longer used for sex; she remained in detention in Podromanija until she was released in Sarajevo in December 1995 under the prisoner-exchange agreements.

Okay.

Now Clare and Vanda have to go back through it all, forensically, for names, dates, durations, explanations, for evidence of command responsibility. It's hard work. Ranković, Ostojić and the others on the Crisis Committee are elusive background presences, shimmering over everything, a frustrating talent for not getting their hands dirty.

But Bannerman can feel that each time Clare winds up to approach another question it costs something, spoken crisply at the old woman, who's facing Vanda, listening to her. Whose car was it. Then what kind. Do you remember what color, at least? How were you secured to it. If you were facing down on the car, how did you know it was Dastunić. Where was Ranković when this was going on. Why do you think that. Did you ever see Ranković actually *in* the Partizan.

But there are different agendas here, and the old woman is pressed to say that they were all involved, maybe sixty men besides Ranković, all as guilty, they are going to be indicted as well, yes?

Clare's used to this one, replies that they're collecting evidence on everyone, that they'll bring to trial everyone they have evidence on, starting with the most obviously guilty, the field commanders, and work their way up to the politicians and down to the soldiers. It's technically true, while also a blatant lie. Clare delivers it perfectly. The old woman is comforted, sits back and lets out a long relieved breath, almost an exhalation of demons. No wonder Clare's got neu-rotic imposture.

"And were there other intermediaries between the guards and the Crisis Committee? A woman? Tell me about her. Do you know her name? Nevertheless, every lead is useful. How old. Height, weight. Did you feel that she was at all sympathetic to the women in the sports hall? Not even slightly? Surely she must have felt *sorry* for you, in some *vague*—Not even a little regret, that things had come to this? Yes, but Serb women are still *women*. You surely don't think that she really approved, of—. But seriously, are you saying that this woman—"

But Irma has exploded, gesticulating, screaming in Bosnian. Vanda has stopped translating. Clare is horrified. She strayed from the foren-sic questioning, the situation got away from her, and now everyone looks to her but she doesn't know what to do. But soon Irma's fury blows itself out, the internal struts of her face crumpling, and Ban-nerman smoothly slides onto the sofa beside her and a mighty hug results, and then wailing, and hiccups of sobbing. But Bannerman's got her, he's got her. Un-Islamic and unseemly, her head burrows into his chest.

The force of his hug showing in his wrists, and a steady gaze up at the hut's rafters that refuses to meet anyone else's, breathing deep and keeping his eyes as wide as possible to blank any possibility of being dragged into tears himself . . .

They rode back over the mountains in silence and smoke, signed the car back in, and walked the length of Zmaja od Bosne to Bannerman's flat. A misty late afternoon, trams lumbering past, occasional roofs up the hillsides catching the sun and shining gold through the blue pastel. Great clouds of birds, Bannerman doesn't know which kind, having a last turn round the sky before coming home to roost.

Up in Baščaršija, Clare drops her briefcase, collapses onto the sofa, and fires up more cigarettes. Bannerman comes in with a glass of wine, and there's still no eye contact.

"Then *that's* brave."

But Clare won't accept this. "Not when you're in a room with—someone who," gesturing uselessly.

"I disagree," says Bannerman forcefully, and Clare does look at him. "It is brave. Emotionally if not actually physically also."

She nods slowly. "Thanks."

"Not sure what for," returning her look. Then: "You're a good person, Clare Leischman."

Thin smile, "To avoid confusion with your other Clares?"

"Just take it for once," a little irritated, "it's not nice having all my compliments slapped out of my hand like that . . ."

Clare's lips fold onto themselves, she puts a hand over her eyes. Looks like maybe she's going to cry; instead she whispers that she's sorry.

Being in that DP camp strips out so much of her—how can it not? This exercise in empathy, of sharing, isn't she just a type of mop, with a finite capacity to absorb? The West using up her natural resources same as everything else . . . her mind's getting rangier, and now Irma's memories seem, literally, to have bled into her own. When she reaches for the memories these days, Clare can remember seeing her *own* reflection in that curving windshield—she recoils in horror, but can't stop it from playing out, in all of its infinite detail—the eyes are in shadow but it's her own blotchy forehead, vertical smudges of soldiers slipping across the wide gloss panorama behind her, her knuckles marbling into purples and whites, fingernails breaking against the paintjob. And an evanescent presence on the other side of the glass, sitting inside the car, that shook its head and whispered to her: Your life is no better than provisional, your future as wishful and improbable as any other magical kingdom . . . maybe you could have avoided this. An improbable stairway of correct decisions, at best, between you and the future you took inadequate steps to avoid. Look at you! You could have fled anywhere, you could have joined the others on a bus to Austria, you could have married a wealthier man and bought off your fate, back in the time for decisions . . . and what home that in your simplicity you stood by, thinking your world civilized, what home will be worth returning to now?

No scarves or parties for her now. There can be no warding off of
memories, not even with candles, and Clare's problem has turned,
like other occupations, from one of defense into one of coexistence.
She is in her boyfriend's flat, but the cheap dark furniture of her boyfriend's landlord holds no warmth for her—nor her boyfriend's bed,
nor his food or his cases of beer . . . even with the thought of him
crowding into her head, Frito's great clumsy feet on everything, telling her too boisterously that she's perfectly ok—she is still alone.

But here in the room is a poor American boy that blazes for her—
even with the wrong type of eyes she can see the fountain of sparks
that roars off the leeward side of him, strays bouncing across the carpet, burning nothing and giving off no smoke—an American who
talks to her without using words—and when he looks at her like
that, all these coldnesses seem to be, temporarily anyway, warmed
away . . .

So Clare moves over, tucks her hair behind an ear, sits in his lap,
puts a hand on his neck, and, timidly at first, lets herself be kissed.

* * * * *

Small hours. Two Land Cruisers pull over onto the side of the Sarajevo road, perhaps 500 meters outside the village. Hours until first
light, and snowing gently. Eight figures in jeans and dark cloth coats
get out and start tabbing toward the village on foot.

Half-jogging. The figures are carrying weapons, pockets bulging,
imaging equipment swinging from shoelace necklaces, almost certainly wearing flak jackets underneath, the heavy swishing of material absorbed by the snowy acoustics.

Though there are no rocks painted red at the side of the road,
denoting mines, the figures stick to the paved road, thin bootprints
in the settling snow. They travel past a handful of houses, silent, no
lights on, no dogs bark. They have practiced on their mock-up thirty
times.

They come to a small redbrick bungalow on its own. Three fan
out around the building, over rickety fences, one for each of the other
sides. One man slides into shadows and kneels, pointing an MP5K,

submachine gun with collapsible stock, back down the road they've come. The other four approach the door of the bungalow, pause. Two in front with shotguns.

Look around. Thumbs up, weapons ready, safeties off.

"Anyone not ready," whispered into a Bluetooth headset, held on with elastic headstraps. Motorola phones, conference call.

Thumbs up. Thumbs up. Barrel-mounted maglites on.

Thumbs up.

Three fingers. Two. One—

Remington pump-action slugs at the handle, two boots and the door's a fucking memory. First man in ducks round, three steps in, ducks left BEDROOM LEFT CLEAR. Next man is already at the end of the corridor, opens the door, two three men pile in there, LIVING ROOM RIGHT DOGS DOGS shotgun rounds, TWO IN BED, shotgun rounds, lights right in their fucking faces, KITCHEN CLEAR, third man in the bedroom steps through to the other door at the far end, PANTRY CLEAR, it's a closet FUCKING DOG the other door's a bathroom, looks in, BATHROOM CLEAR. A man and a woman in bed, covering their eyes DOGS DOWN DOGS DOWN screaming showing their palms white in the maglite spots LIVING ROOM RIGHT CLEAR

DONT FUCKING MOVE DONT FUCKING MOVE

A moment of nothing but heavy breathing.

IS THAT IT. SENTRIES?

Cooper clear over. Geddes clear over. Deuchar clear over.

PUT YOUR HANDS ON YOUR HEADS

FRONT ROOMS CLEAR

HANDS ON YOUR FUCKING HEADS

Brick, get the ties on him.

THIS OUR MAN ANIMAL?

This is our man.

OUT OF BED HANDS BEHIND YOUR BACK

DON'T TAKE YOUR EYES OFF HER JEFF

Animal your taxis are here, and the meter is ticking over.

Give us twenty seconds, Edgar.

Neighbors are coming out, starting to take an interest over.

HE'S NAKED ANIMAL

Grab some blankets, Jeff.

Vane Novane comes stumbling naked out of his own house crunching the snow, hands tied behind, a soldier on either side holding a bicep. He gets shoved into the back of a Land Cruiser. Two more follow them out of the house, the last holding a bundle of blankets ripped from the bed, and pile in.

Come on Jeff.

Made a sorry fuckin mess of those dogs, Flameproof.

Let's get going lads.

The sentries reappear from around the house, jump in, and the last man, Andy Deuchar, exits the house and climbs into the second Land Cruiser, its wheels already turning in the snow, his hand shaking from having had his weapon and maglite held point-blank into the face of a woman, mid-thirties, with brittle dyed-orange hair, her face crumpling in the spotlight, and who has now, as everyone can hear, even the neighbors stepping out of their houses, begun to cry hysterically.

Tekija Prnaša Esoterika

THE FIRST FRITO knew about the arrest of Vane Novane was when he rolled up at the warehouse one morning to find PAZI SNAJPER spray-painted across the doors.

"Suboptimal," he murmurs, and sharply applies the brakes. Egzon the security guard wanders over to Frito's VW Golf, leans down to the window. "Dobro jutro, Frito," he grins, his breath white against the glass.

"Dobro jutro," pointing at the graffiti, "what are we paying you for, eh, Egzon?"

"Yes O.K., nema problema!" And Egzon goes about opening the aluminum gates. At the scraping of the downbolt against concrete, Maza looks out of the warehouse, comes over to the VW, and gets in.

"Thought people didn't joke about that sort of thing?" Frito says.

"They don't," she says. "Go away from here. Now."

She explains on the way back into town. Frito's none too rattled. "So who ratted him out?"

"They think you."

"Alright. Is that so. Let's just swing by ViKA, set em straight, eh?"—"I don't think this is a good idea."—"Aw come on. They're reasonable people."—"Not today."—Frito frowns over at Maza. "Alright. What about the flat?"

Frito pulls up outside his and Bannerman's flat, against the opposite curb. Looking up, a face behind the net curtains, looking down into the street. A moment of eye contact, then the face disappears.

"Bugger."

"What?"

"Think you might have had a point," shifting into gear, pulling out into traffic. In the rearview mirror, a figure bursts out of Frito's front door, comes running up to the Golf.

A snarl-up by the taxi rank. Frito's stuck. Maza looks wildly around. "Lock the door, Maza."

The man reaches Maza's side, starts trying the handle, knocking on the window a little harder than polite. He's shouting and gesticulating at them. "Maza?" says Frito.

"What!"

"Any hints about what he's saying?"—"He wants to speak."—"Sounds reasonable."—"No, this is a lie. Go. Go." Frito considers this. Looks at Maza's wild eyes, and behind her the man knocking and pointing. He's got a diamond earstud. The light goes green. The traffic ahead pulls away. Frito hesitates. Earstud knocks insistently, saying, "sad. *Sad.*"

Sod it. Frito taps his watch at Earstud, shrugs apologetically, and accelerates away. Earstud stands in the street. He pulls out a pistol, fires it in the air. "Crikey." Frito accelerates harder. Earstud levels his pistol at the Golf, fires a single shot into the rear nearside wheel.

"JESUS—*CHRIST*, MATE!"

The wheel's a flapping rim, it's pulling right, but Frito keeps going.

"You see. They are angry."

"I do see."

"What shall we do?"

Frito's Golf is drawing eyes all along Marshal Tito Street. He's slowed down to 30 kmh, grinding along with a loaded tram dinging its bell behind him. "You're about to earn your pay here Maza. Where can we go where Vedo won't find us?"

"I suppose . . . out of town? Perhaps we should go to the coast. Spend a week on Korčula, or Vis?"

Frito looks sidelong. "Get a little cabana, eh? Just you and me?"

"I think that is most safe."

Frito turns right up Alipašina Street, away from town, sparks and strange looks all the way. Digs out his phone, hands it to Maza. "Here, give that little Sufi urchin a call. He ought to know a place in the wop-wops we can get away from it all. Look under Unknown Caller."

So they take refuge, at reasonable expense, at the Sufi Child's alma mater, the Tekija Prnaša Esoterika, up on a hill behind Zuč. Physically, it's a strange collection of hopeful shacks standing on each other's shoulders at the top of an ice-and-mud lane, clustered obediently around a severe concrete minaret come to teach them all ComEcon. Behind and around, steep diagonal snowfields. Muslim gangsters aren't likely to seek vengeance on holy ground. Are they?

The Hodža is head of the tekija, small and delicate, a University of Chicago man as it happens, white-haired with half-moon spectacles and looking like an old Wild West bank teller. He smiles sadly as he takes their credit card payments.

"I fear there are elements within the Izet," meaning the Islamic Community, "who do not feel the tekija is sound on the five pillars. They feel that drinking alcohol is in some way, 'un-Islamic.'" With a bewildered shake of the head, and goes on to explain that ever since the war there's been a growth of fundamentalism, which he puts down to the attempted genocide, Bosnian Psychosis, and the tidal wave of Saudi money that's helping rebuild the place. Female beneficaries of Saudi grants have to cover their hair and so on. "Wahhabi tendencies are creeping in, people are less 'European' in outlook, and maybe the holiness of the tekija will no longer prevent them from— let's say, capping your ass. But you are very welcome to stay. Breakfast at seven. You'll find the minibar uncommonly well-stocked."

A good time to be here. The next day Frito and Maza are joined for dinner by Clare and Bannerman, and all are sat at one end of a table in the little refectory hall of the Tekija Esoterika, furthest from the door. The dervishes—seventeen of them—and the Hodža taking up the rest. The other tables are filled with big-eyed orphans, sat in strict height order, and as such resembling some kind of adorable musical instrument, played upon the heart, each orphan's sadness eliciting a different tone of pure human melancholy—and at other tables jovial hobos, scarved old women with collapsed mouths, junkies, gypsies, merry amputees, blind folk, Down's Syndrome girls playing pattycake with boisterous dropouts of one sort or another. At half-meter intervals sit enormous carafes of slivovic, which everyone's hitting early and hard, and now slapping backs, laughing louder than each other, building momentum for what looks like a godalmighty pissup. It's Kurban Bajram, the big feast day in the Bosniak calendar, and Muslim day of maximum charity.

Maza explains, "This is the day when Ibrahim was going to sacrifice his only son Ismajl to God. But an angel stopped him, and he saw the sheep caught in the tree, and he sacrificed this sheep instead."

"I thought it was Isaac?" Clare wonders.

"Ismajl," Maza says firmly.

"Pretty sure it was Isaac . . ."

"No. This is wrong!" Maza looking to Frito to put an end to this madness. Maza and Clare's eyes lock with a hiss.

Frito shrugs. "It's their party."

"Christians and Jews say Isaac—Muslims say Ishmael," Bannerman says airily, "Ishmael was the firstborn, but he was illegitimate. Born to the handmaiden of Sarah, Abraham's supposedly barren wife. Then Sarah *did* conceive, and that was Isaac. Think it specifies the firstborn in both the Torah and the Koran," squinting to remember, "so the question is, do you count his kid by the au pair? Muslims say you count everyone, is all."

By the end of this little speech Clare's got a sarcastic smile on. "Give me that," leaning over to reach into his lap, where he's got a new phone, the XDA, tuned to the Wikipedia website. "You get the internet on a *phone*? That's amazing!" marveling. Bannerman glows with pleasure; it's not often technology wows the ladies.

"Yeah," he agrees. "Hitch-Hiker's Guide, no doubt about it. It might be my favorite thing in the world."

"I'm sorry to hear that," Clare twinkles.

"Second favorite, then."

Frito looks up sharply. "What's your favourite?"—"Chocolate milk."

"Yeah," Frito scanning the crowd thoughtfully, nervous of sudden movements by the doors, "say what you like about Bannerman, he likes his technology."

Clare, gazing gorgeously into the PDA-phone: "I do say what I like about him."

"Right." Frito flares his eyes. "And how."

"What," Bannerman craning forward, "what's this?"

"I say what I like about you."

"And what do you like about me?"

"I like a lot of things about you," smiling sweetly. "Most of all, you're such a good, moral person, and such a loyal *friend*. Frito's so lucky to have you."

Bannerman's genuine smile turns without any physical change into an empty photograph one, and he nods too enthusiastically.

"We have each other," Frito winking at Bannerman. "I love you, man."

"Love you too Frito." Out come some glasses of slivovic, and a high clink amongst the four of them.

Presently the Hodža dings a glass and gives a little speech, Maza translating in their corner that on this day of commemoration we offer sacrifice, normally a lamb, and divide it into three parts: one part for our house, one for our poor relatives, and one for all poor, whoever they are, regardless of their religion or their ethnic thing.— There follows a longwinded enumeration of the tekija's many blessings, its friends, supporters, hopes, plans for the future, etc. Bannerman keeps hoping Maza will start freestyling, start clean *making up* an alternative speech for the Hodža, preferably obscenely pornographic, but no dice. She's a professional.

"She's an amazing translator," Frito massaging her shoulder warmly, once the speeches are over. "I don't know how you do it, it's like circular breathing, she can listen and translate at the same time . . . amazing to watch, she shuts down, concentrates so hard, it's like she's *channeling* the talker—like in a séance."

"I hear it's more of an art than a séance," says Bannerman.

"And she can do it in German as well!" enthuses Frito, "German English Bosnian, any combination. Unbelievable."

At least Clare liked it, turning to hide a smile behind a curtain of hair.

Lunch is an orgy in the key of red cabbage, modulating through eye-watering onions, cheese, slippery bullets of garlic, roast tomatoes that *taste* of something, tomato's local name being *paradajz*, "I mean, they're good," Bannerman chewing away, "but isn't 'paradise' a little much?"

"It's a sexual thing," Clare speaking with a mouthful, "tomato's clearly the most sexual vegetable." Which creates a four-way schism, Frito going for potato, Maza embarrassingly enough cucumber, Bannerman the perpetual controversialist denying the tomato's a vegetable at all. "Seed, look," Clare dissecting it carefully, "swimming in its own juices . . . chambers on either side like ovaries . . ."

"God you're *ri-i-ight*," Bannerman's voice now lazy and postcoital, and looking up, he's got tomato smeared all over his face and forehead, "that's fan*tastic* . . ."

It's a wonderful time, everyone is happy. For once Frito will lean back and exhale, relax his grip on his quests. Clare and Bannerman are getting along fine, and this makes him happy. Slivovic has given way to Sarajevsko Pivo, which is working its magic, its warm golden overlay of the fantastic dimensions no longer seeming like magic, and joined today by a whipped-creamy vision of Islam—of an exhilaration of peace and whiteness in the sense of Light. It's probably just Frito's own version of the *važd*, Ecstatic Enlightenment, as with any transportational phenomena, even orgasms, everyone must experience it differently. For him, there come the single flashes of it—tiny caesuras in the flow of his attention of suffocating joy, when his system hangs, when he can't speak for love. It's something to do with the beer, and Bosnia, and everything Bosnia suffered for, all made right—

"Life is good in the tekija," the Hodža says cannily, appearing next to him.

By the end of lunch Maza and an acolyte called Drago with the seven worst teeth Clare's ever even thought of are cossack-dancing to BH Radio 1 being piped out on loudspeakers, then everyone piling into a van to hand out lamb parcels at the Displaced Persons camp in Rajlovac, then playing football in the snow with the Sufi toddlers, Bannerman keeps getting mobbed by them, or sometimes Clare will shout something that makes him Charlie Brown the ball—then back indoors for a woodfire in the hearth room and baklava, cookies, coffee-sludge, and all manner of Believers with smiles like cracked windscreens to see the original Sufi Child again—not least the Hodža, who hugs him like his own child, and who is hugged back with similar intensity. Clare sighs to see it. And people are down and facing Mecca at all hours, even a couple of elderly eccentrics who identify themselves as Krstjani, Bosnian Christians, a sect thought to have died out under the Turks—while Bannerman teaches the kids to sock-slide along corridors, comet's trail of cake crumbs behind them, and putting them to nap in a room with the curtains drawn while puppies with fat paws curl up as sentries and raise heads sharply if anyone comes in . . .

"The djinn are plentiful today," observes the Hodža, doing the rounds after the orphans' bedtime.

"Is that who they are?" Bannerman with his hands behind his head, receiving a fireside footrub from Clare.

"No, those are the cleaning staff," says the Hodža. He knows about bathos, he studied economics. "The djinn maybe you are not seeing, I think."

"Only your initiates are, I bet?" playfully.

"I am wise to you, young man," smiling, kindly, "you are intoxicated with your own intelligence. But you are foolish in other ways. Mostly: you do not listen to your heart. You cannot feel it in you. You hear only the noise in your head, and it deafens you, and you find yourself very often sad."

Bannerman has a coughing attack. "Who *are* you?"

"Marvelous that our teachings are so controversial!" the Hodža speaking generally now, "for anyone can learn to hear them!"

"Hear who?"

"Whoever it may be," the evasions of a prophet, "and how strange that all cultures in the world have a tradition of speaking with the dead, except for your magnificent West!"

"Like all cultures have failed to invent computers," replies Bannerman, "except for our magnificent West?"

"These are undoubtedly connected," concedes the Hodža.

Inevitably, talk turns to Kemal Novane's djinn-woman Djelja. Though the Hodža and Kemal Novane knew each other, they were never friends, and the Hodža protests he knows nothing more than what was common knowledge in these circles: that Djelja was said to have delivered its adherents from certain death, once during the Second World War, and once again during the siege.

"The siege?" Frito sitting up.

The Hodža shrugs. "That's what they claim. Myself, I don't know that djinn are so powerful. They are not angels."

"Different things entirely," says Bannerman.

The Hodža ignores him. "Angels are very powerful. But this djinn was so powerless, she was bound to the Djelja punch, you see, as djinn may be to any substance . . ."

"Like the green fairy of absinthe?" says Clare.

"Or the tiger of Frosted Flakes?" says Bannerman.

"The question of djinn in Islam is not as problematic as many think. If you search for 'ghosts,' actual human ghosts, I believe this is erroneous," the Hodža speaking only to Frito now, he has selected him to be the beneficiary of some sort of ad, "because here at the tekija we train ourselves to feel for 'presences,' yes, but ones without shape, and that are only detectable when they pass through the body of the observer, as personal and unverifiable as, say, jet lag. Nonetheless: existent. Professor Novane said that, in the original Arabic, 'smokeless fire' is only seventh-century kenning for 'emotion.' This sounds okay, yes?"

"For sure."

"For a hard desert people, yes. But Vane never thought so." Wistful. "But there is something approaching a demonstration. In fact, if you'll allow me to introduce you to a man," taking Frito by the hand and leading him out, Maza taking Frito's other and following.

The man the Hodža knows is in one of the schoolrooms, apparently playing some elaborate form of three-way chess with his friends, involving drinking, dancing, arm-wrestling, song-based forfeits, and the occasional move. He must be seventy, and his hair is the thing about him: he has a magnificent *Nimitz*-class superstructure of jet-black hair. Eventually they are able to pull him out of the fray, sit him down at a table, and watch thick white spittle concentrate at the corners of his mouth as he remembers Kemal Novane to them, recollections which come out odd—it's either him or Maza, or both, who's very drunk.

"He was very big man, he gave many things to poverty people. He was involved with tekija very much," Maza's hand brushing occasionally on Frito's thigh, "he worked very big at brewery, his death was very brave . . . philosopher's death, he achieved much with it, it was famous scene. You have seen? No? Oh it is very scintillating, I have tape, you come and watch. You will be my guest, Maori, you and your exceptionally beautiful translator. Let us—"

Jetblack shouts at someone, and someone responds, and there is a lot of handshaking, and downing of sliv and more shouting, and presently through the blur Frito and Maza are sat in front of a TV somewhere, watching a TF1 logo come and go, and then they're back in the siege itself, watching some aimless camerawork through scratchy tracking, fishing for establishing shots, panning back and forth along the Serb positions on the southern ridge. It's summer, early evening; the sky is pink with puffy clouds, the shadows long and blue. The occasional far-off thump of an artillery piece, the answering crash of its arrival, much nearer. This seems to excite little interest, certainly none from the cameraman. Sporadic small-arms fire. But even this is drowsy; the atmosphere is of a long warm evening, when no one's really in the mood for fighting.

Then there's a few comments behind camera, some muttering, then: *un mort qui marche! là-bas!* and the camera swings wildly left and down, zooms out, and picks up a figure, coming into the open space of Vojvode Putnika. We're maybe ten stories up here, no doubt the Holiday Inn, looking almost straight down. The figure's in a broken old coat, a beige scarf tight around his neck, a dusty figure against the blue-grays of the city walls.—*C'est un violon?* An old, old man. The wind flattens his tracksuit bottoms against rickety legs.

It's not faultless playing, Kemal's concentrating more on it than the walking, occasionally missing a note, going back and doing it again, stopping walking while he does so. The effect is of an antique clockwork figure, one of many such Austro-Hungarian relics, whose mainspring drives both its walking and its playing. The camera zooms in all the way. Kemal's bald crown is tilted away from us, over the violin to his left. We can't see his face. His figure lengthens as he shuffles, by no means carelessly, toward the Vrbanja Bridge. *Le mic. Le mic directionnel.* There's fumbling for almost thirty seconds before the sound picks up: quite distinctly: woven through the thick white hush of atmospheric noises, birds roosting, distant mechanical sounds, the evening breeze and the whirr of old magnetic tape, a bright thread woven through that gray din: the lonely clear wail of Kemal Novane's violin.

"Trinklied," says Jetblack.

"Drinksong," says Maza.

"Drinksong?" says Frito.

"Das Trinklied vom Jammer der Erde," says Jetblack.

"The Drinksong of the Sadness of Earth," says Maza.

"Drinksong?" a slow realization creeping over Frito's scalp . . .

"Gustav Mahler," Maza translating for Jetblack, "This is the Song of the Earth. Kemal Novane played this very much at the brewery. The song says: life is very good but it is very short also, and so, we drink!" Jetblack grins and demonstrates with a bottle of rakija.

Kemal moves past the sniper blankets, weaves slowly around the banks of cars. There is no small-arms fire now. He stops in the middle of the bridge, continues to play. The sound is barely audible now, only the higher notes coming through. The tension is appalling, on the one hand, of waiting for Kemal to be shot, the harsh rifle-crack and stumbling fall—which Frito knows *has* to happen, he knows the ending already, but as with any movie has allowed himself to forget . . .

They sit, mouths slack, watching Kemal for another six minutes or so, just playing. The transports of a suffocating love are inside of Frito again, he's done heroin and it's similar, it blooms from his chest through the rest of him, feels like his shirt might actually be wet with it.

Finally the shot comes. It's quiet, soft as a dropped book. Kemal Novane is spun half round, hand grabbing at air. Then he puts down his violin and lowers himself to the ground, carefully, as though conscious of arthritic knees, and lies down. He squirms a bit on the bridge, visibly panting for a while, is shot again, and is still.

The camera stays on his body for a further minute. Frito and Maza watch in silence.

Finally someone says, *tu l'as eu?—ouai.—chouette*. And it's static.

Bannerman and Clare stalk the rooms, at first looking for Maza and Frito, before, led by a rhythmic chanting, straying into the tekija itself. Stealing silently in the door, Clare pulling on a head scarf, and watching the dervishes sat in a perfect circle on their carpets, chanting indecipherably, bodyjolting, dreamy lopsided smiles, and not a little drool.

"Are they all right," Clare drawing closer to Bannerman.

"I'm sure they're fine," hands on her shoulders, advancing cautiously, "looks like a grand mal, though, doesn't it." Some dervishes have eyes open, but their sense is shut. Murmurings, strange bursts of laughter, occasionally flailings with balance, eyes clenching in pleasure.

"Got to give it to them," Clare taking Bannerman's hand, "they look happier than we do."

Bannerman squeezed back, and for fully ten minutes they watched one dervish, a kaleidoscope of the summer emotions passing across his face, "like he's in love," every bit as emotionally affecting as a song, and specially when Clare leaned her head onto Bannerman's shoulder, fine cold hair spilling out of the headscarf and onto his collarbone.

"Don't worry about it," by now out in the inky night, having stumbled out of a firedoor, and dancing silently in the snow. "Frito'll turn up." Slow rock and roll, a few swing moves to imaginary music, over the arm, twirl her round—dip—back up, twirl her again. But it's good, it's fluid, Clare's moving like calligraphy against him, there's basic agreement on the time signature; and the rush, for Bannerman, every time their eyes catch, hers dark with mascara and wet with beauty, the rush is so good it's giving him stomach cramps.

There are few absences in the starfield tonight. The frozen air is still. He's barely experienced such a pileup of beauty. But her breath comes out in long spinning ghosts that swim around him, examine him, and though they smile they also shake their heads sadly, and dissipate with their conclusions back into the night.

"You good?" he says.—"I'm good," she says. Spin, twirl, the crush of new snow.—"You dance well."—"You lead well."—"Thank you."—"That's okay."—"So how's it going with Frito?"—"How's it going with *me*?"

"I guess," says Bannerman, "guess I'm doing better with you than you are with Frito."

"What! Really?"

Clare's stopped playing now. Bannerman frowns, rolls his eyes at himself. He's always doing this. "Oh, I don't know," exhausted.

"No, tell me."—"There's nothing to tell!"—"There's always something to tell."—"Fine, but I don't know any of it."—"But you're his best friend!"—"*You're his girlfriend!*" yelling it out, falling to his knees like a tragedian.

"We're not *officially* going out," after a while.

"Whatever."

"So technically we can see other people."

Bannerman watches her carefully. "Do you?"

"No.—Does he?"

Bannerman looks away. "Don't know."

"Come on, you live together. Tell me. Is he sleeping with Maza?"

"Clare . . ." Bannerman's heart's being torn in two, shakes his head sadly, puts a hand to her hair. The pain is directly proportional to distance from her.

Clare nods, acknowledges his defense—then decides better of it· "Come on, don't be discreet with *me*, you're screwing your own best friend!"

"Actually, it's more like *you*—"

"Ach! I knew as soon as I said it you'd go for that joke," shaking her head at him, genuinely disappointed.

Bannerman makes a comic "nagging" face.

"What? You don't think by screwing me you're *betraying*, then, your best friend?"

"We haven't screwed!"

Clare waves a hand, *details*. "We've done enough. Full sexual intercourse can't be far away."

"To be honest—" but he can't keep the smile down, accepting defeat, "all right, lawyer." Disavowing everything. A final twirl, then dipping her low, sheer girlhair brushing the snow, blank throat out to the night, a single slow kiss on it, and holds her there while he says:

"I've never known love to 'take' with Frito."

"But that was the others. It's different with me, isn't it?"

But Bannerman pulls her up, and lets her go, makes to move away.

"Oh come on Bannerman, don't be such a—"

"Jesus, Clare! I'm not going to tell you about—"

"I know it's difficult for you—"

"Difficult! It's—"

"It's not like I'm going to—"

"This is—Percy Sledge territory, it's not like I can refuse anything you—"

But Clare has fallen silent, is searching in his face while Percy Sledge lyrics scroll down the surface of her eyes. "Ah," softly.

"Obviously." A serious silence. "Clare." She has frozen wide-eyed, a daughter scolded. Her cheekbones white with moonlight. "So, yeah. There it is. I love you. It's been what, two months. It hasn't let up at

all. I loved you the minute I saw you. I mean, you don't have to tell
me how messed up this all is. Between me and Frito and everything.
I know what's involved. But I've thought about it, and I've taken the
decision: I would do anything, *anything*, to have you."

"Bannerman—"

"Hang on. Despite Frito being my best friend. And Clare, frankly,
I love him. He's been all I've had for a long time now, in my life, until
you turned up, and I just—I've collapsed in the face of you. I love
him. But I'd still rather have you. Because it looks very like I can't
have both of you. But either way, please don't ask me to spy on him
for you, because I won't be able to refuse . . ."

Clare comes up and holds him lightly by the forearm, searching
in his face, but still not, for the time being, saying anything.

Which is fine because Bannerman's got plenty more: "And Frito,
you know, I mean he's been very loyal to me, in his way, and I have
an obvious vested interest here and everything, but listen to me
Clare:

"You should absolutely not be counting on him. There is just no
way I'd let my sister, say, go out with him. Even though I love him,
and though I pretty much hate my sister," tucking her hair behind
her ears. "Clare, you *can't*. Don't pin your hopes on him. That guy is
not normal. God knows I'm not either, but Frito's a frontal lobe case,
you seen the drugs he takes? Antipsychotics, antidepressants, depres-
sants, uppers, downers, beta blockers . . . his mind is held together
with fucking *tape*. His emotions do not follow like, human channels.
When he's through with you the end is swift and terrible. He's out
of there, never looks back, no let's-be-friends, nothing. I have seen
dozens, no . . . probably one hundred, girls—women—come and go.
Always bewildered when it happens, they think they're all in love,
everything's peachy, then one day he just hands em their papers. This
one girl said with hindsight she didn't think he felt anything the
entire time. She said he went through the motions, said all the right
things, but it's like he's *pretending*. The guy is just not all there. He's
half a person. I have no idea what the other half is. Republican, or
something . . . and frankly Clare, and you might not like this part,
but women tend to have one of two reactions to him: either they see

all that, damage and emptiness and lack of self-knowledge, pretty much immediately actually—or they're so attracted by all that charismatic, confidence—the money, the alpha tycoon—they think he's just the most dreamy dreamboat ever. And the girls who like him, the dreamboat ones, frankly they tend not to have their shit all that together . . . and, Clare Leischman, you are squarely in that second category."

"I have my stuff together."

"Nope. You are one of the most insecure, panicky, goofy, adorable girls I have ever met, but you in no way have your shit together. Not when it comes to boys. You're great at your job, speak two hundred languages, whip smart and all, but you are in *trouble* with boys. How many soldiers you fucked out here? Actually, I don't want to know. Christ look at you Clare, 'technically we can see whoever we like'— what are you, fourteen?"

"Hey—I don't see your life all that together?"

"Right, but I'm not even *pretending* to have it together, I've already thrown my cards all over the table: given a choice, I'd take you over Frito. Because—and I can repeat another important part of this conversation, in case you missed it earlier—I am in love with you."

Clare's eyebrows up, manages to take delivery of this one without buckling, without squirming out of the moment with a joke, not even a joke face, not even slightly comedy eyes. Just her lips, taut perfect lips just—parting very slightly, looking at him, nodding to acknowledge it.

Felt so good he does it again: "I am in love with you, Clare Leischman."

"I heard."

"And you know and I know that I'm in real trouble with that. And though I know it's going to mess me up for years, that I know I'm going to get my heart trashed, still, I have no choice. I am caustically in love with you and I'm taking whatever I can get."

Clare looks down at the snowy toes of her moonboots, bashful, chin into her shoulder, wondering. Eventually she looks up again, sprays of hair caught in her lips. A smile.

· But it's not the smile he wants, it's got sympathy in it . . .

And here comes the pain again, someone's turned up the gravity, sudden lack of oxygen necessitating deep anxious heaves of air—and the only way to keep it away is by drawing near her; get his heart as close to the center of her as possible, and exhale. What will it take to peel her off of Frito? More jokes, charisma, money?—anything, he'll do it. He'd go out and arrest Ranković himself, if he could. Sliding his hands round her waist, letting her head wriggle into his chest and muttering into her hair, and trying to keep the levity up, because through all the pain management Bannerman can just about remember the Rules-level importance of avoiding neediness here:

"Anyway, Fräulein Leischman—I'd like to go back over the statement you gave a few moments ago, where you said 'full sexual intercourse' was not 'far away.' Could you expand on that?"

But no. She leaves early; she has to work the rest of the week. The Prosecution never rests. Bannerman stays up at the tekija, tonight because he's drinking like the damned, tomorrow because his hangover's such an atom-splitter he doubts he could physically survive the journey back. Instead the day is spent lolling like a crash-test dummy, babysitting Sufi infants. Being used as a climbing frame by a dozen rugrats aged two to five, puppies gnawing at his feet, trying above all to keep his cigarette from getting bent in two, it's about the best displacement activity there is. The proximity effect of children and dogs is, well, it's not Clare, but it's something.

That evening, the kids abed, swigging gratefully at more sliva, cooling his butt in the snow when Frito comes up and sits beside.

"Alright."—"Hey."

He realizes it's the first time they've been alone together for a while now, and they spend the time in silence, exhaling in each other's company. Staring up at the distinctive Ottoman shape of the TV mast on Hum: just a higher-tech minaret, the better from which to call the faithful.

"Seen any djinn?"

Frito shakes his head. "You?"

"Maybe a couple, last night. Think one of em held me down, the others got busy with bats."

Frito nods. It's like all of Bannerman's lightness passes straight through him these days, like neutrinos, disturbing nothing.

"How would we know, Bannerman. How would we know, is the thing."

A squint at the corners of already deep-set eyes, a particular rhythmic touretting in his jaw, the crêpe roughness of his skin caught *exactly* by the orange streetlight down the hill aways . . . Bannerman can read that easy. For a second there it's as acute as his own pain.

"You know the feeling, Bannerman? Waking up from a dream, before you've forgotten it—you have to re-remember it, to set it down? The memories are in a—temporary file, or something, you have to copy it across to the C drive."

"Sure." This is Frito on odd form—earnest, loquacious even.

"The first few minutes you still have access to memories. If you had a flying dream, you still know how to fly, which muscles to use . . . the knowledge is there, you know *where* it is, like a book on a shelf. But you reach for it, and it turns out to be an illusion after all, a book painted on the wall . . . Well, what if you had that feeling *all the time*? Of memories"—rubbing fingertips—"evaporating? All of them?"

"Suckular," slapping a hand across Frito's big deltoid muscles, "what other memories are you losing?"

Frito shakes his head, goes "waaa" softly, meaning stupid question.

"Oh yeah," wry grin, "forget I asked that. See if you can't lose that one."

Frito and Bannerman hash it out for a while, slow and warm, the best of friends, bitterly hungover. Frito's thirty-six, or so he claims, says he's lived more life than he can account for, wants to know what's happened to all that life. He can work it out where it must have been, but there is no data attached. A week here, a month there, completely empty. Estimates the accumulated loss at three years.

"Beginning to think the djinns operate in the memory, Frito, actually *inside* the brain. Angels and djinns, adding and deleting . . . leaving only nagging feelings, déjà vus, weird residues you have to shake your head clear of . . ."

"Angel dust." Frito smiles, listening in profile. "That's what my mum called sleep—you know—that stuff comes out your eyes. 'Oh! The angels *have* been dancing the night a-wee on *your* eyes.' "

Frito has never, ever talked about his mother. Bannerman doesn't want to scare him off now, just sits there, their gazes parallel down into the city, saying nothing. His memories cannot be drawn. So Bannerman waits in silence, Clare-pain temporarily moderated by his old friend, and by each wash of frozen air into his wounded lungs. The end of their friendship is coming, in fact may already be here, invisible and sitting companionably on its haunches between them. But for the moment its presence is something they have in common, and for now, he's barely felt closer or warmer toward Frito in his life.

But there are no more memories. It was a single drop, squeezed from stone.

"But Frito," tentatively, "how do you know it *wasn't* angel dust?" Frito, first time in forever, laughs.

"No seriously, you spend your childhood waking up covered in PCP, I'm getting a theory where those missing years went . . ."

*   *   *   *   *

Next morning, too early, the Sufi Child prods Frito awake with a single index finger. "Come. *Alimovci* are here."

Frito pulls on a few sweaters, wanders across the corridor into Maza's room, enters without knocking. Maza stirs luxuriantly in smileyface pyjamas, looking at him, realizes he really *is* standing there, and yanks the sheets up to her chin. "Frito!" she exclaims.

"Get your togs on beautiful," says Frito. "Vedo's boys are combing the place. Urchin's going to hide us somewhere, I think. Rattle your dags." He goes to the window; there's two saloon cars and a black all-terrain vehicle, licence plate JE 61 CE—an injunction to readers of Cyrillic everywhere—blocking the lane back to the main road. "Quick as you can."

In the corridor, the sound of commotion below.

"This way." Sufi Child beckons them with a flashlight to the end, opens a door, looks around, beckons them through. Then down a spiral staircase, vibration of the metal too loud, Maza with her heels in her hand. Across the main hallway that leads to the refectory and the front door—at the end of which, silhouetted against a square of blinding white, black torsos come and go. Through the library, into the annex, and to a small triangular space under some stairs.

Sufi Child opens a trapdoor in the floor, climbs halfway in, and signals to Frito to shut it on his way down. Inside, a metal ladder bolted to rock. Sufi Child's flashlight below them is the only light, and shadows dance sickeningly around.

Maza moves slowly, distressed. At the bottom, a dark wetness— dripping—the flashlight in quick ellipses across stratas of rock, foam-yellow, marbled, gross white rock-tumors bubbling out from the wall. "Welcome to 'Real Bosnia.' Everything important is in the under-ground." A fairly large cavern, roughly level, whose floor dips then descends abruptly at one end, at which Sufi Child points as he hands the flashlight to Frito. "It comes out further down valley. It is cold and dark, but okay at the finish. We play here all my life. We called this tunnel život, life. Not be frightened. Dovidjenja, Frito. Maza."

"Dovidjenja." Frito shakes the Child's hand, and turns it into a hug.

And over the next ten minutes, the feeling grows. It's some kind of epiphany, a nauseating upswell of love for the Sufi Child, for Maza, for everyone—that brings with it an LSD-level feeling of everything suddenly *connecting* . . . a step forward along the path of what he's been looking for all this time.

Because the name "Bosnia" supposedly comes from an old Ursprache word for water. Bosnia the Water-Kingdom, the entire country a mountain-citadel built on a wealth of it, its hoards of trea-sure stashed as ice upstairs or in vast underground vaults hollowed out of the world's largest limestone karst formation beneath, the Swiss cheese of rock formations, a bedrock shot through with who knows what holes and topologies, vaults never lit nor disturbed, completely ineffable, never any animal let alone human to hear its waters chattering blackly amongst themselves, licking stalagmites and flos-ferri in their cavern-worlds, deposits calcified into a kaleidoscope of the wonderful colors . . . Within an otherworldly dimension of caves, waterfalls, overhanging valleys, thermal fissures running in counterintuitive directions, are underground rivers whose magic waters run black, not from lack of light but actually black, ink-black, their clarity internalized, temporarily stored in a different form. But the blackwaters *bing* turn crystal-clear the instant they are observed. Prove that wrong. It is reassurance of a high order, that even in such a world there can exist such things. Frito is absolutely sure of this, as he hustles along the slippery ledge over a deepening trickle, the walls and floors sweating water out at them, Maza Cukić whimpering along behind, her stockinged feet ice-cold in the water. And somehow Frito knows how pleasantly warm her feet feel *to the water*, because he has become abruptly aware of a relationship with the water, an actual personal relationship, which seems to be telling him things . . .

This is not so crazy. Not here. Sarajevo's a city with unexpected fountains at every turn, and no small percentage of them have been, at one time or another, miraculous. The Brezumulja Spring on Vratnik, most famously. Because the water is amazing: mineral, salt, fresh: so many different water systems vein through the water-kingdom's geologies, leaching different suspensions from their aquifers, collecting and depositing transition metals like any currency transactions, and sulfides, fluorides, potassiums, leads at Olovo, silver at Srebrenica, chlorides at Tuzla, maybe even at Bihać nursing a certain depleted uranium content, and all of these traded up and down the country . . . Bosnia's snow income and ice assets made liquid, and through infinitely complex transactions following a set of broad curves characteristic of any economy. Not an idle comparison in the Dinaric Alps, where the currency was until a few years ago the dinar.

And at that thought Frito can suddenly no more avoid the certainties being revealed to him here than avoid following this tunnel of life to its debouchment further on. It all makes sense, all part of a vast and perfect symphony: the Bosnian overworld and the underworld, the literal one this time, as two manifestations of the same identity, an identity hovering somewhere else, in what Sufi Child would call the Seven Skies—and which is almost reachable, like a word on the tip of his tongue, and the agony of reaching for it is ecstastic . . .

Something to do with iterative systems. Iterative systems have feedback loops, like the water-cycle, which gives them a basic irritability. To say the least. For as a capitalist Frito knows that markets don't just exhibit irritability, but *sentience.*

An identity with a personality, no less. Frito can almost—if he listens hard enough—feel her trying to say something . . . *"her"*? Why not? The aquifer he's standing on presumably collects its water from Mount Moščanica, which towers above them to the northeast, and somewhere else it must merge with runoff from Mount Trebević, and together feed the lake under the brewery. The brewery is only a few kilometers downstream from here.

Right. It's coming together. There's some tangle of events around that first Bajram of the siege, May/June 1992. The odd failure of the Yugoslav People's Army's last big attack on the city, and its transformation into the Bosnian Serb Army, the VRS; the "death" of the protecting djinn Djelja, the sudden outbreak of Bosnian Psychosis. Is it not suggestive, to put it no stronger, that Kemal Novane, the djinn's keeper, had, thanks to the artesian screws at the brewery, two-way access to what was suddenly the city's main supply of water? And from which Sarajevsko Pivo *is still made*?

He stops, and Maza stops behind him, whispers, "What?"

He's got it. Frito gets what Kemal Novane must have done. It's not cast-iron, but as Kemal would have agreed, provability is a weaker notion than truth:

At Bajram, the faithful are enjoined to distribute one third of their sacrifice to their household, one third to their poor relatives, and one third to the needy of all religions. By Bajram 1992, Sarajevo *was* Kemal's household, it *was* the needy of all religions . . . and to believers like Kemal, djinn were no less real than rams. In the face of certain death—Karadžić had promised them that—how could he not have run the artesian screws backwards, emptied Djelja down into the aquifer, a rerun of the Communist communion before the Battle of Neretva—so that Djelja would have been present in *all* beer, *all* drinking water, and thrown her protection over the whole city? This would have happened just before the scarcely believable failure of the Yugoslav People's Army to capture an entirely surrounded, unarmed, unsupplied town . . .

That's got to be it. Communion, submission: a religion as syncretic as everything else around here. King Solomon had a battalion of djinn in *his* army.

The trickle beside them has widened to a roar, a proper waterslide with tributaries and branchings, disappearing off into blacknesses that the Child's flashlight can't reach. Frito could reach the aquifer under the brewery from here, had he rope and scuba tank and courage enough . . . but the thought is too much, he shudders at claustrophobia even of the idea.

He turns to Maza, says "pretty swift, this tunnel, eh?" and wraps her in a great meaty hug, to fill her with several different types of warmth, even planting a kiss on her neck, before breaking off and leading them both onward to an exit that he just has to trust really is there.

Dajmond Dancing Club

BANNERMAN CANNOT SHAKE his head free of what Witness
H-7, Irma Sandžaktarević, shouted in her emotional outburst at the
DP camp. He's emailed Clare's boss, Marc van Xanthe, to get Vanda
the language assistant's details, and confirmed his own shaky translation with her.

"It's an open secret," Vanda said. "But it's not the *same*. If they
really wanted to get away, they could."

Bannerman clicked his tongue, *too bad*. "If only they wanted to
bad enough."

Vanda looked suddenly very tired, sliding helpless toward translucent: eyelids purple, surgical-green veins near the skin, black hair
in this daylight seen to be thinning on top. Shale and gravel dust
swirled up from the construction site next door, an enormous hole in
the ground.

"Maybe not," she concedes. "But I am powerless. You are American. What are *you* going to do about it?"

A good question, and one Bannerman has been putting, rhetori-
cally, to Zaim Spaho all morning.

"You knew about this?" Bannerman can't believe it.

Zaim won't look away from his computer screen. "We try not to."

"*Not* to? Like Albert *Speer*?"

"SIPA knows about this, EU Police also . . . what do you want me
to do? Make a challenge to—whole Serb mafia?"

"I don't know, I guess not just *put up* with it . . . wait, the EU Police
Mission knows about this? Does Ketyl?" Bannerman stares. Zaim
doesn't look away from the computer. "Does she?—Oh, Jesus."

But Ketyl Gaarder's office at the EUPM is concerned with problems that register on the scale of politics: forged euros and passports,

car-theft rings, property restitution, and so on. Crimes of wealth. Not *prostitution*. "Which after all is a legitimate export," honestly trying to persuade them, "in the economic definition, Ketyl. It brings money in."

"Yeah, except it's not prostitution, it's slavery."

Ketyl fields a few glances from colleagues around the office, smiles them away, and leans in close to Bannerman and Zaim. "Let's get a drink."

A few minutes later they're at Café Feigenbaum, getting settled into the black leather loungers. Even at four thirty in the afternoon the place is half full, with a good working ambience that a lot of restaurants can't even achieve Friday nights. "All the borders are fuzzy," says Ketyl. "Look around."

And she's got a point: there is a class of local women here, often seen at these tonier establishments, swapping High European witticisms with the colonial class, manicured nails nonetheless playing on epaulettes, flicking their hair back and forth. Recognisably a demi-monde. They avoid the eyes of their male and less beautiful female friends, who sit in dark corners in other bars, nursing beers, watching these scenes play out.

"All right," concedes Bannerman. "What about it?"

"These are the parameters *here*. Metropolitan, educated, rich. Relatively speaking. Now: Republika Srpska has no industry. Only smuggling. The only primary production they've got is illegal logging. They are gangsters with nothing to do than kill for the fatherland. You see? This was the same in Northern Ireland I think, the solution is: you improve the economy, make jobs, a reason to not fight."

"Awesome. Don't fight, rear slaves."

"Bannerman, I don't agree with this. I am explaining the official thinking. Besides, many of their customers are Americans, English, men on the bases. There is not the "Institutional Will." Dayton is a big plan Bannerman, a rearrangement of nations, a whole David Lean movie. Inevitably there are individual persons who get broken under the wheels. This is the theme of all "epic" stories. Okay. We try to stop this where we can, but we cannot stop all of it."

Bannerman doesn't buy it. "This is a little different, though."

"Yes. It is." Ketyl flushes the hair out of her face. "When the International Police Task Force was formed, by the UN, all the member nations were invited to contribute members of their police force. In Norway, it was a great honor to be selected. Competition for places was very strong. Every country sent its finest officers, apart from America. In America, you know, you think 'government is the problem,' so instead of sending the NYPD or whatever, the government subcontracted it to DynCorp, you know, this big defense contractor?" wearily, eyebrows up. "Now I don't know about this company: the main owner is also chairman of the Enron Finance Committee, on the U.S. Council on Foreign Relations, Harvard Board of Governors, bla bla bla."

"One of them."

"Not someone who smells good. Anyway, the IPTF officers, in order that we can do whatever needs doing, without being afraid of the local police or whatever? we had immunity from local law— arrest, or detention, or prosecution. We are above Bosnian law," glancing at Zaim, who's keeping silent. "But we are still subject to the law of our home countries, so there is this.

"But not the DynCorp guys. The DynCorp guys are not in the U.S. government, so the Uniform Code of Military Justice doesn't work, and they are on a UN mission, so American criminal law doesn't cover them," counting on her fingers, "and American common law does not cover crimes committed abroad. So the only authority in charge of these guys is their own *personnel department*. The worst that can possibly happen, is they get fired." Deep breath. "What we had was guys who were completely above any law.

"So what do you expect? You have fifty thousand soldiers suddenly here in East Europe, all on Western salaries. Naturally there is a big explosion for prostitutes. Girls start coming in from Moldova, Ukraine, Romania . . . anywhere poor. Real passports, fake passports— no passport? nema problema, we smuggle you. But smuggling people is expensive, the gangsters who do this want to get their money back, they keep these girls prisoner until they have paid off their debts. O.K. Then they keep them longer. Then they think, oh well! this is good money! I will keep them forever. Because there is no business in the mountains. Only viski, dizel, cigarete. These Serbs have nothing but their patriotism. No one misses the girls.

"So everyone under Dayton goes to use these girls, they are in every nightclub out there, in Prijedor and Banja Luka and Višegrad, everywhere, they say you can buy a girl 'hourly, nightly, or permanently.' And everyone buys them hourly or nightly. O.K. After a while though, they think, it is more economical to buy them permanently, the IPTF guys think, well, no one can touch me, I'll take a really nice girl, and then in a few weeks, if I am bored, I will sell her to a friend at a profit, or maybe, what is it, 'swap-pay' for a new one. It's like cars. Passports are ownership papers. Soon there is an entire industry trading these girls, it makes lots of money for Republika Srpska, and the DynCorp officers are in the middle of it."

Bannerman's fixated. "This *happened*?"

"It's all online. Look for yourself."

"Jesus . . . how'd it come out?"

"Oh, you know . . ." suddenly tired, waving away the exhaustion of even talking about it, "there was a whistle-blower, it was in the news, DynCorp moves the guilty guys out of Bosnia, fires the whistle-blower. End of."

"Wow."

"Again, the borders are fuzzy. Your buddies use prostitutes, O.K.— they *buy* prostitutes?" balancing her hand, "*just* O.K. Conditions in the brothels are very bad, it's not clean, healthy, you know. There *is* an argument there. But the DynCorp whistle-blower finally went to the police when one day his buddy comes in and starts bragging that his new girl *is not a day over twelve years old.*"

A long pause. Bannerman genuinely doesn't know what to do with this. "That's almost exactly the same as—"

"Yes."

"In Foča."

"Not the *same* same, but . . ."

But the world keeps turning. What can you do?

"Pedophile slave traders," Bannerman whistles, "these guys would not enjoy jail."

Zaim is sitting bowed, hand on the crown of his head.

"And it's still going on?" asks Bannerman.

Ketyl says *ja* on the inhalation.

"Americans, trading, slaves . . ." Bannerman half-hypnotized. "Listen. Clare's spending every piece of energy she's got, her whole *soul*, on the Foča Crisis Committee, she got the Ranković indictment, she got the U.S. State Department to post a reward, and now she's trying to get SFOR to bring him in. If she finds out that the same thing's still going on, only this time it's *us* . . ." shaking his head.

"I understand," Ketyl dragging on a cigarette, "but the difference between Ranković and the DynCorp guys is, no one will pay one million euro for the DynCorp guys."

Bannerman frowns, tilts his head at her. "Thought you Scandinavians were supposed to be idealists?"

"That's why the suicide rate is so high," stubbing it out. "In the police, you fight the battles you can win. I think that where there's an army, there's prostitution, and where there's prostitution, there's exploitation. I think these are facts of life," shrugging, "and the Bosnian legal system, it's not good, when the girls escape and go to the authorities, they get arrested for prostitution. It's not good. They do not prosecute for trafficking here."

"So fuck that, why not just keep busting up the clubs?"

"*Battles you can win*, Bannerman. Anyway, we tried this. There was a big raid, IPTF and SFOR joint, we raided three nightclubs in Prijedor, lots of jeeps and tanks, and we freed dozens of women. Maybe forty. Sick, diseased, cigarette burns, fractures . . . we brought them all down to the IOM shelter in the city. The Serbs were very angry, the RS police, and the bar owners, the whole Bosnian Serb mafia. This was a big income for them. So the Republika Srpska, the minister of the interior held a press conference, he said we exceeded the mandate, which, yes this was true, though on some silly technicality—but the RS demanded action, and the IPTF officers who planned this raid, the best guys, they were sent home." Ketyl looks lost. "The next week, all new girls. Same names, different bodies. Now no one does anything. In the end, if Republika Srpska wants to be like this?" shrugging. "And you know, the UN guys go there and use the girls anyway. No one rocks the boat. It's out of the Acquis."

Bannerman doesn't reply. Ketyl looks miserable. She looks at Zaim, who's been silent, smoking steadily. She takes his hand.

"There's nothing you can do," he says.

"No," Ketyl agrees.

"There is, you know," Ketyl's own grandmother, speaking to her from Oslo. "One can always be a 'neutral ally.' The thing is to try."—"But Beste, these are big things . . ."—"Ketyl, I know this is why you called. To find from me the strength."—"Beste, it is not strength I lack, but authority!"—"Your mother's money has come through. She has bought you a dress."—"What," Ketyl starts to choke up, "with her insurance money, she has bought me a dress?"—"The loveliest you have ever seen! White with red trimmings, it comes just below the knee, and a lovely bow. Expensive, but so lovely!"

Ketyl sobs silently, holding the receiver away.

"Animal and Edgar," Bannerman tells her. "Definitely. We know them pretty well by now, they're always looking for new ways to kick ass. You claw out some budget, get the arrest warrants, surveillance in place, clear it with SIPA, that sort of thing, File 13 would totally supply the firepower."

"What!" Ketyl looks doubtful. "I can't just *hire*—" but stops. She looks at Bannerman, who spreads his hands disarmingly. *Ball's in your court, lady*.

"We know about the nightclubs, brothels, what-have-you," says Animal Elliot-Maitland. "Crazy Horse and Mascarada. Harley's. But look at it from our point of view: International Police Task Force guys go in and get RTU'd in disgrace, what do you think's going to happen to us? We're not DynCorp, KBR, one of these cut-outs, we can't weather storms like that. Hanging on to accreditation as it is."

Ketyl stands looking out of Animal's window, smoking with trembling hand. "I understand." Far below, on the other side of the river, trucks go in and out of the brewery. "Even for the money?"

"The money's fine. We just *can't.*" Animal's surprised to find himself not taking that opportunity to chisel more out of the EUPM. Something about the frail will-to-good of this woman. She's out of her depth. These things can't be changed; the crumbling rationality of another Bosnian Psychosis case. But something about her makes him want to help:

"Whereas—now if there was an *indictee* involved—well that's another story," turning on the Lazenby/Bond charm for this Nordic lovely, "under Dayton, we're cleared. ICTY will defend us all from SFOR. You understand?" Ketyl's eyes bright with hope suddenly. "Show us an indictee, and we can *really* have a talk . . ."

She recharges from Zaim Spaho. No puppyish craziness there. He gets her, he gathers her in and protects her. He knows absolutely what's needed, seems to know more about her than she does. Their words are few but well chosen, predominantly English, but a growing number in each other's language. Or languages, rather, for there's a strange mirroring there too, what with the disintegration of Serbo-Croat into its components, and the intractable Norwegian tussle over its own variants, Bokmål and Nynorsk.

And she loves his body. In contrast to her own embarrassing flesh, there's no fat between his muscles and his skin, out of which veins bulge, and whose semicircular paths she can trace with fingertips, in bed at night after making love, all along his inner arm, shoulders, calves, waist. The veins at his waist she likes best, that run down into the channel of gristle between hip and crotch.

"Easy, then," Zaim says. "Can you get a—what do you do, you apply for a licence?"

"A warrant," Ketyl exhales heavily through her nose, "but don't worry about *that*," rolling over, the streetlight smooth on the small of her back, "SIPA has almost branch office at Telekom Srpske. It's not like at BH Telecom—Schengen compliance is a joke. The Intercept-Related Informations (IRI) List, this is updated every morning, new setups and teardowns all the time. Probably there will be something already in the database, it's good on the kriminalace, they're easy to track," a finger coming up to tickle Zaim's chin, "but I think you know this already, no?"

Zaim frowns. "No. How would I know?"

"Idi u pička materinu," turning the tickle into a slap, "again and again, it's the same people: girls, diesel, fake money. Admittedly, we weren't looking for indictees, though . . ."

"Really?" Zaim sits up. "Why not?"

"Off mission. Very. Don't think I've ever even seen an indictee list."

"Wait. Europe, the EUPM, is not looking for indictees?"

She shakes her head, a rustling in the bedroom black, hair backlit by streetlamps into a sodium halo. "Not our job."

"So who is looking?"

"Only the Americans, I think. I don't even know how many indictees there *are* still."

Zaim strokes her back. "On the public list, twenty? The sealed list, maybe another ten."

"Get me one tomorrow. I'll go through the system, compare it with IRI transcripts. There's bound to be some overlap between traffickers and indictees. There are hard copies of the transcripts, somewhere on the EUPM level, but if you can get into the system, there are rudimentary indexes. We compiled them as we went along."

"So then?"

Ketyl props herself up on her forearms. "The system will log my access," searching in his eyes for something she clearly isn't finding.

"Fine.—?"

"But they can't not put it together." Zaim still isn't getting it. "Say Mascarada gets a raid from mercenaries, Internals goes back to look at the Mascarada file and see that I accessed it all last week, you see?"

Zaim and Ketyl look at each other. "So you're taking a risk with your career."

Ketyl nods seriously.

"Can you think of a better thing to risk it for?"

Ketyl's still looking in his eyes, but presently there's a change: a satisfaction, a certain measure of hopes met. She shakes her head.

The UN Building on Zmaja od Bosne, halfway between the city center and the airport, is a nine-story towerblock with three wings in a Mercedes sign. It used to be a university student dorm, and indeed there's an identical but more dilapidated building immediately next to it, which still is—and, the joke goes, it's a moot point which building sees more sex. ICTY and EUPM, as well as other more usual UN brands, have offices there.

A model of resource sharing, the EUPM and Office of the Prosecutor Investigations share a sub-strata of language assistants to do the raw language work. Ketyl tasks two assistants to trawl for mentions of war-crimes indictees on lines relating to the brothels—the presence of PIFWCs providing justification for any Dayton-affiliated forces to intercede, not just SFOR but also EUPM, OSCE, Court Police, even private military companies. On Tuesday, the report comes back, they've got two matches, the most significant of which is at the Dajmond Dancing Club, in the small RS town of Vlasenica: Ažni Stevanjurović. He scores lots of mentions, possibly only because his distinctive name leaps out of the background chatter. Ketyl relays developments.

"We know him?" Bannerman flicking through the indictee list.

"Grave breaches of Geneva Four, Violations of Laws & Customs. Korićani massacre. The one where they shot everyone, threw the bodies from a cliff."

"Ažni Stevanjurović. He'll be there?"

"Seems that way," Ketyl shrugs. "There's talk of a council meeting, though council of what, who knows. Friday's the big night at this club, though, everyone turns up. I'd give it forty percent."

Bannerman nods. "Odds I'm familiar with."

He and Clare have started screwing in earnest now. She comes round to the apartment looking for *him* now, wanting nothing so much as to come in his face—but then Frito turns up and she's mint-cool, just hanging out around a cigarette is all, and she lets herself be led upstairs and blown away a second time.

"I feel sort of sorry for Bannerman," when she and Frito have come back down, making playful eyes at Bannerman, "you and I keep going off to have sex and he's all alone down here and doesn't get any."

"Ban-O's alright," Frito giving him a playful punch on the shoulder, *way* too hard, "he knows what he's doing. He gets plenty of game. Mad shagger, our Bannerman."

"What!" says Bannerman.

"Is that right," Clare evenly.

"God's truth—ask him about Ketyl Gaarder. Got to rush."

A silence after the final slam of the door downstairs. An apologetic shrug. "Comes with the territory," she says. "Repeatedly."

Bannerman points a long arm out the door. "The shower," in a monotone.

An hour later, Clare lies on her front, naked, reading the thick, peaceful sort of novel that favors archdukes and aquiline noses, little-girl princess fantasies transposed into adult. Bannerman's further back on his heels, running fingertips down the pale keel of her thighs, up to the smile where legs meet ass, down to unfreckled orange soles, back and forth. Her freckles dance and flash and keep him prehypnotic so he won't stop. If he does to maybe complain that princess fantasies are only about getting rich, just dressed up in romance and schlossdeutsch, she groans and kicks at nothing until he shuts up and starts again.

Even allowing for Frito's weird droit de seigneur, Bannerman's okay with the status quo. Keeping it subterranean. Because a showdown with Frito would be a total disaster right now, partly for the friendship, partly for the living arrangements, partly for the big F&B deal going down with ViKA, but mainly because he doesn't totally *have* Clare yet. Hasn't quite dislodged her.

"Is it his money?" Bannerman has asked her.

"Absolutely not," Clare angering at the suggestion. "He seems to have some answers," is the best she can do. "Having half a million euros in the bank, I think, is just a side effect of having his life together, of—" shaking her head, lost, she keeps coming back to it, "having answers."

Which is where Ketyl & Zaim come in: when this raid on the brothels comes off, how can she not see it—that Frito doesn't have answers for shit; he has antipsychotics. A man who busts up Serbian trafficking rings, that motherfucker has *answers*.

Marc van Xanthe, afterhours at the OTP offices, has relatively little sympathy with Bannerman's plan. "I have a good working relationship with Clare, and I don't like to keep things secret from her." Nevertheless releasing a bundle of biographical detail, including photographs, on Stevanjurović.

"Marc, there's no reason she ought to know."

"You spend a lot of time with her, you're doing this, basically, *for* her, no?" Bannerman wriggles on this pin. "She's not so vulnerable. She is not—we have a phrase in Holland, 'as fine as dollpoop.' She knows some realities of life. But you're a friend Bannerman, and people can be hurt by their friends. Often she's speaking of you. Consider that you will hurt her more, if you would keep things *from* her."

"Speaks of me, huh?"

Marc lays a hand on the files, still on his desk. "Stevanjurović, Dantić, these are small guys, you know."

"So am I."

"So I agree too," smiling not malevolently, "although there are many people I respect, besides Clare Leischman, who are thinking you are—a real big guy. The Great Bannerman."

Bannerman shakes his head like they're all mad.

"You know," leaning forward, wondering how to say this: "if you really wanted to impress her, you would find Karadžić."

"That better impress her."

"It's not so hard, I think. Karadžić has friends. The 'Preventiva' Network. They all know each other, they are talking on the phone. You know what I mean?"

"I'm with you."

"It's all the SDS Party, you know, in the RS Parliament? Krajisnik, Plavsić, Rogac, Ostojić . . . many others, all implicated. OTP is running investigations on them all," patting his desktop computer, "but they won't get indicted. Not by us. Paddy Ashdown puts them on the Visa Ban List, but there are limits . . . he throws them out of office, but after that—? You see? They all know. Karadžić's own wife too. They speak on the phone."

Bannerman frowns. "So you have a lead?"

"*On the phone*, Bannerman."

"Oh," beginning to twig, finally. "I see . . ."

"Inshallah," Marc waves the backs of his hands, frustrated, in the air. "Everything we know, we tell everyone, hope someone will find them. But ICTY is powerless. SFOR is risk-averse. OSCE don't care. EUPM don't even deal with this. The embassies know nothing. It's all higher. The spy organizations, the National Intelligence Centers, they know. But Karadžić made a deal."

Bannerman wrinkles his nose. "You buy that?"—"Sure."—"Unlike the CIA to stick to a deal."—"A deal is a deal."—"Noriega made a deal."

Marc laughs. "O.K.! But there are other reasons. If Karadžić or Mladić testify, it's a disaster."

Bannerman shifts uncomfortably. "All seems a little out of my league."

"Then five million dollars is out of your league, too."

"Ain't gonna argue with you."

"Actually, Bannerman, we think you are well placed for it."

"We?"

Vaguely, "My Dutch friends. Jens, those people. You are building your—your," waving a hand, " 'spam engine' with Vedo Alimović. No one suspects you of serious work. But they have also watched you build your cell. They were impressed how fast you turned Ketyl Gaarder."—" 'Turned' her?"

"Classic, what I think John le Carré would say, 'tradecraft.' And you're having the necessary motivation," glancing across the hall at Clare's empty office, "to do something really crazy."

Body otherwise immobile, Bannerman's eyes wander around the room. "Marc, are you a spy?"

"No no." Marc shakes his head, smiles engagingly. "No more than anyone else."

Thursday night, International Army night out, Flameproof Cooper and Andy Deuchar, two of File 13's truest stanchions, find themselves in a car with Bannerman Tedus of all people, going clubbing in Vlesanica, a small town just over the Inter-Entity Boundary Line in the RS, and at the tip of the Javor badlands, where the majority of the illegal logging and indictee-hiding is believed to go on. The Dajmond Dancing Club is a square black building, white neon lettering, angled off one end of the slick wet main street. Streetlamps reflect in puddles, pinpricks of rain black against the sodium-orange.

Inside the doors with diamond-shape windows, a brief shakedown by the doormen, and then down into the smell of stale beer, a black-purple bodyscape and a wall of sound—a distinctly old sound at that, Ace of Bass playing when they come in, closely followed by The Eagles, then Abba, then ZZ Top . . . alternate American and Swedish groups. The DJ evidently knows his crowd, constituting much of Multi-National Brigade North (MNB-N), that's the American sector, spiced with Russians, Poles and Swedes, each immediately identifiable, whether by suit jackets over T-shirts or beige slacks and golf shirts. Now and again a peculiar piece of classical bombast gets put on, brutally remixed to a military-industrial bassline—which turns out, on polite inquiry, to be a mashup of Tchaikovsky's *Slavonic March*, once known as the Serbo-Russian March, commemorating the massacre of Serbs at the hands of their Muslim oppressors. Crowd goes wild for it.

"Best get a few in, wouldn't you say?" says Flameproof Cooper.

"Aye," says Deuchar.

It's a gritty scene. Lots of locals besides the Dayton men. No Dayton women. What women there are strut around in high heels glowing in ultraviolet lights and not much else, turquoise light flowing

over skin, pulling Dayton men out of conversations and through a set
of black double doors at the back. Plenty of traffic over there. A few
RS police officers, two-headed eagle on their shirtsleeves, pistols in
evidence, enjoying a drink at the end of a long week. In a niche off
the main dance floor, some sort of VIP arrangement, where a number
of bearded, shaven-headed or otherwise indictee-looking men have
adopted poses of varying degrees of malevolence, drinking from tiny
glasses and big bottles, watching the writhing on the dancefloor and
not saying much.

"Stevanjurović," says Bannerman, "that's Stevanjurović. There."

"Easy," says Deuchar, "take it easy. We got all night."

"That's him though."

"Put that fucking finger down."

"Sorry." Bannerman stands about for a bit.

"You're sure now?" Deuchar says at last.

"Positive." Bannerman digs a photo out of his jeans back pocket,
squints at it in the light of his cell mobile phone. "Yep."

"Okey-dokey," Flameproof leans back against the bar, swigs some
more Lav Pivo, "subject acquired."

"Nice work, Coops," says Deuchar, and they clack bottles.

Bannerman stands there, practically hopping from foot to foot.
"You want to call the others, come bust the door down?"

"You *are* a yank, incha?"

"He might go!"

"Just sit tight. Nothing we can do now."

"There is, there totally is! Call the others!"

Flameproof Cooper wraps a thin but hard arm around Bannerman's neck. "Heya, 'buddy,' what say we sit down and have us a little
chinwag?"

"Listen up, you septic prick," Deuchar speaking into his face,
"more men won't help. What happens is we wait till he goes home,
fall in behind, tap him on the shoulder, pop him in a bag, home for
tea and medals. *Awright?* Something like that."

"All right," croaks Bannerman, and Flameproof lets him go. When
he's out: "But the whole point is to free the girls!"

"Free em from their undies," and Deuchar and Flameproof clack bottles again.

Fuck that. Bannerman's out the door and on the phone to Animal, 1 a.m. or whatever, finger in his other ear, stamping his feet in the cold. A voice graveled with sleep. "What can I do for you, Bannerman?"

"We found you an indictee, your boys want to take him nice and quiet."

"What's the problem."

"The trafficking. The girls."

There's a long pause at the other end, some feminine murmuring, Animal's deep reassurances, before turning back to the receiver.

"Alright. You've got me out of bed and in the other room, Bannerman. Tell me again? You're upset because Flameproof and Deuchar aren't going to double-header the entire club?"

"There was an understanding. You told Ketyl, if she gave you an indictee, you would bust up a brothel, free some sex slaves."

Another silence, interpreted by Bannerman as Animal applying pressure to his eyes.

"Ažni Stevanjurović, you say."

"Ažni Stevanjurović."

"You're sure he's there?"

"Positive."

"And you reckon he'll still be there in an hour?"

"Well I can't be sure, but he *looks* comfy. Deuchar and Flameproof have got him covered, anyway."

"Christ." A long whirring of digital static, clicks and anxieties. "Alright, pass me over to Deuchs. This is unlikely to be surgical."

*　*　*　*　*

Armored personnel carrier wheels slick on the winding road, finally free of its skids of brown ice. March 7, and 1 Battalion The Highlanders has been in-country a matter of days, a Scottish regiment of the Line, recently rotated in to relieve the Spanish garrison at Butmir. Major Jamie Kells-Cameron, 2i/c 1 Bn, follows behind in a Land

Rover, velcroing himself into his kevlar. Good God: days in, and already Elliot-Maitland, the old bastard, is calling in favors.

"Let me get a few more bodies inside first," Animal tells him down the phone.

"Understood. Our ETA thirty minutes. Let me have the layout once you're in."

"Copy."

Jamie would be iffy about this zero-notice raid, but it's Animal E.-M. He's known him since School. Even there, Animal had the knack of making things happen. Their paths have crossed intermittently since. Not least just after the war: Jamie was out here with BRITBAT, stationed in Banja Luka, July 1997. Two years of indifference to international justice ended abruptly when New Labour swept into power, and first thing Blair & Cook did was send the SAS in after the indictees. Animal arrived with 47 Squadron, part of the ten-man team that nailed two players, brought one back alive. They'd been hanging around at base for a week, on continuous ten-minute notice to move, when the Ops Officer came into the TV room, said, "Gents?" and they all faded away. Three hours later they were back with a player and a corpse. Well, that's the sort of efficiency the Army could use a lot more of, and this raid may well be the making of Kells-Cameron. The timing isn't terrible either: there are big SFOR raids just launched in Pale, thirty minutes ago, part of Operation Balkan Vice, trying to bust up racketeers, freezing assets, flushing out indictees . . . so the touchy non-government actors aspect of this raid will be easier to disguise.

Flameproof crumples the cup, alcohol runs down his fingers. "Have they gone mental?" looking around, "you got the entire fuckin Serb army in here?"

Deuchs shakes his head. "Told him."—"Enough gear to start it all up again."—"Told him."—"For that fat bastard?"—"Aye," stoically. "How much he worth again?"—"Hundred thousand."

"Oh for fuck's sake," Flameproof's disgusted. "*His* doing." Deuchar not even tilting his head, but Flameproof looks around to stare at

Bannerman with renewed loathing. "You realise we're going to be right here, between two sets of men with big fuckoff gats, when the fun starts?"

B Coy, 1 Platoon The Highlanders achieves formation while traveling. The Saxon armed personnel carrier in front will travel twenty feet beyond the Dajmond Dancing Club, and park across the road. Second one directly outside the door, third one further back on the Sarajevo road. The men will stream in the door, with axes if necessary. Officer Commanding Lieutenant Morrison. Major Kells-Cameron supernumerary.

Animal, Edgar, and Brick park the Land Cruiser, jeans and T-shirts, and saunter smiling down into the club. Girls attach themselves, they peel them off, wander over to the bar, where Flameproof is picking his teeth. Deuchar stays with Bannerman in the corner.

"Alright boss," says Flameproof, "Edgar."

"That our man in the corner," says Animal, without having looked.

"Aye, fat bastard in the beard, blue shirt with the white things on."

"Everyone got him? Alright."

Girls are still sashaying over, hands out, introducing themselves as Natasha and Anna.

"Hey my boys," Jefferson Penny comes stumbling up, "thought you fellas were whiter than white," cackling. Jefferson Penny is black. Pilot with an American subcontractor at Eagle Base, Tuzla. "Didn't have the Dajmond down as your total exact scene, know what I mean?" but at the lack of boisterousness here, Jefferson cools down sharply, "aww shit, there's something going on, am I right? Jesus. Give me time to get out of here," turning sharply, "and order some drinks, why don't you? You big boys are drawing *fire*," eyes flaring.

"Dva Sarajevska," Edgar says at the bar.

"Nema Sarajevska. Jelen Pivo?" says a big Serb, head like a basket-ball.

"That'd be swell." A stupid error. The Bosnians are as loyal to their beer brands as to their sexual persuasions, and Serbs would rather go sober than drink Sarajevsko. It's mutual.

Animal and the others talk rapidly. "So how we going to do this?"—"Brawl?"—"Stop looking at him, Brick."—"Brawl. Cameron's going to count us in."—"All right."—"Get dancing. He's fifteen minutes out."—"Magic darts."—"Shit."—"What?"—"Behind you. Too late, hang on."

"Zdravo, Brick, Flameproof," says a burly jovial type, facial hair and chest stubble, "nice to see you here! You want Nataša again? Nataša no work today—dirty men—blacks!—but you? maybe yes! Nataša like you, Flameproof!" slapping Flameproof on the arm.

"That would be on account of my enormous pecker, Predrag," says Flameproof.

"Yes! Enormous pecker, come Nataša, nema problema!"

"In a minute, Predrag," patting his shoulder, "first? a few refreshments," he makes to drink his Jelen Pivo, "nema problema."

"Nema problema, yes!" Predrag turns to look up at Animal, "And you? Nema problema?"

"Nema problema," says Animal.

"*Nema problema*," says Edgar, clinking his beer bottle.

"Big boys!" Predrag reaches up to grasp Animal and Edgar by the shoulders. "Very—American food, big boys!" grinning. Animal and Edgar laugh appreciably. "You boys—you want woman?"

"Refreshments," lifting their beers.

"Take woman," beckoning a girl over, "take Laja, take Laja now."

"In a minute," says Edgar, "we're getting refreshed."

"We'll take Laja now," says Animal. "Hello Laja."

Laja smiles thinly, red lace bra showing over the top of her shirt.

"Laja? thirty eyuro, one hour."

"Thirty euro. Fine." Animal digs out some notes, pays Predrag. Laja is transferred to File 13, but Predrag does not go away. "Okay, come, come now," tugging at Animal's bicep, trying to lead him to a door at the back.

"In a while, Predrag."—"Come now."—"In a while."—"Now."

Animal stares at Predrag. "Now?" holding up a beer, "*Pivo.*"

Predrag shows his palms as he retreats, all the way to the edge of the larger group that includes Stevanjurović. He bends to talk to the other men, and shakes his head, no. Glances in our direction.

"Seems like the element of surprise is gone."

Animal calls Kells-Cameron. "How's progress?"—"Five clicks."

But now a bigger man has come over, ski salopettes on, a thick black buzz cut sticking straight out from his scalp, like Chinese hair. "Gentlemen," he says. Putting his hands together in the praying gesture. "We would like you to leave. Please do not be offended."

"You're chucking us out?"

"Here is your thirty eyuro. Laja," with a jerk of the head. Laja gives a faint smile, and disperses.

"Here, I paid for that," Animal tries, but he can't get the indignation right.

Chinese Hair spreads his arms to usher them out, not threatening, polite. "Please." An RS police officer floats up from somewhere, stands some way off Chinese Hair's right arsecheek.

Edgar and Animal look at each other. "What now?"

"We leave."

A glance at Deuchar and Bannerman, still in the corner. Bannerman's watching, eyes like eggs, Deuchar pointedly not. "Tell hello to Vedad Alimović," adds Chinese Hair, from the door.

"Bugger," says Animal, the three of them out on the street.

"How's this going to work now?" says Flameproof.

"Let's get tooled up, get round the back." A pair of eyes watches from the diamond-shaped window in the door as they get into the Land Cruiser, start her up, pull to the end of the street, and disappear towards the main road.

The Saxon APCs and Land Rover are in traffic towards Vlasenica. Salt- and slush-dirtied windows briefly aglow in oncoming lights. Slow trucks working up inclines. Men promenading in their own villages watch the Saxons roll past, put cigarettes to the sides of their mouths, and take out phones.

"Over the last high ground," says Kells-Cameron. "I can see Vlasenica. Four minutes."

"Alright Flameproof, park it here," says Animal. "Pointing the other way." Everyone loads and cocks Browning pistols. Edgar uses a Glock. Tuck them into their jeans' waistbands, get out. It's an alley, set about with plastic crates of softdrink empties, trash cans, SUVs listing with two wheels on the kerb. The bass thump of the nightclub in their feet.

Animal calls up Kells-Cameron. "Myself and two men at the back door," says Animal. "I have two men inside, repeat two men inside."

"Got it. Two minutes."

Inside the nightclub, Deuchar and Bannerman are sat in the corner. Bannerman's knuckles white.

An accelerating tension. Men and girls dance.

"He's getting up," says Bannerman. "He's going."

"Stevanjurović?" Deuchar doesn't look round.

"All of them."

"Fuck." Deuchar looks round. Stevanjurović and his retinue are filing through the bar's hinged section. Stevanjurović is several men from the bar. "Come on." Deuchar up and pushing through the crowd.

"Wha," but Bannerman's up and following. The thickness of bodies provides some comfort.

Deuchar affects a drunken stumbling, gets to the man in front of Stevanjurović, lands a hand onto his arm, and slurs enthusiastically at him. The man looks round, a moment of stark eyeball contact, but Chinese Hair pulls a pistol and levels it at Deuchar's head. Deuchar sees his point. Chinese Hair smiles, and follows the retinue into the back of the club. The barman closes the hinged section of the bar, and takes all glasses from its surface. Severe dudes in tracksuit tops, something like a home team, fall back and line up in front of the bar, knocking Deuchar and Bannerman as they pass.

"Tits," says Deuchar.

Corporals scream GO GO GO and riflemen stream from the Saxons and up to the door. A gloved hand on the door, it's locked, up come the sledgehammers, alternating thuds just outboard of the lock. Ten seconds of that and the door's fucked enough to get kicked in, the hammerers step to one side and riflemen head in.

Music incredibly loud, in the black and violet no one's noticed or heard the intrusion.

"SFOR, get down," scream the riflemen, SA-80s leveled, "every-one down." But it's useless, the sound isn't traveling, it's only when the dance floor sees them that the mood breaks, an awareness trick-ling through the crowd. Finally there's a rifleman at the DJ booth, signaling throat cut, but the DJ plays it stupid. Riflemen at the bar, putting everyone onto their belt buckles at the point of a weapon, riflemen finding and checking all doors. Riflemen finding the trap section of the bar locked, can't find the bolt, got it and finally through. Riflemen into the back reaches of the Dajmond Dancing Club. Finally the music stops, revealing all the shouting DOWN DOWN GET DOWN.

"Under the terms of Dayton Annex One-A," begins Kells-Cameron, striding over prone bodies.

Rifles up soldiers swarm through corridor and kitchen CLEAR pound up wooden stairs and kick in doors, girls sitting up wide-eyed in bed, ON THE GROUND ON THE GROUND, off-duty GI and squaddie scrambling into jeans and screaming out their nation-alities, and a pounding on walls, the crack of broken glass, dust sift-ing down from floorboards overhead, and still more riflemen pile in behind, lifting up doors set into the floor, carpets pushed aside, post-ers of Ratko brutally unhung from picturehooks . . .

Out in the alley, the door bursts open—figures silhouetted black against a filthy corridor. Animal and Edgar and Flameproof have pistols ready, a grim tableau, but it's a Highlanders rifleman in the door, who sees the figures and ducks back in screaming CONTACT at his fireteam. Animal calls in after him, "FRIENDLY—FRIENDLY," until rapport is established.

"Got em?" Animal coming in the back corridor, pistol going in his waistband.

"Nothing," says Lieutenant Morrison, bemused. "Clean fucking *vanished*."

Two hours later, the clientele are finally filing out of the nightclub, a Highlanders detail at a trestle table taking a list of IDs and serial numbers before they go. A vanguard of EUPM people is up here, including Ketyl Gaarder, interviewing the prostitutes amid talk of a coach, due to arrive forty minutes ago, that will take them to the IOM shelter in Sarajevo. If they wish. Some do not wish. Haggard, underfed, a menagerie of STDs, some want to stay. Soldiers in fluorescent vests and gloves wave traffic past. Boots high combat on the rain-soaked road. Major Kells-Cameron comes over to the Land Cruiser, where File 13 have been lying low, walkie-talkie bleating to itself in his belt. "Hell of a thing, Animal."

"You're sure?" Animal can't believe it.

"The entire place," Jamie Kells-Cameron looking at him pointedly.

"Clearly there's an exit we've missed—or a cellar, or suchlike."

No reply. Eventually, "And *you're* sure Stevanjurović was there?"

"Three positive IDs," thumbing at Bannerman, Deuchar, and Flameproof, "my best men."

Kells-Cameron shakes his head. "Don't know what to tell you, Animal. It's a mess. Brigade North is shitting the bed."

"I imagine." Animal drums his fingers on the dashboard. He's got to keep Kells-Cameron onside, if he hasn't already burned him down. "How do they *do* it, Jamie?"

But Kells-Cameron is not in the mood. SFOR raids fail to find

PIFWCs all the time, but not normally unsanctioned ones, and with fairly large breakage bills to pay. The wheels may have just come off his chances of making CO. Maybe he should have gone into the City after all. He looks mighty pissed off, rain beading on his helmet and nose. "Well—we knew the stakes. Went for it, it didn't come off." He slaps the bonnet of the Land Cruiser. "Best get your lads out of it for tonight, Animal."

In the Red Market

JACKDAWS, BIG AND mean and avoided by the pigeons, keep catching Ariel Alkali's eye. No one else gets the creeps from the jackdaws—but then, not speaking Czech, where the word for them is *kafka*, there aren't the same associations. She photographs them, but they never come out dark and foreboding—they're just birds.

Wet cigarette butts lie thick in the gutters. Here and there they get caught in the few remaining Serbian Flowers, once maintained by the city with red paint, these days becoming indistinguishable from ordinary potholes, and which function as foxholes in which cigarette butts may, for a couple of days at least, escape the streetsweeper. Ariel crouches in the gutter, fingers playing in the cigarette butts, pushing them this way and that in search of an arrangement that Says Something. But there's nothing good happening, and presently she straightens and continues off, tripod and four-by-five over her shoulder, cozy inside Edgar's ski instructor jacket. A face, anything. But she's coming up blank. She's lost something. And in order to find it again, she better find out what it *is*.

For Ariel is a priestess of art. Sylvia Plath, prophet, had it right—had Ariel Alkali *herself* pegged, when she wrote in her 1965 collection:

> And I
> Am the arrow,
> The dew that flies,
> Suicidal, at one with the drive
> Into the red
> Eye, the cauldron of morning.

Red eye? of the camera, dummy: its auto-focus rangefinder, or more literally a video REC light. Ariel knew as soon as she read that. Sylvia Plath was, after all, a prophet. Everyone knows that. Ariel has a first edition of *Ariel*, the British one, that goes with her every-where.

For Ariel's own sensitivities to art moments, what they've agreed to call "poignancy," mirror those of her adorable lunk of a boyfriend's to explosive danger. Two modern sensitives, priest and priestess, Eros and Psyche with the genders reversed, feeding off each other's pow-ers. But Edgar's barely put his big paws on her lately, not even to cud-dle up at night. Maybe that's it. Maybe, given the life≡art identity, her lack of productivity has its roots in her lack of reproductivity . . .

Either way she's blocked, can't take a decent picture. Either the arrow that flies isn't flying straight, or there's nothing in this city for Ariel to be at one with. It's not inconceivable; maybe everything's too done. Ariel could build a whole other city just from the grainy black-and-whites taken of it over the past decade—not a bad idea, itself, for a piece. Berlin-friendly. But every moody art book on this city, that she's seen anyway, has a close-to-ground shot of a fresh red Serbian Flower, normally with people (goodness!) getting on with their lives in the background. Well, there has to be something new out there, some poignancies in Sarajevo that move beyond the old, old, boring old war.

Ariel's art is her life, and versa vice. A commutative relationship. The medium-format photographs she produces are as fully *her* as they are mementoes, each produced with as much pain and soul as any child. Really. Her hi-tone galleries in Berlin and New York, allow-ing them to go at $7,500 per, are frequently sold out. And why not? They are infused with a steep melancholy and grasp of the human condition that only Ariel Alkali, really, and maybe a few other gifted photographers, can put their finger on. As the blurb says: "Within the confines of an ordinary photograph, Alkali creates psychic distur-bances so evanescent that even those with the Educated Eye are sometimes unaware of why they are so troubling."

But it turns out that quite a number of people have the Educated Eye. Tipper Gore, so nearly First Lady, has a print—it's the one of

Ariel's former boyfriend, Piedro, with his penis resting mournfully on the shoulder of her own mother, naked. MoMA in New York has the one of Ariel's father sitting mournfully in the middle of a Prague traffic jam, naked. The Stedelijk Museum voor Actuele Kunst, in Ghent, has the one of Ariel's other boyfriend, Matthias, with his recently used, glistening penis hanging mournfully most of the way down his thigh. The most popular of her oeuvre though, are the works in which she has turned her mordant lens upon her own soul, and photographed herself—mournfully alone, or with other mournfully athletic young girlfriends, lying on a Dalmatian beach or around a swimming pool, in an apathy of existential disgust, naked.

The loss is making her photographs come out wrong. Pat. "Somewhat contrived, liebchen," says Katerina, her gallerist.—"But I didn't contrive anything," Ariel will object, "that's exactly how I found it!"—"Hm, yes, I just feel that whole photographer-as-director movement has had its time, liebchen . . ."—"But I didn't direct anyone, Katerina!"—"Well liebchen," Katerina considering the problem, "in that case I don't know what to say. Is there *no* nudity in Sarajevo?"

That got Ariel pissed, all right. So she set about finding herself a new direction. A good place for it. Because out in town, the vibrations are unique in this little rockpool of Viennese sophistication, left behind when the tide ebbed on the Austro-Hungarian Empire. Without getting too *National Geographic* about it (*leathery old peasant women bring in the nettle harvest with their toothless mouths, a way of life unchanged for a thousand*, etc.) Ariel thought she could get some great shots here, help forge a city identity that moved beyond the war. Balkan Gothic. Bosnian Psychotic. Sarajevan Psychedelic.

But it hasn't worked out. In every surface of the city's walls a ponderousness from having been viewed, considered, adjusted, a million times. And on top of that, a lot of it has been recently arted up by—who knows—conceptual students from the Art School, or someone. Ariel creeping corner to corner, hunting for some chunk of raw authenticity. But what she finds is: roses and lilies hung from lampposts, in *nooses*; photographs clothespinned to wires; the Dangerous Ruin scaffolding and orange plastic netting with which the old Hotel Europa is trying to cover its nakedness, sporting ribbons; a teddy-bear tied to a chair, as though for interrogation; a Pepsi cabinet standing on its own in front of the cathedral, absolutely full of books; a hair-raisingly elaborate maze, twelve feet square, drawn in red ballpoint on the side of a wall. Authenticity, but the wrong sort. An ars longa vita brevis complex of a type she's never even heard of before—wow, imagine that! if: surrounded by serial killers giving press conferences saying you will be counting not your dead but your living—you found the *visual arts*, flimsiest of mediums, your best hope for riposte, if not survival . . .

"Lost something?" says a low voice behind her. She looks round to see Frito Cooper, a big slab of man, checking her out from behind. "If it's a cigarette, I can let you have a new one, all of your own," tapping out a pack of Drinas.

"Lost something, don't know what," her hand lightly on his wrist as he lights her up, then eyes flicking up to catch his, sucking on the cigarette as she does so. A rite holy to the Nouvelle Vague liturgy.

"Your mojo?"

"Something like that. I am not sure what, exactly."

"Hmm," Frito pretending to think but really checking her out, a smile near his face. "You don't know what you've lost till it's gone, all the authorities agree."

"Yeah. But with me it is the other way around."

"You don't know what you lost till it's found?"

"Right." Ariel smiles, and Frito smiles, and they stand a while longer, making smalltalk about where she's looked already, what it might be, and gossiping about all the relationship fusion and fission going on, and, always in a conversation with Frito these days, why Sarajevo never fell. Ariel likes him.

Finally: "In Berlin I would go to see my therapist, in Prague it is the Tarot lady. In Sarajevo," all B-movie starlet innocence, "I do not know *what* to do . . ."

Frito drops his cigarette, grinds it beneath a boot, "I've got a young man back at the flat, he's pretty good at rooting out the truth. Fancy consulting him?"

Ariel smiles devilishly, considers him for a long while. "Why not?" taking his arm.

Back to the apartment in Baščaršija. Inside the cobbled courtyard, at the top of the enclosed wood staircase, white-yellow cases of Sara-jevsko Pivo are stacked eight high and two deep along the hall, nar-rowing the entry corridor; in the living room, Sarajevsko Pivo cases form a two-by-two-by-four-block coffee table, almost lost under a weight of Bosnian banknotes, and Sarajevsko Pivo cuboids of other sizes form side and occasional tables, chairs, TV stands. A black trashcan by the door is full of brown Sarajevsko empties. Under them, on a butternut suede sofa, clutching a bottle of orahovac walnut brandy, is an adorable green-eyed Sufi Child.

"Aw," begins Ariel, "let me get my camera—"

"Jewess!" the Sufi Child shouts, without preamble. "Frightened! Empty! No children! Where are your children?"

Ariel freezes. "Scheiße."

"Have you lost any children lately?" asks Frito, quite calmly.

"Fly away home!" shouts Sufi Child, veins coming into his fore-head. "Fly! Fly, Jewess, *fly*!"

"Yeah I'm sorry about that," says Bannerman later, calming Ariel down. "Sufi boy's kind of unpredictable, you should try waking up with him still there. Him and Frito stay up all night long sometimes, drinking with God—you're like, 'Good morning,' and they're all, 'Your heart is doomed Bannerman,' and I'm like, 'All right, coffee first, guys. Seriously.' "

Ariel's got a soft spot for Bannerman, the boy has a love in him that rages, it spills out of the emotional and into the nearly visible. "How are things with Clare?"

"You tell me," clinging to a cigarette on the rooftop.

Behind him, across the river, the Gothic yellow dome of the Art School. Ariel has started a side project, taking black-and-whites of Bannerman Tedus every day against this same backdrop of mountain and city. An index, like a stock chart, of the changing fortunes of his heart: progress, setbacks all set down in a growing matrix of photos, like Warhol's but bigger. It's okay. Certainly it's the only piece with any soul she's done here. Shooting Bannerman, she has the right sort of Eye, but only when looking at him in miniature, upside down, and focused on the rear projection panel of her 4 x 5 . . . then, aligning with the previous day's shot, she's got something again.

"Well you have to stop doing what you're doing. Hey! Bannerman! Stop it, already!"

"I'm just standing here!"

"Standing there *needing*. I can feel your neediness from here. Play it cool, man."

Bannerman gives a flat smile. "Easier said than done."

"Leverage the jealousy. Let her know what she is missing."

Gazing wistfully up at the old Jugoslav Army barracks on Vratnik, high above the city, "Don't think she works that way. She's not threatened."

"You are joking?" Ariel straightens. "*Everyone* is threatened. If you find yourself a really, *seriously* hot chick, who is really beautiful, great legs, tits, everything"—indicating her own assets—"you go to have a great time in public with her, you don't even have to fuck her, it can all be a pretend—Clare will come around in a *second*," snapping her fingers. "Done it a thousand times," a glamorous smile, "trust me."

"Offering your services? Jealousy management?"

"Jealousy management is the name of the game, Bannerman. Supply and demand. You cannot let supply outstrip demand. Ask De Beers."

Bannerman tries, really he does, but the mask is heavy. There comes a point when he's in bed with Clare, his heart can't maintain its distance—and tiny shivers spiral out of his chest, dancing capoeiras in front of them, confetting through the air, over the erect points of her hip bones, shivers brilliant green and yellow, little fluttering softnesses, homing in on her sleek wet face, her chin rucking up as she looks down her body, swatting lightly against her eyelashes like they're looking for friends . . . Clare indifferent to all this, her face gone a deep cardiac crimson under the freckles, lips almost grossly swollen, and staring Bannerman clean through the mind while she fucks him. And how can he not arc his torso back down to meet hers, translucent Rorschach blot of love left in the air behind him, enter her again with the biting of lower lips, shutting of eyes, pastel butterfly presences dance double and triple helixes in the rising air above their bodies . . .

"You're a lot gentler than Frito," is the first time she says anything connecting them, moving beyond her tendency to compartmentalize. It's hope. Even when it's mostly bad news for him, Frito being such a dominating presence in her bedroom and mind, and with such a whopping middle genitalium, still it's these confidences, lightly worn between them and with such light hearts, that will accumulate into a cartilage.

"Do you find it strange," lying post-coital beside her on her rich gray sheets, toying with her damp hair, "that when the sexual organs become excited, one becomes hard, the other wet?"

"Wet's pretty annoying," she says, cheek on his chest. "*You* don't have to keep changing your underwear."

"I mean aren't they pretty arbitrary qualities? Where's the sex organs that turn, you know, green, or furry? You know: 'I'm so hairy for you right now, baby, how you doing?' 'Honey, I am *viridian*.' "

Clare giggles and writhes and tries to bite her way into his sternum. Wouldn't be surprised if she could. There are rips opening where he didn't even know there were seams. But in the way she looks at him, she understands his problems, the depth of his need for her, everything. Even as she gets up to put some milk on the stove, skipping across the room bashful in her nakedness, and dives back under her duvet; he is giddy with future. She might not come to him now, not fully, but she will, she will. For she can see the world and all its arrangements, her mind's eye ascending to an altitude where the curvature of the planet asserts itself, a curvature so vast, can discern the problems of viewpoint as relating to the spinning of the axis, the fixed and moving stars . . . she gets it. She sees they will end up together. Soul mates, and cell mates. Prison with this girl would be fine. A curvature so vast. Once he gets her he will never let her go. So Bannerman doesn't hassle her about leaving Frito. It's all coming his way.

She takes to text-messaging people right there on his chest, tiny shoulder twitchings and hair playing on his ribcage—and his eyes slide shut, and he sleeps.

Oh, dear. Ariel's seen *this* situation before. She clicks her tongue, hangs up her prints in the darkroom. Maybe it's just that her sensitivities, so special in Berlin, aren't special here. The Bosnian Psychosis of which Edgar is frightened—she doesn't know why frightened, love is a psychosis too, God knows he's probably frightened of that as well—correlates with the Educated Eye so widespread here . . . but isn't that a plausible locus for the Eye? If a psychosis gives you a hypersensitivity, whether to sun, heights, being followed, explosive danger, mendacity—isn't that sort of empowering? To have special sensitivities, side effects of what are in clinical terms traumas, but which in themselves approach superpowers—the classic superhero backstory—isn't that something? And has Bosnian Psychosis turned the whole city into hypersensitives of one sort or another—which is to say, artists?

"Well it *was* an art-war," is Rachael Drikkevand's point of view.

Rachael's from an Old High Danish family, currently playing at International Development, and involved with distributing WTO/OECD money under the Doha Development Agenda. Snooty as hell, uses money like a cudgel, and over lunch will never, like the rest of the expats, go Dutch.

Which is fine with Ariel, with whom she lunches at least once a week, manifestly eager that Ariel's beauty and art reputation rub off on her, and together they drink bottled water at Restaurant Beban, high on the southern ridgeline, the whole of Sarajevo spread out beneath them like a map. You could snipe whoever you wanted from here.

"What was I saying?" says Rachael.

"Art-war," says Ariel.

"Right," and Rachael Drikkevand sinks into a strange, well *cri-*

tique of the Bosnian War, assessing its aesthetic qualities vis-à-vis previous attempted genocides, praising it for challenging our assumptions about war and beauty. When she talks about its violence being "graphic," she's not talking about its extremity . . .

"It was a masterpiece. The entire thing was fought on television. Wasn't it. Real television, demotic TV, not the faux coverage of Gulf War I, sanctioned by generals—no, this was grassroots art . . . cameramen more effective as defenders of Bosnia than the mujahedeen who came to defend their faith. Television at least as important as any other weapon. A whole front in itself. A genuine art-war. And the only weapon the Bosnians had . . ."

Ariel frowns playfully. "Not much good against artillery?"

"On the contrary." Rachael Drikkevand sneers, looks at her hard. "Television *saved* this country. Europe was letting the Serbs do whatsoever. War crimes are piling up. No one is doing anything. But cameramen are getting it all on TV, getting it out to the world, to The People, *us*. And we clamored for action to stop it. Eventually we got it. It took America three years to act, but they did." Rachael's voice has become a filmic whisper, her quietness not an absence of volume but a positive, an intense quality, her nude-lipstick mouth a small tight line: "America did come. Clinton did stop it."

"Why 'art,' though?" Ariel asks.

"WHAT IS WRONG WITH YOU?" a vicious reaction, but Rachael has become used to people pooh-poohing TV's claims to high-art status, in comparison to canvas, photography. Ariel just stepped on a sore point, is all. The misunderstanding is swiftly cleared up:

"Well it *looked* cool, didn't it . . . the palette was so muted, all those fady grays, the smoky city, the blue hills . . . you don't get film grading like that by accident. And it wasn't just the war. Rwanda, at the same time, remember?, wasn't even vaguely good-looking. It had terrible aesthetics. Their violence wasn't graphic at all. You know what I mean?"

"Sounds more like a race thing."

"Well yes. This is clearly true. But more than that, the Bosnia angle was—how do you say—*worked*. All the footage, it all looked like, I don't know, commercials. You know what I mean? Designed to hook you. Not necessarily by the Bosnians, either. It was just so . . . packaged, to an extent that eliminates any idea of conscious design. Just its emergent qualities. You had banks of cameramen in the Holiday Inn, lenses pointing all along Snipers' Alley, waiting for someone to cross the street—I mean *eagerly* waiting, *praying* for an old lady to come out with her groceries. Agencies paid thousands for a headshot. And on the other side, the snipers with their bounties and sick sense of humor. So you had these strange mirror-worlds, War and Art, their interests aligned, if not identical . . . no government could arrange that. No, this was something larger, perhaps the city-state herself, doing whatever she had to survive, sacrificing thousands of her own lives if need be, to give the message form . . ."—painfully quiet now, in awe at the invocation of this most holy authority, "—rousing The People Of The World to her defense . . . it could only be by TV. Such insight. Some conception of mind too broad for our Western definitions. She was a *real* artist . . ."

Rachael Drikkevand stands on the bench, statuesque now in high-heeled moonboots, looking down at the misty city-valley. "Art saved this city. The Serbs knew it too. Knew the city was too well covered with cameras, that what they did at Vukovar, they'd never be able to do here . . . they knew that if The People Of The World saw it, tomorrow the skies would be black with American Wrath . . ." waving a hand from Mounts Igman to Hum, spinning round to follow the ridgeline with her fingertips, all the way around . . .

And that's it. The claims of art finally pushed too far, and in a second Ariel suddenly doesn't believe any of them. In a world of violent unhappiness on all sides, she only hopes she doesn't seem as preposterous to others as this silly bitch Drikkevand does to her. Wants to claw her eyes out. Instead, with a grace that surprises even her, she only says: "Frito's collecting reasons the city didn't fall. You should tell this stuff to him."

"What, that Maori alcoholic?" Rachael looking down at her, horrified, "I won't go *near* him. Worst case of the Psychosis I've ever *seen*."

*

"Good day?" said Edgar, that evening. "Been seeing anyone?"

"Terrible. I think I'm going to give up art."

"What, really?"

"We're *scum*." Ariel putting her hands over her eyes. " 'My art is my life'? I mean, what?"

Edgar was amazing and looked after her, as she floundered in her crisis that evening at the apartment. Her photographs weren't children. Not nearly. "What have I been *doing* with my life?" she wailed, face melting off and splashing on the sofa.

Edgar hugged her and whispered, "You've been making me the happiest man alive," and mopped her eyes.

"Does this mean you're not going to take that naked picture of my dad saluting?" Edgar asked later, holding her in bed, when calm had returned. Ariel sighed at the ceiling, pushed her hair back from her forehead. "Girl has to make a living."

*   *   *   *   *

Zealotry and doubts. Clare doesn't return Bannerman's calls, sometimes for days. He sits around developing Ghost Phone, which is to say, the erroneous belief that his phone is ringing. He quickdraws for it at lunch, and plates jump on the waxed pine. Zaim and Ketyl catch their glasses, then each other's eye. He's taken to putting it down near audio speakers with the volume turned up, so the near-field interference will make the speakers stutter if anyone even thinks of calling. But even that's not enough. *Any* sound whose attack gradient is insufficiently gentle and Bannerman's an inch above his seat, his paperwork wafting autumnally to the floor . . . . He's maybe even developing *premonitions* of phone activity, though it doesn't look like he knows it; whenever a phone is seen to ring it tends to have been preceded by an uptick in Bannerman's fidgetiness, general caffeination. Not a strong enough effect to predict an incoming call, but an unnerving correlation anyway.

It's after a few weeks of this that he caves, and corners Zaim at the F&B warehouse, where Zaim and some of his sub-coders have been writing the server-side software. Midmorning one day, after Frito and Reza the delivery guy have gone off, Bannerman ushers Zaim into the toilet. "That cell-tracking program of yours," Bannerman getting out a scrap of paper, "here's Clare's sim number."

"Oh man," Zaim whines, his shoulders sagging. "This could be really big trouble for me, Bannerman . . ."

"How big?" Bannerman unmoved, licking his forefingers, and leafing through a stack of twenties.

Listening in is too difficult. And too much. Knowing what neighborhood she's in is good enough stalking for now—it'll help, as Al Mudhill once put it, "engineer fate" a little. Soon he's rigged up a whole other computer screen just for her transceiver cell readout, which he starts checking out of the corner of his eye every third second, more addictive than online poker sites, and which he watches mostly never leave cell 118, the UN Building area.

Somewhere he got the idea that the not knowing was worst of all.

"Wait wait, her cell's just come on," Bannerman calls out at 8:30 a.m. at the F&B warehouse, where they've been hard at work for an hour. "Cell Seventeen Five . . ." checking the cell coverage map. "Seventeen five". . . a finger stopping near Vratnik. "There's nothing up there. What's up there?"

"File 13?" Zaim not looking up from his screen. Then realizing.

A pause. "The fuck is she doing up there at eight thirty in the morning?"

Zaim looks uncomfortable.

"Seriously? What business could she possibly have up there, at *any* time, let alone first thing in the FUCKING MORNING?"

"Man, maybe you should cool it a while."

The pain is giving him the strategic thinking of a moth. So a rash of coincidental meetings ensues, not foolproof, given the low resolution, covering maybe ten possible bars or restaurants—but with dramatically increased peculiarness nonetheless. Bannerman keeps happening to run into her on a morning Walk of Shame, or at dinner, or after work with her boss, Marc van Xanthe, hanging around with other Francophones, letting the day fall off them at the underground pool bar, Billiards Club Action.

"Yo Leischman," swaggering up.

"Bannerman again! Are you following me?"

"Sure am," jokingly but nevertheless, "you avoiding me?"

"Oh *stop*," Clare pushing him away, chin back down to the magenta baize. Marc van Xanthe leans on his cue, scrutinizing Bannerman carefully. Around them, a huge matrix of pool tables upholstered in all colors of the rainbow, and more, some with actually fluorescent baize, dozens of games in progress, and ducts and piping on the low ceiling barely visible through the cigarette smoke; and beer bottles, hips jutting out, the busy clatter of balls—and panning back to the foreground: an idiotboy unable to leave things subjunctive.

"Well are you?" he says.

So she has to answer. "There's not really anything to *avoid*, you know? It's not like we're—" glancing at Marc, "*look*," sotto voce, "*I just don't want anyone to get hurt.*"

"Get hurt?" smiling hugely. "Why, because you know it can never work out between us?"

Clare is silent for a long time. "Well—"

In the darkroom, a still red-black scene silent but for the lapping of developer and stop bath, Ariel sees it all. She hasn't lost anything, but found it. A classic, almost drug-induced moment of clarity, of seeing all the world's systems in perfect balance. Rachael Drikkevand drove that home all right, made clear what this was really all about: Westerners jacking off over the Bosnians' misfortune, wave upon wave come to sit in cafés peddling views that all begin "The thing about Bosnia—." A patronage the Bosnians bear with weary resignation, much less angry about Dayton than they should be. Than *Ariel* is. They were about to defeat the aggressor once and for all, when the West finally chose its moment to act, and froze the action *inches* before they got their comeuppance. That's Dayton. And because the Nazis still don't think they lost, still won't play nice, the West somehow thinks there's something innately wrong with Bosnia—an attitude neatly codified in this idiotic urban myth "Bosnian Psychosis," like there's something uniquely schizoid about this place.

Gives Ariel, seriously, the fury. Has no one read Kafka. It's the same failure to understand that she's seen in the Ashkenazi community in Brooklyn—where her entire extended family, even the goys, think there's something in the German psyche that's uniquely prone to evil. Won't buy Mercedes. She tells them every time that in that case they've *completely missed the point*—what about Ante Pavelić— but you try telling Jews of a certain age they don't "get" Shoah. And Rachael Drikkevand won't ever understand that nothing magic happened in Yugoslavia. Tito fucked the economy, inflation hit 2,000 percent, and people were left with nothing but their patriotism. Anyone who thinks it's to do with "evil" is either under ten or liable to the exact same thing themselves.

And these are things she can now *see*. Clothespegging and tilting her head at prints of people, Ariel's eye has become educated to a radically new level. Its loss was maybe only a cocooning, while it metamorphozed into some new form. Arrows into butterflies. She feels very much the witch in her cave, bent near double over red cauldrons of developer, sending her eyes fluttering out into the world, to do her knowing for her. Sylvia again. Because the things she can see about people in these prints are not pretty. Especially the ones of herself . . .

The "Bannerman" series is nearing its end. He's trying to save a girl from herself, and make her want him at the same time—well— soon his heart will be dead, and that will be that. High hilarity among the expats at the spectacle of his car-crash attempts at love, not least among those of his supposed friends—transparently acquisitive creeps like Khan Kerensky and Dmitri Lautz—who take every opportunity to mock him behind his back, and on rare occasions to his face:

"Cameras, bollocks. Enormous pile of shit," says Dmitri Lautz, smiling at Clare and Bannerman. "TV didn't *save* this country. TV almost wiped it out."

A wind has picked up. A copy of yesterday's *Oslobodjenje*, dropped at Sebilj among the pigeons, seems to get the idea and also starts flapping its wings—and out fly pages, two at a time, cartwheeling down Sarači Street, and they become wetted, get caught against blackened blocks of snowdrift, long since turned to ice, plaster themselves upon windows, or are trodden back into a pulp that grouts the cobbles. A tourist-wife holds onto her husband's arm and the top of her own hat, slips on a slick double-page, and ends up on the ground. Locals rush to help, pick her up and offer them both a coffee, but as usual the tourists think they're being worked somehow, and decline and hurry on with a degree of scorn that is presumably perfectly acceptable in the West. The locals shrug, and with no one else to be hospitable to, take to offering each other cigarettes, and accepting with easy grace. In the foreground, Dmitri Lautz, from the German Ministry of Economics and Labor, is talking, often in German, but Clare keeps making him speak English, for Bannerman's sake.

"As you wish, gorgeous. So imagine you're Radovan Karadžić—a subtle man, remember, a psychiatrist, a poet, a *green*—and your ultimate aim, remember, is an ethnically pure, enlarged Greater Serbia. What you really want is the land next to Serbia, everything along the Drina, the Sava. Maybe also the Krajina, Banja Luka, places like this. But you're not really interested in Sarajevo, this irredeemably Muslim town. Never in a million years is Sarajevo going to be a Serb town. So you let journalists and cameramen in *here*, you saturate the West with pictures of Snipers' Alley, where you fight a relatively clean war, and you confuse the issue with supposed Bosnian *government* atrocities as well, and Croat atrocities in the south and what-have-you: total confusion. International deadlock. The media can be trusted only to see what's put in front of it. You have beautiful hands, by the way."

Clare leans forward, looks blankly down at the table.

"And it worked. If you remember, all the press reports said: well there was such-and-such an atrocity by this side, but then there was supposedly one on this side also, and here are some bodies, and here is a widow, look how sad she is, and it's all very tragic, and everyone and no one is to blame, and it's all down to ancient ethnic hatred, and so on. All that bullshit. Which leaves you free, out in the mountains, where there *are* no cameras, to do the Nazi thing all along the Drina—at Goražde, Žepa, Foča, Srebrenica—which, as you see, is what you really want anyway." Dmitri Lautz spreads his arms as though expecting applause. "Clever, no? Hey, schatz?"

Clare's emanating pure sadness.

"Sounds like you're making a parlor game out of the facts," says Bannerman.

"No no. You should read more, Bannerman. The Serbs were clear about this: Nikola Koljević said as much. *They never wanted Sarajevo.* Armchair diplomats forget the *Ostpolitik.*" With a smile that makes Bannerman want to smash his perfect fucking nose in. "Guys, I would like to talk about this more with you sometime, with either or both of you, but I must go—I have just found out I can bring one guest to Berlin in April, for the Chancellor's official, ah you know, banquet—would one of you like to come with me? Bannerman?" Bannerman and Clare look at each other, sadly. "Or maybe Clare, I think despite the accent dein Deutsch ist ein bisschen besser, oder?"

But when there's no comment from either of these two suicide-watch cases, Dmitri stands up, the *Feral Tribune* tucked under an arm, leaves some coins on the café table, winks a ciao, and is gone.

Air-djinn watch the scene and moan their dissatisfactions under the gaps in doors. On Kazandžiluk Street, hanging copperwares chime discordantly amongst themselves.

"Clare," says Bannerman at last. "Don't let him get to you. I've got you. I got your back."

She gives him a distant smile.

Leveraging the jealousy bears a heavy cost, is its own form of soul-rot, trying to convince everyone, including himself, he's okay with all this indifference. As in the case of Zanna Agneri, who he sees again, Zanna from the abortive double date in January.

Clare goes, "What, the date-and-a-half? At Rotop?"

"That one. Oh man, it was nightmarish. It was the end. It was the freaking Twilight Zone. Stop laughing. So I take her out to Kibe, and dinner goes fine. Well, we're both so kind of *horrified* to be out with each other, after last time, it's clear neither of us can get anyone else to go out to dinner, so by kind of mutual agreement we hit the wine pretty hard, and so the main course is all fine. Mainly just the sound of drinking. And then dessert comes, and the first sign of trouble is when she leans across and sticks her spoon in my ice cream. You know those tall ice-cream glasses they have? Yeah, so I'm just getting going on my ice cream, three scoops, when she leans over, sticks it right in, and it's not like she's helping herself or anything, which'd be fine, it'd be cool, a good thing. No, she just starts stirring the ice cream around really slowly, and I'm looking at this, and my flavors are getting all blurred together, and I'm like, The Fuck? And I look at her, and she's staring at me with what she thinks is a sexy little grin, and she goes, I like your sweet, Bannerman. No seriously. I SWEAR TO GOD. So I go, well have some then, while it's still three flavors, and not, you know, *soup*. And she's like, I want your sweet . . . a lot. I SWEAR TO GOD. So at this point I realize she's just, fucking nuts. I mean, she's not unattractive you know—no okay, I know—well you—you've got your own—yes yes bitchiness aside, she's good-looking. She's fine-looking. So it dawns on me, the reason she can't get anyone to date her, is cos she's cold fucking crazy. At this point, and for the rest of the night, I'm scared. Actually scared. Picture that. We're dancing, I'm trying to dance, she's rubbing herself all over me like she's, I don't know, trying to *mark* me or something, and I'm kind of trying to pat her down for weapons. The whole thing is hideous.

"So we end up back at her apartment, and we're necking on her sofa, everything's going fine, she's been basically normal for a good thirty minutes. Then she stands up and tells me to make myself at home, that she—yeah. Yeah. She actually says it. I tell her don't worry about it, c'mere and kiss me some more, but she's adamant, she's going, so I beg her, Clare Leischman—I get down on my knees and beg a girl not to take off clothes. I *implore* her. But she thinks I'm kidding or something, and she touches me on the nose and takes off. Yeah, that little, *aww, you're cute* thing. I almost imploded right then from—I don't know, pure shame. On her behalf. So she's in there, I swear she's gone for like ten minutes, enough for me to sober up a little, meanwhile she's clearly getting herself all fired up in there,

there's the sound of spraying and blow-drying and like heavy *machinery* coming from the bathroom, and I'm debating whether I can just take off now, but I decide I better wait until she comes back out. So she comes out wearing something just—actually I'm not even going to—yeah, it's too shaming—so she comes out and I start my little speech, look it's been swell, and all that, but she just shushes me, I SWEAR TO—. She shushes me and throws me a little packet, from across the room. Yes. And I'm like, oh sweet christ she's just thrown me a condom, before I've got my *shoes* off, it's now so awkward I'm practically *English* with embarrassment—she's totally fine, of course—and this is when I notice that this is no ordinary condom I'm holding. No. She has just given me a—. Yes. Okay. Enough's enough, edelweiss. It's not that funny. So by this point, the deal is so massively broken, I'm like, you know Zanna, I'm not sure this is going to work out, but she's not taking no for an answer, she's not even really asking any questions—she's just: what's it going to take for you to make love to me. And things are so excruciating by this point, I think, I'll just kill it dead, and get gone. So I'm like, 'to be honest Zanna, a quart of vodka.' "

A moment listening.

"Course not. I drank it, fucked her and left."

The photographs of Bannerman grow starker, more deranged. Ariel fingers them tenderly. The boy is in free fall. He knows what he must do, but cannot . . . Ariel bends close to the print. "There is valuation in the dating scene, Bannerman, same as the black market, gray market, eBay, whatever," she whispers. The acoustics are strange, an insufficient reflection, as with snowy days. "We all have our currencies. But it's hard for people, I don't care how well-meaning, to avoid this squash-ladder thing, that some people are worth more or 'above' others. Your valuation can be manipulated. Every teen movie says so. You are flooding the market, you keep chasing her like this. Ease off, man."

That night Edgar blunders into her darkroom, finds it nearwallpapered with pictures of Bannerman, and, for the first time in weeks, screws his girlfriend like he means it.

"Bannerman, listen."

Oh he's listening. He's listening to Clare's voice, not her words: listening for the tone that presages the comma-but. It will be unmistakable and absolute. The clauses that follow are not the preamble to the end, her explanation of why it's not working out; they're not even the beginning of the end, not even, in her formal repudiation of him, the end. They're not even relevant. Already off the map. And here they are, as deafening as the tolling of the Liberty Bell, and with as total destruction for his heart:

"Bannerman, look. You're a really amazing guy—"

*   *   *   *   *

That'll do. Ariel won't take any more pictures of the boy now, with a smile that reads like a scream, almost vanished behind some lens-flare. They talk to you, Ariel, they ask you to stop rubbernecking at our misery. Yes the aesthetics of misery are wonderful, but please. Enough.

Ariel finishes up, switches off the red light, and gets into bed with the man she has chosen.

Because you know Ariel, soon there will come a time, alone in a room, when you'll take down your old copy of *Ariel*, red white and blue dustjacket ragged at the edges, and slowly read, a frown deepening across your eyes . . . as you move away from thirty, which is as far as Sylvia Plath ever got, you might find other connections between you and her etiolating and snapping too . . . and that most famous poem in *Ariel*, "Lady Lazarus," might address you less directly than before:

> *Dying*
> *is an art, like everything else*

you'll read, and it might be it just seems less profound now you're a mother, ennobled by the defense of your little ones, maybe you don't have the stillness of mind anymore to really get it. But doubts creep in anyway, about whether Sylvia Plath wasn't, eventually, just a silly little girl?—playing chicken with death, frolicking among these Oscar Wilde-isms, and soon enough you'll read "dying is an art" and by now you'll have seen a few actual deaths yourself, and think, hmm. But nevertheless want to get into it more, read more of what Sylvia foresees for this year, but there will be dinners to cook and stories to read, lives to be shepherded toward happiness, and soon the book will be tidied away into its place, a place it will end up keeping for decades, its spine fading to white, lonely of company, and with only a postcard bookmark to hug.

Kriminalace

"TWAT," FAT MAORI finger quivering over Animal's desk, "you almost got me fatwa'd."

Also furious it took him four weeks to find out who arrested Vane Novane. His own *pals*. Animal got going right away with a barrage of agreement to all Frito's complaints: the underhandedness, the cavalier values attached to First versus Second World lives, all while signaling imperceptibly to Brick Lahoussaye. Brick slips out of the room, comes suaving back with a tray of freshly foaming Sarajevsko Pivos, Frito takes a sip and the anger drains right out through his feet.

"Well—hope you're not going to make a habit of it," Frito mumbles to a close.

"Absolutely. Terribly important. All sides *do* have to face justice."

"I know, I know . . ." Frito looking pained out the window.

"Cept us," says Brick.

"Naturally," Animal agrees.

"Well sure, but," Frito waving such niceties aside, "guess I just don't understand," his confusion turning back at them, "why you didn't involve me?"

Ah, so. Brick and Animal interglance, and start the routine. "In a job like ours . . ." Animal's sausage fingers interlaced on the blotter in front of him. It's a pretty insulting speech really, featuring need-to-knows, implicit acceptances of risk, facts of life, and worst of all "that's Bosnia for you" shrugged off onto him like contempt, like he's some kind of warzone tourist aghast at—a-actually seeing some *war*! Frito nods quickly, trying to hurry them through the whole demeaning spectacle, but he did ask for it. Poor Little Civilian. Didn't Get To See The Gun Fight.

"Besides," Brick with a bit more sympathy, "not many people want to get their hands dirty for Vane Novane. We asked around. Everyone said basically what a tosser he was."

"Certainly not Vedo's people," adds Animal, "there'd been a dust-up with them a few years ago. And, let's face facts, Vedad Alimović isn't an idiot. He knows which side his bread is buttered."

"Meaning what?" suspiciously.

"Oh come on man," *man* in the Noël Coward usage, "everyone knows what you and Bannerman are up to. Vedo's far too canny to chuck you now. *You're* alright."

Frowning, Frito takes a deep breath, his mana's being seriously impugned here, growing into a taua warrior ready to avenge himself at any of a number of insults—but collapses, exhales noisily, whines, "What, *everyone*?"

"Break out the whiskey," sighs Animal.

Yes, in Pareto-optimal town, everyone. F&B Consulting has pulled together. Exhausting and closely argued negotiations with ViKA Spekulacija finally stabilized a venture capital deal for F&B Consulting's online pharmacy, incorporated in Bosnia as "FB Lijeka, d.o.o.," investing 1 at 1. Which means: Frito's managed to convince everyone that the value of their online pharmacy, properly discounted, whose assets are basically a client list, EU funding agreements, and suspiciously high "goodwill," is €1.000.000—and to persuade Vedad Alimović to invest a further €1.000.000 on top of that, in exchange (this was the hard part) for a 49 percent share. Frito went to the line insisting on a one-million-plus valuation for FB Lijeka, eventually settled on €950.000 funding. He refused to cede control.

For his money, Vedo gets two directors on the board below Frito and Bannerman, but *above* them in the management hierarchy. This very Dayton arrangement means that Bannerman and Frito, demoted to Development Managers, will keep new clients coming in, Internet marketing and all that, which according to the Business plan is something they know all about. Zaim Spaho is given the honorific title Chief Information Officer (CIO), but is still not even a full-time employee. Okay. Everyone's ready to knock heads together.

The street-gang tradition. GlaxoSmithKline got a thirty-year lockdown on AIDS drug AZT? Not a problem. AstraZeneca trying to extend its expiring patent on Prilosec? Screw em. Indian drug companies like Cipla have been doing the same thing, producing generic versions of patented Big Pharma drugs at a fraction of the cost. Unashamedly ripping off the West, it's lives that are being saved after all, but it's as clear as anything that these Indian operations are going to be shut down soon. The Indian government knows what's what, will never make Security Council while it's pulling that kind of anti-capitalist crap. Leaving a gap for the phoenix of Bosnian industry to take over where they'll leave off in, say, 2009 . . .

It'll get nasty. Intellectual Property Law has been a knife fight for ten years now, and ViKA's attorneys will have their work cut out, but getting sued by the likes of the Pharmaceutical Research and Manufacturers of America (PhRMA), the European Federation of Pharmaceutical Industries and Associations (EFPIA) and the International Federation of Pharmaceutical Manufacturers Associations (IFPMA) is the sort of thing gangsters' lawyers are for. They enjoy it.

Yes the dream is grandiose, if it comes off even a 1 percent market share will sort Frito and Bannerman out with sports-team-owning money, so correspondingly Frito fought tooth and nail to keep 51 percent ownership. He knows the road from gangster to industrialist is littered with the bodies of insufficiently paranoid business partners. Not that, in the end, that knowledge helped much:

"Our disagreement over Vane Novane was not with you," Jasim the majordomo told Frito over the phone, "but with your language assistant."

"What, Maza? I thought she was cool with you guys?"—"We also."—"Look, even if Maza did finger Vane,"—"Yes."—"Which I know you believe,"—"Yes."—"even so, Vane would still have had to turn himself in."—"Which is his choice."—"It's not like it's a major upset . . . you seen the sentences ICTY are handing out."—"Yes."—"It's nothing. Two years, four, tops!"—"Modest, I agree."—"So then."—"May I speak?"—"Go for it."

"You have hide Maza from us. On the other hand, we have placed great trust in you, by buying your business Mr Frito."

"Not all of it."

"We have great hopes for this business, but you endanger these hopes against Vedo's anger. You think: politics is politics, but business is business. You are wrong. Vedo does not need your business. He will lose every his businesses, every KM, before he loses his beliefs."

"Don't doubt it."

"As always, there are arrangements. The peace process needs appearance of balance, so Serbs do not feel victims. So the Tribunal needs Bosniak indictees, to make numbers to be more same. But in reality, numbers are not same. Yes, bad things are done by all sides. All. But this is true also in Second World War, no? You English burn Lübeck, Dresden, more dead than Hiroshima . . . you are not proud of this, I think. But it does not mean that you are as same bad as Germans."

"I'm a New Zealander."

"So this is situation. Vane Novane will go to political trial. He was good lieutenant of Juka Prazina, before Juka goes," searching for the *mot juste*, "clinically insane. There are many. Also Naser Orić, defender of Srebrenica, he will be arrested soon. Ask your woman at OTP. The prosecution builds strong cases against this men, and defense? not so good. So Vane must make his own defense, but he is not ready to go to The Haag, because he is looking for his witnesses. These men are disappeared; they are all in Frankfurt, Oslo, Dearborn . . . who knows? Without these witnesses, Vane might get—who knows?— ten years. In order to make Serbs feel less 'victims.' Commander of SFOR, General Ward, we have spoken to him, and he understands this, and he gave Vane Novane more time. So you see. This is annoy- ing, what Maza Cukić has done, to sell his location to File 13 Con- sultants, who get him like *this*!" a snap of the fingers. "This is bullshit, you see. Vane is hero of Bosna-Hercegovina. So, I think it is necessary if Vedad Alimović will speak to Maza Cukić, he will decide what to do."

"Don't suppose if ICTY put Vane back, that would . . . ?"—Jasim Bukić chuckles politely. "I just want to make sure that you're not going to get tricky with her."

"No, no," dismissing the absurdity of the idea, "it will not get tricky, because we have her father."

*

What else? A settlement to smooth the matter over, extremely out of court, and worth 2 percent of FB Lijeka, a "token of friendship." Well, phooey. That's what happens when you get into bed with the kriminalace. Maybe "control" was always going to be an illusion, even with 51 percent. While Maza, chastened, gets her dad back, and they rejoin the swim of life, tentative in their own neighborhood, Maza helping him carefully across the pitted cobbles to the supermarket, while soulful eyes watching from cafés know the whole story. For selling the information to File 13, Maza got €500.

"Five tons? *I* coulda given you that."—"I am so sorry, Mister Frito."—"Aw not with the 'Mister' again."—"Sorry, sorry."—"There there Maza, no worries. It's all over now. Long as your old dad's in good working order, and looks like he's got a few miles left in him eh?"

Frito knows which way the wind's blowing, it's only a matter of time before they get edged out entirely. In June FB Lijeka will be "merged" with ViKA Lijeka, the euphemism by which Vedo's laboratory interests are known. By July Frito'll have sold out to his partners, leaving Bannerman facing some dilemmas on his own finally, for example the project called "Mala Kula," which formally comes under the Research & Development budget, but whose breakdown is all off the books, and which no one will talk to him about. He'll be like, ¿WTF?, to put it mildly. But he'll have gotten passable at speaking Bosnian by now, and wise enough to spot that there's a lot of hiding behind the language barrier going on. Ostensibly yes, they're pending license approval from the relevant government agency to synthesize opiates from morphiates, the legal, and expensive, process. The new CEO will have explained the regulatory structure to Bannerman: the hoops to be jumped through; what *will* happen. Talking patiently while apparently possessed by some kind of Alien Eyebrow Syndrome, semaphoring something radically at odds with what was coming out of his mouth, which was no doubt technically true: ViKA Lijeka will produce high-purity chemicals for clinical use: codeine and so on. Many of Bosnia's hospitals have indicated they're interested in whatever's going, as long as it's cheap. As have, unofficially, any number of aid outfits: the auditing of restricted drugs is a lot less thorough in hospitals built out of stacked shipping containers.

Well, O.K., message received, Bannerman's not going to look too close. Their chairman is a powerful man who made his first fortune running arms, which left him with plenty of contacts inside Afghanistan, monoculture country if ever there was. Paperless transactions, *hawala* or blood honor banking all the way. Right. It's not Bannerman's patch, but he *is* a director. So now it's *him* in the Kenneth Lay position, strong suspicions about funny business within his own organization, and what's he going to do about it? Turn a blind eye, is what. Sure. What else can he do? He's not in *charge* charge. And he has no *moral* objections to certain plant extracts over others. Still, that's how quick a peek at the trough will knock the corners off his idealism.

Because at thirty he can no longer deny that there is a point at which wealth stops being irrelevant to the heart, becomes genuinely problematic if not for happiness then for comfort, not to mention relationships, the stuff happiness is built of—and what intelligent, tender, funny girl in her late twenties can let herself fall in love with an old man of promise? He knows Clare likes him, is physically attracted, finds a security inside his arms—but if there's no financial security, is it really security? He'll be the first to admit: if his twenties were all about railing against that, well he's out of breath now, and maybe it's time to take life as he finds it and start building some reserves. If he doesn't start making money now, when will he. She wants to *escape* her Swiss prison.

The fulcrum of many compromises. So he'll go along with the Mala Kula arrangement, its legality ragged around the edges, not least because it's the only one on offer.

"Don't even tell me, man!" Khan Kerensky shouts, pre-emptive, when Bannerman is on the point of worrying aloud about these things. Khan takes off his pointy hedge-funder sunglasses. "Not *me*, anyway—I got fiduciary duties, disclosure or jail, crap like this. Besides. There is not a single company in the whole of the Former Yugoslavia, that I've seen anyway, is clean as a whistle. Listen to me: whenever you have this attack of scruples, go hang in a Wall

Street bar on a Friday night, get talking, see how you feel Saturday morning."

Frito's more *polako* about it than Bannerman is. "Just the entry costs to business in a frontier town. The laws have higher elastic limits, mate. They're like the ropes in a boxing ring, they're there to be used. Just got to make sure we're not bending too much of our own stuff eh," Frito twinkling, "but in the long war for Clare, it's probably worth it."

Bannerman's straightface is impeccable. "The long what for Clare?"

Frito grins. "Don't even bother, Ban-O."

"Of course this is worth it! Everybody has business with ViKA!" Vedo himself, coming round to the warehouse in person, time to time, to check on progress, remind everyone about the Golden Rule. "You have seen *Dani* newspaper this week? They are writing these— many lies about me!" waving the offending issue around, carefully opened to the correct page and outlined with thick black marker pen, arrows pointing at it, "So today Haris will go to shoot office of *Dani* newspaper. It is how we do business! No, do not worry," to pre-empt Bannerman's vocal discomfort, "they do not mind. It is—little game. It is good for business, we shoot office of *Dani*, no one is hurt, just the bricks, you see—they sell magazines! Also, more people read magazine, so they are fear of me, ha ha! Good for everybody! And I give very good price! Oh—" his face darkening, "too good, now I think of this. Haris, make a note."

His arrival preambled by the arrival fifteen minutes earlier of some of his colleagues in Porsche Cayennes. Gives the boys time to put away the PlayStation, sweep the stock creep into orderly piles and drape tarpaulins over, and make sure the Comprjon Lijeka encapsulating machine's going to at least start this time. All it does is compress active ingredient and powder into pills, with a little F+B indentation (the pride!), but jesus it makes a song & dance about it. Zaim Spaho and a whole sub-routine of other engineers he's personally hired will have been working on it for months by this point, weekends and evenings all summer, cash in hand and as much burek and beer as they can handle, while they tinkered, ratcheted, screwed and otherwise hammered away at the fucker.

It's an idiosyncratic machine. Chugs like a locomotive. When it starts, you want to shout All Aboard! Bannerman sort of starts to do that, but peters out, halfway through, like his heart's not really in it . . .

"And what are this pills?" Vedo scooping a handful of the little white tablets collecting in the stamping tray.

"They, uh—Bannerman?" Frito asks.

"Uh, they're," Bannerman's been a zombie all day, something wrong with him, "uh, prolly-like," he croaks, "finasteride?"

"Finasteride," Frito tells Vedo decidedly. "For baldness."

"Baldness, famozan, famozan!" Vedo's smile goes all the way round his head, the outside edge of all eight premolars, including the gold one, clearly visible. "In all history, no man is losing money selling cure for baldness!" he cries in delight, then says it again in Bosnian, for the benefit of his jaranes, who find it hys-*terical*, bent over gasping for air, slapping each other on the back. But Vedo's on a roll: he shouts another wisecrack, indicating his own thinning patch, and crams maybe two hundred pills into his mouth—at this, his men are just *dying* laughing—and then something completely unidentifiable, spraying soggy tablets all over the warehouse, and the men will surely need hospitalization.

When comedy hour is over, Vedo gets taken through some spreadsheets, initials pages and signs off on accounts, likes everything he sees, slaps everyone's cheeks, and is about to go, when he sees, written in luminous green paint-pen on the breezeblock end wall, Frito's little ongoing *rapunga*, or quest, represented by a complex flow diagram of circles, arrows, connections, and boxes, in the middle of which, spraypainted in bigger, are the

REASONS SARAJEVO DIDN'T FALL

1. PLUCK
2. US / AQ ARMS SMUGGLING

3. VRS Timid After Vukovar

4. 360° TV Defense

5. Decoy War

"What is this?" smile flying off his face and out the door. "You boys write shit on my wall?" stomping over to it, voice climbing to a shrill scream when he sees "VRS" in there, "*VRS? Why you write this?*" now veins-in-neck screaming, "WHY YOU WRITE VRS ON MY WALL?"

Which takes an amount of uranium-grade care until Vedo is soothed back into human form. Everyone knows the corpus callosum story.

"But this is—all wrong, this TV, Vukovar, nothing," fat hand forming a teardrop, five fingertips together. "We survive because Chetniks are shit, and we are strong. This only."

Frito looks from Bannerman to Zaim, back to Vedo. "Takes a little more than strength, right?"

"No. Strength. All Caco had was strength."

"Ćaćo?"

"No, Caco . . ." the droogs nodding in solemn reverence at the name. Vedad's eyes glaze over. "Caco was musician. This only. From Sandžak. But like me, he sees war is coming, so he makes whole brigade to defend Sarajevo. He has no money, no weapons," Vedo banging his fists together inches from Frito's nose, "he gets both. This is strength! hey! boy," pointing at Zaim, "you tell to them about Caco!"

Zaim stares back at Vedad for a dangerous length of time before turning to Frito. "Mušan Topalović, 'Caco,' was a notorious *kriminalac*. Gangster. He made his gang into a private army. Yes, he defended Sarajevo, and yes, he saved it. Probably. Caco and Čelo and Juka and all these many kriminalace, all these friends of Mister Alimović," bowing slightly at him, "they saved Sarajevo. At first. Then it's the mafia as usual. They make money. They fight their own little vendettas, against police, the army, each other, they trade with the VRS. They sell things to VRS, the VRS sells them guns, they sell guns to Army General Karavelić . . ."

"Sorry hang on, the VRS?" says Frito. "The Serb army was selling them guns?"

"There is mafia on all sides," Zaim shrugs. "People think it was Serb siege of Sarajevo, but most time, it was really *mafia* siege of Sarajevo."

"Er—"

"Mafia everywhere. You know this. *They* don't want to fight, they want to make *lova*!" rubbing his fingers together, to sheepish pride among Vedo's crowd. "The siege closed the city's whole, what do you call it, white market. Black market prices were as high as the sky. Field commanders made very much money selling rakija, dizel, guns—and Caco, Mr. Alimović, Hasan Čengić, they are all buying weapons from VRS. Everyone is happy. And like this, Sarajevo will never be captured."

"That's just—" Bannerman's astounded, "wait, they persuaded the *enemy* to sell them *guns*?"

"Nobel Prize territory," agrees Frito, "peace or economics, take your pick."

"Trust in wisdom of market," Vedo beams.

Which is also what he used to say during the war, being shown around the lines he had helped arm, pausing occasionally like the dignitary he suddenly was to chat to the troops, bestowing kind words, taking on certain wise-old-imam inflections: "Trust in the wisdom of the market, for it shall provide." Handing out Hands of Fatima stamped from melted-down plate, talismans to protect against the evil eye: a hand with two thumbs and three fingers. An old Islamic symbol, worn around the neck. "The fingers also represent three pillars of market," kindly hand on a boy's shoulder, "viski, dizel, cigarette." A deep breath in the gloam, hair whipped against the falling evening sky, ink-blue setting for a whitewhite moon the color of Faith, and moving on . . .

"We really made these hands for Serbs," Vedo chuckles now, "you know they have—salute with three fingers? Yes? *He* knows," doing the Serb three-finger salute at Zaim, who gazes evenly back.

Zaim's mother was Serbian. She spent the war in the city, under the same siege as everyone else, a siege that took its toll on the embattled city's ideals of coexistence, and by the time she was shot—not by a sniper, at close range—in late 1993, Zaim had begun to slip into other viewpoints. His Muslim defenders were starting to look like what Belgrade had been telling him all along: hard-eyed janissaries stalking the streets, looking for some new Osmanli abominations to perpetrate. He could shake his head clear of it, see them for his friends again, but as they all left the Orthodox cemetery that time, lighting cigarettes for each other, he wasn't sure how long he could keep it up . . .

Executions happened. The gangs were taking Serb men and women from their homes, single round to the occipital lobe. It was hard to find someone to take a stand against it; there were undoubtedly VRS sympathizers, even soldiers, in the city. And as the siege wore on, the multiethnic character of the defense began to crumble under the pressure. The Muslims were fighting to the death, but the ethnic Serbs would be looked after if the city fell. Over the years of siege, these faultlines became cracks and then canyons, and soon front-line soldiers refused to fight alongside ethnic Serbs. No doubt in these bitter fragile minds, hemmed in to their narrow prison-reality, waking to find the day's probability for annihilation had crawled a few yards closer in the night, every night, every night for years, death "closer than their shirts," in the Bosnian—the pressure never, *not once* letting up—wasn't it reasonable, as the mosques fell and Chetnik threats were made good around your country, as your people died in the fields even as you huddled in your prison-city, the rest of the world quite prepared to watch you die and not lift a finger, the likelihood of your own child's survival dampening to zero— might it not seem merely due caution, necessary even, to eliminate anything to do with this implacable menace? Military pragmatism only, on a par with disrupting their lines of communications? And whose fault, really, was it? If there hadn't been a Caco, wouldn't we have had to invent him? Wasn't it us, after all, who prayed for some- one strong enough to save us, for an unscrupulous bastard who always came good out of any deal? And isn't that what we got?

But no. Ethnic Serbs who believed in a multiethnic Bosnia enough to stay behind, innocent people caught up in the war like the rest of us, were being executed. It could not be tolerated: this was what characterized the enemy, not Sarajevo. Ours was a defense not just of lives, but—when our children peered out of our broken apartments, open to the sky, trying to see the enemy invisible on the black mountains around—of nothing less than civilization itself. Caco was killed by the government in the fall of 1993.

After that terrible winter, by the spring of '94, it finally became believable that the city would not fall. It had been a time for strength. But there were plenty of other gangs besides Caco's, those of Čelo and Cile and Juka, and the commanders of all the other brigades, bad blood brewing between the Novo Sarajevo, Novi Grad and the Ilidža brigades, all competing for minimal resources, all smuggling their own logistics, stealing from civilians, working the Dobrinja-Butmir tunnel beyond their allotment. With no army at the outset, how could there not be clashes between our street-gang defenders? More than once there were mass confrontations, symphonically complex Mexican stand-offs, more than a hundred men all pointing weapons at each other, locked in a trembling hair-trigger tableau in the street outside Corps Command. Caco and Cile front and center, muzzle-to-muzzle with each other, in this most absolute of zerosum games . . .

For that was the year of *Reservoir Dogs*, released only months before and popular in the barracks. General Vahid Karavelić, ARBiH Commanding Officer of 1st Corps, had to run out of his own headquarters and onto the cobbles of Danijela Ozme Street, hands up and unarmed, standing at the wrong end of every single weapon out there, and talk every last one down.

Vedo was there.

"I saw this. This are men who has saved Sarajevo. Men who are strong."

Frito gets up, starts rattling the agitator ball in the can of green spraypaint, then stops and looks over to Zaim. "What do you reckon, Zaim?"

Zaim, arms folded, unable to look at Vedo, is silent for a long time. He reddens. It's clear he is flattered by Frito's gesture; even overbearing Vedad Alimović pauses as well, puts his hands behind his back, lowers his head, waits on what the young man has to say. There is a respect afforded to the dead. We are all doing what we can.

Finally Zaim nods. "General Karavelić was good man."

Frito rattles the spraypaint, and turns to the wall.

6. BEING BADASS

Prep

APRIL, AND THE butterfly gods have returned, as foretold, to liberate the city from its cast of ice. Kids pull Vespa wheelies amid the tires of Carabinieri jeeps, lines of laundry flap flower-smells through the air, spate has turned the Miljacka River to caramel, and suddenly the city squares are full, entirely full, of parasols, café tables, euro-techno, ripped-out banks of cinema seats and people thronging them, as miraculous and promising as new shoots in old weed-beds.

Animal Elliot-Maitland is one of them, who stands up to greet his breakfast companion warmly by the hand, even when Bannerman begins: "Things pretty shit for you, I guess?"

"Ciao, Bannerman. We're . . . getting traction."

"Is that army slang for 'fucked in the ass'?"

Animal smiles, orders the coffees, and wonders aloud to what he owes the pleasure.

Bannerman leans forward, puts his ten fingertips together. "I want to establish terms."

"Another highly professional foray into the bounty business?"

"Stevanjurović was *there*."—"Hmm."—"It's not my fault your boys are too cool to ID him themselves."

Animal waves it all away; they've been through this. "You had a proposition?"—"No, I was asking for one."—"I'm listening."—"I asked you first."

Animal sighs. "All right: if a third party supplied intelligence to File 13 that led directly to the capture of a PIFWC, for which a reward was paid out, to File 13, we'd be prepared to pay out twenty-five percent of any profit made."

"Profit," Bannerman tilting his head, "no one takes points of *net*."—"Look, it's negotiable."—"You'll have to do better."—"When I know nothing at all about what you're offering?"—"I have a meeting with a *very* interested PMC later today."

Animal makes a face like he's licked piss off a nettle. "*Who?*"

"Carbide International."—"Those clowns?"—"They're highly capitalized."—"Just tell me what you've got, *then* let's play hardball all we like."—"You're offering me monkeypoints! Forget it, where's Edgar? I want to deal with Edgar."—"I fear I'm all I can offer you."— "My question was, where is he?"—"In bed, most likely."—"Screw this, I'm off to see Carbide."

"Bannerman, sit *down*," a patience now demonstrably worn. "Look. I see that my very existence is offensive to you. But I suspect I'm going to like what you're offering. This could work out for both of us. So, to eliminate these obstacles, let's get it out in the open. Yes, I've slept with Clare Leischman, and yes, I enjoyed it. Of course. She's a wonderful woman."

"How many times?"

"But look at yourself! You're in the grip of fairy-tale ideals. Learn a bit of give-and-take, this is Bosnia! It can be rough, and women need to blow off steam, no less than you or I. Out here, perhaps more so. It meant nothing. *I* mean nothing to her, other than maybe, you know—" how to word this, "maybe she finds the fact that I'm over a foot taller than her . . . poignant."

"All right all right."

"You're clearly very important to her. Whenever we've been together—which, believe me, hasn't been that much—she spent half the time talking about you."

Bannerman tries to keep his face level. "Yeah?" at last.

"Honest engine. Blissfully unaware of it. But it was always, 'A friend of mine has this theory—' and, 'A friend of mine did this funny thing—' Clearly you. Jolly annoying. Ticked us right off."

"Us?"

Animal realizes his blunder, puts up a hand. "Just—let it go."

"No seriously—'us'?"

Amused, "You've been tapping her phone, and you didn't know about Marc?"

"Marc *van Xanthe*? Wait wait—tapping her *what*?"

Animal taps the side of his nose, points at Bannerman roguishly. "Why would you think—"

"Oh, don't deny it, look at you, you've a face like a slapped arse. Can't be that surprised, surely? We know all about the Gaarder-Spaho show. Two telecomms people stepping out, it's the talk of the town."

At this, Bannerman can only goldfish. Eventually: "I have an NDA here—" rummaging in a briefcase.

"Put it away."—"It's just a—"

"Put, your bloody, Non-Disclosure Agreement, away."

Bannerman glumly complies.

"Tapping your girlfriend's phone," Animal shaking his head.

"We had to try it out before bringing it to market, there was always going to be milk runs, betas, you know."

"Betas," amused.

"But seriously, who told you? Not Zaim and Ketyl?"—"No no."

"Carbide International?"

Animal leans forward. "What have you told them?"

"Nothing."—"Then no, clearly. Berk."—"Then how? What is this, common knowledge?"

"Not common. It *is* knowledge, though. In specialized circles."

"Fucking tell me already!"

"Let's call it Gulf War II brain-drain," airily, "everyone's being pulled out, you must have noticed. Dayton is yesterday's carcass. There's only a handful of people left running certain systems, the NICs"—National Intelligence Centers—"at Butmir are a ghost town, a lot of Chinese Walls have come down."

"Systems? Does Clare know?"

"No no, she'll be the last to know. Have no fear on that score."

Bannerman chains another cigarette. But Animal's sanguine about it, about its operational security (OpSec)—even in the city of perfect knowledge, it's fine, it's not compromised. The importance of not burning down intelligence streams. As of not involving Clare.

But it's a total disaster. Bannerman's scrambling to think through what this means for their own safety, him and Ketyl and *Zaim* who after all has *family* here—but his mood improves enormously when

Animal reveals that the "systems" don't, in fact, know anything beyond badly informed surmise:

"Anyhow, you've been following her around. How were you managing that?"

Ferhadija Street is a pedestrianized showcase of Imperial bombast and Western lingerie, set about with the usual run of apotekas, bakeries, frizerski salons, and Rafeissen Banks, and thick with teenage girls with red sinuses and go-thither eyes and jeans that fit too well. Sideways up a little alley and down a half-flight of crisp creamstone steps lies the basement door to Ponts Sans Rivières, a sassy little bar and the language assistants' main hangout in Sarajevo, where there's a free and lively exchange of gossip, alcohol, clients, dictionaries, the latest idioms, favors, slang, and abuse amongst the girls—all with floating values, naturally. There are no gentlemen language assistants. At least, none that ever come here.

Maza Cukić clacking down the steps in two-tone stilettoes, patent white and suede: "Zdravo zdravo, girlfriends—" and the reception when they enter blows Bannerman's hair back. A surge of hugs, airkisses, compliments, and comparisons on jewelries too samey for Bannerman to tell the difference between. Maza has evidently become something of a big cheese; not just running with someone as studly and wealthy as Frito but getting herself into trouble with Vedo Alimović seems to have given her a certain celebrity staus. Maybe it's just dreamy for these translators, so long Dayton's transparent people, to have one of their own become solid for once—actually to interact, however passively.

Eventually the crowd is scattered by the entry of a wiry woman, descending heavy-lidded into Ponts Sans Rivières, dressed up in a metallic-red pantsuit, with cheek and eye shadow to match. A cosmopolitan appears on the bar at her approach. Her lack of effusion, color control, and ease with the concept of article bespeaks a higher status, here.

"Fancy Miss Cukić, slumming with us in our little hovel!" she says. "We are 'plowing in tall cotton'!"

"You are 'all dressed up and nowhere to go,' Malina?"

"I 'dress for success,' Maza; you look like you 'undress for success.'"

"Resettled peasants might think so. A Canadian called me a 'living doll' today."

"A 'goo-goo doll,' I think he must mean."

"Ha! What English! Goo-goo doll does not mean covered in goo, Malina."

Malina shrugs, aware she's strayed off firm ground. "A chacun son goo," sipping her cosmopolitan. "Canadians can go to hell, anyway. They don't know shit." Downing the rest in a one-er. All the language assistants have their Lieutenants Pinkerton.

"Malina, listen, I'm 'hitting the road' up to Banja Luka tomorrow on business . . ."

"And you want a gig?"

"If someone wants to swap?"

"Doubt it, Iraq is 'killing the golden goose.' Maybe Selma. Selma!"

"Eh."

"Selma, you're translating at BL tomorrow?"

"For OSCE—" Selma looking Maza up and down, "—what have you got?"

Maza pulls a personal organizer from her handbag. "European Disability Symposium?"

Selma breaks into a broad smile. "Go fish," turning back to her friends.

"Magasins Sans Frontières?" Selma shakes her head from behind. "Peace Implementation Council?"

"Don't have this accreditation."

"SFOR is O.K."

Selma considers this. "No again."

"Partnership for Peace."

"I need money this week," Selma turning round on her stool, "Sorry. And I already looked to catch ride tomorrow, no one else is going to BL, so if you want gig, it is 'my way or the highway,' and my way is the 'buy' way."

"Sorry," Maza pretending not to get it, "the *what* way?"

"Buy way," Selma's chin coming up defiantly, "You must buy it."

"Ah." Maza turns to Bannerman. "You have lova?" she whispers.

"I have lover?"

"Cash." Maza rubbing her fingers.

"Well hang on," frowning, "you want me to *buy* her job off her?"

"Thirty percent discount is standard, for travel, hassle of working, these things."

"Forty percent in this case, I think," Selma smiles. "I think you want pretty good."

"Way way wait," says Bannerman, "you want me to *pay* for you to get a job for which you're going to get paid anyway?"

"Poor American boy," Selma pinching his cheek, Bannerman failing to swat her away, "think of your daddies in big finance towers buying and selling debt, O.K.?" Her hand letting go and trailing off and down his cheek, eyes full of an ancient sadness, "I know *I* do . . ."

A 6 a.m. start and out past the Koševo Stadium to Banja Luka. White morning fog draining from the valleys, a slow reassertion of color. Frito and Bannerman are in a camouflage, assured to be effective, of shiny gray-green suit, baggy at the shoulders, geometric-pattern necktie, gel in the hair. Cell phones in belt holsters. A two-hour slog through the winding mountains, an attempted though failed breakfast of čevapi in Zenica, and descending the hills into the fractured grid-world of Banja Luka, the capital of Republika Srpska. The National Assembly is a long white-concrete bunker, set behind tailored lawns—

"The fuck?" says Frito. "Their Parliament is on Karadžić Street?"

"Different Karadžić," says Maza. "The good one."

"Still," Frito shakes his head. "Hitlerstrasse, eh."

Bannerman stays with the car while Frito walks Maza up the steps, slower objects in a faster tide of delegates, journalists, observers and translators, all tumbling into the Assembly Building and a conference center vernacular: brass and glass doors, a lobby of gleaming parquet,

black leatherette chairs, pot plants, brass light fittings, and everywhere the double-headed spreadeagle of the Republika Srpska, which
with its red, white and black color scheme, and its central cross, tal-
ons out and wings up, looks somewhat, when you catch it out of the
corner of your eye, like it's beginning to acquire a familiar 4-rota-
tional symmetry . . .

Inside the actual Assembly Hall, there are rows of tables, micro-
phones, comfy swivel chairs, facing a high school stage with curtain
backdrop, where a succession of SDS deputies in manufactured outrage and genuine sweat are bustling around, slapping each other on
the back, laughing, muttering in clusters. Frito and Maza stand at the
doorway, scanning the room, until their eyes settle on one Staša
Rogac: a small man in a big suit with a crewcut, eyes set at random
about his face, and currently chortling with a colleague. Maza turns
to face Frito, but Frito gets his reassurance in first:

"You can do this," Frito straightening an imaginary imbalance in
her lapels.

"I can do this," holding his wrist like it helps.

"But it's O.K." Frito looks at her seriously. "You don't have to. We
can try something else."

"No, it's—we've been over this. I owe. I want to."

The semaphore is universal. Into a gray leather handbag so decked
with buckles, swatches and toggles that it looks military issue, Maza
makes a show of searching for something—timing it for when Staša
Rogac's bundle of delegates comes past on the way out to lunch—
flinging her head up in slo-mo, hair in an upward waterfall around
and behind her, eyes flashing and the beginnings of a smile. Male
radars all swivel off their heading. She taps two fingers against glossy
lips, and the group scrambles into a scrum around her, rubber soles
squeaking basketball-style, fumbling in a swirl of polycotton and
oaths, elbows in the face, heels on toes, the clattering of carkeys, cell
phones to the floor—culminating in a delightfully chivalric tableau
of proferred cigarette packets. Staša finishes second, his personal

space ruthlessly appropriated by a burly delegate with shaved head and goatee.

"Boys, boys," goes Maza, all Marilyn ingenue, before selecting a York brand from Staša. Staša preens. Goatee and the others grumble, take one themselves and light up.

"You're new here," says Staša.

"Why yes! And it's all so *wonderful*!" Maza hammering the Evkavski accent. "Until now I've been kept almost *prisoner* in the UN Building in Turktown," unhappy pout, "translating the ditherings of old men . . ."

Back at the Hotel Ekspidijent, Frito and Bannerman hang out in the room smoking Lucky Strikes, chatting about datastreams, firewalls and military frequencies, how it's all going to work, and talking more broadly around the issue, general cell-phone exploits, *that* fatal Sidekick weakness . . . fielding the occasional text from Maza, and comparing the butterflies each is getting at this scheme that will graduate them into full Bosnian patriots. For Frito that's motivation enough—and, Bannerman has to assume, he thinks it's enough for Bannerman, too.

"Big thing Maza's doing," says Bannerman.—"Sure."—"*Big thing*," Bannerman loading the words with as much meaning as they will bear.

Frito shrugs. "She does owe us."—"Us meaning you."—"Whatever."—"For five hundred euro."—"Aw get off the grass, *her dad's life*, you mean."

"They were never going to stiff her dad . . ." But Bannerman knows he doesn't know.

"Anyway. What's it matter—if it's to bag some Serbs, it's all good."

Frito's insouciance is getting to him. All the time Bannerman's spent with Clare, seems like her monomania about violence-to-women is rubbing off. "You think Maza's doing it for international justice? Or you?"

"Chill out, Bannerman. I'd lay someone for my country."—"You hero."—"Aw c'mon . . . don't reckon it's all that different for girls."—"Sex? *Rape?*"—"Rape, sure. But this isn't rape, this is consensual. The girls *I* know impale themselves on anything. No, c'mon, don't be like that. There's a sort of symmetry, eh? Isn't this what we've been taught all this time, equal and opposite effect, and all that? Though I grant you, it is literally more invasive, which I guess implies certain other," waving his hand around, "things."

"I think it's pretty bad. Sleeping with the enemy. Her mother died."

The boys look at each other thoughtfully.

"No you're right," Frito admits, "I haven't a clue what kind of weirdness this involves for her."

After an hour or so of this, Frito's phone goes *bing* again.

"They've finished lunch. They're coming."

Bannerman opens the window, Frito sprays the deodorant, Bannerman wafts a pillow around, Frito his arms, until presently—

"Okay. Under the bed."

The window is shut, everything put back, and they hide under the bed.

Voices outside. A key turns in the lock and Maza's patent whites step in. Black lace-ups following. Murmurs in Serbo-Bosnian, giggles; exclamations of mock prudishness; rustling; low groans of admiration for each other's bodies. The glistening sound of mouths, a spill of footsteps over to the bed. Maza sits on the edge of the bed, her heels inches from Bannerman's nose. It's a pine flatbase; so no getting their heads bounced on. Directly in front of the patent-whites the black lace-ups take a position, scuffed tips curling upward, looking almost eager, before being abruptly obscured by the seat of Rogac's pants. Shortly thereafter they are joined by underwear, and before long, a series of loud affirmations, directed at nothing.

Bannerman and Frito keep silent.

Then the suit jacket comes down, some shirts, a bra, the rest. Maza is making a lot of noise, enough to cover some pocket-rifling, but so much that Staša comments on it, taking credit. A steady commentary of *da da, doboro . . . ne ne . . . sada!* keeping Staša happy while providing some guidance for Bannerman, who by now has fished an ancient Nokia 6120 out of the trousers, and draws it back under the bed. From a backpack full of cabling he selects a nine-pin serial and plugs in, the other end of which leads to a laptop with a disabled fan, and begins to attempt to communicate with the thing.

Frito shakes his head, and with a small penlight and notebook starts to take down numbers. Hi- and lo-fi.

Oh but it's vile. Fingers that dig. A dry, muscular tongue that drags her flesh this way and that. A vigor presumed exciting but that touches violence. She presses on the peculiar stripe of hair across the small of his back as he humps her, holding him tighter to restrict his motion and maybe dampen the feeling of being beaten . . . but she remembers her breathing exercises, shuts her eyes, whispers *bismillah* and retreats, with occasional lapses at sharp pains, from the taut exterior of her own skin . . . It's O.K., it will be O.K. Staša Rogac can fade out, a memory already half-gone. No, on a level above this, there is something fine about it, if she can hold on to an element of—if not fantasy—then sacrifice. A coming home. For she is not the firstborn, no; she is no son at all. She is the sheep in the thicket, and content to be so, a throbbing carcass stretched into a long H upon the altar, that another be spared. A form of martyrdom. Lesser in the scale, of course, than her brothers, but she is no sehid; her life is not her greatest gift. As a daughter she has only her honor. The sword that plunges into her frees it from her guts. Honor rises from her now like cigarette smoke, twisting into turbulence and evaporating back to the Skies, to the blinding company of fathers and mothers . . . how she will weep to see you again. Thousands of you, forever lining up on your own soccer fields, squinting into the sun, breath coming into tighter chests, watching grease guns being put onto tripods, ammunition belts fed, and grace beginning to come upon you now, grace, or understanding, at least . . . and Islam meaning something more than "submission" finally, revealed as the white exhilaration you'd heard was behind everything, and beginning to show through rips in the sky. No room for anger, not now, just all the love you've ever felt come rushing back upon you, forming their own tears, and there's no shame in them, not now. The people you have loved deserve to have heard that fact aloud, from you, one last time before you went. Your own father in a room, alone, yellow hands clutching at spilled insides, calling for someone to be with him, even his captors, at least it will be human company in the face of that blackness . . . won't you go to him now? Or are you still proud in your childish way, do you still fear nakedness before your parents? No anger and not even a struggle, just acceptance, as we have been taught—so we will line up on this summer field, emigrants in the green, fully content with the loves exchanged while we were here, and now only waiting for a Chetnik hand to drop . . .

Bannerman's not having much luck with copying the memory. He can't understand what's wrong. Checking the connections. Nothing. Signals to Frito he wants to reboot the phone. Frito grabs him by the wrist and shows him his most unamused eyes—and gets back to taking down numbers. Commotion continues above.

Lot of numbers, and it's slow work. Approximate spellings. But he's being methodical, it's going to be okay, while Bannerman has entered the acceptance phase of computer rage, shaking his head, listening to the storm overhead. Which, despite Maza's best efforts, is already reaching its outro . . .

Frito and Bannerman freeze, look at each other. They're only at the M's.

"Not yet—a little longer," Maza abruptly leaving off the rhythm.

"No, don't stop!" cries Staša. His eyes widen as he finds himself stalled right on the cliff edge of orgasm and he lets loose a bloodcurdling shriek, fingers pressing the blood out of Maza's skin, and a thrashing of sheets that soon dies into nothing, followed by the slow *whump* of a body onto the bed.

Bannerman beckons for the phone. They've only got a few seconds. Maza is shushing and cradling her aggressor. Bannerman starts going through the phone himself, and Frito's eyes go wild, he's pointing at the pile of clothes. Bannerman holds the phone away, keeps browsing through the phonebook. Frito, silently, explodes.

Bannerman scrolls through to the R's. But the name he's looking for isn't there. Shit.

Faint stirrings, reawakenings above.

No Ranković. Oh wait wait: this is a Nokia 6120, address book only has one field, *course*, so it's sorted by first name, not last name— so we look under P, for Petar . . .

"You've had a good day so far," Staša says as he slaps Maza on a thigh.

"Wait . . . stay a while."

"No, I think you've had enough fun from me, *bula*," wiping himself on the duvet, getting out of bed, reaching for his clothes. "You think I didn't know? Ha, ha! So it's true what they say about the UN Building, public service, public house?" Public house, *javna kuca*, meaning "brothel." Staša cackles like he just thought it up, finishes putting on his suit, pauses at the door to say in English, "Bye bye, *bula*," and is gone.

"Disaster," Bannerman groans, driving back to Sarajevo.

"What? It was great," insists Frito, "what's your problem? We got half of Staša Rogac's phonebook. Staša *Rogac!*"

"It was worth it?" asks Maza.

"Oh totally, *totally*—" Frito and Bannerman both leaping to reassure her, again. Frito leans forward from the backseat and puts his arms around her shoulders. She hangs on to them.

Maza was near catatonic when Rogac left. Eventually she got up, showered, dressed. Smoked. All without breakdown, or emotional affect in any direction. And *then* she had to make it through the afternoon session, while Rogac pointed her out to his snickering SDS friends.

"No no, the whole thing was wildly successful." But Bannerman can't keep the postmortem entirely upbeat. He shakes his head reluctantly. "I mean, we didn't get *Ranković*, but Rogac didn't get wise to it *either*, so the numbers will still be good . . ."

"Banko Ranković, from Foča?" asks Maza.

"Right."—"How much is he?"—"A half million dollars."

"But we got Milan Lukić!" says Frito. "Lukić, mate! The fuckhead wiped out Višegrad!" slapping Bannerman's headrest.

"How much is he?"—"Five million U.S."

"Aw screw the *money* guys, this guy's like, chief Serb twat! We'll be carried through the streets! We'll be promenaded up and down Ferhadija at head height for *days*! Hang about—" Frito reaching forward to hold Bannerman's shoulder, "Ranković, isn't that the one my girlfriend got indicted?"

"Uh yeah I think it might be."

Frito applies pressure. "Why you interested?"

"Well, the thing about Petar Ranković . . ." thinking fast, then, "wait—Maza—what'd you call him?"

"Banko?"

But Bannerman's already grabbed the notepad and is flipping through it while driving, eyes going back and forth, thumb moving in jumps down the panicky pencil-scrawl: Anto D, Antonije Krakić, Badunić, Balkan Restoran, Balić, Banejević . . .

Which is how they find themselves back in Witness H-7's hut at the Tuzla DP camp. With a verified phone number for Ranković, Ketyl Gaarder will be able to access, without a warrant, Telecom Srpske's SIM number index, and load Zaim's program to channel the data out. Maza's recuperating at home with her old dad, too rattled to deal with any more of this, for the time being—so Ariel Alkali has been dragooned in to translate, Bannerman now the caring face of Western repentance, and Frito standing around useless in the Bannerman role. Bannerman removes an iPod base station from a rucksack, presses "play," and the ringing at the beginning of a call fills the room. Irma the witness's eyes vacate.

"Molim?" says a gruff voice.

"Prestani," nods Irma, eyes filling, and signaling for it to be switched off.

File 13 Consulting Ltd

CIVIL TWILIGHT IN the mountainways of Serb-held Bosnia—whiteknuckle pursuit of a road that leads the way, only just ahead, slaloming among cliffs, guardrails, walls of rubble held back with mesh fencing, swerving rock buttresses, darting nimble across re-entrants, out of debauches, into defiles, wheels skimming gravel over the edges of embankments, the valley broadening to accommodate junkyards and oxen, skeletal trees still bearing snow high on the embankment overhead—the road occasionally ducking into rock-blasted tunnels, and back out. Blackscape with a point light at the end, every journey's a near-death experience. Inversions of the black-white cliff shimmering inside the river below, the gloss reflections here and there occluded by ripples moving in bands. The exhausts of spirits upon their own highway, in convoy, returning upstream for the night.

—All right. Got it. We're gearing up. Edgar, get us dialled in.

—Yep.

Further along, the gradient gives out to a long stretch of dark evergreen and purple foliage, oil-puddle colors, hugging both sides of the road. The members of File 13 call present one by one, Motorola Iridium satellite phones on conference call, down here using the Mobilna Srpske GSM network, getting headsets comfy under helmets, seven voices at banter, someone singing "Why Don't We D-Do It In The Road."

—All right, bit of hush people. Kalazar One to Charlie Charlie One. Bravo One is mobile. Last-minute change of plan, minor detail, instead of channelling through me, our American friend at the com-

puter is going to be joining us directly on conference, callsign Kalazar Zero. Kalazar Zero, say hello to everyone.

—Ciao guys. Pleasure to be working with you this evening.

—All right.—Likewise.

—Like we practised, Kalazar Zero. Just the facts.

—Got it, Kalazar One. So, like he said, Bravo One is mobile. He
left the Višegrad cell a few minutes ago, has already gone all through
the next cell and he's into the third one and coming strong. Still, at
least twelve kilometers, clicks, east of your position. ETA you guys, I
guess, twelve minutes.

—Alright, thankyou Zero. This is it lads.

Headlights rush past in the gathering dark, and briefly garish
scenes, lit in forensic detail, flash on the retina: Saturated green and
yellow foliage, spruce and pine, birch just beginning to shoot. Black
shadows, white plumes of breath dissipating up into branches, giving
away our positions.

—This is Kalazar Zero to everyone, his signal's gone. He's in the
first tunnel.

—Eyes on the road, Five.

—Got it, boss.

—.

—OK, he's out of the first tunnel. Next tunnel is your tunnel, uh,
Kalazar Five. He'll be at you in two minutes over.

—Ready Four and Five?

Jefferis and Flameproof are parked at the side of the road in one
of the Land Cruisers. Flameproof at the wheel, Jefferis watching
down the road with the headset on.

—Still ready, boss.

At the ambush site the coverage is thick and ascends steeply off
the road. The second Land Cruiser waits half-hidden at the roadside
50 meters west. Hearts beat in our throats. The Sufi Child is crouched
next to Animal, dressed the same as everyone else, in full Green Army
combat gear, helmets and chinstraps, only a bit more short-arse.
What he doesn't have is a weapon. Animal watches him blinking
wide-eyed in the dusk. The only Bosnian they could trust, in the end,

not to have links, angles, vulnerabilities, vendettas . . . a nameless orphan. Animal runs a thoughtful hand over his own submachine gun, the gunmetal parkerized black, settles a finger onto the safety catch, and presses it flush.

—Kalazar Zero to everyone. Signal out, Bravo One is in the second tunnel. You'll have him in twenty seconds, Kalazar Five.

—Indicators on, Kalazar Four.

—You're looking for a green Opel Kadett, Kalazar Five.

—Probably, Kalazar One.

—Probably. Thank you Zero.

—This is Kalazar Four, we got him, it's the Opel, doing seventy kilometers an hour. Far as I can tell, driver and passenger only, repeat one driver and one passenger only, over.

—Positive ID?

—Too quick for that, Kalazar One.

—All right. Never mind, thank you Five. Four, get on his arse, fast. We're a go, repeat we are a go. Safeties off. Ski-ball ready, Three?

—Good to go, One.

Kalazar Three, Eddie Geddes, holds a nylon cord that lies flat and taut across the road. On the other end is a ski-ball, a tangle of nylon mesh and spikes that will burst tires and wrap itself around the axle, stopping a car in feet not yards.

—Don't let that cord flap about, you two.

—.

—Kalazar One this is Five, we can't get up behind him.

—Say again Five.

—There's two cars between us and Bravo One.

—Then get on the other side of em, Five.

—We're trying. But it's right twisty up here—and every time he pulls out, there's some fuckin character coming the other way. Every time, like. Frustratin.

—Five *get on the other side of those cars.*

—Copy. Wait out.

—.

—Kalazar One? We've overtaken one of em, can't get the other.

—Say again Five.

—The one car's tailgating the Opel. Looking to overtake. We can't get in.

—Get in.

—*Boss*. I just don't think we *can*. Try again and we'll spook him, you know?

Animal takes a deep breath, puts his hand over his mouthpiece, "Bugger." He stands up, snaps his fingers at the darkness. "Edgar."

Two yards away, Edgar Radford, Jr., stands up, shakes head and finger at Animal *don't even think about it*, jabs at Animal decisively. Animal nods. They squat back down.

—Five is there just one car between you and the Opel.

—Just the one, boss.

—Alright, ease off a little. Give em space. Everything as planned lads, there's two cars and an ugly prang coming, the second car is going to be today's little surprise. Kalazar Four, you are now covering the second car. Five, on Bravo One as planned. Kalazar Six, let's see you at that door before it's stopped rolling.

—Right boss.

—Let's hope it's today's only surprise.

Sufi Child, kneeling in the trees, shifts his weight. His ears pound. Short of breath. The air-wake of every vehicle thumping past makes him jump. Animal puts a hand onto the Child's shoulder. "Doing fine, son."

—One this is Kalazar Five, we are coming up to the treeline . . . treeline coming everyone . . . Opel's at the treeline . . . now.

—Seconds out.

This will be Animal's sixth PIFWC attempt. First under his own steam. They've all been straightforward so far. One spotter in a row-boat, a team hidden in the sticks, along comes your boy for a spot of fishing, team steals him out of his own shoes, chucks him in the car boot. Only once was there any trouble, an RS chief of police who pulled a gat and shot Flameproof Cooper in the leg. The rest of the boys let him have the good news. Non-governmental teams were routinely getting 60,000 Deutschmarks, per, for that kind of work—

damn sight better than Animal's package, Special Forces and Campaign pay rates included.

Terrific fun and terribly easy, and on the whole no one got hurt who didn't badly need it. Including Flameproof. But by 1999, after the first wave of high-profile arrests, the Serbs were getting bolshy, rumors of revenge attacks circulated, and NATO began to re-emphasize, on the SFOR website, that its mission was not to give in to mission creep but to "promote a climate in which the peace process can continue to move forward."

"We're not police officers," some chummy staff officer told Major Elliot-Maitland, "can't have everyone's Special Forces running about kidnapping people, every time someone's nose gets put out of joint. We're not *Americans*, you know," with that ingratiating remf smile.

One of many excellent reasons. Also perhaps, never mentioned during office hours, a distaste for what the witness list of a Karadžić or Mladić trial might look like . . . but Janvier and Holbrooke's pull with the top people must have dried up by then, because in June 1999 Madeleine Albright's State Department announced a $5 million bounty on Milošević, Karadžić, and two dozen others. Supply-and-demand would suggest that this would do the trick, but there was a strange phoney war: it took two years for Milošević to be turned in, with few "hot" arrests in any sector. SFOR was, at best, sitting on its hands; at worst, in the French sector, actively collaborating to prevent arrests. There was simply no upside for government armies: certainly nothing as compelling as $5 million was to private soldiers, hanging around bored and poor at Eagle Base Tuzla, McGovern, Carreau, Butmir . . .

Carla del Ponte herself, the Tribunal's Chief Prosecutor, has gone so far as to call publicly for "creative ways" of bringing indictees to justice who are "beyond the reach of SFOR." Well, Animal can read PR, a louder call for a vigilante posse he'd never heard—and his backers, City men all, could count the zeros on State Department websites. And so, again, Private Enterprise to the rescue.

As in any financial instrument, there are deceptions. Animal's motivation may not be wholly pure. Which is to say, creating shareholder value. Because he too got caught up in the UNPROFOR debacle back in the nineties, among these enclaves and antique artillery pieces, the forced marches and mutilated genitalia, propagandizing officials and his own Tory government's determination to stop anyone from saving anyone. Who knows what he saw out here. What in particular. All anyone knows is that one day the Union Jack shoulder-flash was no longer on his combat jacket. So more than likely there's something redemptive in this venture of his, a too-late repudiation of orders. Swapping armies.

His country disgraced itself. Maybe what he's really doing with this PMC is declaring for the UN, an organization without "interests," rolling up his sleeves like the man he was brought up to be to get some rescuing done. Too late for actual people. But not for more abstract things, for what Yugoslavia and Rwanda suffered for, to save it from being dithered into irrelevance by the Great Powers. Why not. The money's there. A grand dream, forged somewhere in these mountain forests, for private military companies to form the nucleus of an Army of the United Nations: human ideals, clear objectives, and free from the venal meddling of governments. Grand but still a dream, and dreams are shy and fear their names spoken aloud. Animal will wait for it to come to him. Because now, finally, roaring down the Višegrad road, here it comes.

And the Opel Kadett's in sight, sixty yards from the blind corner, forty, Land Cruiser behind them blocking easterly traffic, Geddes is stood up hauls the ski-ball across the road with twenty yards to spare, the Opel can't react before *Bam* the tires burst, bonnet dips, *flap-flapflap* tires shredding, the netting already wrapped round the axle, the bonnet rises again as the whole rear of the car jams into a skid, the Skoda behind fishtailing to avoid but smashes into the boot of the Opel, now immobile, with Deuchar and Geddes at the doors with MP5s, Animal in and releasing the seatbelts, dragging a bleeder by his collar out onto the road, Radford helping, everyone shouting THE FUCK DOWN THE FUCK DOWN ON THE ROAD DON'T EVEN FUCKING—

The Skoda has rebounded ten yards and skewed round sideways, Jefferis is at the driver's side with slung weapon, has pulled the door open and leaning in and doing something with the driver in there—

SAID ON YOUR FUCKING HEADS GET THE FUCK DOWN

"Ties, lads. Get the ties on. And the hoods. Good."

"Is this him?"

"This is him. Flameproof, get that man's battery out of his phone. You three: car off the road. Day-Glo vests on."

"Sokack? Sho—"

"Let me see." Edgar takes the wallet from Brick. "Recognise it, Animal?"

"Child, get over here, talk to him. All right."

—Kalazar Zero this is Kalazar One, you still there?

—Still here.

—Get onto OTP, run the name Šokac, S with a thing, O K A C with no thing, Šokac Marko, past them. Let us know soon as you can over.

—Got it, out.

"How are things over there, Jeff?"

"Not good, boss."

"Christ."

The second driver's face is a mess, lolling back where the headrest should be. Blood pumps in cardiovascular time out of what used to be a nose, the occasional bubble of blood and snot bursting, hands fluttering at his own face.

"He's in bad shape."

"So I see." A first field dressing across his face, morphine in the thigh, check the time and "M20:45" in marker pen on his forehead. Animal and Jefferis lift him out, carry him round to the passenger side, get him settled in. He's conscious but not making much noise.

"Bad sign."

"Anything else wrong?"

"I didn't have a poke around, just threw it on."

Animal nods briefly, thinking. "All right. Keep his airway clear. Watch for choking on the blood. We'll have to get him to hospital, somehow."

Jefferis and Animal straighten up, look at each other, briefly around.

"I'll take him," says Jefferis.

"We need to get him back to Višegrad."

"I'll take him," as evenly as before.

"You're sure?"

"Yep. No problem." Animal won't look away from Jefferis' eyes.

"No problem," Jeff says again. "We broke it, we fix it."

"You're a man, Jeff," Animal puts a hand on his shoulder. "His car drive?"

"Can't imagine—"

"Faith, man. Says Skoda, it's a VW underneath."

"Radiator tank's leaking. I'll need some water."

"Deuchs. Cooper. Give the man your flasks. Jeff: get on the horn to Bannerman, he'll sort you out with directions to the hospital, phrasebook, the lot. Thanks Jeff. Better let me have your gat. Chest-rig. Better hold on to your money. Anything else you want to give me? You've got your ID. All right. Get going. If he gets lippy just give his nose a tweak. Whatever happens, don't lose heart. We'll get you home. Good lad."

"Maybe Sufi should go with him, to translate," says Edgar.

"I have a funny feeling we'll be needing the Child ourselves."

Brick Lahoussaye stands in the road in a fluorescent jacket, waving cars past. Car crashes being the national pastime, they slow right down to look, a small queue stretching toward the east. File 13 playing the SFOR patrol, MP5K sub-machine guns very much in evidence. Terrorist-looking little fuckers, an edge taken off by the foldable stock, which gives them spurious length. Definitely not General Infantryman kit, but they'll work fine, as long as no one knows too much about NATO issue.

Ranković and Šokac are bundled into the backs of the two Land Cruisers. Questions, abuse shouted from cars with SCG stickers. Sufi Child instructs them to move along in his best official-military, and deepest, voice. Perplexity at his youth helping divert curiosity. Gun barrels and unmistakable gestures backing him up.

—Kalazar Two, this is Zero. Šokac is not on the indictee list.

—No, alright. Thanks Zero. Not an indictee.

Deuchs drags Šokac's hooded body out of the Land Cruiser, back onto the road with a thump. Šokac cries out in pain. Edgar looks round.

—Deuchs, the fuck are you up to? He's coming with us.

—Thought you said he wasn't an indictee.

—We can't leave him here, talk to the police and shit. Help me get him back in. We dump him later.

Šokac is hauled back into the Land Cruiser. Deuchar climbs in after him and holds out an elbow and a big grin as he drops onto him. Edgar shuts the gate chunk behind him, climbs in the driver's door, and they start in a spin of gravel toward the west, and the West, and past a sign saying CAPAJEBO 88.

"Bannerman, do not be a dick."—"I'm not."—"Then tell *me*."— "Clare, I can't talk now. Let's do this tomorrow."—"Sorry: I think I have a right to know. You call me up about random Bosnians—what are you, arresting people now?"—"Clare, I'm hanging up."—"Do not hang up on me."—"I'm hanging up ri-i-ight now . . ."—"If you hang up on me, Bannerman, don't ever . . ."—"Any second now . . ."— "I'm coming round. What are you, at the warehouse?"—"Ašenova Street."—"Fine."

Half an hour later, the sky blue-black, the File 13 Land Cruisers are eating up the road. Weapons and uniforms packed away in one of the underseat compartments, Ranković cuffed and fetal in the other one, a case of Lav Pivo out and cracked open along with some high spirits, just off-duty boys out for a drive is all, fielding the usual looks of curiosity from locals hitchhiking village to village. Sufi Child won't touch it. Serb beer. So Flameproof tosses his out as they pause at the Goražde junction, shouts *živjeli* as it plops into the mud in front of some locals, to blank looks.

And after a few kilometers, pulling off to a concrete roadside apron—the landscape empty of people—and with no headlights approaching—the rear Land Cruiser slows to a walking pace, opens its door, and spills out an unbound but still hooded Šokac. He stumbles, rolls, and comes to rest in the mud, the cloth over his face periodically bright in the headlamps of passing cars. He doesn't move, and soon the Land Cruiser is just a pair of red tail-lights.

Animal calls up Jamie Kells-Cameron of the Highlanders, at the UK National Intelligence Centre at Butmir.

"Cooking on gas," says Animal.

"That's not what we're hearing," says Kells-Cameron. "RS police channel's going mental."

"Is that right?"

"I'm afraid it is. Where are you?"

"Between . . . Goražde and Prača," signaling for the others to be quiet. "Half an hour from Pale. You coming to escort us home?"

"Bit of a wrinkle . . . you can't cuff it through by yourselves?"

Animal clenches his jaw. "I don't have the information for that. What's chatter on the RS channels?"

"They know Ranković has been nabbed and they know it wasn't SFOR. They're on the lookout."

"Are they? They have a description?"

"Ivana?"—a pause on the line, presumably a language assistant—"No, no description, just 'mercenaries.' They've set up vehicle check-points."

"And where are these VCPs?"

"Ivana?—Haven't said. Best guess, Inter-Entity Boundary Line."

"That's Pale. In fact that's *every* road back to Sarajevo. In which case, no, Jamie, if they are looking for us at VCPs then I would say we cannot cuff it through."

"Right, yes, I see."

"We are going to need that patrol you promised. I thought A Squadron was already out."

"Like I said, a wrinkle . . . can I get back to you in a mo?"

Animal clenches his jaw. "Quick as you can, Jamie."

"Right you are."

Flameproof relays developments to Edgar in the other Land Cruiser. No one's drinking now. The Land Cruiser fills with the hum of tires peeling off the slick wet road.

Kells-Cameron calls back.

"Tell me."

"Animal, this is Rory Duggan speaking, IO for The Highlanders. Jamie's asked me to give you a bell. Is there somewhere you can lie up for a few hours?"

"Patrol's off?"

"It's from above Dougie," meaning the Commanding Officer, "there's a lockdown on the vehicle pool, supposedly from Division. No one knows what for. Adjutant's·trying to get to the bottom of it."

"All right. We'll pull over. Call soon as you can. Thank you, Rory." Animal hangs up. "Bugger."

"Cops and robbers?" says Flameproof.

"Cops and robbers," Animal peering at the map. He calls up Edgar. "There's a lay-by two clicks up the road. Pull up there."

"They found the other guy already?" says Edgar.

"No knowing."

Edgar darkens. "Guess we should have gone to Filipovići," the German SFOR outpost near Foča.

"You're thinking in the wrong direction in time," says Animal briskly. "Alright, lads," once at the lay-by, "it would seem that the element of surprise is denied us. Again. Chances of smuggling the Rapist through a checkpoint I now think are too slim to be worth a shot. So I reckon we'll be going for a little bimble. Which soft bastards don't want to tab home from here?"

A certain high-spirited joshing among the File 13 boys. Sufi Child sticks up his hand. "Me," he says, "I do not."

"Can we at least *try* shooting our way through," says Flameproof.

"Child, I'm afraid I'm going to ask you to work for your money. You, Edgar, Brick and I will be taking Mr. Rapes for an extended walk uphill. Geddes, get the Child kitted out."

Flameproof shows genuine upset, comes to Animal in the busyness. "You're taking Brick and not me?"

"Thing is," a quiet hand on his shoulder, "I'm going to need you to coordinate getting us out of whatever shit we will inevitably get into up there," nodding at the black mountainside.

"Understood."

"Right. Deuchs, put your boots next to Mr. Rapes's, would you? Yes alright, would you mind lending him your boots. And can we get this lad a slightly less garish jacket. Flameproof, Deuchar and Geddes, you three get the Land Cruiser home & hosed, and put a rocket under those bloody Highlanders."

Edgar unhoods and unties Ranković, gets him into a black anorak, and bowlines a leash around his neck and waist.

"Right then," says Animal. "Lead on, MacDuff."

Bosnia's mountains aren't so very different from the Highlands, steep triangular numbers with rivers in place of lochs, and it's amongst such observations that the lads set south into the Jahorina massif, straight up an appallingly steep incline, using tree trunks as handrail, phones set to vibrate, a leash tied to the waist of their raping & murdering piece of shit, who apart from the moral side of things is otherwise the perfect hostage, behaving exactly according to type, and who even, as per manual, pulls the oh-dear-I've-sprained-my-ankle routine—

"Brick, the honours?"

"Gladly," and that's a big boot on his left hand, his little finger bent backward till the twig-sound and the screaming comes. After that, he's a poppet.

In a deepening darkness and as the road falls away beneath, there's much banter amid the labored breathing, Animal leading a singalong of "Sufi Boy, You're Going To Carry That Weight, Carry That Weight, A Long Time"; spirits high on the danger and nothing more than a biscuit supper, and knowing there's the whole VRS after them, speculating whether they'll have night vision or just set the dogs loose, and if so whether Brick will try to pull said dogs . . . talk of hunting the boar, wolves or wild goat that live up here . . .

And the Sufi Child taking what comfort he can from this bright Western enthusiasm, but shivering as he huffs along behind, only partly from the cold. His childhood has been full of fairy tales of foolish woodsmen who ventured into these mountains at night—tales told in the lulls when mountain forces were not actually, in real time, killing his friends and family. And now here he is, in apparent intentional search of such ghoulish fates, keeping company with a man whom the mountain ghouls—perhaps his former victims, Sufi Child's own parents, whoever they were—might stop at nothing to haunt.

"It's going on now?" Clare says. She came straight round to the File 13 building at Ašenova 25.

"There was a screwup. Don't know what. The guy I asked you about, Šokac? They left him on the side of the road, I guess the RS police got to him. Quick work."

"So who do we have?" Clare bending over his laptop. Bannerman lowers the screen a little.

"I . . . can't say."

"You're not going to tell me?"—"No."—"But I'm already involved."—"Sorry."— "*Operationally* involved."—"Not my call."— "You're going to need me from now on, somewhere, right?"—"Don't think we are."—"You are."—"I'll call when we do."—"You owe it to me, Bannerman."—"For *what*?"—"It's *me*, Bannerman. You love me. You can trust me with anything."

Bannerman chuckles grimly. "Those two statements do not follow."

Clare looks at him slyly. "Is it Karadžić?"

"No!" bemused. "Crazylady."

"All right, one down. Do you have an indictee list here?"

"Clare, stop. Please don't do this. It's important to keep OpSec in as tight a circle as possible—"

"OpSec? Man, what is this! Are girls not allowed in your gang, is that the problem?"

"Clare, look around you. I am the only person in File 13's control room. It's *that* sensitive."

Clare looks around. He's right. She's never seen it without at least two Sarajevans smoking up a storm in here. "He doesn't trust his own guys?"

"Right. His Bosnian employees, anyway. Get that. He's been employing these guys for *a year*, and *they* don't even know."

"What's sensitive? Why, how'd you track him down? Oh come *on*, Bannerman! Don't you want to be doing this *with* me? Together?"

"Clare, and I mean this from the bottom of my heart—" Bannerman rubbing his eyes "—fuck off. Seriously. It is not my call. You know what Animal's like." Then, looking up at her pointedly, "More than anyone."

Hip cocked, flaxen Hitler hairdo held with a pink clip, Clare looks at him a long time, then away, disgusted. "Not now, Bannerman." Then, bright as a new day: "Hey, have you eaten?"

"Can you see squat," says Edgar.

Balaclavas rolled down and scarves pulled tight, gloves on but hands in pockets anyway, File 13's prisoner detail has summited some kind of high ground. Subarctic wind raging from the east. A difficulty with the map. Animal and Edgar on their knees and comparing theories under a red maglite. Off to the east, the bottom of the valley is marked by streetlamps in a join-the-dots. In every other direction, a darkness of trees that the moonlight doesn't penetrate. It's hard going. The Highlanders' Rory Duggan got back in touch halfway up, told Animal he was frightfully sorry, but there was nothing to be done until morning. Took every ounce of grace Animal's ever collected not to tell him to fuck himself.

Now Brick stands to one side, MP5 angled at the floor in patrol position, holding Ranković by the leash, looking everything like a scrapyard Doberman that's turned the tables on its rangy master. Ranković, in deference and physical fear, talks in a low voice to Sufi Child. Sufi Child giggling companionably back. Brick watches them for some time.

"Witty fellow, is he?" Brick says at last.

"Good sense of humor, yes," the child replies.

"What sort of thing?"—"Nothing much. 'Trash-talking.' "—"Yeah? Like what."—"The usual."—"Go on."

Sufi Child sighs. "That as soon as he gets to The Haag he'll tell his friends to go to the Prnaša Tekija and cut throat of the Hodža slowly over the sink while spooning his blood over his head, the same as was done to my father."

Edgar and Animal look round.

"He is only making fun." Sufi Child staring him dead in the eyes. "I tested him. He does not really know my father," tickling under his chin. Ranković swats his hand away with bound wrists, and another comment, a seemingly more elaborate one. To which, again, Sufi sighs happily. "Oh, silly Banko."

"Kalazar Zero, this is Four," says Flameproof.

"Yeah no sure," says Bannerman, "your name comes up on the phone."

"Right. So I've got Six and Seven here, we're moving through Pale, there's a VCP up ahead—"

"VCP?"

"Vehicle checkpoint."

"Right, sure."

"Frankly it's not looking like a belly of laughs, so if I don't call you back in the next half hour, assume we been pinched."

"Great. What should I do about it, in that case?"

"Fucking Christ," Flameproof mutters, though not far enough away from his mouthpiece. "Get us out, ya gobshite. Chib something together. Get onto SFOR, The Highlanders, the Embassy, the policija, maybe Marijan at the newspaper, fucking anyone. Maybe get Isfan to get a crew up here," File 13's Bosniak employees, "anything. Go on a rampage. Make like Godzilla, get everyone out of their restaurants and fucking *doing*."

"Right. Do you have—"

"Numbers on a big fucking list, top left corner of the pinboard. Seen?"

"Seen."

"All right. We clear on everything? Any questions? Good. Out." The line goes dead, but Bannerman can still hear Flameproof shaking his head.

Clare lounges in the other swivel chair. On the desk around her, empty takeout containers, one and a half empty bottles of Herzegovinian red, a bottle of slivovic, a full ashtray, lighters, Kleenex, pens, the extraordinary contents of a handbag debouched onto stacks of official-looking A4. Dried red wine in the cracks of her skin-colored lips. A slow grin, hair collapsing into her eyes. "He's pretty nuts and bolts, that Flameproof."

Bannerman squints. "Another double entendre?"

"What! When have I ever made one of those?" playfully, "though he *is* pretty, admit that."

"Tell me you haven't." Bannerman shakes his head clear. "Actually no, don't even—just don't answer that at all. I don't even care."

"Sure you do."

"Clare," exhausted, "you see how serious this is. Please just stop, for tonight, torturing me."

"Of course," topping up her wine, "if you tell me who you've arrested."

"Enough," coming to stand in front of her. "Yes I am into you, but you need to wake up to the fact that tonight, I have other things on. Either behave, or get the fuck out." Pointing at the door.

"Okay okay."—"I'm serious."—"All right."—"So are you going to behave, or leave?"—Clare shrinks into herself. "Sorry."—"So you want to stay?"—"Yes please," in a small voice.—"And you're going to help me with this, help me get Flameproof and Co. out, if they get arrested?"—"Yes please."

Bannerman uncocks and reholsters his finger. "Right then." And he's on the phone to the duty officer at Butmir, finding out about the VCPs, if they're cleared by SFOR. Apparently so. Watching the location traces for the phones of Flameproof, Deuchar and Geddes stall in the Pale transceiver cell.

"You all right, Leischman?"—"Yep."—"I didn't mean to shout at you, but you were being annoying."—"I know. Sorry."

No sign of the others, last seen mid-mountain, a weak signal near the hamlet of Kamenica. Tracking southwest up the mountain range. Bannerman tries to raise them on the phone. No joy.

"It's not going to work if you're just going to sit there feeling sorry for yourself."—"Sorry."—"I can't concentrate."—"Maybe I should just go," Clare repacking her handbag.

Bannerman's turn to relent. "You don't have to *go*."—"You want me to stay?"—"Are you going to help?"—"It's clear you don't want me here."—Bannerman sighs. "No, I want you here."

"But why?" unshouldering her bag. "If I don't know who we're bringing in—no hang on, I'm not getting at you again, I'm just being, straight—essentially my knowledge base is useless. So what do you need me for?"

"Looks like I'm going to be up all night, I could use help staying awake?"—"You've got coffee."—"And the company."—"So call Frito."—"Yeah, I totally would but," Bannerman shrugs, "you're already here."

O.K. In the competition to trivialize their relationship, it's a winner. "All right. What else. Just the company?"—"You could hand me that bottle, I'ma need a shot of clarity?"—"Okay. What else."—Rubbing his deltoid muscles, "really sore shoulders . . ."

"Division has got wind," says Kells-Cameron, "they've got a bit shirty about it."

"*Shirty*?" Flameproof almost spits it out.

Two a.m. and Flameproof, Deuchar and Geddes have arrived, at last, at Camp Butmir. A protracted shakedown at Pale from the RS Policija, who combed through every angle of the Land Cruiser, while the boys were separated and questioned. Bannerman no sodding use, as predicted. An hour later the local SFOR unit checked in, Dutch lads with well bling weapons, came by and saw the situation, checked out File 13's accreditation, and persuaded the Pale authorities, with some difficulty, to let them go. A wall of text messages from Bannerman, all read by the VRS, when their phones were returned. His callsign Kalazar Zero, presumably for zero common sense.

"Yes," Kells-Cameron with emphasis, "*shirty*. CO's talked to Division. There was talk of suspending the entire battalion—don't ask, I don't even know what that means. It wasn't a pretty meeting, the word 'collusion' was being bandied about, Division practically blamed the CO for Bloody Sunday, the CO got pretty hot himself. It's supposed to be a very delicate time with the Serbs, they've been caught selling weapons to Iraq, in breach of *God knows how many* laws, Paddy Ashdown's been removing the kingpins from public office left right and centre," enumerating on his fingers, "the Serbs are very twitchy. The last thing they need is this. COMSFOR's white-hot. Upshot, everyone's agreed to meet at eight. Nothing's getting worked out any time tonight."

"We can't get a vehicle out?"

Kells-Cameron shrugs. "Speak to wheels yourself, if you like. Spaniard. He was pretty inflexible a few hours ago, I'm not sure being woken at two in the morning by merc gloryboys is going to make him any more inclined to see reason."

Flameproof folds his arms "Animal's on a mountain, and you're going to help yourself to some kip?" with an undisguised sneer.

Kells-Cameron looks down, rearranges the weight on his feet. Looks up. "Cooper. So you were in the Det, well done you, but *I* am second-in-command of the Sarajevo garrison, believe me I have other things going on, and I have wound my neck extraordinarily far out for you boys. I have burnt a lot of goodwill, pursued every avenue open to me, and I will continue to do so when the camp gets up in the morning. As of now however, the situation is firmly out of my hands, and I will be much more use to you, and Animal, and everyone, if I can get some sleep. So you boys will now turn on your heels and walk away from here, and while you're walking, think about this: If you ever take that tone with me again, Cooper, just once, as God is my witness I will bring the hammers down on you and your entire outfit, including Elliot-Maitland, so hard, you will never work with the Ministry of Defence again. Are we clear?" Eye contact with each of them in turn, and some mumbled apologies. "Alright. G'night, lads."

*   *   *   *   *

Brick stalks the mountainside, night vision goggles on, moving tree to tree, watching the gray panorama moan in the mountain wind.

Occasional pairs of mammal-eyes, bright as torches, stare from distant undergrowths. Wolves or foxes. Above, the Milky Way burns like a flare. No clouds means a cold night. Someway down the western and leeward slope, the others are asleep under the fir trees, dead tired, having walked for six hours straight, all four in bivvybags and cuddling against the cold. Brick smiles at them, spooned together, as innocent and gone as children. Ranković and Sufi Child the Lucky Pierres.

He continues his circling, a slow 100-meter diameter of their evergreen spinney. Bare mountain below their sleeping point. Chosen for such.

Then, on the wind, a single bright note over the white noise.

He adjusts the magnification on the NVGs. A crowdscene of swaying treetops, branches, and—somewhere moving inside it—along the line File 13 took—the occasional shape moving to a different rhythm. Smooth curves. A helmet, an elbow; a rifle cradled horizontally across the chest. Maybe a dozen. The occasional high clink of metal drifting far on the cold night air.

Brick moves swiftly back to camp, lifts the NVGs onto his forehead, brushes into the trees and squats above Animal.

Animal is fast asleep inside his balaclava. And then starlight is glinting off his eye. "Bit early, Brick."

"Visual. Four hundred metres."

Animal rubs his forehead, sits up. "Edgar. Child. Wake up. We're moving on. Silently. Quick as you can. Child, don't let on to Rapes that we're moving under duress."

Either the hurried repacking of rucksacks, Brick scattering handfuls of needles and pinecones over the flattened ground, or perhaps one glance too many in the same direction—because Ranković starts calling out at the top of his voice. Brick steps over and drops him with the stock of his MP5. The noise cancels.

"Thank you, Brick."

"Can I try?" Sufi Child offers.

Animal puts a hand on Sufi Child's shoulder. "My lads know this and you had better get hold of it as well, clearly and immediately.

There will never be anything personal in any of my operations. Are we clear."

Sufi Child nods quickly, flushing. "Yes Animal." Sober, he doesn't have as good a feel for the emotional seas.

"Good lad. Everyone ready? Brick, could you make sure they don't come on too strong? All right then. Edgar? Onwards through the fog."

Brick gets Ranković to his feet, unsteadily and leaking blood from his forehead. Brick offers a gauze bandage but Ranković waves it away, gathers his composure, mutters something at Brick, and falls into step behind Sufi Child, his leashmaster.

Ten minutes later Sufi Child pipes up: "He says he deserved it and it was good and strong."

Brick pats the Sufi Child good-naturedly. "I can let him have another if he wants."

The phone goes. Bannerman gets it on the first ring. "Animal?" A long pause.

"This is—Kalazar One, here," says Animal.

"Oh, yeah. One. Right. How's it going. In fact, how are you calling me?"

Pause. "On the phone."

"I mean you're not on the GSM network—oh, sorry, they're sat-phones also, right."

Pause. "Zero, are you drunk?"

"Absolutely not," waving a hand at Clare to shut the fuck up, "just been dealing with Flameproof, and now the whole Highlanders situation."

"Kalazar Four."

"Shit, right, Four. Sorry."

A silence heavier even than the sat-phone lag. "Now listen up Zero. Tonight we covered twenty clicks, over the hills, in what is it? Three thirty, in six hours. Serious going. We just put our heads down for a bit of kip, and got bumped by a VRS patrol."—"Right."—"In other words, in the entire circle, diameter forty kilometres, from where we started, the patrol that was looking for us, found us."—"I see."—"So, something funny's going on."—"Clearly."—"We've taken the battery out of his phone, searched through all of Ranković's clothes and belongings, and short of something very *very* high-tech, we couldn't find anything that could conceivably be a bug."—"Right."—"Is it conceivable he's swallowed something, has an implant?"

"The Bosnian Serbs?" doubtfully.

"Well that's what I thought. But there's definitely something up. If you could find out what, please. Get onto your GSM people. Get onto our friend from the American Embassy. Literally if you must."

Bannerman smiles. "I'll see what I can do."

"What's Kalazar?" Clare asks when he's hung up.

"Just a name."—"For what?"—"Callsign prefix. Just a codename."—"Chosen at random?"—"Don't know. Something Animal came up with."

"Goodness," mistily, "he is a real man, that one."

"What?" Bannerman paused mid-dialing. "Why?"

"You don't know what kalazar is? Or Kala-Azar, rather?"

Guardedly, "No . . ."

Clare nods, looks away. "Kala-Azar is a disease that was diagnosed by a scientist," dreamily, "called Leishman. Spelled like my name, but no c. So now Kala-Azar is called leishmaniasis. Very nasty. Like the plague. You see? And Leishman was Scottish, too, like Animal! I think this isn't a coincidence. So here is a man you see, who named a bounty-hunting operation, I'm guessing, after the girl he has a 'mania' for . . ."

Bannerman's body temperature plunges. *That bald Scottish bastard.* "Except it was *me*."

"Shit," Clare looking at Bannerman, "maybe that means Animal decided to go after Ranković, for *me*? Has he got Ranković? Bannerman? He does, doesn't he?"

Bannerman doesn't know where to start with this. "Except it was *me*!" he explodes. "*I* found him!"

"Ranković?"

A sigh. "Right, Ranković. I got you Ranković."

She lets fly a high squeal, runs at him, and hugs him. "Ranković!"

"Thought you'd be pleased."

"Pleased? I'm—" but a hand to her chest, frowning, "Oh goodness, what *am* I feeling . . . ?"

Fear. Ranković is staring at her.—It's been too easy, in the comfortable *klimatizirano* UN Building, to feel like an onlooker, just historians pushing data around—but here it is, she has changed the world. Ranković himself has been jolted out of his orbit, and he will no doubt now come looking for his persecutor, cold eyes turning to stare Clare Leischman clean through the head. But Animal Elliot-Maitland has Ranković prisoner; as long as Animal's there, there's nothing to worry about. But if Ranković should get away . . . she curls closer to Bannerman, but it's only instinctive anxiety. All her hopes and fears, many of them about physical safety, lie with Animal Elliot-Maitland now.—She breathes. A good place for them. A man of strength.

"Animal has him," a hypnotized voice, "Animal caught him . . ."

"Well, sort of," Bannerman still hugging her, "really it was *we* caught him."

"I got the indictment . . . Animal got the arrest . . ."

"Right but Animal and *me* got the arrest."

". . . and he called it leishmaniasis. A mania."—looking up—"he's crazy about me!"

"Well hold on—"

"A bounty hunter so in love with me, that—"

"Maybe *he* chose the name, but *I'm* the one—"

"No, better: an SAS *colonel* so in love, he's capturing the bad guys for *me*—Oh, mein Gott!" hands to her mouth, wide eyeballs at Bannerman, "I'm a Bond girl!"

"You hearing me? We found him because of *my* technology, me and Zaim's, which—"

"My man is running around in the snow with a gun, and when he gets home, he's going to *devour* me! Ooh!" in mock fright.

"It was *me* hid under a—" But she's not listening. Bannerman can't start in on this now. He has to make this call. He puts a finger up at her. "Just—stop thinking like that. I'll tell you all about it. First I need to call Mudhill."

"Don't try to steal credit," shaking her head at him sadly.

"Just—hold on—"

"File 13, *buongiorno*," says Al Mudhill, answering on the first ring. Wide awake.

"It's Bannerman here, Al."

"Bannerman! What's my favorite cohort doing at File 13—Oh! *Is this a booty call?*"

"This anything to do with you?"

"Is what?"

"No sure I get it," says Bannerman. "So . . . if it *wasn't* to do with you, you'd say no, or yes really, either way, but you'd still know what I was talking about. Or at least pretend to. But you're not, so, I deduce: you must be involved. How's my aim?"

"Are we talking about Dmitri Lautz fucking Clare Leischman?"

"We—" Bannerman's heart lurches, but he keeps ahold, stiff exhalation, he glares across at her acting out play scenes with an imaginary friend on the other side of the control room. "I am interested in what you have to say on that subject. But not right now."

"Yes, in a dark corner at Colorscheme. Apparently she came."

"Enough. Right now I'm talking about File 13."

"Aren't they planning an arrest?"—"Cut it out, Al. Why is SFOR throwing them to the wolves?"—"Really?"—"I said cut it out."—"I've got nothing to cut out."

Bannerman takes a deep breath. "Al, I promise I will give you whatever you want, and I mean whatever, just help us out here. Why won't SFOR get them out?"

"No but this *is* news. SFOR *is* throwing them to the wolves, present tense, so File 13's in the middle of an operation, tonight . . . and there's nothing contractual, it's unlikely to be the building sites, so they must be arresting an indictee, *hmm*. And presumably they've already secured their man, otherwise there'd be no wolves . . . so

SFOR *is* preventing them from coming back in. How *interesting*, Bannerman, do reveal more?"

"Did you hear me about the whatever you want?"

"Oh, a world of yes. I'll be replaying your little cri de coeur over and over again later. I might make it my new ringtone."—"What is it you want?"—"Me?"—"You. SFOR. The States."—"Not sure 'we' want anything."—"What can we do to get you to help us bring in this guy?"—"I'm sure SFOR would be only too delighted to assist in the apprehension of any indictees."—"What about the U.S.?"—"The U.S. is irrelevant. SFOR is a NATO force, not an American one." Bannerman rests the receiver against his forehead. "So how are they being tracked?"—"Who?"—"File 13."—"They're being tracked?"—"Is it conceivable Ranković has some kind of transmitter on or *in* him?"

"*Ranković?*" squeals Al Mudhill. "I don't think there's anything more you can tell me! You have the loosest lips in the business, Bannerman. I can help you with that, if you like."

"Crap." Bannerman hangs up, leaning all his weight on the receiver, but it doesn't make it any more hung up.

Clare paces in the background. "What'd he say?"

Bannerman turns around. "Dmitri *Lautz*?"

Clare frowns, genuinely doesn't know what he's talking about. Then gets it, angrily tries to brush it aside. "Stay out of my life, Bannerman!"

"Real fucking piece of work," as he turns to try the cell phones of Animal, then Edgar, Brick, Zaim and, for luck, Banko Ranković. But it's all voice mail.

"What looks like a hamlet over the next ridge," Edgar says. "Either sat reception on the top, or a phone mast down in town. Double-ended draw."

Animal peers at the map in its plastic sleeve, spots of rain appearing. An unnerving simulation of ranging shots. "Agreed." Standing up. "How's morale, boys. One more hill then a bit of kip?"

They try to follow the low ground, to stay out of the wind. But they hadn't counted on the sat-phones not working at the bottom of the valley. They've been moving fast, faster than sensible given the darkness, the patrol that bumped them at the rest stop presumed long behind.

Laboring up the slope and back into the wind, balaclavas down and just their lips and eyes freezing: 4 a.m. and the first beginnings of light on the east horizon. In the hollow at the bottom of this slope, two or three kilometers distant, a few lights in the hamlet of Pomoroc.

"Oi, Sufi. Come down from there, will you," says Brick, squatting a few yards down the slope. Thumbing at the hamlet, "You're silhouetted."

Up here, the satellite connection comes on strong. Animal receives a text message from Bannerman:

> Mudhill involved. My guess is they will not lift a finger to help. At best. Don't know whether "they" means USA or SFOR. Wait for Highlanders or do you have helicopter friends?

and from Flameproof:

> Butmir vehicle pool locked. no dice. kalazar0 useless. maybe the Fiat best bet. resupply tomorrow am. locstat?

Animal replies to Flameproof:

> Beg borrow or steal a helicopter. locstat from kalazar0.

Animal and Edgar have a brief confab about developments, then bed down again. Light flurries of snow which don't settle. Another hour's rest to mop up some raggedness. Some appreciative comments about how Banko hasn't made a grab for weapon 1. But he's held in check by the cold, the pitiful state of his swollen fingers, and a certain acceptance of fate. Maybe it's nice for him at least to be "Banko" again, to be special. Nevertheless cuddling up tight to Sufi Child and Brick.

Soon everyone's dropped off. Edgar's on stag. He's stalking the rocks, yards from camp, playing around with the night vision goggles, when his phone starts vibrating.

"Al Mudhill, what's up?"

"Edgar Radford, Jr., the 'Outside Dope.' Sorry to call you so early, *do* hope I didn't arouse you."

Edgar steals away from the sleepers. "Just doing my morning stretches."

"I bet those muscles don't tone themselves."—"You're not wrong."—"Edgar, I just had a *fascinating* chat with Bannerman Tedus, who tells me you boys are in an absolute *pickle*."—"Does he."—"Among other very interesting things."—"What sort of things?"—"Oh all about Banko, your signals intelligence, the whole deal."

Edgar purses his lips. "What do you want, Al?"

"You may know that the authorities in Republika Srpska are not at all happy. I might even say, *un*happy. No, I would, actually. Republika Srpska is decidedly unhappy with the events of last night."

"I'ma hang up now."

"The TV is talking about, quote, 'American death squads.' They're calling it an act of war."

"Serb cranks."

"Edgar, listen to me. You are destabilizing the country. Do not even think about coming in with Ranković. Put him back where you found him like a good little boy."

"Nice talking to you Al."

"Wait wait. You still there?"—"Yep."—"Edgar, I'm sorry about that last comment, it's early, we're all getting excited. But listen to me: *we badly do not need this right now.* And I don't think you do either. What's the deal? Money? Not even real money—what—five hundred thousand dollars, of which you'll get maybe ten percent, fifty thousand, *if you're lucky?* For fifty thousand bucks, you're prepared to push the whole theater back into war?"

"He's a war criminal! He needs to be—"

"Oh please, you musclebound idiot, don't justice me. You're in it for the money. You are prepared to risk war, in order to line your pockets. Which puts you in exactly the same category as Milošević."

"That's such bullshit."

"Actually it's not. You are trying to make money for yourself by going against the policy of your own country. We have the indictee situation completely in hand. You are making an enemy of your own country, Edgar Radford."

"You're not my country."

"Sorry Edgar, but I am. In this conversation, I am the fucking voice of America. And like the wonderful democracy I am, I'm giving you a vote: are you with us or against us?"

"It's not a choice between—"

"Oh but it is. You're going to shit on the flag for some chump change. Daddy *would* be proud."

"Don't bring my father into it."

"Your father's *in* it, dipshit, and he's *against* you! Daddy's company kept the Bosnians *alive*—" but Al breaks off, composes himself, and starts again: "Okay. Officially, yes, State Department is committed to capturing all indictees at once. Unofficially, as you should have fucking worked out by now, State doesn't know shit about it. Dayton is a precarious thing, Edgar, OHR just fired the Serb president! You read about that, dipshit? We just overthrew some country's democratically elected head of state for being an asshole, and—god knows how—the Serbs swallowed it. *Whole.* Maybe because he *was* an asshole, but SFOR was expecting riots—retaliations—assassination attempts, anything! And just when we think we might have got away with it, like, okay, Paddy Ashdown's not going to get home to find everyone dead—suddenly there are *American death squads* on fucking TV? You get the picture?

"Radford, I just can't even begin to describe . . . So far you've cost, ballpark, five million in fuckup money to the peace process, and so help me God if you don't let Ranković go right now I will stop at nothing to make sure you personally get busted by the RS. Understand *that*. You have no idea what deep shit even *looks like*."

"Is the Embassy with you on this?"

"I *am* the Embassy! You fucking trigger-puller, I'll see you thrown into some Chetnik hellhole, and you know how much the Serbs love Americans. Animal and his goons will be fine, oh the Brits are their *friends*, they fought at Salonica, but they'll take a real shine to *you*. You'll learn *all about* American state terrorism. And yeah, the State Department will make all the right noises about getting you out, no doubt Daddy'll kick up a fuss, have lunch with *lots and lots* of senators, but I guarantee you you'll be there for at least a year. Think on *that*. A year in Serb gulag, and Ariel all teary-eyed and getting jodied by every guy at Eagle."

Edgar has stopped walking now, phone to ear. Nothing on the line but breath and static for almost thirty seconds. Eventually—

"Anyway, so glad we had this chat, Edgar. Let's do lunch." Dial-tone.

Dazed, Edgar drifts back to the camp. He squats by the sleepers, wonders what do to.

"Will he retrieve us?" says Sufi Child.

Edgar lifts the goggles off his eyes. "Awake, huh."

"It is difficult to sleep in this cold."—"You manage, sooner or later."—"Will he retrieve us?"—Edgar rubs his jaw. "Not exactly."—"What did he say?"

Edgar, eyes defocused on the horizon, starts to speak, then stops. Really sees Sufi Child, calm Sufi Child and his clear complexion, spooning comfortably behind Banko Ranković, and he's humbled.

"Ahh," squinting into the coming day, "just trash-talking."

Eagle is Eagle Base Tuzla, HQ for Multi-National Brigade North, and capital of the American sector. Seventy miles north of Sarajevo, where a large proportion of Dayton's air assets are stationed, not just those of the U.S. Air Force and Army, but also those of the Poles, Swedes, and a slew of other denominations: Brown & Root, DynCorp, Blackwater.

Land Cruiser parked in the visitors' lot, Flameproof, Deuchar, and Geddes, the backbone of File 13, pick along concrete walkways to the canteen hut. Inside it's any neon-lit diner, lino floors, the heating at full whack, inspirational posters where the o in ALL-AMERICAN HEROES has been amended to a P, a few other solitary figures at plastic gingham tables, insomniacs, sentries, patrols just in, roughing up their greasy helmet-hair, attempts to transform from soldiers back into boys . . .

Their black pilot friend Jefferson Penny is there, bleary-eyed & getting outside of some vending-machine coffee.

"This better be worth it."

"Trust us, Jeff, you will never do a more financially together thing in your life. Let's go get your flight suit."

"The crews aren't up."

"Then let's go, let's go," Flameproof clapping, "this cannot fucking wait, my man, it cannot wait."

Jeff shakes his head. "Pull up some coffee. This ain't the Air Force no more. Ground crews don't get out of bed just cos you ax em to. First takeoff, first light. And in case you're wondering, civil twilight? 0541 hours. Jefferson waves a flight plan on a clipboard, "Now I assume you don't just want a hop back home. Maybe you better tell me something about this, so I can figure out how to lie least on the paperwork."

Flameproof looks at the clock on the wall: 0437.

First light. Edgar's on stag, watching from their position in the trees uphill of Pomoroc village. The air thickening with birdsong, dew beginning to fall. Below, houses are waking; distant cockerels, dogs barking, a grinding of gears, diesel engines throbbing against inclines.

Edgar feels a vibration in his jacket. A text from Al Mudhill:

Its going to be ok. Am fond of you & AA so have pulled strings.
Let R go & will bring in F13, recoup you personally. Call it 50k.
Secret of course. Delete this. Let me know. Axx

Edgar rubs his eyes, tired, doesn't know what to think. But even as he selects "delete," he knows the slope he's on is just as steep as this physical one. He just needs to work it out. A little time to think. Just when he's decided to reject it, another text arrives, and the offer's up to

100k

Animal, woken by the activity below, pulls himself out of his bivvy-bag, rolls up his balaclava, eyes fat with sleep, and makes his way over to the edge of the trees where Edgar's standing to get a clear view of the village from there, see what's going on. But Edgar's staring at his phone, unaware of Animal's approach. Animal comes closer, treading noiselessly, but Edgar's lost in himself.

He gets to within ten yards of his 2i/c, and squats. Watches him for upward of thirty seconds—sixty—before, taking a routine look around him, Edgar finally catches sight of Animal—

"CHEESES CHRIST—oh wow," holding his heart, "oh man, you scared me."

Animal watches him levelly. "That's what concerns me. The Edgar Radford *I* know doesn't let people sneak up on him."

"Pretty fazed by this text Al Mudhill sent me."

Animal watches Edgar carefully for a long while, before, finally: "Tell me."

"He doesn't want us bringing in Ranković."

"Yeah?"—"Yeah."—"In as many words?"—"Incredible, huh?"—"Never had him for such a sloppy operator. Well, don't delete it, might come in useful at a press conference."

"For sure," Edgar stowing his phone.

"I came to see what the racket's all about—" field telescope pointed at the hamlet. "Oh, Christ."

Edgar peers down. Gray jeeps parked around the largest house. "Oh shit—Well, maybe it's okay."

"Those jeeps are empty." The muscles at Animal's temples are working overtime.

Edgar looks again, and sees that they are. They know what this means.

"Fuck, Animal, I am so sorry—"

"Not now." Animal shows something close to scorn. "We can do all that later."

"Right," as they make their way back to the others.

"And try to work out how they keep finding—oh, god *dammit*." Animal stops, a hand on the top of his balaclava.

"What?"

"We are a *load* of *imbeciles*."

"What? How are they finding us?"

"Lads, lads," once he's back with Ranković, Brick and the Child. "We cocked up. Everyone, take your batteries out of your phones, pack up, no trace, no food, we are going absolute elsewhere as of this fucking instant." Animal slings his rucksack up onto one arm, lengthening his stride through the forest, and dials Bannerman.

"Kalazar Zero, this is Kalazar One. The biter is bit, repeat, this channel is not secure, I have to assume via the same liability we exploited to find Bravo One, and for either GSM *or* satellite comms."

"Holy shit." Bannerman at Ašenova understands at once: their own phones are being tracked.

"Right. Another patrol on our case. So that's my conclusion, and until we work out a way to talk without giving away position, we'll have to be incommunicado. We're going batteries-not-included now."

"I understand."

"I'll be in touch shortly to arrange what I hope will be a final RV. That will perforce be my last communication until, with any luck, we get picked up. Can you send text messages to, ah, let's call him, Kalazar Minus One?"

"Kalazar Minus One . . ." Bannerman works it out. "Sure."

"You understand the reasoning?"

"Absolutely. Does he *have* his phone?"

"Hold on," hand over the receiver. "Oi, Child!" hissing, "do you have your phone with you? Sufi Child, listen to me! Do you—answer me, dammit. You do?—Yes he does. All right. Speak on that in a mo. Adios." Animal disconnects, takes the batteries out of his phone, then turns back to Sufi Child, who's been gesticulating oddly. *"What?"*

"Listen," says Sufi Child, and when Animal finally falls silent, a distant whine can be heard, inhuman and wavering against the distance, but growing louder over the trees.

"What's going on?"

On the floor of the File 13 control room, two sleeping bags have been zipped together to make a double. Miscellaneous olive-green bundles used as pillows, a tartan travel rug over everything. Clare wrapped up in several T-shirts and curled into the side of Bannerman's naked chest.

"Animal's phone has been being monitored," getting up, stepping into his jeans, "and the VRS have been being tipped off."

"What?" up on her elbows, hair everywhere, eyes not fully open. "The VRS are tapping his phone?"

The neon striplights come back on, Bannerman angles up the laptop's screen. "I don't know if it's the VRS . . . or how any of it works, really. Either the VRS are monitoring Telekom Srpske *themselves*, but I don't know, if that was a standard battlefield move, you'd expect Animal and Edgar to know about it, right? So I doubt the Bosnian Serb Army are doing it. Possible but unlikely. Or they're monitoring the satellites . . ."

"Satellites?"

"They've all got these sat-phones? that use the terrestrial network if there is one, otherwise they go satellite. And I don't know who has access to that."

"Jesus."

Throwing Clare her cell phone, "Ketyl Gaarder might."

Clare peers bewildered at her phone. "You're going to let Ketyl Gaarder in?"

Bannerman thinks. File 13's local employees will start showing up for work in an hour. "At this point, I think pretty well the whole of Bosnia is in."

*

A Gazelle, the utility light-reconnaissance helicopter of NATO forces, distinctive encased tail rotor, appears over the trees, its equally distinctive banshee wail flooding the mountainside.

"Flameproof already?" says Animal.

"Nice to see a friendly face," says Edgar.

"Stay down a minute." Animal looks up. The Gazelle hasn't found them; is picking slowly through the bare forest a few hundred yards to the north. "We don't want to be caught with our pants down if this doesn't pan out."

Animal shuffles out into a clearing, gets behind a fallen tree, three feet thick, leans slightly forward. Gets down, goes back to the others.

"What's up?" says Brick.

"Edgar, Brick, correct me if I'm wrong, but that's not one of ours."

"What?" Edgar's confused. "That's a French flag on the tail-plane?"

"Not sure the French have blue in the middle."

Edgar squints back up at the helicopter. "Nuts."

"It's a Soko," says Brick. "Yugo version of the Gazelle."

"All right then, no sudden movements, people, let's get out of here. Edgar? Lead on." But the forest here is deciduous and therefore bare, and though they slide briskly through the branches, pretty soon the Gazelle Soko has swung abruptly around, and springs across the distance toward them.

The feedback spike of a loudhailer being switched on.

—ATTENTION.

Brick grins at Edgar. "Think he means us?"

—YOU ARE SURROUND BY ARMY REPUBLIKE SRPSKE.

Animal stops against an outcrop of rock, leans against the far side. The others join. The mountainside is a long mossy slope, dalmatianed with old snow, with the forest continuing some distance away. "All right. Let's get rid of this joker. We'll dash across to that evergreen block, move under cover of trees. Ready?"

—DO NOT RUN AWAY OR YOU WILL BE KILL.

"*Those* trees?" says Sufi Child. A hundred meters of bare mountain away.

Animal gestures up at the Gazelle Soko. "No weapons on the hardpoints. He won't get us."

"They said we're surrounded."

"It's the sort of thing they say."

A shot and its echo clatter across the mountainside.

"Ah!" A child's scream has escaped Sufi Child. He stares at the sky, quivering.

"Toughguy," Animal drops a hand on his shoulder, "don't let em rattle you. Bloody hard to use sights out of one of them. Automatic fixed to the back is their best bet, but you run quick enough, jink a bit, it's a damned lucky shot that clips you. Airframe's too light, even if they *want* to hit us. Bags of reasons not to worry," and nodding at Ranković, "just make sure he doesn't drag too hard on the leash. Ready?"

More shots from the Soko. Singles.

Sufi Child can't cover his worry here. "Banko is tired now, Animal. His feet . . ."

"Yep. Hand him over," holding out his hand. "Brick, hang back to help me with the Serb gentleman, would you? Alright lads." By now the Soko is hovering almost directly overhead, the noise and down-wash intensifying our fear. "This'll be exciting!" shouts Animal, an irrepressible grin.

Brick offers Edgar his MP5K. "I got one-bit," meaning a tracer round every other round, "you want one-bit?"

"Sure." They swap. Edgar leans out, fires a burst up past the Soko, the tracers not igniting until they're well above it, curving over into kilometer-high parabolics. Nonetheless. Enough for the Soko to tra-verse away skittishly.

"Good then. Don't dawdle. Over the top on three?" Animal looks, hard, in each of our eyes in turn. Even those of Ranković, who's understood what's about to happen, and has a mortal terror himself. Now he's playing along. But Animal's confidence is a warm hand on our hearts, and when he shouts *three* the adrenaline kicks in and we stream in our millions out of cover.

—STOP. WE SHOOT TO KILL. More shots, singles at first, then bursts.

"Not effective!" Animal bellows. "Keep going! Come on, Rapes!"

Ranković is wincing as every step sends shocks through his broken finger. Enormous bangs on Sufi Child's other side, he panics, but it's only Edgar firing back at the Soko, which climbs abruptly to 300 feet. Edgar trotting along comfortably, jinking left and right.

Sufi Child sees this and copies, but his enthusiasm for running diagonally gets beaten down fast, he doesn't want to waste any time getting to that treeline, his mind filling with the dark abstract shape between two firs.

But fifty yards from the darkness, curling bright across it, is the momentary flash of a phosphorescent tracer round. Going away from them, parallel to the ground.

Sufi Child understands at once what that means. He looks round in terror.

Dawn. Layers of peaks ascend in a tessitura of smokey blues to a flare of white at the horizon. Down here on the plains, inside the perimeter fencing, diesel engines idling, refueling trucks, ground crews staggering around in boilersuits and circles, reluctantly treading out embers and moving headphones from necks to ears. The control tower a hundred yards off. Main radar spinning surely too fast. On helipad 4, Jefferson Penny has completed the external and pre-start checks on his Huey, and there's the low hum of an engine climbing up the octaves.

"Tower to Starlet Seven, how you doing?"

"Starlet Seven to Tower, stabilizing at flight idle."

"Copy Starlet Seven, let us know when you're ready."

Jefferson Penny works down the checklist on his thigh, putting his finger against hydraulic controls, fuel boosts and carburetor de-icer switches one by one, deliberate as an infant. Progress is slow. Next to him in copilot, Flameproof has restless leg.

Eventually Jefferson Penny looks around at his passengers. "All right! Ready guys? *Fantastic.* Starlet Seven to Tower, we are good to go. Request permission for takeoff."

—.

"Starlet Seven to Tower, did you copy my last?"

"Hold on, Starlet Seven."

Flameproof throws up a questioning hand. Jeff shrugs *dunno*.

"Tower to Starlet Seven: you are not cleared for takeoff."

"Thank you tower, standing by, let me know soon as the coast is clear."

"Tower to Starlet Seven, yeah, the thing about that is, just had this MP sergeant on the phone?, sounding like somebody took a dump in his Cap'n Crunch. Mud puppies on their way out to see you now."

Jefferson Penny looks left at Flameproof. Flameproof starts shouting impotently. Jefferson leans over and turns on his microphone.

"Let's go, Jeff. Fucking make it happen. Now, like!"

Jefferson grimaces, hands on the sticks. "Shit, I dunno. It might just be something small . . ."

"Jeff, the monkeys are coming! Go!"

"You can get in a lot of trouble." Jefferson sits for a moment, unreadable behind his mirrored aviators. Tics in his left cheek. Stubble rash.

"Jeff ya gobshite, go on! You'll be minted!"

Jeff takes a deep breath. "Starlet Seven to Tower, we have received a five hundred kilohertz distress signal at this time, I am proceeding in accordance with NATO distress signal procedure."

"Five hundred kilohertz? What, at sea?" says Tower.

"*Yes!*" shouts Flameproof.

"Thank you for your cooperation on this matter."

Tower lets out a hollow chuckle. "Godspeed, Starlet Seven."

But Jeff hesitates. "Are we really doing this?"

"Fucking, GO!"

And stumbling out the swing door, MPs in navy overcoats and white helmets clattering onto the concrete, a lean older man pulling on a T-shirt striding out toward them . . .

"Aw shit, Colonel Kolleen."

"Let's go, let's go!"

"I dunno man . . ."

The MPs have leveled rifles at the Huey, standing a polite distance from the main rotor. Colonel Kolleen is dragging his finger across his throat at Jefferson Penny.

"The monkeys won't take fucking potshots!"

"No, they just going to throw my ass in brig for twenty years."

For a few moments, against the monstrous screaming of the helicopter, no one moves.

"Twenty thousand dollars to take off," says Flameproof.

Jefferson grimaces. "Shit." But makes no move. Colonel Kolleen is gesturing some MPs to approach the helicopter.

"Forty."

In the back, Deuchar and Geddes look at each other. *Forty?*

"Sorry guys. We are already in the deepest of shit." Jefferson's aviators look round at each of them, an apologetic smile as he cuts the power, and then there's a white glove knocking on the window.

Flameproof looks round at Deuchar and Geddes. "Any more ideas?"

"Animal!" screams Sufi Child, as more tracers curl past them.

"Keep going keep going!" Animal some way behind, dragging a stumbling, grimacing Ranković, going on a bad foot. "Too far away! Brick!"

Brick takes over Ranković's leash. "Got him, boss."

"Hey Sufi!" shouts Edgar, trotting beside the Child. "Run in front of me!" Edgar moving behind the Child, who swerves to avoid, but Edgar's persistent, and the Child finds himself accepting the arrangement. "Sufi, see these tracers disappear? Tracer rounds burn out at a thousand meters, right? They're a click away. Don't sweat it!"

Sufi Child skitters into the trees, ducking through the catching branches, and doesn't stop running for a hundred yards inside. The going's hard, the branches start at half a meter off the ground. Darker in here, no wind, stony earth littered with pine needles, even the sound of the Soko muffled by the thick cover overhead. It can only see them when directly overhead. Occasional shots fired blind into the trees.

"Don't stop, keep walking," says Animal, blowing past the Child. "Get your breath while you walk. Brick, how's he doing."

"Cooking on gas." Banko himself grins, gives Animal a double thumbs-up.

The morning continues, moving fast through fir and melancholy pine, fading into bald stretches of apparently infinite birch forest. Occasional detours up to high ground to plan the most evergreen route, the beating scream of the helicopter drifting, by slow drives and reverses, further away. Scrapes of persistent snow in hollows and wheel ruts. Chains of electricity pylons bounding over the mountainside. Old fences. Lost mountain huts. Occasional service roads of turbulent mud, frozen hard, leading to clear-felled sites of logging operations that they edge around.

"You say Mudhill's involved?" Animal coming up alongside Edgar.

"Well . . ." wrinkling his face, "he wants us to put him back, sure. But I have a hard time thinking he'd actually *try* to get us caught."

Animal considers this. "Wouldn't put it past him."

"—Um, Animal, listen. I have some concerns."

Animal makes sure no one else is in earshot. "Go on."

"Not complaints. I just want to be helped out here. My feeling is, this particular mission is beginning to conflict with File 13's more general aims. You know? Specifically, what I don't get, is: regardless of whether Mudhill is or isn't a good guy—if we're bringing Banko in against the wishes of the U.S., how do you expect us to get any business out of them in the future?" Edgar's palms up like he genuinely wants an answer.

Only a question, but Animal's not too happy. "We're not after contracts from Mudhill's people. Only the Pentagon." And he strides off ahead, to take the Ranković leash back off Brick.

"There aren't a lot of suspects." 7 a.m., and Ketyl Gaarder has kicked Marc van Xanthe out of bed at his apartment on Kulovića Street. He's pulled on a pair of jeans and no shirt, smoothing down his lustrous hair, and they're standing bleary-eyed around the stove, smoking the first of the day's cigarettes, waiting for the kettle to whistle. The TV runs repeat footage of the car wrecks on the Višegrad road, interviews with locals, close-ups of the "metal hedgehog" wrapped around the Opel's axle. Evident anger. Accusations and gesticulations. No comment yet from SFOR, but a press conference called for 9 a.m. More footage of the car crash, plus a historical roundup of other Serbs murdered by ICTY and their lackeys in SFOR. A spell interrupted by the first tentative wail of the boiling kettle.

"I think there is only one suspect in fact," Ketyl pacing on creaking floorboards; "you have seen the NICs down at Butmir," the National Intelligence Centers, "the Americans have one of those golfball listening posts."

Marc nods. "A radome. You think the Americans?"

Ketyl shrugs, she doesn't want to think it. "Who else? Only Echelon has this technology." Echelon being the U.S. government's eavesdropping program, run from radome stations all over the world.

"Ah Echelon," Marc smiling warmly, "whenever Echelon is appearing in a conversation, I know things turn religious really . . . Chomsky fans wanking off to these paranoid fantasies—no, there really are men in headphones typing down every conversation in the world," Marc shrugs, "if this fantasy didn't exist, it is necessary to invent it, I think?"

Ketyl hits the stove with a pan. Marc jumps. Her mouth is a short, tight line. "It is time to take this seriously. You were in NATO. Who else can do this?"

"Everyone," bewildered, "even the Serbs. Of course. SFOR found a VRS intelligence unit inside the National Assembly, intercepting calls. Last month."

"That was eavesdropping. Calls *inside* the Assembly. If you are in Banja Luka you can't intercept a call in Goražde. Not without huge dishes."

"But Echelon though . . ." Marc's reluctant to go along with this. "I don't buy it. The Americans are the keenest to catch indictees."

"State Department, yes this is true."

"Oh, so. You think the CIA?"

"No. The Pentagon. They are at war with the State Department and CIA, both."

"But that's about Iraq! If anyone, it's the French. The French have been colluding for years, actively tipping off indictees before arrests and whatsoever. And they have their own Echelon, you know, 'Frenchelon,' so it's no problem." His laser eyes narrow at Ketyl. "How did *you* do it?"

A beat, and she gives in. "Through the Internet. GSM networks have very bad GPRS backdoors." A lie, but a quick one, to protect Zaim. Above all else, she has to protect this sweet, sweet honest boy silly enough to have fallen in love with her.

"So then. Why not everyone else through the backdoor also?"

"These exploits are not known. The first people to find these things are hackers, always hackers. Then intelligence agencies, then companies, finally armies, but by then it is all secure. The way Zaim hacked Telekom Srpske is very new. In a year it will be old. Trust me, this is all way above the EUPM, the Policija, SIPA," being the Bosnian FBI, "and definitely the VRS."

"The DB?" the secret police of Serbia proper.

Ketyl shakes her head. "Hackers in Belgrade, if anything."

She paces on the creaking floorboards, exhaling twin nostril-plumes of smoke. Out of the double windows, a spring-haze morning in the city: the mountaintops fading to the same misty brilliance as the sky, roofs up the hillsides catching the sun and shining golden through the blue pastel. "I still think the Pentagon. Sarović has been kicked out, OHR wants to merge the armies, VAT and so on, the timing is very bad. The Serbs need to be reassured. The OHR has the motive but not the technology. Only the Americans do. That Pentagon Intelligence Unit, the neocon thing. And they *would* do it, and they wouldn't include SFOR, the High Rep, even the CIA, I think. No way the army and ambassador. These people we can trust to be okay, share their projects, you know? They are very different from Al Mudhill, or Dmitri Lautz with the Germans, these guys. Different agendas."

"O.K."

"It's conceivable for the same reason they don't bring in Karadžić, they also want this arrest to go away."

"They don't want them testifying against Chirac?"

"No. For stability." And in that exchange Ketyl finally understands, on a gut level, that for anything there will be as many entirely convincing explanations as there are people: the ICTY investigator, the police officer, neither convinced the other person sees the whole picture. And in that tantalizing glimpse, the sudden crushing futility of ever trying to sort anything out—of, in fact, doing anything with her life beyond trying to be happy and in love. A sudden longing for Zaim, a crushing regret that she ever cheated on him . . . she never will again. Not even with Jens Asselijn. She will stamp out her lingering need for Jens' body, but which hasn't quite—yet—dissipated . . .

"O.K.," she says, "Americans or French, it does not matter. Animal and everyone have turned their phones off, so maybe they will not be found anymore. But we agree: there are non-local forces, who do not want Ranković brought in."

"Agreed," Marc going ugly at the sludge power of his coffee. "So what do you need?"

The sun now hot on their backs, they stop at a stream to drink, refill water bottles, lie around on the ground. Animal lies prone and begins to encode a message with a onetime pad; Edgar dispenses dextrose tablets and biscuits. Brick takes off Ranković's shoes and socks to tend to some fearsome blisters.

"Ew," goes Edgar.

"Soft feet," says Brick. "Don't tab about much, Chetniks, do ya?"

Sufi Child relays this. Ranković says something back. Sufi Child nods thoughtfully.

"Good comeback, were it?"

"He says even your feet are not hard enough for the ground ahead."

"Aye." Brick nods, applying a Compeed to Ranković's heel. "That was a good comeback."

"What does it mean?"

Eventually: "Mine country."

Edgar looks up, pissed off. "Aw, nuts."

Sufi Child looks at Animal. "There are mines here?"

Animal scratches his face. "Former Confrontation Line does go through the Olympic slopes."

"But we are not going that way? They have cleared the mines at Jahorina?"

"Yep." Animal's lips move as he encodes. "Mostly."

Edgar's searching in his webbing. "Animal, I don't have a mine map on me. How about you?"

Animal shakes his head. A long silence.

Sufi Child doesn't want to break it, but eventually can't not. "How shall we go through it?"

"Carefully," Brick with a grim smile. He looks back down at Ranković's feet. Sharp inhalations as dead skin is cut away, pulling at pink flesh underneath. "Sorry pal." Putting away the knife, breaking open a capsule of red desiccating antiseptic. "This might sting a bit."

Ranković makes a point of showing disdain for the pain. He sneers at his feet, brings his wrists up to his mouth, taps two fingers against. Edgar pulls out a Lucky Strike, lights it, passes it across.

When Animal's finished encoding he looks up at them. His eyes are beginning to rheum up. "Okay people. In a mo I'm going to put my batteries in just long enough to send this text out to Bannerman. It's our escape plan, and it tells him to have us picked up here," pointing a pencil at the map. "Eleven clicks as the crow flies, a bit of up and down, we ought to be able to make it inside of six hours. Everyone happy?" looking from face to face, "everything running like a Swiss watch?"

"I think Mudhill might pay us not to bring him in," Edgar says.

"What?" Animal turns sharply at Edgar.

A drop of temperature and a sudden silence, swiftly followed by a longer, harder silence. "You do, do you?" Animal narrows his eyes. "How could you have got such an idea?"

"I told you. He sent me a text. I deleted them, though. Offered us money *not* to bring him in. Not the whole amount. I reckon he could be haggled up some. I mean if the U.S. *really* doesn't want him brought in, you know," hands up, "they're a lot stronger'n we are, plus it's a whole lot cheaper for them just to pay us the half million than for them to spend the same amount and more on ammo, putting the warzone back together, and all that."

Animal sits back on his haunches. "What's your point?"

Edgar spreads his hands. "Hell, we got Ranković. We got the ace."

Animal is near white-hot with rage. "You're considering as one of your options, letting him go?"

"If they want to pay us the same amount anyhow," a shrug.

"There are other considerations besides the money, Edgar."

"Yeah?" a sudden teenage defiance. "Well maybe you better let me know what some of them are."

"Christ." Animal knows where this is going. No option but to meet it head-on. "Crimes against *humanity*, Edgar. Not just some county court judgement—rape camps."

"Never anything personal in any of your operations?"—"Rape camps, Edgar."—"Little Clare, that's not personal?"—"I'm married, you berk!"—"What difference does that make?"—"All right, then. It's not just the money, no. It is also bringing an indicted slave trader in."—"Finally. And you always said like you were superrational about ops."—"I am."—"That it was all about cost-effectiveness."—"They were investors. You have to say that kind of thing."—"You also said it to me.

"Instead, now I find out I'm caught up in someone else's passion project. Animal, this is a serious misunderstanding, here. You're always talking about the scope for moral choice in a private army, you know, feels like you haven't been entirely straight on this one. Denied us *our* choice. In fact, it feels like *our* interests," a finger and thumb seesawing between their chests, "are no longer exactly aligned."

"Well," for the first time Animal doesn't seem in total control, "I'm sorry you feel that way . . ."

"For the same money, you want to take us through the minefields! Well, this is the point at which I believe I'm entitled to say: hold on. I think it's time we considered turning him loose, taking old Mudhill's money instead."

"You want to turn him loose?"

"Yank," mutters Brick.

Edgar looks back from Brick to Animal. "No, if you listen, I do not *want* to turn him loose. But I think we should consider it. I think we ought to have a failsafe for getting ourselves out of this snafu. We ought to decide at what point we're going to let him go, take the consolation prize, live to see another sunset. I mean, this guy—" gun muzzle held ARVN-style at Ranković's temple, "—is not a do-or-die situation. Or am I wrong?"

No answer. Edgar looks around.

"Brick? You prepared to die for this character?"

"Don't get rhetorical," says Animal. "Of course it's not do-or-die."

"How about a foot then. Those AP mines, the little plastic ones? them suckers'll only take your foot off, maybe your nuts, too. You ready to lose your nuts for him? Brick?"

"Come to the point, Edgar."

"That is my point. Let's agree what we're ready to lose for him. All right?"

Animal clenches his jaw. "Alright."

"You first."

Animal considers his words. "If it looks like mortal danger, we'll think again."

"And having Sokos chase us into a minefield, does that look like mortal danger?"

"It's not a minefield. It just hasn't been verified *definitely clear* of mines. Different things entirely."

"Pretty fine distinction to me."

"It's really not. Chances of our treading on anything are so minimal as to be . . ." but even he can hear that it's not a strong argument, so he switches tack: "Alright look. We'll stick to the high ground, where the ground's frozen. Nothing can go off up there."

"The high ground. Where the trees thin out, and the Sokos can see us better?"

Animal loses it. *"Radford, belt up! You want to be in this company or not?"*

Edgar walks around, draws his hands down his face, eventually turns back to Animal: "Am I doing this for the buzz? No. Do I want to get paid? Yes. And I'm not doing it for the 'justice,' neither. Fucking kangaroo court anyway. I want to get *paid*. I have a girlfriend I want to *marry*, I want to raise *kids*, and yeah, frankly, I do want all four limbs and two testicles to raise them with. So. Do we have a problem here?" Edgar shrugs off a poisonous look from Brick. "Animal? I said, do we have a problem here?"

"No problem," concedes Animal.

So this is it. Edgar, hulking easygoing Edgar, has pushed Andrew Elliot-Maitland into a corner.

"Brick, what about you. Do we have a problem here?"

Brick's looking at Animal with a certain forlorn intensity. The eyes of a dog in the rearview mirror as you abandon it in the forest. Animal looks at the ground, and Brick turns to square his jaw at Edgar. "Bird in the hand," growls Brick.

"Now just what in the hell does that mean?"

Animal's system comes alive again. Blood rushes to every part. Good old Brick. Fucking champion man on the planet. He's saved Animal's life more than once. Rearmed, Animal turns on Edgar.

"Means you turn him loose now, you'll be lucky to see *any* money."

Edgar immediately sees the fatal weakness.

"Ever again, actually. No one will take you seriously."

"He gave an undertaking . . ."

"I don't know what Mudhill told you, but you want to be a player in these circles, you've got to achieve what you set out to do. Show people they need to get you onside beforehand or stay out of your way. You show weakness to people like Mudhill, it's over."

Edgar's shaking his head. "I don't believe he would, just . . ."

"That's not even how the Company works."

"Mudhill's not CIA."

"Whatever he is. There are paper trails. They can't just bung someone a few hundred K. There's no way Mudhill can swing a payment like that."

"He's skimming like a motherfucker. He's got a ton of money put away."

"You think he's going to dip into his own money?"

"We can use Ariel! We'll get Mudhill to give the money over to Ariel, and she can count it, right, and then she'll tell us everything's okay, and *then* we'll turn him loose . . ."

Animal doesn't even have to reply to sink this.

"Animal, I still think this is one we need to go around and not through."

"I didn't want to do this," Animal holding out his hand, "but may I have your phone?"

"My phone?"—"Your phone."—"What do you want with my phone?"—"Edgar. Give me your mobile phone."—"Animal, let's stick to the issue here . . ."—"Your cooperation would be appreciated, Edgar. Let's not have this turn ugly."—"Ugly? What are you, going to pull a piece?"

The two stare at each other. Ranković sniggers, Brick clips him round the head.

"Edgar. Let's not have total breakdown."

But Edgar sees that he has stalled. It's a humiliation he'll have to swallow. He shakes his head like it's too bad, pulls his phone out, hands it over.

"Before I look at this, is there anything you want to tell me?"

"Like what?"

"Is there anything you want to tell me?"

Animal and Edgar, once such a friendship, suddenly degenerated to a hostile alliance. Animal has stripped him of trust, and that only takes one to tango.

"No."

"Good. That's what I was hoping." Animal stows Edgar's Motorola in his combat smock. "You lot, get going. In thirty seconds I'll have sent this message, and I want to have to catch up. Go."

*　*　*　*　*

Clare's pacing, her polkadot hand round a giant mug of chocolate, vacantly looking out the window at Ašenova 25, staring into alter-

nate lives. She's just heard the news from an OTP colleague: over-
night, an email from Milan Lukić has been traced back to an
Argentinian ISP. The butcher of Višegrad. What's he doing out there?
she wonders. What *is* there to do? Is he on a beach, as bashfully modest about his escapades as any of the Great Train Robbers? Absolutely
happy now, with his wife, reaching over from his deckchair just to
touch her hand, no words passing, just the sun and the breeze and
the serenity of growing old together . . . his wife putting down her
book after a half dozen of these touchings, playfully exasperated, to
give and receive watery-eyed looks of love, actual soul-deep love,
perhaps more lifelong and closer to True Love, whatever that is, than
anything Clare will ever experience . . . oh, that's where the horror is.
Not in their evil, but their humanity. To know that ordinary decent
people, bumped by the crowdian motion and taking their cues from
those around them, are capable of such things . . .

How can she not think of herself? Doesn't that mean that she's
susceptible too, her father, Frito, the police officers outside, everyone?

In the control room, Bannerman's whining about the Highlanders.
"They're doing nothing! They're totally hanging Animal out to dry!
Fucking *turncoats*, colluding with the *Serbs*, I thought these Scottish
guys were all supposed to have known each other from when they
were like, sperm?"

"Bannerman."

"No room for moral action inside an army. It's completely amoral.
Your choices are made by men with budgets. A private army is the
only—"

"Bannerman, I think we're getting raided."

Bannerman comes over to the window. Parked twenty yards off:
two white SUVs, men in expensive waxed coats standing on the door-
sills, talking on phones and shooting occasional glances up at the
File 13 building. Coming up the hill, slowing to stop, a navy Policija
VW Passat.

"Why would the Federation raid *us*?"

Striding over to the laptop, folding it up, and sliding it into a
rucksack, "Take everything. We'll go out the back." He shoves in

leads, spare computers, external disk drives. Clare takes a map off the wall, random stacks of files, puts them in a shopping bag, still bewildered.

"Seriously, why would they try to stop us, from—?"

"I'm sure it's all a terrible misunderstanding, now come the fuck on," holding out a hand, to take hers and head fast out of the room.

"The lights," says Clare.

"Let em burn."

"They'll know we were here."

"They already know the lights are on," as he unbolts the door. "Let's just fade away."

They emerge into the alley beside the house. Bannerman pushes her over a fence into a garden, alongside the house— children's shoes in neat pairs by the doorstep—and into the next street, an alley of cracked paving stones and handrails down steep steps. The move downhill toward the Centar. In the sliver of landscape they can see between towering apartment buildings, Mount Trebević rises precipitately on the other side of the Miljacka. Somewhere behind that mountain, Animal and the others are lost.

"What the fuck!" hisses Clare.—"I know."—"Ranković has an in with the big boys."—"I know."—"So, why is all this happening?"—"I have no idea. Haven't heard from Flameproof in a while, that can't be a good sign."—"So, where do we go now?"—"Somewhere with a connection. I suppose the warehouse. Hang on," as his phone pings. It's a text from the Sufi Child's phone.

9EPD0 6JOQ0 WZEE7 LMFWP 5NJRT 4LI9M TPQ3M
R8YWM IDQMR V8ZZK K2MR9 E4RGT EJJYV
C2AUY MLTY4 IUNFD FR

"Oh shit."

"What. Let me see."

"The onetime pad. We left it."

"You can't decode it?"

Bannerman pushes his hair back. "Shit."

That's it. That's the last message Animal said he would send before taking his phone batteries out for good—and it's indecipherable.

"Seriously, what the fuck are we going to do?" They stare, searching for clues in each other's eyes. They go down Širokac Street, double back up, but there's a car with EUPM plates parked in the turning into Ašenova, and men in camouflage are consulting with suits in the road.

"No good," says Clare, turning sharply on her heel.

"Wait up. Look interested," Bannerman holding her tight by the bicep. She frowns at her bicep and then at him, reddening under the freckles. Outrage or interest. Beside them, a bored police guard watches from his booth—then looks back down to his magazine. "*Now* let's go."

Transference

THE ONLY TRAIT Frito's ever found common to the great money-makers is getting up early. Something he does anyway, often with a hefty jog out to the tekija—and on his way back down, 8 a.m., sweat in a bib all down his T-shirt, Frito pauses at the top of Koševo Hill to look out over his city, and run his mind over its textures, its temples, divisions, the hardness at the Ilidža end . . .

Another peculiarity of Dayton: the city turns out to be ghosted by some doppelganger called "Srpsko Sarajevo"—because the Serbs wanted one, too. Only there's no real city there for them to *have*, and like many realities out here it's difficult to say if it even exists. Oh it's on maps all right, but that's something of a sop, as the Inter-Entity Boundary Line wriggles crazily around the western and southern suburbs, leaving the Srpsko parts widely separated . . . so it's not a town, it's *kind* of a region but with an evanescent formality, its notional capital Pale, a miles-distant town on the other side of Mount Trebević . . . still, it's *there*. You can feel it, sustained by the fervent belief of ethnic Serbs, a whole other city without locus, a new capital in fact, cleft from an existing one and widening the division between their identities. And, going by the new road signs directing drivers to Belgrade, and *none at all* to Sarajevo, the division isn't getting any milder, either.

The metaphors are all brain architecture, psychiatric. What's going on?

So there's a long history of, let's say, being able to see both sides of a question here. The fibrillation of mind that overcomes a person in big cities, the inescapable fizzing caffeination very useful for getting things done, also for partying, making jokes, picking people up—well that's the opposite of Bosnia. The serenity is absolute. The trees are green, the clouds white, friends shake hands, and there is never any need to worry. Ironically enough. Frito sees the world and all its arrangements. And it is perfectly possible to see both sides of a thing simultaneously, which may normally be considered admirable broad-mindedness, but, to be strictly literal about it, to see both sides of an object simultaneously requires two heads, so it's more like *split*-mindedness—like the creepy double-headed Republika Srpska logo, just a transposition of the Imperial Austrian eagle, though no longer in the yellow-black color scheme of Habsburgsigns.

"Land of Contradictions" perhaps but Bosnia-Herzegovina is a uniquely schizoid nation. Any SFOR soldier knows this. Double-named for the kingdoms of Herzegovina, in the Mediterranean south, and Bosnia, *kind* of in the north, jurisdictions whose borders no one can exactly agree on, along the lines of "the Midlands" or "the Midwest"—it's been the dotted line for who knows how many divisions into two: between Joseph II and Catherine the Great, Turks and Austrians, Cvetković and Maček in '39, the German and Italians shortly thereafter, most recently divided into two completely new entities, the Federation and Republika Srpska, jurisdictions whose borders were also disagreed over, rather violently if you recall, in the 1990s. Bicameral division is everywhere. And especially when this sexy city-valley appears to be calling out for him—he doesn't like to talk about this, but—*personally*. To *be* with her. He knows it's probably to do with coming off the antipsychotics; but she does, she appears to have a mind—and to be in pain, and to love him, and—here's the thing—to be making *him* fall in love with *her*. He fights it but it's hard, and against such a barrage of suggestion: djinn in the water, Rachael Drikkevand's thing about higher sensibilities orchestrating the city's defense, and now Maza's dad and his talk of drilling into the city's head . . .

Yes, Gospodin Cukić, father to Maza. Frito could no longer put off the hospitality Maza has been insisting he accept for weeks now.

G. Cukić is a solemn, rickety old fellow with misshaven salt-and-pepper jowls, few teeth, and thick black spectacles that wildly distort his eyes, the whites of one an astonishing cherry-red. But his dignity is as indomitable as the city he defended a decade ago, and, Frito suspects, not unconnected. He has served the coffee in silence, placed the brass džezva back on its copper tray, drunk his whole cup, and set it down, before he shuffles forward onto the edge of the leatherette settee, beckons Maza alongside, rummages for her hand beside him, and, safely holding it in both palms, begins to address Frito. Maza translates:

G. CUKIĆ'S STORY OF "TUNEL DOBRINJA-BUTMIR"

"So absolute was the siege of the city of Sarajevo that we were compelled to dig a tunnel to escape. The same as in the prisoner camps in Germany. Each citizen was a prisoner. As in Trnopolje village, where Chetniks simply put barbed wire around the town, and said: now, this is a prison. This was what the Chetniks were telling us when they let the psychiatric patients loose in the city. We were all prisoners now, with no claim to normality.

"It took months to dig the tunnel, through a maze of trenches and almost a kilometer of wet mud, under the flat killing zone of Butmir aerodrome, and out into the kitchen of the widow of a friend of mine in the suburbs on the other side. In the shadow of Mount Igman, still vulnerable to Chetnik fire, though in the relative safety of blackout, our chances of being shot were reduced to the chances of anyone being hit by any unaimed round or ricochet. This was acceptable.

"From the other side of the airport one could drive in convoy out of the valley and down to Konjic. This was the only way that food, medicine, and ammunition got in, and the wounded got out. UN soldiers and journalists did not use the tunnel. The Chetniks allowed them to cross the airfield, but not us.

"Hundreds of people gathered at the tunnel-heads every night, carrying sacks of food, letters, children. You had to shield your cigarette embers. There was shit and litter everywhere. There was always a loud noise of people, babies, soldiers. Everyone talked as softly as they could, but the effect was loud. Small-arms fire and mortars continued as during the day. The army slid gurneys of ammunition into the tunnel between every few people. The only way through was to push them along the rails in front of you as you walked, bent double.

"The tunnel was opened in August 1993, and the first army officer commanding the tunnel used it himself to escape. Tunnel passes changed hands for thousands of Deutschmarks, for apartments. Most people were not allowed to use the tunnel, or the city would have emptied. The army had to defy the People's wish to run away. If it had not, the city would have fallen. And unless you had very good connections, and a vehicle, there was nowhere to go on the other side.

"All the crossings were at night. There was never any light.

"The tunnel was dug just in time to save us all from starving, or from surrendering and being exterminated. Just as a surgeon must sometimes drill a hole in the skull of a stroke victim to relieve the pressure of the blood inside, the tunnel allowed us to live a little longer. We had been bleeding inside for a year and a half before the tunnel was dug.

"I thank you for your help with my daughter. I love her more than anything in world."

Gospodin Cukić refills his cup of coffee, drinks it, puts it down, sits back on the leatherette settee, and looks at Frito.

Frito knows by now comments are not necessary. His function is only to hear. Perhaps to repeat what he has heard to the insular West. He puts his hands together, thanks Gospodin Cukić for his hospitality, and leaves.

Summer will come. Money will change hands; loves be traded, stockpiled, lost. Butterflies will throng the city. Somewhere along the way Frito has learned that "butterfly" in Ancient Greek is *psyche*—also the word for "soul"—and now can't shake the image of thousands of minds fluttering around, trafficking their own economy, neurons at play in a brain the size of a city. New faces appear in the streets. As the weeks go by he feels less and less a part of the scene, feels something moving him on. But when pressed, he'll say it's not so much something, as some*one* . . .

How can he stop himself? How can he look at the shape of the

Republika Srpska today, two lobes joined by the Brčko Zone, and not think: brain scan? Even at the time of the Austro-Hungarian occupation in 1878, the finest minds of the Dual Monarchy's kakanian bureaucracy couldn't decide which half, Austria or Hungary, Bosnia-Herzegovina should fall under. So Bosnia developed a Janus-like status, known as *Corpus Separatum*, and uniquely in the Empire, was administered jointly by the two sides. And what country doesn't claim to be "Crossroads of East and West"—but BiH was a bit more than that. Along the lines of the corpus callosum, the neural structure connecting the two halves of the brain: leftbrain Austria with its Teutonic rationalizations, its schools of engineering and monuments to commerce; and right brain Magyars, fiery tempers from unknown bloodlines east of the steppes, untamable nobilities, indecent dancing and worse language. Or consider Brčko itself these days, the most fudged city in a fudged "peace" settlement, postwar intersection with all its Customs officials, razorwire, index fingers on trigger guards and buildings with ←MINES→ spray-painted on broken walls, connecting the Bosnian Federation to the Republika Srpska, and so vulnerable to any attempt to sever. And is not the symbol of the Republic, chosen back when Bosnia-Herzegovina was still in Yugoslavia, the Old Bridge at Mostar, high sixteenth-century arch over fizzing turquoise waters—i.e., the joining of halves?

And, of course: the Old Bridge, like Vedo's corpus callosum, was severed during the war.

Frito is not so far gone as to think this proves anything. It's almost certainly an attack of pattern recognition, just faces in the moon. But this is the ambient noise against which he is trying to stop himself from thinking of her as having some kind of higher intelligence, "sensibility" at least, with which she is gamely trying to lure him into something.

Something along the lines of: "I *am* your father"? He tries to joke it off, but there *is* a family resemblance, beyond the schizotypal: at first helped but now strung out on Dayton medicine to keep her sane, increasingly divided against herself, and unable to join the EU, or the WTO, or the whole main sequence of twenty-first-century life, if things keep up as they are.

Djinn and shaitan are known for exacting their price. What price Sarajevo's deliverance from death? Hard to say. But Frito's no longer inhibited against having a go: this little rockpool of Imperial sophistication, so exiled within a desolation of rednecks, it's got nothing else to leave—it's going mad in solitary. Like the university, it has lost its faculties. For Frito the professional exile, a Wandering Jew never able to find intimacy, his life one long sequence of departures and startings afresh—perhaps this explains his unusual affinity to Sarajevsko Pivo in the first place? A recognition of his own kind, cognate blood circulating through another exile, their eyes meeting over slinky 33cl non-returnable glass . . .

Oh it's too much, all connected in some huge geometry in too many dimensions. When reduced to the one dimension of a line of words, it stops making sense. The shape is too elaborate and delicate to fit out of a mouth, to exit the comfortable environment of a brain— but the overall pattern makes *sense*, dammit.

But yeah, he knows what it looks like from the outside. He has a little trick, not unlike wishing on the first star. First thing in the morning, *ding* eyes open he's awake, head washed clean by sleep, he can ask his heart a question and he'll get a straight answer:

Must I leave everything behind?

And it's an answer that makes him stay fetal a bit longer, drag the covers up to his nose, until courage enough comes online to get up & doing, go free up some energy with a run to the caves . . .

"I think you are not quite well," says Sufi Child in June, at Club Bill Gates, removing the earphones of his new MP3 player. Not hostile or anything, just without any adult bashfulness or politik.

"I'm right as rain."

"No, your mind is very—" flapping his hand like a luffing sail. "Maybe you are drinking too much the sliva."

Frito resigns with his eyebrows and settles on an elbow to enjoy his coffee. Well, Sufi Child's at that age when his bullshit antennae are permanently erect—and the feeling that this bipolar old dude on all the meds might, after all, be completely insane, and therefore somewhat full of shit, must be pretty compelling.

"You're going to take off aincha," Frito tells Sufi Child. "Take off aincha?"

Who half nods, half shakes his head.

"You see? You're not the only one who can read minds, mate."

Sufi Child doesn't want to upset Frito. "But I have no—there is no more games here for me, I do not—"

"It's alright," Frito squashing this defensiveness with a palm, "it's alright. You've got no reason to stick around. I'd take off if I was you." Frito's taught him everything about the hunter-gatherer fundamentals of trade that he knows, really. In six months he's earned more than Frito will all year, plus he's fought off a bizarre legal action by the Tekija Prnaša Esoterika to have him returned, animus revertendi, to their ownership. He'll most likely head to London, soft bullseye for illegal migrants. Frito's sorted him out with a few names and addresses, directions to the Grosvenor Victoria poker rooms, and has acquired from Belgrade, epicenter of these things, an artfully worn Slovenian passport in the name "Jovan Axl Rosavić."

"Jovan Rosavić," Sufi Child trying it on for size, looking proudly at himself, then doing the calculation, "I am—eighteen?"

"No reason to piss around, Axl. You'll be a European in a year." When Slovenia will join the EU. Leavetaking in the Information Age is a different thing entirely, it's only been a few months since they met and they'll never be further away than a Please Update Your Contact Details, but it's still sad to see him go.

"Take it easy, Axl," says Frito.

"What is this Axl?" says Sufi Child.

"You got carte blanche, take any name you want, you want. Might as well go for something a bit more dominating than Jovan. So people'll remember you. My Christian name's Lewis. Lewis! Plenty of Lewises, only one Frito. And since you're a poker player, your name has to begin with A. Like the Aces. Get all your money in. Scrawny little troublemaker like yourself. Axl. The weapon. Under a vehicle."

"Axl," says Sufi Child, impressed. "Very pleased to meet you, my name is Axl. Bitching."

Frito has an odd way of reprogramming his brain with this—"Sufi Child" find-and-replaced with "Axl," all the way back to the first meeting, which kind of throws Bannerman when Frito reminisces, Bannerman who never saw Sufi Child between his being renamed Axl and his departure.

FRITO: This one time, it was just Clare, Axl and me down in
    Konjic . . .
BANNERMAN: Axl?
FRITO: Axl Rosavić. *You* remember him. Little fella. Rent boy.
    Drank like a fish . . .

Axl's all fired up for the off. Watching him disappear from the Dobrinja warehouse, knocked-off rucksack on his back, Frito at the curtain door puts an arm round Maza, half out of the cinematic conditioning of the moment, half because she's genuinely upset. Even Egzon the security guard seems a bit down.

"Oi Axl," says Frito.

"What." Turning round.

"What have you given the O'Ryans to thank them the O'Ryans?"

"I have tried, but . . ." with a weak lift of the shoulders. Then, in answer to Frito's look, "Jamie will not take anything! He is too proud!"

"Find a way. You can't just leave. Don't give me those eyes ya tight little bastard! If you leave, it *will* follow you. Doppelganger. Trust me. Vedo's adamantine. What's the first rule of Islam, or whatever? Hospitality. Doctor of the hospital. You. Make it better."

Axl Rosavić accepts the point, nods, waves at Egzon, and is gone.

Frito versus the world. The template in his head is of a psychiatrist and patient at loggerheads, one convinced that he's Elvis, the other convinced that he's a psychiatrist, and both convinced the other is wrong. The discussion has become futile. The only safety lies in numbers.

He has not found love. He has looked, and he has tried to find something worth more than money. He has tried *so* hard to find love. Someone to generate within him a love that would weather decades. But out of intolerance or megalomania or Disinhibited Personality Disorder or some other failure of self, it has not worked for him. How long do you keep looking in all the places you've already looked?

It's been a meager fulfillment, at best "busyness," this endless chain of one- and ten-night stands, during this long, exhausting adolescence—which, sure, normality regards as perfectly viable behavior for the antechamber. A procrastination most fine before Deciding Who You Are, even while your future watches you, non-judgmentally, though not without a certain kindly impatience— nothing serious, on the order of a dad come to pick you up at the swimming pool. But at this point Frito's going to have to put his elbows up on the side, and confess: really sorry, but interpersonal love just isn't for him.

But *still* can't he just pike out, find his way back to the herd, opt in to the pleasant mediocrity of growing old, find a person of the opposite sex to keep him company doing it? Even—with some massive effort of will—attempt to remain faithful?

But no. His morning heart also tells him:

You don't have to go forward but you cannot go back.

Any faithfulness wouldn't be to her; not even to some moral principle. It would all be in the name of, what? Conformity? Sparing her feelings? He simply does not have the necessary fear of loneliness to care. Sure, he recognizes these symptoms as classically psychopathic. But it *feels* radically different from the inside. There is a radiance that pharmaceutical psychology is not interested in—the word "love" will have to do—in everything to do with Sarajevo, and especially its wonderful, transcendent beer. His blood. The landscapes are all psychedelic.

He shuts his eyes and feels airborne, drifting through the ceiling of the Baščaršija flat, its rusted armatures and bullet-scarred walls taking their place among the nightscapes below: floodlit mosques,

EnergoInvest cranes, queues of headlights—and tonight, this constellation of city, its lights floating into position, vast and symphonic, each point the voice of a crisp metal instrument, together describing the curvature of city here laid underneath him like a lover.

Within an arrangement of streets he has come to know so well, shapes now as instinctive as the shape of continents, down in all the tenements, towerblocks, the graffiti'd and busted pillboxes, teenagers in killer bodies with big bro's leather jacket and a pair of hopeful condoms still joined at the perforation—what capacities for love? This very night how many pairs of people are removing clothes, are delaying to touch the goose-bumpy surfaces of what will very soon become their lovers—because once that first touch's repercussions are felt, the sudden chromatograph in your chest fading away underneath the touches that come after, isn't it all downhill from there? To feel that, to absorb all *that*—for Frito to be immanent in all these lives, to remain forever on the leading edge of all these bright topnotes of lust, swelling deep loves, bass as oceans—and better than that: the *anticipation* of all this? The hope that what may come to pass between us will weigh so much as to split open the mountain beneath?

That's what Sarajevsko Pivo does for him. At least, those are the only terms in which others seem to be able to understand it.

And still he floats away into the black night, aeroplane winglights moving diagonal past him, and can come to see the entire kingdom and all its waterways, over- and underground, lighting up in infinite dendritical patterns, detail cascading down to the smallest trickle. Because when he stops resisting it he knows he's not seeing Bosnia the water-kingdom at all, but *his own brain* in incredible resolution, axons all lit with luciferase aglow to the far horizon, where what looks like the city of Prijedor in the far north, but is actually an enormous complex of loves he can no longer feel, leaks a peaceful yellow light into the starfield above. Loves now sealed off from him, from when "Frito" used to be someone else, someone whole.

But—a shining snaking through to this valley—he does love Bannerman. Maybe he can remember them kissing. (Not Bannerman and *him*, Bannerman and Clare. Please.) Bannerman holding her with such gentleness and Clare responding, not much of her at first, but with a timid reciprocity that's been building. Frito has a touchstone and can assay these things. He can reach out and grab at what Bannerman feels for her, bunch it up into a nugget and drag it across a low black slate, and it comes back pure. It's fine. It's everything he has been unable to generate himself. How can he not feel such love for them both that as he inhales his chest fills with stars, his own eyes for once shut in pleasure? A distillation of all that love coursing through him, that in the magnanimity and broad-mindedness of his current state of mind he doesn't need to keep to himself.

And Bannerman so very, very unhappy.

All right, so maybe Frito overcooked that a bit.

Frito met Clare Leischman last October at a soirée at the Swiss Embassy. Some Italian from the OHR had invited him, back before he'd really started in on the beer. Hell, he was in town, so he thought he might as well throw a few back with the Paddy Ashdown crowd. He was a little tipsy by the time he showed, nothing serious, though maybe having a little bit of an "episode," because he found himself creeped out in a back-against-the-wall kind of way by how much makeup had been troweled on by the ladyfolk here. As if seeing it for the first time. Half the people in the room had *paint* all over their *faces*! and were grinning with manic ferocity like it *wasn't there*! and Frito went round subtly tapping his face at various ladies, the "ahem you have a little something on your face" routine, and they'd check themselves out in the mirror, fine, look to Frito for confirmation only to find him doing it more insistently, and go round again, by which time Frito would be basically punching himself in the face. Scared clouds of them off to the lavatories. Caused a bit of consternation, but these people weren't just Swiss but *diplomats* too, compromise-ninjas, and one of His Excellency's entourage wafted over to Clare and wondered if she might like to soak up some of this Maori's attention, keep him away from the straights. Clare has always been a team player.

"But it's like—look at *that* one," Frito's manic eye peeking over Clare's shoulder, "how can you tell what shape her skull is? Could be an alien under all that slap."

"That's the treasurer of the Serb Unity Party."

"Christ a-bloody-live, what is she, in hiding? Anyone know if she really looks like that?"

"That is what she looks like."

"I dunno, wouldn't be surprised if it was bloody Ratko under there. Here, I'll go get a sample—" and Frito drifted over to the treasurer of the Serb Unity Party's circle, pulled an eyelash off his own face, said "excuse me but," clamped a great hand on her shoulder and gouged a furrow in her foundation with his thumb, and held up the eyelash on a different finger. Awkwardness all round. "You make a wish and blow it away eh?" explained Frito. "Go on then. Made a wish? Then give it a blow." She puffed it away. "There you are, well done," Frito admonishing her flirtatiously now, making a singsong of it, "but I hope your wish doesn't involve artiller-y . . ."

Frito came back with his thumbful and huddled over it with Clare. "Bloody orange, eh."—"Not a very natural tone," agreed Clare.— "Let's see how it looks on you."—"No!" Clare trying to squirm away, but Frito managed to get her wrists together, and burnish small orange patches on her cheeks while she kicked and flailed delightedly.—"Not too bad eh?"—"I look like a burns victim," wailed Clare.—"You been tango'd," agreed Frito.

"Clare, a word?" said someone from the Embassy.

But before she could respond, Frito said "we're just leaving," and when he grabbed Clare's wrist and pulled her out into a night of anticky Western hedonism, she let herself be led.

And in the crater of the next morning, eyes glued shut with sleep and angel dust, Frito and Clare helped each other limp down to the lobby of the Holiday Inn for breakfast, the courtesy of strangers passing between them—last night's memories were still drifting overhead, searching for somewhere to alight—and with his rational brain still shut for business, and this Clare girl bent over a Bosnian glossy, her fresh-washed hair falling in her face trying to read an article about

SEKS, in those days still full of good intentions about learning the language.

At the next table, some hatchet-faced peroxide types were chatting animatedly amid a flash of jewelry and acrylic nails, and between them on the table was a small, ratty dog-in-a-handbag, head poking out of a very undignified pink feathery thing. The doggy let go a small, high-pitched sneeze. The women twittered in the air above him, but Clare looked up from her magazine and across at the little dog and said gesundheit.

Causing Frito to realize that here was pretty much the exact female transposition of his best friend, Bannerman K. Tedus. Intelligent and warm and fierce and all good things but endearingly, heartbreakingly incompetent. Such a good clean heart, but only half able to deal with life, which is to say· unable, without someone else to hold her heart for her.

And clearly having a very shit time with guys. Perhaps she'd managed to convince herself, taking her cues from the way things went around her, that getting laid a lot was just her having fun, but somewhere inside the cliff-face of her desolate island heart, and pointed outward so she wasn't aware of it, this girl was signaling distress.

Frito locked up staring at her, ketchup-covered meat product halfway to his mouth, feeling the idea of her and its textures, marveling at how the spectroscopy given off by this girl was practically identical to Bannerman's. Then she looked up and caught him looking and was like: the fuck are you looking at?

"How beautiful you are," said Frito. And she melted. Yep, this was Mrs. Bannerman all right.

But then he remembered that Bannerman's specialty lay in missing open goals like this. It wouldn't be enough just to introduce them. Wrinkle No. 2: Bannerman was in London, Clare was in Sarajevo. Well, that wasn't insuperable. Bannerman wouldn't kick up too much a fuss about moving down here if Frito sold it right. Sweet as.

But even if all this were arranged, how could he trust Bannerman not to cock it up, in either direction? not to somehow alienate her while also not convincing himself that she was too short, freckly, too—christ, *anything*. Too circumspect. Bannerman, Idiotboy, could not be trusted with his own heart. It wasn't that he was stupid, or disingenuous, he simply had a block; he kept losing interest in the girls he'd chased down, and after it was all over and they found someone else, *that's* when he went crazy with loss. Frito watched this cycle again and again, with mounting disbelief.

Bannerman had always had issues: insane mother, absent father, never much in the way of a family life, except for Frito. Frito had been his life for a long time now. It wasn't that there was anything sexual about it, and their friendship wasn't that weird really, except maybe for its exclusivity.

Touching. But not healthy, not in the long run, and not good for either of them. Being inseparable chums was getting lame by their thirties. Frito had thought about what would happen to Bannerman if he, Frito, had ever found love, back in London. Bannerman dumped, not by a girl this time but by his only friend?

Luckily it never came up. More immediately, how could he prize Bannerman's childish deathgrip off him and onto this perfect girl? So Frito hatched a plan, which called for the Transference of the boy's feelings, as delicate a psychiatric operation as any: psychiatrists often experience Transference effects when their patients transfer their unrequited or oedipal or psychopathic feelings onto the facilitator, the psychiatrist. It's a standard part of the therapeutic canon; it has to be handled right, not abused, and has in the course of therapy to be redirected back at the right targets. Often, merely back into themselves, to correct a neurotic failure of self-respect. Or in this case, redirected at a wonderful girl.

Frito, enlightened Renaissance man, had just the plan. He would start seeing Clare, and Bannerman would be as full of jealousy and resentment and lust for her as for all the other girls Frito'd ever dated. Because Frito would keep telling him *she's the one mate*, and spending time with her, taunting him with the prospect that this girl would remove the only crutch from Bannerman's life. And in Bannerman's mind, she would be able to do this because she was *better than him*, and therefore, in his naïve boy-heart, worthy of his love.

It would demolish him. Bannerman would see in Clare the most precious, powerful entity in the universe, the sun around which he would revolve, and that's before he even got his teeth into how miserable and funny and dejectedly optimistic she was, with such a heartbreaking faith in everyone's capacity for goodness . . . and how pretty she was. Kind of.

Frito just had to keep shagging her, selfless bloke, until Bannerman was weak with need, until he scraped together blood, guts and spunk enough to cash it all in for what he wanted—to stand up to his best friend and take her and make her happy and never forget the clarity he had before he got her—never get to thinking that maybe he could do better. Then Frito would stand aside, and let these two hearts lick themselves clean and get on with the rest of their lives. What could go wrong?

Čišćenje Mina

THE VALLEY HAS turned brown, wet and gray. Roofs weep for the passing of winter. Under the receding snow are whole riversides of dead ancient undergrowth, now seen to have been clawing for air with twisted burgundy branches. In the valley, cargo cranes dangle still hooks over the water. The occasional circular chimney-stack of blood-colored bricks. A lugubrious sky finding redemption further west, breaking into a scribble of cirrus clouds shining in steep perspective against the sun's weak glare, struggling to be felt.

But the wind is savage. Wet jeans, numb feet, the File 13 prisoner detail takes a course broadly west by southwest, up streams fat with snowmelt, onto and off paths, victims of paving attempts, past red-painted rocks—everyone's taken the Mine Awareness Course, they know what an unplowed field means—past broken old houses, roofless, collecting corners of snowdrift—and up into the snow-line.

The topology is complex. Animal's GPS would pinpoint their location, but on the assumption that it's compromised along with everything else, he's turned it off. Anything imponderable descends to the level of superstitions when NATO is your enemy. Antagonist, rather. Animal going so far as to remove its batteries, and even then regarding it with shamanistic misgivings.

It's not until three hours later, resting in a burnt-out chalet, and after a half-hour rest that Animal announces:

"In a few minutes I'm going to check phone reception, send a message. We'll have to skedaddle fair sharp thereafter."

When he does so, Mobilna Srpska gives him five bars. The Jahorina cell phone transceiver is nearby. He picks up Bannerman's text:

Asenova raided. 1 time pad still there. Try another code.
sorry.

"Shit!" Animal shouts.

Everyone looks up. "Everything alright, boss?" Brick says.

Animal takes a few deep breaths. "Yet another change of plan. Brick, for the next five minutes, I have to encode a message and then I'll have to turn the phone on again. So as to lead the VRS a merry dance, I'm going to head back the other way. You boys head northwest, stay on the treeline, I'll catch up with you in a bit."

"No worries."

Animal looks at nothing, pulls out a pencil, begins to write.

GET COJONES VICTOR RV AT BASE LAMDA EONACH HOLES SPETH YEARS HER HOUSE PHI DJELJA CROSSING WINNING HAND ARIELS FORMAT T QUARRYMEN STOP DONT USE GPS OR GSM STOP ATT HELIS END

Bannerman and Clare's faces are pressed together over the screen.

"The fuck?" says Bannerman

"It's definitely English, is it?" she says.

"Yeah. All right.—Let's go see Shiny and Jamie. Now where'd I park the car?"

Bannerman explains on the way. "Jamie O'Ryan won this like historic game of Cojones—totally stupid game—he won like forty thousand euro or something crazy. So the message says: Get Cojones Victor, that's Jamie—RV, Rendezvous—lamda's the symbol used for latitude, or longitude, one or the other—eonach holes, no idea—speth years?—no idea, but you get the idea. I have no clue what this stuff means, but I bet Jamie and Shiny do."

"But he mentions Ariel," says Clare.—"Yep."—"But what would he know about Ariel Alkali? That you would also know?"—"It's a code, see."—"But, what, you two know private stuff about Ariel?"—"A few things."—"Has Animal hooked up with her?"

Bannerman shrugs gaily. "Who knows?"

Clare pinches her lips, eyes moving vacantly on the billboards as they pass the windows. "Have *you*?"

They need to get onto the other side of the mountain, the southern slope, but can't risk breaking out of the trees and crossing the bald summit. Not with the Sokos patrolling the bare high ground, creeping up past them twice an hour. Instead Edgar leads them along the treeline, more or less, the thick undisturbed snow inside the trees making it hard going, breaking cover now and again to traverse a gully, and back in. The slope is more white than green, and after stumbling mostly noisily through the trees they come to the end of another block, and see a pair of skilift cables, lifeless black against the white sky.

"Jahorina," says Sufi Child. "I know this place. There is a skilift over the next hill." Ranković agrees.

"Working?" Edgar asks.

Sufi Child shrugs. "It is late in the season."

"Lots of snow recently." Brick looks uphill. "We'll get picked up for sure we try to cuff it over the hill."

Animal arrives through the pines. "That sodding hill."

"We could wait it out?"

Animal shakes his head. "We have an appointment."

At his and Shiny's flat, Jamie O'Ryan unfolds a 1:50,000 map, Bjelašnica-Jahorina, onto the kitchen table. It's laminated, the plastic gone white at the folds, with shaded red polygons in solvent marker denoting un-demined areas. Jamie uncaps a pen. "So what have we got?" he says.

"Enough holes—eneach?—" Bannerman tries. "*That* word."

"Eonach," Jamie reads. "Golf course. Just up the road from us in Scotland."

"That'd be eighteen then," says Clare.

"Eighteen, eighteen," Jamie following the longitude marks at map's edge. "Eighteen West, makes sense," writing it in the corner. "What else?"

"Speth years her house phi."

"I'm thirty," says Shiny.

"Shiny Dryhten!" Jamie admonishes.

"two," crestfallen, "but I shall be having words with Mr. Elliot-Maitland upon his return."

"Speth?" says Clare.

"Elspeth—Good. So—which puts us sort of *here* . . ."

"Her house phi." "Phi is latitude." "Her house, then. What's the number of your house?"

Jamie and Shiny look at each other. "Gornjovakufska Four," says Jamie.

"Flat B," Shiny adds.

Bannerman gives a tight smile. "This is Animal. Would he know your house number in Scotland?"

"Absolutely. Ambercloutie 4502."

"Fantastic," writing it up. "This line.—Now, latitude."

"Djelja? Djelja Crossing? Djelja Crossing winning?"

"I think it's going to be Djelja Crossing—Winning hand, which is probably the Cojones game again. Jamie, can you visualize your hand at Cojones that time?"

"Every time I shut my eyes. Four–three of hearts."

"Excellent. Not sure we need the suit. We are the *shit*."

"Sure it wasn't three–four?" Clare says.

Jamie and Bannerman look at each other. "Higher card first," Bannerman says presently.—"Agreed."—"You sure Animal knows that?"—"Yep," after a pause.—"All right. Four–three."

"And—if you look—our latitude is going to have to start with forty-three North, whatever it is. So I guess that's what winning hand means. So what's Djelja Crossing?"

Difficult silence. Fingers skid back and forth across the Jahorina mountain range, a triangle defined by vertices at Sarajevo, Foča and Goražde—a long icicle pointed at Sarajevo.

"All right. We'll come back to Djelja. Ariels format t quarry-men."

"The Quarrymen were John Lennon's group before the Beatles," says Shiny. "Knowing Animal, has to be."

"Right. So, what does that mean, numerically?"

"Nineteen sixty maybe? Sixty-one?"

"You don't know when they were?"

"Google it."

"And ariels format has got to be her four-by-five camera. Forty-five."

"What about the 't'?"

Difficult silence. "Most likely the numerical value, where A is one B is two, so on. Which makes," counting on his fingers, "twenty." Bannerman wrinkles his face, another silence. "Maybe he couldn't think of a twenty."

"So," Jamie O'Ryan summing up, "we've got: we need to meet him at a *base*, longitude 18° 32' 45" and 2 hundredths, and latitude 43° 45' 20" and 59 hundredths. Up here, by . . . Pavlovac."

"Excellent. Go go go!" cheers Shiny.

"But we left out Djelja Crossing," says Bannerman. "It can't be right."

"Maybe that's what he's calling this operation," suggests Clare.

"That is easily the stupidest thing I ever heard."

"If it's a rendezvous, aren't you going to need a time to be there?" asks Shiny.

"Yep yep. Course! She's good, she's good," Bannerman shooting her with his finger, "So 't' is time. Quarrymen is the time. When were the Quarrymen?"

"Wikipedia says 1957–59."

"Which is what. Eight o'clock. Easy."

"Which makes ariels format, 45, the seconds—43 is the minutes, and so Djelja Crossing is the degrees, which we know has to be 43 anyway. Did you Google Djelja Crossing?"

"Kind of. *Djelja* is Croatian for 'multiple.' "

"Oh wait!" Bannerman and Clare getting it together. "That's that beer-djinn!" says Clare.

"Battle of the Neretva, 1943," says Bannerman.

"Okay great: 43° 43' 45". Which puts the RV *here*."

"But then you've got greater accuracy in the longitude than the latitude. What's up with that?"

"Not sure I'm happy with your house, Shiny. Every other clue has two words, which gives us a two-digit number, apart from that one. You sure that's right?"

Shiny looks blankly offended. "Ambercloutie 4502, that *is* my number. My parents' number."

"And the street number?" Clare asks.

"No numbers, just words," says Shiny. "Lots of words."

"Big house," whispers Jamie.

"So maybe it's double zero. Which puts it here. That makes sense?"

"Doesn't feel right," says Bannerman. "Her house, zero zero. You're supposed to *know* when you've got it right, regardless of where it comes out."—"Yeah."—"Is there anything else you can tell us about your parents' house?"—"It's Georgian. Pale blue. Seven bedrooms?"— "And no numbers in the address?"—"Well there's the postcode: PA35?"—"Thirty-five sounds good; 35's here. Right? What do you think?"—"I guess so," says Bannerman," not a *world-class* clue, you know . . ."

Shiny shakes her head, at a loss. "Well, it's the only two-digit number in the address: Elspeth Dryhten, Fife Dean, Ambercloutie, Oban, Argyll and Bute, PA35 7KT."

Everyone assumes different postures of thought.

"The man's a genius," says Clare, turning to Bannerman.

"Not this again."

"Fife Dean," she repeats, with emphasis.

Oh, the near-ecstatic pleasure of walking on a paved surface. The Sufi Child's feet are terribly sore. He paces happily down the winding road to the center of the resort, pausing now and then to stomp snow from his bootlaces and push his jacket sleeves back up over his hands again.

The pistes down here are thick and well combed, people are out and smiling, knock-kneed children are on the baby slopes, pop music blares from cafés, the treble picked out in eidetic clarity today, off-duty snowboarders in jester hats lean back with beers, ski boots angled onto their heels. RS police officers stand around beaming. Sufi Child heads over to Pension Sport, hires a pair of skis and two snow-boards, buckling them sideways under the compression straps on Brick's rucksack. It is heavy and difficult to carry. He also buys five lift passes and four packs of Drina cigarettes, spending Ranković's KM all the way. Gets on his skis and onto the ski chair to the top of the mountain. For a few minutes, he can relax. The air and the view are beautiful.

At the top he turns left, and slides diagonally down toward the second station. It's very fun to be skiing on real skis finally. Suddenly in the middle of hands-down the most extreme experience of his young life, here he is skiing like a Westerner. Falling down occasion-ally, sitting hard onto his bottom, the wind in his hair, goodness *he should have bought sunglasses too*! squinting against the sun, teeth bared to the cold.

Halfway down the Super-G he comes to a stop and sits in the snow. He's just realized.

He could go. He could escape from all this, just slide down to the station and get away. He would survive. For sure. Whereas to go back is to choose a fate already "tits up"—an idiom new to him—where weapons are involved. Vojka Republika Srpske is after him. Of every-one, not being international, he is most likely not to survive if caught. He could turn and ski, carve large womanly curves into the snow, wave to the Westerners as he schusses past, giggle at their expres-sions, escape. They would be fine. And he would live on, he could go back to Frito, learn more about business, about cards, not be chased by Serb gangsters his whole life, become rich.

He realizes he has never, ever asked himself what he wants. Beyond getting warm and fed, it simply never came up. He looks around the mountainscene, blankly, for clues, toe-to-toe with what is suddenly the absolute and only question. But for the first time he has no reads. His instincts are blank, he doesn't even know where to *begin*.—A recognition that this blankness must be what the grown-ups have been talking about all this time, and probably the reason they do such silly things . . . no one has the first idea about *anything*. And now, especially, himself.

But maybe those teeth bared against the cold—maybe that's not a grimace, young dervish, could it be that that's actually a smile?

He stabs his poles and skis down, taking a right fork, to the second station.

Not so nice over here. Old cable-car stations, rusted iron flywheels, concrete housings pockmarked and grafitti'd. Grand hotels burned out. Bars and restaurants closed, small wooden chalets boarded up; suspended building work; a village home only to djinn and ghul. Undisturbed snowlanes wind through the trees.

—"CHILD."

He looks up. Edgar and the others are lounging on the porch of a closed wooden chalet, waving to him. He skis over; everyone's looking much better. Shaved. None so much as Ranković, who's lost his mustache, his leash and his wrist-ropes, and is looking extremely happy and agreeable.

"Morphine," Edgar explains.

"I hear good things," says Sufi Child.

Edgar and Brick get the snowboards. Everyone gets Drinas. Weapons and webbing will barely fit into the rucksacks; alarming bulges in all directions. Animal takes a deep breath, pulls his arm around Ranković, gets comfy. Below them, the chairlift station, whirring mainwheel under giant yellow V-braces, has a short queue, and is being operated by a pair of bored guys in white one-piece ski suits.

"How drunk do we look," says Animal.

Jamie O'Ryan runs a finger down the latest MICC mine map, south from the city and into a tangle of contour lines. "Three hours," he says. "Plus or minus three."

"Plus or minus?" Bannerman looking at his watch. "So we could arrive any minute?"

Jamie's briskly preparing the Land Rover. "Get yourself a few coats from the rack. Shiny, a few tools from the gun cupboard, if you'd not mind. Clare, it's been a pleasure." Pausing to kiss her on the cheek. "He's a brilliant man, your—" waving at Bannerman, then catching Shiny glaring at him, "—your acquaintance."

And out into the garage, a blue long-wheelbase Land Rover with a white roof and ČIŠĆENJE MINA in great stickers on all sides. Jamie loading a spare jerrycan of diesel, throwing in some pointy sticks, metal detectors, blast shields, other bits and pieces of mine-clearing kit, possibly out of habit. Shiny arrives with a pair of pistols and a matt-green ammunition box. Clare with slivovic. Bannerman buttoning up a Barbour as he comes.

"Be careful," says Clare. Then, "Both of you."

"Animal's been out there for a day," says Bannerman, "how bad can it be?"

"Yeah but he—" Clare begins, then stops. Bannerman's smiling, he doesn't care. "I don't care so much about him," she says.

"Save all that nonsense for later," says Shiny. "Jamie? Stop by the Lady Di Café on your way out of town. I've placed an order for a few čevapi. I expect the boys might appreciate it."

"Farewell, Mrs. O'Ryan, my love," says Jamie, "you think of everything."

"Jamie?" says Shiny.

"Yes, my knife and fork?"

"You know how Andrew—Animal—and I, our families, knew each other growing up? It's probably nothing, but I suppose worth mentioning—" and Shiny barefoots gingerly over the gravel to Jamie and whispers in his ear.

Jamie frowns, turns a death-ray pair of eyes on her, but can't for the moment actually speak. Shiny backs up and dips her head and hides behind her hair. "I've been meaning to tell you," she mumbles, "but you never noticed, and it just became one of those things . . ."

"Thirty-*three*?"

"Nice job, Sufiboy!" Edgar shouts to the chair behind. Sufi Child waves in return, him and Brick bobbing against the blue sky. Brick gives a jolly nod. In front, Animal bends round, does the *quietly* gesture. Ranković lolls happily against Animal, hanging on to the red safety bar.

Edgar fiddles with the weapons rucksack. A moment of powerlessness. They can't go any faster than the chairlift. Bare of trees, cloudcover for the minute gone, the sun banging hard off the crust of snow crystals. Blank of feeling in their feet, jeans dark with wet, faces numb with the stinging wind that gusts off the mountaintop. The thrum of helicopters comes and goes further down the valley. The top approaches steadily.

Then, fifty yards from the landing, the chairlift stops. The boys are left swinging in the blue. Look from one to the next. Empty shrugs. Ahead of them, a wooden shed. The chairlift operator emerges, listening to a walkie-talkie, looking at them.

"It's fine," Animal shouts back. "Don't stress."

"Totally," shouts Edgar.

The operator gestures for Animal and everyone to be patient. "Nema problema," shouts the operator.

"Nema problema," Animal shouts back.

"Nema problema," mumbles Ranković happily.

"Oi Edgar," shouts Brick. "The Child dun't like the look of this. Tell Animal."

Edgar looks to Animal; the Child and Brick look to them both.

Everyone looks down. The slope is steep, with maybe four inches of new snow. Further down the valley the helicopters have turned toward them. The chairlift operator, a tall rangy guy in a lilac one-piece, is watching the helicopters approach, mumbling into the walkie-talkie.

Everyone looking at everyone else, swinging helpless from the cable.

"We got to, boss," shouts Brick.

A moment of thought. "Yep," Animal calls back.

Brick chucks his rucksack uphill off the chairlift. "This'll smart," he says, lifts the bar, and drops into air.

*

Back at International HQ, on Churchillplein in The Hague, it's been chaos at the International Criminal Tribunal for the former Yugoslavia for almost a decade. The smooth course of justice has been repeatedly hijacked by budgetary shortfalls, video-conferencing snafus, translation failures, speechifying witnesses who answer their own questions, fainting prosecutors, unscrupulous Texan defense attorneys ("cross-examination is a contact sport"), judges taken ill, witnesses crippled in untimely road accidents, inter-suspect assassination, obstructionist NATO governments that won't share intelligence, and finally a whole other *war*, in Kosovo. And that's not even the Milošević case—whose witness list stars Bill Clinton, Warren Christopher, Douglas Hurd, and goes on down from there. These people will never allow themselves to be examined in court, so it's all but untriable. It's slowly dawning on Churchillplein what NATO has been telling them all along: that it was a horrible mistake to arrest Milošević in the first place, that in pure legal terms he's in the clear, and now no one knows how, short of an unexpected death, they're going to wriggle out of the corner they've painted themselves into. More than once, a judge has turned his gavel on himself.

The lobbies outside the courtrooms are thick with chain-smoking clerks of the court, lighting each other up with trembling hands, comparing notes on these scarecrows of cases that no man alive understands, least of all the journalists. Then there are the indictees: not long ago there was a case in which one fired his court-appointed defense lawyer for not giving him a big enough kickback of his ICTY fees. Themselves pretty generous. True story or not, you might be in jail for crimes against humanity, but that didn't mean you didn't have leverage.

Meanwhile, out here in Sarajevo, the first Bosnian government war-crimes trial—because yes, they're running their own trials *as well*—has condemned two Bosnian Serbs to death for murder, only to have their alleged victims turn up alive and well. Further down the food chain, deciding who to investigate and who to let go on with their lives occupies a whole division of the OTP, Westerners all with no real understanding of the Bosnian arcanities, frequently homesick in this snowblind city and more or less constantly hungover to boot, fatally mixing up all the evidence files and operating what seems, at times, a lottery method for raising indictments. Investigator Marc van Xanthe, trying to concentrate in his little corner office, whose glass partitions shut out only the most obvious kinds of noise, sees himself trying to assemble a balsawood contraption of a case, without instructions. . . . because putting together damnations sturdy enough to survive the flurry—the devil's advocates always get the benefit of the doubt—what thanks is there, what can he draw from all this, where everything is frantic and subjunctive and liable to cancelation right until the gavel hits the knocker? What is there for *him*, other than to throw his hands up at it all, and take his victories where he can.

Marc picks up the phone. "Jens," he says, "are you busy?"

Ranković is in no state to walk uphill, even over the last thirty yards of crisp moguls. Brick slings him fireman over his shoulder. Edgar hustles up to the operator's shed, ice in sprays as he toe-stabs up the piste, opening the rucksack full of submachine guns, leaving one on the snow as he goes. Animal collects it as he passes. "You're a legend, Brick," calls Animal from near the top. The operator has scarpered. Spectators watch from the stalled chairlift.

The lead helicopter is whipping up snow further along the ridge. Brick is working hard.

"Nothing else for it," says Animal, loading a magazine into the MP5K. He stands behind the operator's shed, takes aim at the Soko.

"Jesus Christ Animal, don't start shooting *choppers*—"

Animal's aiming eye swivels over to Edgar, swivels back to his iron-sights. He fires two shots, a double tap. The Soko rears up, pauses.

"They can't set down here anyway. Too windy." He keeps up a light suppressing fire.

"You'd be amazed what they can do. Come on Brick, you fucking hero!"

But the Soko has moved away, sixty yards, hovers twenty feet above the broad mountaintop. Dark figures bale out into snow, weapons on slack slings falling with them. Brick arrives, panting, sets Ranković back onto his feet. Edgar grabs hold of Ranković's ankle, fixes it on one of the snowboards. Animal fires a few rounds at the figures, who drop back down into the snow.

"We getting a ruck on?" says Brick.

"Child, you know that side of the mountain?"

"I think no one knows this side."

Shots returned by the helicopter's fireteam crack as they pass. "Effective," calls out Animal. Child is pressed flat into the snow.

"Edgar—leave him, no time to go tandem. Just get off the top. Brick, take yourself, Rapes and the Child, get some distance behind you. Head west. Get to the treeline. Ready, standby standby go." Animal fires a few more shots. And heaving Ranković fireman over his shoulder again, Brick stamps off across broadly level ground, Child gliding along on skis squatting on his heels first, then as the ground begins to drop, straightening up, looking round, circling Brick.

Buddy-buddying backwards along the ski trails of their friends, Contact Drills, familiar as old hymns, in the teeth of a not particularly dedicated enemy, providing covering fire from a series of comfortable fire positions: prone in the snow, behind outcrops of rock and little cornices of wind-sculpted ice, an eternal blue day flying off the top of the Dinaric Alps, south across the vinelands of Herzegovina, the Montenegro massif just an inaccuracy on the horizon—with maybe even, in that shining haze to the right, the Adriatic Sea . . . the happiest time of Animal's life. Dimly aware of it approaching, descending upon him. And a special quality to the light, almost a filter . . . out here above the clouds, Ascension-white snow taking up two thirds of his field of vision, albedo so high the sky's the darkest thing he can see, he's now struggling with snow blindness too. An affliction like angelic visitation. The day already fading to white, dog-eared at the edges from having been, at some point in the future, loved too well.

"Stoppage."—"Got you."—"Clear."

Still, the VRS—if indeed that's who piled out of the Soko—have cottoned on to File 13's squeamishness about actually hitting any of them, and are beginning to convert that into bravery. Animal and Edgar trying to keep a mellow hundred yards between them and their antagonists.

"Getting a bit concerned," Animal glancing at his watch. "Don't want the others to get too far ahead. Brick heads down the wrong valley, we're in all kinds of clip."

Edgar lifts his chin. "You head on back. I'll keep em warm a little longer."

"Hell of a thing, providing covering fire for one."

"I'll be okay."

"—You're sure?" Animal buying time, thinking through the possibilities it might leave them vulnerable to Edgar fucking up.

"Go on. I'll give you twenty minutes, catch up with you later on." Animal nods. "It's a plan. Where'll I meet you?"

"Let's see your map. Alright. Planning to follow the high ground over to here, drop down into this valley, and into what I hope will be trees, about here—we'll wait for you on this stream here, where it crosses the most obvious geographical feature. A treeline, ideally. We'll hang about until five thirty. After that, you're on your own."

"Got it."—"See you there."—"Sure."

Animal looks down, licks his lips to indicate a change of gear. "We've had a result, Edgar. Everything's coming right. Here's your phone back. And the battery. Don't put em together unless you're turning yourself in, understood?"

"Understood."

"Sorry about all that ugliness earlier, but I am pleased you jumped the right way in spite of Mudhill. Not that I doubted you, but still. It's nice when you can count on your muckers." He puts a hand on Edgar's shoulder. "Solidest man I ever knew, Edgar Radford."

"Thanks."

"Thank *you*. Five thirty."—"Sure."—A round cracks overhead. "Let em have it, Edgar." And he's gone.

Finally, Edgar has some time to himself. Exhales. He hadn't realized until that shouting match with Animal how much he meant what he said, about wanting a family, and with Ariel. Now he just wants to get back and get on with his life. Instead, look at him—Jesus

H. Christ on a *stick*, how'd he get into this mess? They're all here to fix this broken country, and here he is shooting them. RS have got every right to be pissed. Only holding em off, sure, but how long can they be held off, with limited ammo and no exit strategy? With their whole police force, and army probably, on the lookout, checkpoints on all the roads, patrols combing the narrowing sector toward Sarajevo, sweeping them toward the minefields on Mount Trebević, Animal's own Highlanders confined to barracks and the door to SFOR shut anyway—realistically, this is Slim-to-None territory. When your upside looks like a prisoner exchange agreement, you probably ought to quit what you're doing.

The best way out *has* to be the Mudhill route. Trust Uncle Sam. Well, he knows where Animal's going to be at five thirty—that's good enough. Al Mudhill will get them out. If Animal and Brick don't go in for any heroics they'll get arrested and handed over to SFOR; the RS will keep Ranković; File 13 will be shut down. It's not a disaster. Animal's way too finicky to make it as a private military subcontractor anyway. Even Edgar can see that. Bottom line, everyone will live.

He puts the battery in and turns on his phone.

As it boots up, he reflects on the strange path that has led him to oppose Animal Elliot-Maitland. Really such a noble-minded man, capable but so stubborn. Won't see that while he's pursuing his own self-interest, he's bringing a resumption of hostilities that much closer. He thinks he's doing Bosnia a favor! Actually it's *Edgar* that's doing that. What Edgar's about to do isn't a failing, it's him finally waking up and smelling the coffee. Dad would be proud, for once.

The phone has booted up at last. The screen says

!Insert sim card

Edgar gives a weary smile, and puts his head in his hands. That was one last test from Animal, and he failed.

Jouncing along in the Land Rover, Jamie working both gearsticks, Bannerman steadying himself against a handle bolted to the roof, their snowchains crunch along the broken old roads above Lukavica. The valley winds southeasterly off the Bosna plain, the social-realist suburbs and glossy billboards giving way immediately after the Inter-Entity Boundary Line to half-built houses, outbuildings patched with breezeblocks, rusted old machinery, firewood slumped into the road, and advertisements saying AUTOPRAONICA spraypainted on piles of tires. Meltwater trickling in sheets down the road. Soon after that the tarmac gives out and it's rocky mudpaths from hamlet to hamlet, persistent scrapes of snow appearing and then multiplying. The old badlands on the southern slopes of Trebević. Vistas occasionally open up of Sarajevo herself, far below, an evening mist settling in the valley. Lengthening shadows of pine and spruce strobe orange and blue across the Land Rover's windscreen, dust and wipe-marks picked out in infinite golden detail.

Silent houses, the gradients of their roofs mimicking the hills and sometimes cliffs that guard them, appear less frequently through the trees. The last of them to seep ochre smoke has fallen away below. The rest are all dead. Graffiti about Ratko and the 4 C's cover roofless hamlets. Red splashes of paint on the trunks of fir trees. Then into the upland meadows, with more lesions of war: partially filled-in trenches, pitted land, the remnants of old Olympic fixtures. Broken bunkers filled with rubbish and shit; craters ten, twenty yards across. Destruction on a more giant scale than anything down in the valley, legacy of the NATO airstrikes.

The Land Rover picks a route through areas of maximum destruction, pitching like a ship in a storm, down into craters, spinning the wheel, across, rev up and clutch out up the far side, a sudden braking, sliding back, revving again, wheelspinning, Bannerman having to get out and push, snowchains biting, and finally rolling safe over the lip, and sliding sideways down into the next one.

Bannerman comes up behind the Land Rover, walking tightrope along the skidmark, and looks in at Jamie, clearly not wild about being a pedestrian here.

"They're almost all antipersonnel anyway," Jamie says.

"Terrific."

"In the Land Rover you'd have been fine."

And drumming toward them like a coastline, the yellow MINA MINA tape staked across the track. They drive through and retape with their own roll. Unofficial through routes have been established, used by the de-mining community. Officially, Mine Action Center hasn't cleared them yet; but according to Jamie's understanding of the frontline, this is probably one of those gangsterized "suspected minefields," which is to say, harmless. Probably.

"So here we go," Jamie reaching over to pat Bannerman on the thigh, "excited?"

A silence has deepened—not just a silence, more a natural-world omertà. Midafternoon and everything is unnaturally still; a strange quality of light. Only the thick diesel working of the Land Rover. High overhead, inaudible, kestrels wheel across the sky.

"It's like Hades."—"Everyone knows to stay away. I imagine that's what Animal has in mind."—"Chickens."—"You want me to show you a mine?"—"No."

At seven, they clear the last ridge, and falling away beneath them is a small dell, overlooked on the north side by a steep tumble of rocks, on the east by the mountain's long slow debouch. Open, but broken ground.

"This the place?"

"He does choose his spots." Jamie looks around.

"Base base base. We're looking for a *base* . . ." muses Bannerman. "Seen any of them?"

"Not so much."

"I spy withmylittleeye . . . a base. Double bass? Baseline?"

"*At* base." Jamie points, wrist on the steering wheel. "Base of cliff?"

A precipitous cliff rises sharply above the steep tumble of rocks, overhung with black trunks above and snowdrifts below. Bannerman nods. "That sounds right."

"Best we can do is get the Land Rover out of sight, and go sit it out."

"When you say go sit it out—you mean, get out of the Land Rover, wait somewhere else?"

"Given that the Land Rover's pretty visible, we don't want to be in it if it gets rumbled."

"Wait *outside*?"—"Sure."—"In the mines? And the cold?"—"I told you to bring a coat."—"But not mine-proof boots."

But it's golden hour, the last spectacular flaring of the sun, and they huddle up the rocks with a flask of coffee, legs braced against boulders, where it would take someone thirty seconds to scramble up to them. They chat about this and that, and soon the sun has disappeared into the last layer of cloud, there is only the radiance above Igman, then a deepening twilight, cold that descends like a curtain, and then dusk.

"Might try one of those čevapi now," says Bannerman.

Brick waits in a bush at the edge of the treeline. No stream here but there's a trickling under the snow. The valley below is still rolled in muted winter colors, browns and sodden purples. Thawing clumps of snow drop unexpectedly from branches. Occasional VRS four-wheel-drives toiling up and down the valley floor, but it's hopeless. No doubt the roads are still checkpointed, but there's too much area. The search is over. The minefields are easy. Depending on how Edgar managed, it's all looking good to be home & hosed in a couple hours. For now it's just Brick and his MP5K.

Twenty minutes behind schedule, not bad given the distances involved, Edgar Radford, Jr., comes over the hill, walking fast along the treeline. Weapon cradled in his arms, periodically consulting a map. He stops a quarter mile short of Brick, kneels down, looks around, and then creeps into the treeline for a more thorough wait. Brick gets up, walks over to his location.

"Boo," hisses Edgar, as Brick comes past.

"Edgar. Nice job."

"Didn't creep up on me that time, didya Brick?"

"You shake em off?"—"You tell me."—Brick nods. "Didn't see anything."—"The others?"

Brick sighs, stares a while, looking for a tell. Finally: "To be honest mate, it's a fair old tab from here. Back uphill. Seven clicks or so."

"Seven—what the hell? How are they getting the old guy to do that?"

Brick nods sadly. "We're the ones doing two sides of a triangle. Down a different valley." And in response to Edgar's look, Brick lifts his eyebrows once, looks away at the setting sun. They both know what it means. Animal's faith in Edgar has fallen to such an extent, he felt it necessary to insulate the real RV from Edgar with seven kilometers of mountain. For Edgar, that's probably the end of working with Animal. For Brick, nothing but a shitload of extra tabbing.

"I see."

"Come on, Ed. Chin up. We're going to have to peel one off to get there in time."

The snow pocked with dripmarks and dusted with pine needles, the black soil beneath crumbling to an orange that gives the Miljacka its color, a towering wall of evergreen on three sides creating a west-facing suntrap, and the feeling that they're all going to lose their digits finally ebbing. Ranković has his boots off in the afternoon sun, the bandages unpeeled and leaking pink goo. The Child, next to him, double-barrels two cigarettes and hands one over. Animal's dozing vaguely with his head on a rock. Sufi Child and Ranković murmur, burst into laughter.

Sufi Child turns to Animal. "He says, he thinks he might make some noise, maybe you should give morphine again!"

Animal looks up. "Getting along famously, you two?"

"Ha, ha! He says, hurry up and take him to The Hague, Milošević owes him money!"

"Polako, polako," Animal calming them down. "Slobodan's got a bodyguard now, you know."

"Naser Orić." Banko smiles, dragging on his cigarette.

"Naser Orić," savoring the name. Naser was Milošević's body-guard before the war; but he fought for Bosnia, became a general at twenty-five, and defended Srebrenica against the Serbs. It fell after he was withdrawn by the General Staff. He was arrested in Tuzla last week.

Sufi Child translates: "Banko thinks it will be nice in The Hague, Slobo and Naser are good friends, it will be like this: hey, my friend, nice to see you! Sorry about all that shit! Never mind, I made good money! Me too! Let's have a drink! Ha, ha!"

"I hear the squash court is excellent." Animal smiles, basks in the sun, enjoys the drying of his clothes. A little stream foams down these rocks, as the ground here falls precipitously away, even though the tops of the firs maintain their gigantic height. Possibly forty meters. There's something terrifying, holy, in this landscape. Far below, the Lukavica-Pale road crosses their route home. Beyond which, a hundred vertical meters away, if everything's come right, a Land Rover ought to arrive before eight o'clock. The last helicopter is far to the southeast, and in the dimness of the sound it's easy to infer a certain resignation. Sunset, and it'll be over.

"Excuse me, Sufi Child," Animal lifting his chin, "how's he feeling?"

"He is okay," looking at Ranković's feet. "He can do it."

"I meant, about all this," circling an index finger.

"Oh, the politics?" Sufi considers this, head on one side. "He is fine, actually. I think he was bored, before." But Ranković has understood, not least the word *politiks*, and lifts his shoulders good-naturedly, begins to speak without malice. Sufi Child turns to Animal: "Okay. Banko asks you: they invade countries because Muslims attack, UN says no this is wrong, and bad things happen, there is torture and prisons and this stuff, so what is difference between—Ratko Mladić and Tony Blair?"

Animal snorts, amused. "Just for starters? Tony Blair's daughter didn't top herself out of horror at her father."

Ranković replies. The Child doesn't want to translate any more. Still when he hears, he laughs, small hand over his mouth, and turns to Animal, "Banko says, everyone hate Muslims, but everyone hate Serbs more! We deserve each other. Welcome to Bosnia!"

"Dobrodošli u Bosne," confirms Ranković, with a stately nod of the head.

Hours later, Edgar and Brick have returned to a mellow welcome, cheeks furnace-red and hair matted to scalps, and the five of them clambered on stiff legs down the rubble to connect with Jamie and Bannerman—who watched the team coming in, and had a noble tableau and an outstretched palm ready for them when they arrived. "Colonel Elliot-Maitland, I presume?"

Moonlight on Animal's enamel grin. "Home, Jeeves."

Nightfall in the Trebević minelands, the Land Rover's V8 grumbling against the clutchwork, čevapi being wolfed, slivovic glugged, a carton of Luckies turning the air blue, a pitch-black celebration in a vehicle so full of hot bodies Jamie has to drive with his head hanging out of the window, and even then the night vision goggles keep steaming up. It's a hell of a feeling, being driven through a minefield with the lights off, which is, Ranković pointed out, not unlike life. But with Jamie O'Ryan at the wheel, there's no point worrying. He's as good as there is. Periodic stops to get out and check lumps in the ground, eventually they get onto the stony riverbed, and then back onto roads at first mud and then metaled, headlights on and down through the high hill-villages, glimpses of Sarajevo through the trees, rusting yellow guardrails and rickety log fences giving way to new three-story chalets and dogs that watch from the middle of the road. At last they come to Lukavica, the million city lights in the valley beyond burning the night sky orange, down onto the main road, and finally left toward Camp Butmir, built on the Inter-Entity Boundary Line, now only a few hundred yards away.

"We sodding chibbed it!"—"A half million bucks!"—"Fuckin A!"—"Fuckin B!"—"Jesus, we caned it across those mountains."—"Brick, man, you sure know how to go uphill."—"You do pretty good for a Yank, yourself."—"Yeah, thanks Edgar, you really held those bad boys off!"—"And Sufi Child! How about the *Child*! Put us to *shame*! You got the right stuff, man."—"And Bannerman! Couldn't have done it without you. Did you like my code?"—"Aw man, we nearly came unstuck, Jamie didn't know how old his wife was!"— "Oh, Jamie: three cheers for Jamie fucking Specky Four-eyes O'Ryan! Tight driving! Don't hit an IED *now*, Jamie!"—"And let's not forget the man who made it all possible—he's a murderer, he's a banker, but the man can tab—gentlemen, I give you: Rapes Ranković!"

And Ranković is loving it, what with slivovic, tobacco and the company of soldiers being a few of his favorite things. His fate is not so bad. He goes to a comfortable Valhalla, to keep the company of other warriors fallen in battle, where all foes have turned to friends, where they will compare notes, swap stories, and grow old in comfort, reliving the glory days.

But soon—"What's the holdup?" says Animal, from the back.

To their right, the perimeter fence of the airport hasn't moved for a few minutes. They're caught in a long line of traffic.

"Vehicle checkpoint up ahead," says Jamie. A sudden silence.

"At this point—" begins Edgar.

"Depends who's manning it," says Animal. "Can you see?"

"Looks like Strykers." American armored fighting vehicles. As Jamie says it, the fun drains out of the Land Rover.

Lit by the headlights and portable kliegs, two Stryker AFVs have created a slalom across the road. GIs are peering into cars, waving saloons and hatchbacks past and gesturing SUVs aside for inspection. Raised glove beckons Jamie off to the right. "Sir," as he comes past the window, "pull over and *stay in your vehicle.*"

"What goes on, Officer?"

"Pull over and stay in your vehicle."

Jamie complies; throws a look over at Bannerman.

"Never driven in the States, have you Jamie?"

But the GIs have shone flashlights into the back, and are soon thickly surrounding the Land Rover, weapons leveled, a few burly types looking sadly over from other duties. Bannerman splays his hands on the dash. Jamie likes the philosophy and does likewise.

An officer has been called for, who emerges from one of the AFVs, helmet chinstrap hanging. "Evening guys," jogging up to the window, "I'm Lieutenant Caley, One dash eighteenth. We're having a special roundup on Anti-Dayton Activities, looks like you boys qualify."

"Hey there, Captain Radford, Eighty-second," says Edgar, leaning over Jamie's seat from the rear. "Far as I know, One-AD is Brigade North, so I'm kind of wondering, what you legs are doing so far from Eagle?"

"Sure is a pleasure to meet you, Mister Radford, as luck would have it, I just been looking at a Xerox of your discharge papers, you were quite the shit. Anyhoo—seems you boys have pretty much started World War Three, so if you-all wouldn't mind considering yourselves Mirandized, and getting out real slow like, remembering course to leave all firearms inside, and laying yourselves facedown with fingers laced behind your head?"

"Wh—"

"Right now," opening Jamie's door for him.

Empty eyes, the tailgate is opened, and after a moment's contemplation they comply, even Ranković, gingerly avoiding putting weight on his broken hand. Animal's first in, last out.

"Lieutenant Caley," as he unfolds himself to his full height, offering a hand that's not taken, "Colonel Maitland, Twenty-second Special Air Service Regiment. I'd like to draw your attention to—"

"On the ground."

"Under the terms of the General Framework Agreement for Peace—"

"On the ground."

"—Resolution Eight-two-seven, and—"

"Corporal?"

A corporal in a chinstrap puts a hand against Animal's back and swipes at his shins. Animal steps over it and brings a heel, hard, down on the side of the corporal's knee. Corporal crumples with a wail. Animal keeps talking throughout "—Chapter Seven of the UN Charter, I hereby request that you formally accept custody—"

But Lieutenant Caley has unbuttoned his sidearm and brings it fast into Animal's face. "GET ON THE GROUND NOW MOTHERFUCKER."

"Lieutenant Caley, I don't know what orders you have, but as an extremely litigious—"

"GET ON THE FUCKING GROUND RIGHT FUCKING NOW!"

"If you're going to use your powers of arrest as mandated—"

Another GI has taken his rifle butt to the back of Animal's head, but Animal leans out of its way, tripping the GI and giving him a helpful shove on his way down "—under the terms of—"

But by now Animal is mobbed in a rush of GIs. They bring him down in a hail of punches and cusswords, knock his head against the tarmac, lay fists in his face, get his wrists cuffed, and once he's tied up, a few clarifying kicks in the kidneys.

"All right. Your boys tried to rip off a helicopter up at Eagle, you want to know charges, I think Grand Theft Chopper ought to do it. You like that? How's *that* for charges, you big bald fuck?"

A chain of Zastavas and saloon cars crawling past; a block of apartments with satellite dishes, families watching from diffuse-glass balcony panels, over streetlamps hunched in poses of perpetual grief. GIs in woodland battledress wave traffic on; the tarmac glistens yellow-black against sodium lights, the seven suspects facedown with one cheek or the other against it, trying not to catch each other's eyes, and an Army lieutenant stepping over their heads, reciting the usual parody of the *Miranda* warning: "You do not have the right to an attorney—if you cannot afford one, tough shit, get a job—"

Clare sees the text from Bannerman, and the world goes silent. Shiny keeps talking, unheard.

She's suddenly not sure she'd be able to move her life on, if Ranković is not sent to The Hague. She's invested so much of herself, she may have painted herself into a corner. Could she even *enjoy* life on the outside—or would it feel unclean, unsafe, everything pure debased, wouldn't she fear retribution from Ranković himself, even back in boring old Zurich? Suddenly trying to find a way back, to compromise: so what, in the end, did he do that makes him the worst person in the world? Isn't his behavior common to financiers everywhere—grinding out profits, commoditizing humans, scraping the bones for every last cut of meat? Everything in her screams she's not up to it—she should crawl away somewhere, pretend she never got the text. But come on come on schatz, Bannerman is in trouble and needs you—

Clare stands up and runs from Shiny's house, dialing a number. Outside on Radnička, she bumps into Joren, the weird Dane from the OHR, who stops her—"Hey Clare, yes! They are saying every time you have sex, you get another freckle! Ha ha yes, you think so!"

Clare knees him hard in the balls, and keeps jogging down the road toward the river.

The phone is picked up. "Guys," she says, "it is time to drop sack."

*　*　*　*　*

A short convoy of white SUVs, OSCE plates with enormous bull-guards, approaches the roadblock from the direction of town. A GI holds up a hand; the first slows down; the GI steps to the driver's side to speak in through the window, but there's only an SFOR pass pressed against the glass as it accelerates away toward the AFV roadblock.

"Hey—!"

It stops at the Strykers, by which time a dozen rifles are leveled. Out get four men in all orders of dress—jeans, webbing, kevlar, sneakers, led by a taller man, weaponless, in a French cap badge but a flecktarn combat jacket. He advances directly on Lieutenant Caley, walking ponderously, hands behind his back.

"Stay in your vehicle! Stay *in* your vehicle! What the fuck?" says Caley. But the men continue to flow calmly from the other vehicles and wander amongst the GIs with an exotic array of semiautomatic pistols and bullpup weapons to the fore: FAMAS, Steyrs, SIG-Sauers, even one with a long-range Barrett sniper rifle, with tripod. The GIs, who've only got standard-issue M16s, and like any professionals are maybe sensitive to superior brand names being bandied about, don't really know what to do.

"When one of my men gives you an order to stop your vehicle, asshole, you stop your vehicle!"

"Good eveningue Lieutenant, I am Commandant Sommantier, French Army, CIMIC-AF Liaison—"

"Don't care what fucking army you are, you do not—"

"This is Mister van Xanthe and Miss Leischman of ICTY, please demonstrate to the lieutenant your credentials—thank you, and this is Captain Jens Asselijn, of the 108th Dutch Commando."

"Well thanks for telling me your names, because your commanding officer is going to be having a new asshole ripped for him, you know by who? By *my* commanding officer, General Ward, you heard of him?"

"Lieutenant Caley, thank you for intercepting the war crimes indictee. Under mandate from the United Nations, the Dutch 108th will now receive him."

"My orders are to—" Caley shakes his head no, "those are not my orders."

By now the weapons of the commandos have, without obvious movements, come to be arranged in a much less friendly way. A GI responds allergically. "Get that fucking weapon out my face! *I said out my face, assho.* HEY, YOU DEAF, OUT MY FACE."

"Bernstein, calm your retarded ass down! You got a weapon, put it in *his* face, you're even!"

Commandant Sommantier smiles reassuringly. "Captain Asselijn will write you a receipt for the prisoner if you wish."

"Like hell. Specialist—get on the phone, get some more combats up here."

A GI nods, but turns to find there's a couple of Commando standing between him and the Stryker, one scratching his head apologetically. GI turns back to Caley. "Uh, Lieutenant?"

"What the fuck are you doing?" Caley turns to Sommantier, aghast.

Sommantier shrugs slowly. A generous gesture. "There are many armies here. Many times, orders are slightly—" doing it with his hands, "—they bump into each other. Only a little. But it all works, because, you see, we are all United Nations, and because the United Nations has rules we all follow—for example, that there is international law, as this man knows," indicating Ranković, "who must now go to the Netherlands for trial. And these persons are from The Hague, they know that to assist an indictee to evade capture is also an indictable offense, is it not, Doctorandus van Xanthe?"

"Well yes," says Marc, then, looking at Clare, "in theory."

"But no one's ever been that silly," says Clare.

"I—" Lieutenant Evan Caley's eyes dart around at the plainclothes soldiers. "I ought to consult with a superior officer at this time. Do not do anything. *You are not authorized to take the prisoner.* If you attempt to do so, my men will respond with lethal force. But listen, you need to get your guys to lower their weapons. It is not in any way shape or form acceptable for them to—Hey, are they taking *pictures*? Stop taking pictures! Ellis, stop those men taking pictures."

At the sound of her voice, Bannerman decides to risk getting shot, and turns his head over to look. Backlit against the appalling brightness of the klieg lights, stray wisps of hair picking up a halo, she catches sight of the movement, looks down at him, and winks.

Our Snowblind Life

AL MUDHILL IS gracious, as ever. "Delighted. We're all delighted for you. I see no obstacles that the reward money not get paid out. As you know, the President is all about bringing evildoers to justice."

Petar Ranković appeared before The Hague on April 13, 2003, and was formally indicted for mistreatment and killings at Foča; grave breaches of the 1949 Geneva Convention, violations of the laws or customs of war, and crimes against humanity. Provisional trial date set for January 2005.

The news storm created by the capture and pursuit rolled on for a few weeks, not without its headaches, though it served to focus attention on SFOR's lack of enthusiasm for arresting indictees. Also to provide File 13 with a decade's worth of contracts. High Representative Ashdown publicly condemned "trigger-happy bounty hunters" but also took the opportunity to ratchet up pressure on the SDS Party for harboring indictees; and for the first time, the idea of UN missions being routinely manned by private military companies, rather than government armies, was put on the agenda.

Clare Leischman and Marc van Xanthe, riding high, were given the go-ahead to investigate the DynCorp pedophile slavers. Because although IPTF officers had immunity from all Bosnian law, conversely ICTY is mandated to prosecute all "war crimes and crimes against humanity on the territory of the Former Republic of Yugoslavia since 1991," and by ICTY's own 2001 pretrial ruling, which established sexual enslavement as a crime against humanity, the DynCorp employees were faced with the prospect of joining the Serbs at the UN Detention Unit.

"Americans in the dock. Holy *shit* . . ." Clare and Marc burst into unexpected giggles at nothing, for days after they get greenlit. Sheer grandstanding, of course. The U.S. government will have a fit, there'll be legal wrangles over jurisdiction, and close to zero chance the men in question will ever come to trial, let alone inconvenience. At a push, it could even jeopardize ICTY's funding as a whole. Nevertheless, the Chief Prosecutor has had it up to *here* with NATO obstructionism, and she's not above manufacturing a few headlines herself, to concentrate everyone's minds on finding Karadžic and Mladić. Besides, it's an important principle. There's no monopoly on criminal acts. Everyone is liable.

And Frito is happy. The problem of the beer's role in the miraculous survival of the city has been fitted neatly into its context. For a few weeks Frito really passionately believed in it. But it wasn't the beer— it was the *water*. Sarajevska Pivara wasn't the only company that kept going. Cigarettes were manufactured and sold in what paper there was. The university stayed open, as did the Koševo hospital. Books were published, plays put on, festivals organized, football played, Radio Zid kept up a steady stream of sarcasm even as Ahmad Pasha's walls, made of tombstones, collapsed around the loudspeakers ("Call that a grenade?"). The newspaper *Oslobodjenje* didn't miss a day. The oddity of the brewery's perseverance has been crowded around by a tangle of other heroisms. Difficult for him even to remember what was odd about it in the first place. People survive, and they work. Crazier things have happened.

Well it was just a theory, one of many to be filed away. Call it Reasons Sarajevo Didn't Fall #7: Forces "Other." What most people are happy to file under "inexplicable," or, for those with scruples about internal consistency, "Allah." And there's plenty more of *them* in town these days: the suburbs are full of resettled countryfolk; hot chicks stalk the streets in head scarves, and anti-Serb riots are turning fundamentalist week by week. Getting abandoned by civilization and saved by Middle Eastern gunrunners reaped its harvest in terms of the Sarajevo IZ's pan-Islamic awareness. Plus the country's a European colony all over again, and the United States, having one of its four-year fits, has turned dark and hates ragheads. Where else should an oven-fresh Bosnian patriot turn? Who wouldn't be as Muslim as possible, out of defensiveness if nothing else?

So the logical next step, now that Bosnia is Frito's state of mind, is "submission." He's been in touch with the Hodža up at the Tekija Prnaša Esoterika; in return for a modest bequest, they'll let him take the green robe, with perhaps a rod and a staff for company, or as the dervishes say, tespih-dajak. He'll be inducted into the mysteries, insofar as they have been unraveled, and once he's up to speed, he can lend a hand to the unraveling himself. His own Aqidah to enunciate. Above all he wants to explore Bosnia's limestone underworld, starting at the tekija, and try to map the network of rivers and springs that underpin the country which he now sees is him. He'll need a hat with a lamp, a lot of rope, more courage, scuba kit, maybe a below-ground radar, all to flush out whatever secrets hide inside that inscrutable Bosnian karst. He's fully expecting, like his own Maori demigod Maui found, an entrance to the Underworld, the rivers Mnemosyne and Lethe, and possibly Styx. Undoubtedly a shitload of alcohol. His heart is set. He's "sold" Bannerman his share in the F&B killing before second-round funding. Bannerman needed the money more than him, to run that crazy freckly girl, about as stable as a Serb on a wobble-board—while Frito's going to become a spelunking dervish, and couldn't be happier about it.

Away from this overloaded, overstimulated existence anyway. If Axl Rosavić taught him anything it was "too much information, no information."

"Like we're snowblind?" Frito said.

"Yes," the Sufi Child with a slow closure of eyelashes.

Maza catches a rough go. She is thrown back into the pool of language assistants, hanging around at Ponts Sans Rivières, solutions looking for problems. She'd dreamed of a different ending, even tried to force the issue one day at the newly sleek ViKA Lijeka laboratories: now compartmentalized into fume cupboards, darkrooms, blowrooms, extraction pumps, pressing rooms, teak everywhere and a cathedral of Pyrex up on shelves, singing their scales of clarity in the muted sunlight, glass in a hundred different internal-organ shapes, Vedo's chemists moving efficiently about their work.

"Frito," she began, blushing and fidgety.

"Listen Maza, I really don't think you and I . . . oh no, don't give me that look, oh no, don't cry—oh crikey dick . . . oh bloody hell Maza . . . c'mere and get hugged . . ."

Patting her absent-mindedly where her bra divided her back. He allowed it to go on too long. Well, better now than later. This might hurt.

"Look Maza, you should know, the thing about me is: I just want to have sex with heaps of women. And I only want to have sex with them like, two or three times, and then that's it. End of. It's a vanity thing. I *like* the fact that I can have sex with women. I like myself because of that. I think I'm the dog's nuts. I'm really not interested in anyone else, and, much as I'd like to root you good and proper, I don't really give a hoot about you—" bloody hell this is hard, but the thing is not done yet "—not in you Maza, not in your annoying little problems, and not in your pathetic old dad—"

Bannerman and Clare had another few weeks of intensity, of love as deep and swimming as either had known. But soon enough another character appeared in town, structuring finance for EnergoInvest, who caught her eye. Bannerman got crowded out again, and was moving closer to giving up, finally.

She feels terrible about it, really, but what choice has she had? All she's looking for is that giddiness . . . she had it with Frito, with Dmitri Lautz for a while, but only intermittently with Bannerman. Calmness, contentment, sure. She could hold hands with him forever. But she can't go on with this, the longer she leads him on the worse it'll hurt. And yes, she does know, Animal freely admitted that Kalazar was a reference to *Bannerman's* mania, not his, so *here* was a guy who upped and found a war criminal, for you. She knows she'll never have a more giant declaration of love. That's really something. But the beginning and end of it is you can't force yourself to fancy someone. So for now she'll keep in shape, work hard, dress well, back into the blacks and charcoals: position herself to catch a firm hold of the next opportunity for love that brushes past. The fun of shopping around wore off a long time ago.

Bannerman, disgusted, goes about his days empty. He would leave this city, would start again again, but he's finally committed to this life. No more geographical cures. ViKA Lijeka's getting going; the others in the management team are competent and enthusiastic; Zaim Spaho is his new Frito. The expat scene is great. For a Westerner, the quality of life in Sarajevo is awesome. He'll take it.

Things hot up when Edgar and Ariel, for reasons neither will talk about, split up, and Clare's corporate finance boy, rich and dreamy as he is, suddenly seems less compelling now Ariel Alkali's out there loose, and with a proven interest in Bannerman. Zanna Agneri was fine. Clare could handle Bannerman dating that pockmarked laitière, but with Ariel it's different. She's too beautiful.

But she doesn't act on it and pretty soon Bannerman and Ariel *are* being seen around town. When she sees them herself at Colorscheme of Hazardsigns, celebrating the sale of F&B and Bannerman's drug-money windfall, all the flats of Clare's make-believe life clean fall off. She turns cold and her hands shake. *Now* she can't sleep. Oh, goodness.

She's screwed this up good and proper. What was she *thinking*? How had she not felt it? What was wrong with her heart, because good god she feels it *now*, she can see it in the slightest turn of his head, in the way sinews can be seen in his neck when he's talking, in the grace he hides under a clumsiness. His eagerness to please, the brightness of dogs, a heart that beat for her steady as the kickdrum. He's on an eighties TV show credits sequence, he's laughing at something, he turns to camera and grins right at it; his name appears below in friendly yellow letters.

No, no.—*He* is the love of her life. He *is* her life . . . a sudden avalanche of memories, toys from a cupboard unopened for twenty years that tumble down upon her now: the whole life they have not had together. It's not a notion; these are memories that exist in an absolutely definite way, as much as a snowfield they are about to walk through. They haven't yet. But look, there it is. As are the dark rivers they will have skinny-dipped in, dots of pollen dreaming past on the surface; rustling fields of greencorn, cinematically high; they have tackled each other, laughing, into mudpools, Bannerman coming at her with *eoo* a wide-open mouthful of *mud*, black between his teeth, his tongue twisting around hellbent on frenchkissing her, arms pinned by her side, while she spasms, weak with laughter, trying to get him the *fuh offa me* . . . They will have held hands at the funerals of friends, a once manic dog snuffling its nose into their joined hands, wanting reassurance too; they have had sushi fights, and pillow fights, and fights; they have caught each other staring across the clatter of formal dinners, in a quick privacy of love, across whole comas of cocktail-party chitchat. They have pulled over on lonely roads on the Plateau to make love in forests, not a word from either interrupting the torrid solemnity. He has been able to call her within minutes of a cold hollowness creeping into her, to say, "What's wrong?" too many times now, for it to be anything other than what they suspect.

What was she thinking?

Gott he's the one, the One. He held her tight and had an infinite capacity to listen, his heart spooling out like an answering machine while she talked. He liked to watch her paint her nails, he had to be bundled out of the bathroom so she could go in peace, he loved every inch of her compromised tumorous skin. His pain has blazed a hole in the last few months. When she reaches back for the memories all she finds is the burnt edges. He has fallen through. And she left him, her sudden best friend, while she frolicked around, butting her head against a series of walls that she thought were alleys.

"I was wondering," Clare says, all nerves now, after a chance meeting at the Samoposluga supermarket in June, "if you wanted to catch up over dinner some time?"

"FUCK YOU," Bannerman shouts, index finger out to be clear who he's talking to, people in the aisles looking round, "YOU FUCK-ING BITCH."

The inevitable Rhett Butler moment. Ariel Alkali appears quizzical from around an aisle, hair tucked into Bannerman's gray trenchcoat, adorably big on her even at four inches taller than Clare, fingertips poking out and clutching a carton of chocolate milk. Ariel's wolf-eyes full of sympathy. Clare feels the luminescence of communication between them, the sympathies, the daily arrangements— and Ariel's long legs ending in Bannerman's ratty running shoes. Clare, in the full nakedness of her heart, crumples. And she turns and hurries away, past at least three miles of detergent to the end of the aisle, and out of their line of sight.

Hurrying stumbling down the road, around a corner to put a hand to her mouth, crunching down and sliding to the cracked paving, a smile through the tears to reassure passersby that no, thank you, she's all right . . .

And she has nothing, nothing. She would give it all, pink face melting in her flannel, alone with the mocking echoes of her bathroom tiles, give *everything* to take it back, to have another chance. But she has no one to blame but that sagging girl in the mirror, her skin as mottled and bloodless as any fish.

Winter mornings in a rambling lowland house, a gray ocean out the window, weather clawing to get in, but only a soft white-duvet awakening for her, rubbing sleep out of eyes, the ticking of a radiator warming up and Bannerman on hand with a glass of orange juice but which, just as she reaches for it, he drinks himself—to which she angrily lunges for his ticklezones and OJ gets all over the bed and now she's in a *real* temper . . . so Bannerman settles in to squeeze it out of her and tell her that everything's wonderful and maybe screw her and hold her some more until the morning is so far advanced it's *indecent*, their houseguests will all have finished breakfast by now, at which point he'll start to screw her *again* . . .

This is what she has lost. A life of the searingest love with a guy who never did anything but love you.

But how better to achieve enlightenment than by having your ego stripped off? All Scarlett O'Hara had to do was keep pounding, heroically refuse to walk away. And Clare cannot give up. Not once she calms down, sits at the bustling café tables in a clean white dress, wet hair combed into a side parting, smokes a cigarette into the warm evening sunlight, and thinks clearly about that scene at the supermarket. If he had been polite then she might not look back. Civility indicating case closed. But no, passions were still high, and that's the signal that redemption has narrowed to a crack but is not yet closed. And Bannerman still has passion, smoldering in the form of anger. Its direction but not its intensity can be changed. Let him fuck it out or something, receive the submission his amour propre demands, and in the panting return to sanity, in a tangle of bedsheets, their eyes will meet again, and catch, and lock.

Because how can Bannerman, chocolate-milk-drinking boy, defy both their happinesses for long? Watch her turn up for work defeated and practically transparent? How can he not at some point put a hand out to her, and say: stop it edelweiss, c'mere. Arms wide to receive and forgive, and Clare on the other side of the room, putting a half-drunk bowl of chocolate amongst its forerunners on the TV, the cups and mugs, ring-stained legal files, candles-in-a-glass flickering against her moods, and taking a moment or two to absorb the relief and this vista of future contentments, before crossing to be held.

Because she'll know it, finally, when it holds her. The Great Bannerman.

"Seriously, what was I ever great at?" he'll murmur, half-asleep into his pillow, hair in a roadkill and shedding tangular pieces all over the sheets.

"Not knowing you're great is part of it . . ." Combing invisible shinto softnesses down his back with barely there fingertips, a back moley, acne-scarred, with a column of hair from inside his boxer shorts mounting an attack on his spine—while he'll emit soft hunchback moans, each a little payment for the petting. She's grateful for these but far greater pleasures will lie in being taken for granted, as the years advance, small happinesses passing unnoticed between them, synchronizing diaries, dressing for parties, trading turns to do the dishes. . . .

The long summer will approach its end. And on this broad seam between the seasons, their lovemaking, slow and deliberate now and with days to spare, will hollow out new caverns behind her breastbone. The feeling is of the construction of containers, a whole system of vaults that will be able to hold warm liquid contents belonging to them both. How did she not get this before? she'll wonder, lying cat-like on his chest, Bannerman protesting mildly but too at peace now to do anything but sleep—for days and days—and Clare kissing the soft vulnerability of an eyelid, its lashes attempting to blink underneath like her kissing has released frozen parts of him from old storybook curses, now returned to their ancient forms, which when she stops will take off and flutter around the room, randomly at first and with their own joy-maddened whimsies, but soon, finding the window open to the hot mountain evening, will move through it in twos and threes and to the street, to the hills and their flowers, the night's possibilities for happiness, and everything beyond.

LOA

AF	(the formerly warring) Armed Forces
AQ	Al Qaeda
ARBiH	Armija Republike Bosne i Hercegovine
AVNOJ	Antifascist Council of the People's Liberation of Yugoslavia
BL	Banja Luka, capital of RS
CID	U.S. Army's Criminal Investigation Division
CIMIC	civilian-military co-operation
CO	Commanding Officer
COMSFOR	Commander of SFOR
DB	Serbian secret police
d.o.o.	Bosnian limited liability company
DP	displaced person
DPM	Disruptive Pattern Material (British camouflage)
EBRD	European Bank for Reconstruction and Development
ECHELON	U.S. eavesdropping program
ETA	estimated time of arrival
EUPM	European Union Police Mission
FCL	Former Confrontation Line
FRY	Former Republic of Yugoslavia
GFAP	General Framework Agreement for Peace
GSM	Global System for Mobile Communications
GPRS	General Packet Radio Service
HDZ	Croatian political party
ICMP	International Commission on Missing Persons

ICTY	International Criminal Tribunal for the former Yugoslavia
IED	improvised explosive device
IMF	International Monetary Fund
IO	Intelligence Officer
IOM	International Organization for Migration
IPTF	International Police Task Force
IRI	Intercept Related Information
ISP	internet service provider
JNA	Jugoslav People's Army
KBR	Kellogg, Brown & Root
KFOR	NATO's Kosovo task force
KM	Konvertible Marks (Bosnian)
LOA	list of acronyms
MAC	Mine Action Centre (sic)
MoD	UK Ministry of Defence
MICC	Mine Information Coordination Cell
MNB-N	Multi-National Brigade North
MP	Military Police
MPRI	Military Professional Resources, Inc., a large American PMC
NDA	Non-Disclosure Agreement
NGO	non-governmental organization, typically a humanitarian aid charity
NIC	National Intelligence Center
NSE	National Support Entity
NVG	night-vision goggles
OECD	Organization for Economic Co-operation and Development
OHR	Office of the High Representative
OSCE	Organization for Security and Cooperation in Europe
OTP	Office of The Prosecutor
OZNa	Yugoslav secret police

PfP	Partnership for Peace
PIFWC	Person Indicted For War Crimes
PMC	Private Military Company
PTSD	post-traumatic stress disorder
remf	rear-echelon motherfucker
RS	Republika Srpska
RTU	Returned To Unit
SACEUR	NATO's Supreme Allied Commander Europe
SAS	Special Air Service, a British special forces regiment
SCG	Serbia and Montenegro
SDA	Bosnian Muslim political party
SDP	multiethnic Bosnian political party
SDS	right-wing Bosnian Serb political party
SFOR	NATO's Stabilization Force in the FRY (1996-2004)
SIPA	Bosnian State Investigation and Protection Agency
UNPROFOR	United Nations Protection Force in the FRY (1992-1995)
u.s.p.	unique selling point
UXO	UneXploded Ordnance
VCP	vehicle checkpoint
VRS	Vojska Republike Srpske (Bosnian Serb Army)
WTO	World Trade Organization

About the Author

Thomas Leveritt is half-American, half-British, and thirty-three. Raised in Dallas, Texas, he was sent to boarding school in England at the age of eight. He has won the Carroll Medal for Portraiture from the UK's Royal Society of Portrait Painters, and twice been runner-up at the National Portrait Gallery's BP Competition. In addition, Leveritt has programmed computers, aid-worked in Bosnia-Herzegovina, received an Army Scholarship into the 5th Royal Inniskilling Dragoon Guards and a law scholarship into Middle Temple, and held the UK distribution rights for the very excellent beer Sarajevo Pivo. He received a Betty Trask first novel award for *The Exchange-Rate Between Love and Money.*